Wedding night . . .

The wedding chambers had been prepared by the Vatican court and were strewn with fresh flowers, the heavy scent in the hot chamber making Lucrezia dizzy and faint. In a daze she felt herself lifted up and laid on the bed, then divested of her clothing. Giovanni pulled the coverlet up to her chin.

Lucrezia lay without moving, her limbs stiff with fear, Giovanni lying quietly beside her. At first she thought he had fallen asleep, but then she saw that he was watching her. He reached over to the decanter of wine, poured a goblet, and pressed it into her hand. "If you are too tired," he said, "we can wait until morning."

She sipped at the wine slowly, conscious of his eyes on her all the while. When she finished, he took the glass from between her fingers and set it on the table. "Now I will teach you about love."

The stiff limbs relaxed and Lucrezia smiled. In a moment, she thought, he would lean over her and begin to pummel and tickle her, as Cesare had. She drew a deep, contented breath and waited.

She was not prepared for what happened next. . . .

"Historical novelists should have a special kind of empathy . . . to bring alive, in their own time, historical figures as convincing characters. Genevieve Davis possesses this trait . . . in the pages of this colorful novel. . . ."

—Robert Kirsch
Los Angeles Times

A Passion in the Blood

by Genevieve Davis

PINNACLE BOOKS   LOS ANGELES

Although the main characters in this book were real people, and the events herein depicted did take place, in some instances both the people and the events were fictionally intensified to add to the drama of the story.

A PASSION IN THE BLOOD

Copyright © 1977 by Genevieve Davis

A Pinnacle Books edition, published by special arrangement with Simon and Schuster, Inc.

ISBN: 0-523-40255-4

First Pinnacle printing, April 1978

Cover illustration by William Vaughn

Printed in the United States of America

PINNACLE BOOKS, INC.
One Century Plaza
2029 Century Park East
Los Angeles, California 90067

To Bud, who is always there . . .

ACKNOWLEDGMENTS

To Jay Garon, Evelyn Grippo, Ruth Nathan and Alfred Palca, my heartfelt thanks.

A PASSION IN THE BLOOD

PROLOGUE

It was the year 1490, and the ducal palaces of the Italian states were at the height of their magnificence. Columbus was petitioning Queen Isabella for the wherewithal to outfit the ships that would, he believed, find a new route to India; Michelangelo was famous for his frescoes and notorious for his love of young boys; and the Borgia star, with its trail of blood, was on the rise.

The great families—the d'Estes, the de' Medicis, the Orsinis, the Borgias—when they weren't at war, tried to outdo one another in the elegance of their houses and the sumptuousness of their feasts. They dined on plates of solid gold and silver, and dressed in fabrics and jewels gathered from all four corners of a still-flat world—velvets and silks, ermines and sables, emeralds, rubies and diamonds. Their marble halls were hung with costly tapestries from the East, and they coupled indiscriminately under canopies of satin on divans of gold.

They commissioned the best-known artists to paint them and their families. They held elegant salons and

1

supported young poets, who, wisely, wrote verse that sang their patrons' praises.

If they went to a wedding in another duchy, it was with a retinue of thirty or forty attendants—often there were as many as five hundred servants, and as many horses, to be housed and fed and stabled for a week— and they staged elaborate hunts with such exotic animals as giraffes and antelopes, merely to entertain the ladies of the court.

The princes who ruled the separate provinces of Italy made their own laws, created their own justice, and lived from one day to the next, always keeping a watchful eye for the poisoned chalice or the sudden flash of a rapier's point. For if one didn't die at an early age from the excesses of overeating, overdrinking, or that sickness of the genitals euphemistically called the French disease, one frequently met an early end at the hand of an enemy—as often an ambitious brother as an ambitious neighbor.

This was the world into which Lucrezia Borgia was born, a world of unbridled sensuality and violence. She was a product of her time, and the urgencies of the flesh were gratified wherever and whenever it was convenient. For Lucrezia, in whose veins flowed the notorious Borgia blood, it was unthinkable to turn her back on the things that gave her pleasure, whether it was a chestful of pearls, a joint of mutton, a passing ambassador, or her unholy brother Cesare, whom she loved in a way she could never love another man. No, Lucrezia took her pleasures where she found them, for like everyone else, she was racing frantically against an implacable enemy, Time, which would soon enough deprive her of her looks, her passions, and her life.

CHAPTER 1

"Lucrece!" The boy's voice rang out, filled with impatience, through the gray stone arches of the Orsini Palace of Monte Giordano and across the tessellated courtyard to where the girl lay on the grass in the sun.

"Lucrece!" he repeated, the syllables exploding like a crack of gunpowder in the golden air, loud and imperious for his fifteen summers. "Lucrece, come here!"

Lucrezia smiled and chewed slowly on the stem of a flower. Her brother was angry again, some little thing no doubt, a stray feather left floating in a pigeon pie or an unripe wedge of Tellegio cheese. Anything at all, it seemed, could send him into a towering rage so that his dark eyes filled with blood and the deep pits on his handsome face flared into an angry red beneath his auburn hair, earning him the name Lucifer.

"Lucrece!" She was the stream he bathed in, cooling his blood, soothing his anger so that he could breathe without choking on the contempt for others that always lay inside him, just waiting to be unleashed.

"He is crazy in the head like his father," his patron

3

Ludovico Orsini would say proudly, tapping his forehead significantly with his jeweled forefinger. "I don't know why we put up with him," his lovely wife Adriana would answer, nodding agreement, both knowing full well that they could do no less for the son of Cardinal Borgia, who might one day be Pope and who had entrusted his children into their care. The Borgia star was ascending.

"If only he were more like his sister," Adriana said. "A perfect beam of sunlight."

Ludovico smiled. The boy was more to his liking than his quiet, whey-faced sister. The boy was bold and bad and clever. The boy was like himself.

Cesare stumbled in his fury, his anger shaking and blinding him, thrashing with maniacal fury at the fat, stupid pigeons pouting in the yard, so that they rose in a flurry of feathers, their eyes red with alarm. He hated it when she hid from him. She did it all the time. "Lucrezia, come out or I'll thrash you!" He would do no such thing.

A flutter of white caught his eye just beyond the hedge. There she was, the little bitch; he'd make her pay for that!

Lucrezia waited calmly, feeling the force of the sun on the little points of her breasts beneath her bodice, and when she saw him coming toward her she rolled aside nimbly, so that he lunged for her and missed, falling heavily beside her. How she loved to torment him. She removed the stem from her mouth and poked it at his ears, his mouth, his nose, so that he doubled up to escape, his anger choking out in spasms of laughter until he lay spent, groaning with pleasure. The thing that had angered him was forgotten as Lucrezia hovered over him, her ash blond hair hanging into his

4

face, tickling his nose and making him sneeze, his gray-blue eyes alight with mischief.

She pushed out her lower lip at him.

He longed to catch it in his teeth and make it bleed.

She shook her hair in his face and he caught her by the neck and pulled her to him, her mouth soft and warm on his, her lips tasting lightly of salt when he bit her, until she broke quickly away, her breath fanning against his face like a child's.

He must teach her not to breathe when she kissed. "You still kiss like a baby."

She made a moue with her tongue.

"Again," he said, reaching for her.

"No. They'll see us."

He breathed heavily, struggling to undo her bodice. "Let me see your breasts."

"Not now, Cesare," she said, fighting the unfamiliar sweetness stirring in her groin.

"Why not?" he asked.

She pushed him away, frightened of what she saw in his face. "Cesare, you shouldn't have done that to the pigeons yesterday. I saw what you did and it wasn't very nice."

"Who cares," he said impatiently. "Next time answer me right away or else I'll do worse."

She looked at him angrily. "You have another pimple."

He clapped his hand to his face to cover it.

"I'll make you a poultice," she said, feeling herself in control. "A poultice of pigeon dung. Then when I squeeze it, it won't leave a scar. Will you let me squeeze it, Cesare?"

"If you let me see your breasts."

She smiled, her teeth as white as the milk teeth of a little child. "Do you love me, Cesare?"

"Yes," he said. "No, I hate you."

5

She smiled again, her lower lip swollen from the mark of his teeth. "Do you know, you really hurt me." She pulled out her bodice and peered down between her breasts.

He watched her sullenly, his desire for her slowly mounting. He wanted to pinch and bite her all over.

"Would you really like to see them, Cesare? They're bigger than they were last week."

He reached out to grab hold of her, but she eluded him nicely, her slender body arching away beyond his grasp. His desire slipped heavily into anger. She was an abominable tease. "Take care, Lucrezia. You push me too far." He searched her eyes for guile, but her expression was one of innocence, pure and simple.

"I think it's because I'm bleeding. Do you know, Cesare, that I've begun to bleed?"

His anger died away into softness. "It's high time at eleven," he said with a show of gruffness. "Most girls start to bleed earlier. Here," he said, extending his hand, "I'll help you up if you give me another kiss."

Lucrezia glanced anxiously back at the palace. "Carlos is on the terrace waiting for me. I have to do my lessons."

"Just one, Lucrece."

"No. Carlos is watching. Do you want them to send you away?"

"Fat chance! They wouldn't dare." He pulled her close and pressed his mouth against hers.

Lucrezia closed her eyes and smiled, the pulsing sweetness starting to beat again.

He watched her as she ran, her small feet kicking out at the heavy dress so that it billowed in folds behind her. He picked up the stem she'd discarded and put it in his mouth, savoring the gray-blue eyes set in the sweet oval of her face, the flawless skin, the soft sifting of hair. "Lucrezia," he whispered, imagining the soft white crevices of her body which he'd never seen. Did she care for him as he cared for her? It was difficult to know. She was sensuous and quick to love all things, the soft feel of silk, the glitter of jewels, her little spaniel. She loved them all exactly alike, while he loved only her and no other thing in this world, unless you counted the dark wild groping with Sanchicha and Dolores as love . . . He thought of their thick, squat bodies and smelled the odor of musk. No, that was not love. It was a fever, quickly broken. He could manage as well with a mare. But the feeling for Lucrezia was different. It went on and on and never seemed to stop. He thought of Carlos St. Angelo, the pale, well-born young man who preferred to trudge about with books instead of serving in the Orsini barracks at Monte Giordano like the other young noblemen.

The Orsinis, the House of the Bear, were one of the wealthiest, proudest, and most influential families in Rome as well as the most grasping and arrogant in all of Italy. For the last six centuries their fine Italian fingers had been in all the uprisings and intrigues of Rome. Cesare could scarcely wait until he was of age to play such games. The wily Cardinal had done well to entrust the education and rearing of his children to this family. But Carlos, and here Cesare flicked his fingers in contempt, Carlos was a milksop, with the body and face of a man and the fine, tender feelings of a woman. Only yesterday Cesare had found Lucrezia cradled on his lap, pouring out some tale of woe about a rabbit she'd found caught in a trap, and Carlos had comforted her like a woman, stroking her hair and murmuring soft women's words. Even now his chest burned to think that she had gone to Carlos for comfort instead of coming to him. And what would it be like when the summer ended and he had to return to

7

the university at Perugia to resume his studies in juris-prudence.

His father, the Cardinal, had designated for him a career in the Vatican, which was not at all to Cesare's liking. Soldiering and hunting were more to his taste, but he would tilt at that when it came. Meanwhile he was engrossed in the study of law, which Cardinal Borgia deemed more valuable to a Church career than anything else he could think of. For Cesare it was simply another weapon, another way of fighting. Up until now he had fought only with his body, using it as a means of communication when he was at a loss for words, reveling in the hard contact and the vast sense of physical release which it afforded him. Soon he would be able to fight with his mind as well.

He put it to work on Carlos. When he left, Lucrezia would come to rely wholly on the tutor. He was not afraid of the physical part. Carlos did not run to women. Sanchicha and Dolores had laughed over that. Never had he gone to them or to any of the women who were available to men in the huge compound of palace, barracks, and stronghold that was Monte Giordano. No, it was not the physical part, he reasoned, it was the other part, the thing that he had seen in Carlos and in Lucrezia as well, a thing of the spirit, a part he couldn't reach either with his mind or his body. He had seen the same thing in butterflies and in the flame of a candle. They burned brightly, but you couldn't touch them. Once you pulled off the wings there was nothing left but a hairy brown body, and once you snuffed out the flame with your fingers there was nothing left but an ugly black wick and a smear of soot.

He had reasoned thus about Lucrezia. She was actually nothing but blood and bones, skin, hair and teeth, each in itself nothing marvelous to look at. But then the magic asserted itself. The eyes looked steadfastly out of the oval face, framed by the soft, shining hair. And the pomegranate lips parted and smiled, exposing the small even teeth. And after that, there was nothing more he could do. The magic took over completely.

He wouldn't care, though, if he were only certain that she loved him the best of anyone. But he was denied even this. She had a heart too easily made glad. A kind word, a little trinket, or the flowering of a tree called forth twin spots of color on her flawless cheeks.

Of course he could speak to his father . . . "I do not feel," he would say judiciously, "that Carlos St. Angelo is a proper companion for Lucrezia." And Cardinal Borgia, tall and powerfully built, would look amused and enjoy Cesare's discomfiture, and he would say, looking like a hawk down the length of his hooked nose, "What particular thing about our cousin annoys you?" And Cesare would repeat, "He is much too gentle; he is too much like a woman." And the Cardinal would touch the tips of his fingers together, pushing out his lips as he did so, which was a favorite trick of his while pretending to consider a point of view other than his own, and smile. "But that is precisely what Lucrezia needs, someone to calm and gentle her into womanhood, and Carlos is the very one to do it. Perhaps you might do better," he would add, looking at Cesare with eyes that missed nothing, "to lavish greater concern on your studies. I have great hopes for you, my son."

The last two words would be uttered with a trace of sarcasm so imperceptible that only Cesare could have caught it, for Cardinal Borgia had never been certain of Cesare's paternity. At the time of his birth, his mother was still married to her first husband, who disappeared the following year, probably at Borgia's instigation, leaving her to resume her uninterrupted relationship with the Cardinal. That Lucrezia was his daughter was indisputable. Less intelligent than her father, she had the same impetuous Borgia blood, the same heavy surge of sensuality and love of domesticity that marked her father, without his cunning and duplicity.

No, speaking to his father would be fruitless, for the very objections that he would muster against Carlos, his father would turn to his own advantage, using them as arguments to further his own case. Perhaps he could speak to his mother. Vanozza lived quietly, only a few hundred yards from the Orsini Palace. Her physical relationship with the Cardinal had slipped into an easy domesticity, so that the Cardinal would drop in from time to time for a cup of wine or a chat about the children, for she had relinquished her claim to them, giving them over entirely to the care of their father, who was better able to advance their careers. No, it wasn't likely that Vanozza would oppose the Cardinal in anything. Raised by him from the obscurity of a middle-class background, she clung to the security of mediocrity and frugality, quietly investing the Cardinal's gifts of money in real estate until she had acquired several houses, a vineyard, and three hostelries. No, Vanozza was certainly not the one to interfere.

That left only Adriana and her husband, Ludovico. But Adriana was the Cardinal's confidante and not one to go against his wishes, while Ludovico had absolutely no interest in domestic things. The feud between the Orsinis and the Colonnas was rife. Not once, but many times, Cesare had heard the strident call to arms sounding from the barracks, followed by the ringing hoofbeats of the Orsini cavalry upon the paving stones as they dashed out to meet the rival forces of the House of Colonna on the plains outside the city. At times the battles raged right into the city streets, and the frightened citizens had to barricade themselves behind

10

their doors until it was over. Ludovico Orsini had his hands full recruiting replacements for his fallen men. No, Orsini was not a man to bother with domestic problems, Cesare thought ruefully. He would have to think of some other way to rid himself of the tutor.

CHAPTER 2

Lucrezia and Carlos sat with bent heads over the long refectory table in the library. The room was longish rather than square, which made it more difficult to heat, and was paneled in fumed oak.

Lucrezia lifted her head from the Latin couplets and looked toward the window which had been thrown open to the fine June day.

Carlos followed her glance and smiled. "You will not find the answers out there. Pay attention and it will soon be over."

"I don't see," Lucrezia said with a quick toss of her head, "I don't see what good this will do me anyway."

Carlos smiled with a flash of white teeth that lighted his narrow, sallow face. "It will do you good up here," he said, tapping his forehead. "Out there you exercise your body; in here you use your mind."

Lucrezia looked at his teeth. He was quite handsome as Cesare in his own way, smaller perhaps, more neatly made, with close-curling dark hair and brows. "I like it when you smile. I shouldn't mind this so much if you smiled more often."

12

Carlos' smile deepened despite himself. "All right, I shall smile each time that you score a perfect translation. Agreed?"

Lucrezia scowled. It was not what she meant at all.

Carlos' smile turned to laughter. She was a delightful child, a perfect beam of sunlight, as Adriana was fond of saying.

"I like it when you laugh." Her own eyes reflected his merriment. "What were you thinking of?"

"Latin couplets, of course," Carlos answered. "And that is what you should be thinking of as well."

Lucrezia looked at the fine brown hairs growing on the backs of his hands, at the neat square fingers with their closely trimmed nails. "You have nice hands, Carlos," she said, turning them over and running her fingers lightly over his palms. "Cesare's hands are rough and full of calluses. I wish they were soft like yours."

Carlos drew his hands gently away. "Cesare uses his hands. I use my mind and so my calluses don't show."

"That's a funny thing to say." Lucrezia put her head to one side and looked at him through half-closed eyes. He really was quite handsome. His eyes, she noticed, were deer-soft brown, fringed with thick dark lashes like a girl's. She dropped her eyes to his mouth. His lips were full and deeply carved at the corners. What would he do if she kissed him? Her breath came fast at the thought. Dear Carlos, would he kiss her hard like Cesare did? No, she decided, he would not be rough. His mouth would be soft and tender. She smiled and closed her eyes, thinking of how he had held her yesterday when she'd found the little rabbit in Cesare's trap, the matted fur stiff with blood, the eyes still as glass. He had held her tightly against him and when she was through crying she had raised her head and looked at him and then she began to laugh. "Carlos,

13

my tears are all over your face. You look as though you are crying too."

"How do you know I am not?" he had answered.

And then she had laughed some more. She could never be sad for very long. The strut of a pigeon, the set of a dog's tail, the sight of Antonio, the food and wine taster, waddling along splay-footed on his flat, tired feet—anything at all could distract from the sadness at hand, any sadness.

She was like a vial of quicksilver, Carlos thought. She could not sustain one emotion for very long, but must dart restlessly through the whole range so that in the course of a day she would run the gamut of laughter, tears, and anger, dimpling back again into laughter.

"You are really very handsome, Carlos."

"Back to the couplets, Lucrezia." It was difficult to keep her attention for very long. He had to resort to all sorts of tricks or else she would never learn anything.

She smacked her book shut and banged it against the table, giving vent to an excess of feeling. "Do you know, Carlos, that I've started to bleed?"

Carlos suppressed a smile. "Adriana spoke of it. You will make a lovely woman," he said seriously.

That was not at all what she wanted to hear from him. She moved her head so that her hair swung slowly against his cheek.

Carlos pretended not to notice. "We will adjourn for today," he said, gathering up the papers, "and continue the couplets tomorrow. Will you stopper the ink, Lucrezia? And here," he said, handing her a bit of cloth, "you may clean the quills as well."

Lucrezia's eyes filled with tears. He was treating her like a child, knowing all the time how she felt about him.

"No," she said, fighting back the hot sting of tears. "The ink will stain my fingers."

A warm tear fell on his wrist. He pretended not to see it. "All right, then," he said, handing her the silver shaker of sand. "You may sprinkle this on what you have written."

The hot tears came in a flood and she was powerless to stop them.

Carlos sat quietly, making no effort to comfort her. He waited until she had cried herself out. Then he leaned over and gave her a bit of cloth for her nose.

She looked at him with tear-drenched eyes.

"Use it," he said firmly.

"Yesterday," she began, "yesterday when I cried, you took me in your arms and held me." She blew her nose loudly.

"Yesterday," he replied, "you cried for a reason. Today it is different. Sometimes, when a woman bleeds, she cries without reason. Perhaps she is sorry to be losing some of herself."

She dabbed at her eyes with a corner of the cloth and handed it back. Then she took up the silver shaker and sprinkled golden sand on the half-dried ink. In a moment, when it had set, she would give the paper a quick shake so that the loose sand would scatter, leaving only a neatly written page.

"That is good," Carlos said encouragingly. "You may go now if you like."

Lucrezia looked covertly at the curve of his mouth. What would he do if she kissed him and then said, "That is because I love you." The skin across her back tightened deliciously. Did she dare?

Carlos looked up and smiled, the flash of his teeth lighting his narrow face. "I will see you at mid-meal, Lucrezia."

"Yes," she replied slowly, beginning to leave. "At mid-meal."

CHAPTER 3

The midday meal was the principal meal of the day, and it was served in a huge hall plastered in zinc with frescoes of sienna and ocher. Because of the great length of the room, there was a stone fireplace at either end for heating. Consequently, the people seated mid-table generally lacked warmth, but since those seated in the middle were considered of no importance, it really didn't matter.

During the summer months the hearths were rarely used, but were banked with huge bunches of rushes and musk-broom, a dry purplish pod that gave off a sweet, cloying odor to override the ranker odor of spilled food.

There were never less than thirty-five at any meal, since Monte Giordano was the Orsini stronghold and a sort of minor court, so that besides the regular residents there were always distant clansmen, visiting gentry, and the usual hangers-on.

Huge mastiffs lay before the banked hearths, rising only to catch the food that fell from the table. Table manners had not yet come into vogue from the French court. Knives and forks could either be used or ignored. One generally ate with a knife, hacking away at the proffered roasts which journeyed to the middle of the table from either end, spearing the meat with the point of the knife and conveying it to the mouth. It was more genteel than fingers. Pieces of food flew through the air, landing on clothing and hair, staining the rich fabrics, over which a pearl or a semiprecious stone would be sewn to hide the spot. Most of the clothing worn was richly encrusted with such stones. A goodly portion of the food, however, landed on the tessellated floor and was promptly gobbled up by the mastiffs, who served to keep the place neater than it would otherwise have been.

Ludovico Orsini sat at one end of the great oak table, flanked by his captain at arms, Gian Capello, a short, swarthy Sicilian with a profusion of black hairs growing from his ears and nose, and his advisor, Alphonso Orvieto, who thought and ate with precision, always making his Parma ham and melon come out exactly even.

At the other end of the table sat Adriana Orsini, her shining chestnut hair pulled smoothly back to form thick loops on either side of her shapely head. Adriana smiled and said very little, listening quietly to the frivolous chatter of her ladies in waiting. Adriana affected a fork as well as a knife, as did Carlos.

Behind Orsini's chair stood Antonio, the flaccid food and wine taster. Each dish as it came from the kitchen below was proffered to Antonio, who tasted it judicially and pronounced it either good or bad. He was not allowed so much as a grape between meals, since it might affect the judgment of his tongue. Ludovico pronounced his the finest tongue in all of Italy, still waiting, however, the proscribed fifteen minutes before

17

eating just to make certain. After all, one did not reach a position of such prominence without making some enemies along the way. Murder could always be made to look like an accident and one had to look sharp to stay alive.

The fifteen minutes having ended, Ludovico raised his chalice and drained it. That was the signal to begin.

"Congratulations," his advisor said, raising his goblet in turn.

Ludovico looked at Alphonso and laughed. Only yesterday Alphonso had pestered him again to order the new Venetian goblets which were said to shatter upon contact with poison. Leave it to the Venetians, he thought, to come up with something like that. As for Alphonso, he was an old woman. And that wife of his, Seraphina, was cuckolding him all over the place with everyone in the barracks. The latest tale was that she had thrown herself on twenty young infantrymen after they had come in hot from battle, taking from them in great greedy surges all that they had to give, lying afterward spent and exhausted, a vapid smile upon her face. Ludovico laughed as he thought of it. Heaven preserve him from women in their forties.

Lucrezia sat on Adriana's right. She had tried to master the fork in imitation of Carlos, but her progress was slow. Naturally quick and impatient, she finally abandoned it each day in favor of her fingers. "It tastes better this way," she confided to Adriana, who bade her try again. Lucrezia raised a piece of lamb to her mouth and tore it off with her small strong teeth, chewing vigorously until she tired of that too and simply washed the whole thing down with a large draft of red wine.

Huge bowls of rice flavored with saffron and olives lined the length of the table. Lucrezia banked the rice against the meat with her knife, mopping up the food

18

that fell onto the table with large pieces of bread torn from her trencher. Between mouthfuls she glanced surreptitiously at Carlos, who ate meticulously, wiping at his mouth with his lap cloth and making quiet conversation with his companions. Now that she was less hungry, she would try the fork again.

Adriana smiled her approval.

Was it Lucrezia's imagination, or was Carlos really looking her way every so often? Lucrezia, quick to believe what she liked, took as her own any glances that were turned in her direction. She looked over at Cesare and stuck out her tongue. Let him scowl as much as he liked. She would learn to eat with a fork if she had to starve to do it.

Cesare stabbed viciously at his food. What lay in his plate was not leg of mutton, but Carlos, damned fop. Before she had come here, Lucrezia had been perfectly content to eat with her knife or her fingers. Now look what was happening. God only knew what would happen while he was away at school.

Ludovico leaned over and laughed. "What are you thinking, son? You have a killer's look in those eyes of yours." Ludovico had seated him next to his captain at arms, Gian Capello, a rare honor to be accorded a boy his age. It was rumored that when Innocent III passed on, Cardinal Borgia would be next in line for the papacy, and Ludovico was not one to pass by an opportunity. The support of the Church and its vast fortune would be invaluable to him in his fight for supremacy over the House of Colonna. Therefore, Cesare was accorded a place of honor at the table. Moreover, Ludovico really liked him. In the boy he sensed a ruthlessness that matched his own. Someday, he thought wistfully, Adriana and he would have a son of their own.

Meanwhile he treated Cesare as his own, even to

taking him on hunts, where the boy displayed ferocious cunning and fearlessness.

Yes, Ludovico mused, Cardinal Borgia could be proud of this son of his. Why, then, did he seem to prefer the younger boy Juan to Cesare? Perhaps it was the question of paternity that bothered him. Rodrigo Borgia was proud and vain, and even though he had issued proclamations designating Cesare a legal heir, his ego was at stake. In his own wily way, Ludovico realized, he had probably legalized him for personal gain. Male children in families such as the Borgias were distinct assets, since the proceeds of the clerical and secular offices bestowed upon them by the Church were considerable. During Cesare's childhood, Cardinal Borgia had enjoyed the revenues from his son's holdings as well as from six other bastards whom he'd legalized along with Cesare. Ludovico smiled. The Cardinal's legal jugglings were not entirely without point. There were rumors, however, that Cesare was beginning to demand an accounting of his estate. A hothead like that, Ludovico thought, could not be put off much longer. Everyone knew that he hated his younger brother Juan. All the honors and titles that the Cardinal had bestowed upon his favorite chafed. They should by rights have been Cesare's, instead of the few paltry ecclesiastical offices that dispensed only a meager income.

"What is the use of laws that do not dispense justice?" Cesare had demanded of Ludovico as they rode back from a day's hunting. "I am the eldest and am therefore entitled to the lion's share."

"That is true," Ludovico had agreed.

Cesare's face had darkened in suppressed fury. "I know a law," he said, touching his scabbard lightly, "that cannot be disputed."

Ludovico shook his head ruefully. If it ever came to

that, it would be no great loss. Juan was a scoundrel and a weakling.

Cesare speared his meat savagely. He had followed what he thought was the exchange of glances between Lucrezia and the tutor, and his stomach soured with hatred. The talk of fighting continued on either side of him and normally he would have sopped it up as a piece of bread sops up juices, except that he was busy walking in the dark reaches of his own mind.

"There is a new poison," Ludovico was saying, "that acts so slowly that it is sometimes a matter of days before the victim succumbs."

Cesare's ears stood up like a hare's.

"It works on the nervous system like fingers on a lyre, giving the murderer ample time to cover his tracks, and when the victim finally succumbs, the symptoms are almost those of a natural death. Isn't that so?" He turned to his physician.

Sciopine nodded his assent. Each great house, it was known, had its staff of experts. Sciopine himself worked day and night amongst his bottles and vials. Great beakers of glass holding beautifully colored fluids, that could maim or kill, waited to be used. Soft yellow powders that erupted in a puff of smoke, breaking the blood vessels and forming clots or shredding the ganglia and producing spasms and partial paralysis. Gian Sciopine smiled. Knowledge was power, and he kept the doors to his laboratory tightly locked.

Orvieto, the advisor, leaned forward with interest. "Who has developed this poison?"

"The Medicis." Ludovico pushed aside his trencher and pulled at a pyramid of purple grapes and figs, sending some of the fruit rolling onto the table.

"We would be well advised not to dine there," Orvieto said reflectively.

Ludovico peeled a fig and belched. "What a pity.

21

The food is always outstanding. What do you say, Sciopine?"

In the silence that followed, the physician realized that the entire table waited for his answer. Sciopine put his mind carefully to the matter at hand. "Leave it to me," he said. "I'll think of something."

Ludovico smiled sardonically at the grape which he still held between thumb and forefinger before tossing it back on the pile of fruit. "Yes, I was certain you would." Food no longer interested him. His gaze turned idly toward Seraphina.

Captain Capello, watching the direction of Ludovico's eyes, leaned over and smiled. "With such a one as that, you would be advised to try the root of the orchis. Otherwise she will suck your strength, leaving you as weak as a woman."

Ludovico nodded. The root of the orchis was shaped like a human testicle. Impotent old men devoured the harder part to make them potent. The softer part, which killed desire, was fed to nuns. "And which part," Ludovico asked carefully, "which part would you recommend I eat?"

Captain Capello's face remained a smiling mask. "Your Lordship well knows which part he has need of, the same as your youthful charge," he added, inclining his head toward Cesare, whom he hated. "I am told that certain—uh-ladies are much taken with him."

Cesare's face filled with blood. He had not missed Capello's deliberate pause at the word "ladies." The Sicilian captain was known to have no use for women, preferring instead his stable of soldiers, with whom he could do as he pleased. He was especially taken with blood and mutilation, his eyes in the heat of battle shining with lust as he lopped off an arm or a leg. The valet at arms who stripped him of his clothing afterward whispered of ejaculations.

22

Cesare, his face still smarting, reached over and speared the mutilated joint of mutton with his knife, thrusting it under the Captain's nose. "Perhaps this might be more to the Captain's taste . . ."

Ludovico threw back his head and roared. The boy would go far with that agile mind of his. "I propose a toast," he cried, "to Cesare Borgia, the future Captain General of the Church of Rome. May he rule wisely and well."

"I shall," Cesare said seriously.

Ludovico pushed back his chair and stood up, a sign that the meal was over. Carlos sat quietly in his chair, giving the others time to gain the archway. Lucrezia too sat quietly. She was wondering how she could see Carlos alone before her lesson tomorrow.

CHAPTER 4

The afternoon sun slanted sharply through the partially
shuttered window and onto the open book. The book
had lain there for some time.

Lucrezia gazed at it with unseeing eyes. She had
thought at first to study tomorrow's lesson and surprise
Carlos with all that she had learned, but the food and
wine had made her drowsy. She banged the book shut
and slammed it down on the table. She was tired of sitting around and mooning. She would go to Carlos and
tell him exactly how she felt about him.

She opened the large chest that stood beneath the
window and rummaged around in it, throwing everything on the floor until she found what she wanted.
The wrapper was a soft blue and was made of the
lightest silk. Her father's new mistress had sent it to
her for her birthday. She threw everything else back in
the chest, using her foot to stuff it all in. Should she
take a bath, she wondered. No, there was no time, and
besides, her maid was taking her siesta in the alcove off

her room. She would wash her face and her neck, she decided; that was quite enough.

She kicked off her shoes and pulled down her hose. Soon she was in her shift. Should she keep it on or take it off? Off, she decided. She would wear the blue wrapper with nothing on underneath. She clapped her hand to her mouth. Mother of God, she had forgotten that she was bleeding! She put on a pair of linen drawers and stuffed them with rags. There, that would take care of any embarrassment. After she had finished brushing her hair, she pinched her cheeks and bit her lips to give them color. Now, she thought happily, stepping over the clothing she'd thrown on the floor, now she was ready.

There was no one about the wide halls. Everyone was asleep or resting. She padded on bare feet to the opposite wing of the palace, her heart beating quickly. What if he were angry? What if he made her go back to her room? She wouldn't, she decided; she simply wouldn't listen.

She stood for a moment outside the wide oaken door. Then she knocked. There was no answer. She grasped the heavy handle and turned it. The door opened noiselessly. The room with its whitewashed plaster had a look of Spartan simplicity, broken only by a cerulean-blue vase of daisies which stood on a table next to the chair and by a profuse clutter of books.

Carlos was sitting in the chair next to the window. So deep was he in the book before him that he did not look up and see her.

She continued to stand in the doorway, beginning to feel foolish. She coughed, and Carlos looked up slowly, marking his place with his finger.

"What is it, Lucrezia?"

"I didn't mean to disturb you," she faltered, gather-

25

ing the loose ends of her wrapper together. "But please, may I come in?" Now that she was here, she seemed to be at a loss as to what to do or say. "I couldn't sleep, it's so hot." Tentatively she added, "I thought perhaps we could talk."

"Come in," he said courteously, amused despite himself. "It might be better, however, if you left the door open."

"I don't think so," she said, closing it softly. "Cesare might see us, and he is very jealous of you." She stopped to see what effect that had on him. "I wouldn't want him to think that I like you better than he."

"Him," he corrected her.

"Him," she repeated quickly. "I wouldn't want him to think that I like you better than him."

Carlos nodded. "I understand."

"Do you know what I think would be nice," she asked, taking the hassock from under the table and drawing it close to him. "I think it would be nice if you read me some poetry."

"What would you like me to read?"

"Something sad," she said, her eyes on the curve of his mouth. "You choose."

"Lucrezia," he said kindly, "don't you think you had better go back to your room? We can read in the library later."

"No. Please, read to me now."

"All right," he sighed. "We will read the poems of Catullus."

She followed him with her eyes as he picked up the small volume from the heap of books on the table. She saw the daisies and smiled. "I'm glad that you like flowers. Cesare says they are foolish. I'll pick you some more when they die."

"If I am going to read, then you must be quiet." He began reading in Latin.

26

Lucrezia frowned in annoyance. "I don't see why you have to read it in Latin. It's so hard to follow."

He stopped a moment and smiled. "In that case, you must listen more closely."

Lucrezia picked nervously at her fingernails.

"Besides, it was written in Latin originally, and translation robs it of its beauty." He continued to read, losing himself in the cadence of the verses.

Lucrezia looked at the way his lashes fanned darkly against his cheeks. Nothing was going right. This wasn't what she wanted at all. She had lain in her bed after the noonday meal, tossing about on the hot sheets, the small points of her breasts stiff with excitement, thinking of Carlos and the shape of his mouth, imagining the soft skin of his lips pressed against hers and longing for something to fill the sweet aching void between her thighs. Finally she had gotten up in despair. She had never been with a man. She had never given them much thought until the hard swell of her breasts had begun to push forward against her shift, the small tender nipples continuously chafed by the thin bleached muslin. And then last week at her lessons, Carlos had accidentally brushed her bare arm with the sleeve of his tunic and she'd watched in surprise as the skin on her arm rose up in tiny bumps. It was that night that she started the fantasies, using her finger to help bring them to fruition, imagining all the while the heat of his hands and his mouth all over her, achieving her climax alone in her narrow bed, so that when she saw him the next day she looked away in shame, feeling that he must know what she had thought and done.

But he had merely looked at her and smiled as he always did, saying, "Now we will start on Homer," leaving her to glance furtively at the deep corners of his mouth and the clean curve of his jaw.

27

She did not hear a single word that he read. When finally he turned to her, the question he'd asked regarding Homer hanging in the air unanswered, he found her gazing steadily at his hands.

"What's wrong?" he asked her.

But she only turned her head away from him, the color rising from her neck to the tips of her ears.

"Lucrezia, please tell me what's wrong." His arms came around to hold her. He drew her gently toward him, alarmed by the sudden spasm of sobbing which shook her small frame.

The heat of his body went through her, melting her reserve. Throwing her arms around him, she sobbed against him as though her heart were breaking.

"Lucrezia," he whispered, his mouth warm against her ear, "tell me what it is. Is it the rabbit, still?"

"The rabbit," she choked, nodding. "Yes, it is still the rabbit." For all her body's urgency, she could not let him know the real thing that burned inside her, the thing that would not let her rest, for he would only laugh and then she would die.

Carlos had allowed her to cry a bit more. Then he gently loosened her arms from around his neck. When she tried to cling to him, he smacked her playfully on the backside. "Those are enough tears, even for a rabbit. Let us see if you can smile. That's better," he said as she complied rather tearfully, for she would do anything he asked of her. "And now let us return to Homer. He's waited long enough."

Today the sound of his voice fell softly against her ears. At first she tried to pick out a word here and there, but her knowledge of Latin was meager and she finally stopped trying altogether, smoothing her blue wrapper and listening instead to the sound of his voice, letting it enter and fill her until, worn out by the strong

28

wash of feelings within her, she fell asleep with her head on his knee.

Carlos closed the book and sighed. He had been engaged to instruct her in the classics with a little bit of French and simple arithmetic thrown in for good measure. But Lucrezia was a difficult pupil. In the middle of a lesson, her attention was apt to wander. She was unable to sit still for very long; he would sometimes look up from the lesson to find her leaning out the window in search of other amusement or fast asleep with her head on her arms.

Lately, though, he had found her looking at him in a way that made him vaguely uncomfortable. He would talk to Adriana. Perhaps she could think of a way to divert the child. Only recently, rumor had it, Cardinal Borgia had arranged a marriage contract between Lucrezia and Don Cherubino Juan de Centelles, Lord of Val d'Ayora in the kingdom of Valencia. The contract provided that Lucrezia would receive a dowry of thirty thousand timbres in gold and jewelry from her father and brothers.

Two months later Rodrigo, in his cavalier fashion, had decided that he could make a better match for his daughter. Accordingly he broke the first contract and negotiated a more advantageous one for Lucrezia with Don Gaspare d'Aversa, Count of Procida. In a year and a half, if Cardinal Borgia did not again change his mind, they would be married. Married, Carlos thought, and she was only a child. Nor would she be less of a child in a year and a half.

CHAPTER 5

The weeks had passed and the weather had grown cooler. The early October mornings were filled with wood smoke and a curling mist that rolled down from the hills and lay in the basin of forest until the sun burned it away. It was good weather for hunting, though, the dampness compounding the odors of lichen and leaf with a good rich mulch of earth and mold. The horses' hooves would be lost in swirls of vapor, a wildness in their eyes as they hit the hidden ground, and their nostrils jetting steam, lending them the look of demons, as their manes and tails carved out behind them.

Some of the animals had gone into their holes and burrows, not to be flushed out until spring, but there was still plenty of stag and rabbit and a shy fox or two.

Cesare rode out with Ludovico and his friends every morning, his body joyfully succumbing to the hard ride. He gloried like an animal in the constant play of his body, working out his choler like a horse who needs a good run.

"When do you go to Perugia?" Ludovico asked him.

"In January. Why?"

"Nothing. I will miss you, that's all."

Cesare flushed with pleasure. Now might be a good time to mention Carlos. "I would feel better about going away if Lucrezia had a different tutor," he said cautiously.

Ludovico glanced at him in surprise, remembering just in time to skirt a stout branch that barred his way. "What is wrong with Carlos?"

Cesare hesitated, choosing his words with care. "He walks in the woods like a woman, smelling the flowers like a girl. He even picks them and puts them about his room. He has turned Lucrezia's head completely. She minces about now and is constantly smoothing her dress. The other day, she wouldn't even let me kiss her. 'It is unseemly,' she said. 'Unseemly.' That is his word, not hers." His face darkened. "Soon he will have her eating with a fork."

"What is wrong with that?" Ludovico inquired.

"Fops," Cesare sputtered, "French fops eat with forks!"

"So do the de' Medicis, I'm told."

Cesare's rage was complete. "Who gives a damn what they do? Someday I'll grind them all into the dust!"

Ludovico threw back his head and laughed. "By God, I believe you will!"

Cesare was not anxious to leave the Orsini stronghold. Since Lucrezia would not submit to him or even tumble any more in play, he had started a liaison with Orvieto's wife, Seraphina, which was very much to his liking. The woman was positively insatiable, and in Cesare she found her match. It had all started very oddly. He was walking the grounds one night as she

31

was making her way back from the barracks, her hair disheveled, her clothing awry. He had recognized the cloaked figure immediately and called her by name.

"How was it?" he bantered. "Good as always?"

"Out of my way, bantam. I'm tired."

"I'll bet you are. Is there anything left under that cloak?"

She spread open her cloak obligingly.

Cesare caught his breath. She had nothing on underneath.

"What is it?" she laughed. "Have you never seen it before?"

"I've seen it, all right," he said, the fever in him rising.

"Not like this, I'll wager."

He stared at her breasts. The nipples were full and bruised.

She smiled. "Come, let us see what you're made of."

Cesare unfastened his codpiece and she pulled him down on top of her.

"You're big," she said, "much bigger than I thought." She reached her climax almost at once, but she pressed against him, unwilling to stop. "Keep going," she panted greedily. "If you keep going, I can do it again." She achieved her second climax with a long shuddering sigh.

Cesare fell wearily against her.

"Again," she urged. "Again."

She sent for him the following day. The room was darkened, and thick with the odor of incense. Seraphina lay stretched on a leopard throw, her thin, feverish body all hollows and angles. "Don't bother taking off your clothes," she said, watching him like a hungry cat. "I want to see how it looks sticking out of your pants."

He entered her almost at once. There would be time to play with her later . . .

32

He lay on his back and looked at her. She really was a fright. Her hair lay plastered in damp strings against her face. Her skin was pasty and pitted with pocks.

"Did you like it?" she asked, watching him anxiously.

"It was all right," he said. "Not bad for an old woman."

"I'm not old. I'm only thirty-six."

He crossed his arms behind his head and smiled. She had given him the upper hand without so much as a struggle.

"You did like it, didn't you?"

He continued to smile and say nothing.

She grabbed a lock of his hair, but he was laughing so hard by now that he scarcely felt it. She started to tongue him, from the soles of his feet up to his thighs. When she reached the thatch of auburn hair she stopped, breathing fast at what she saw.

Then he pulled her over on top of him.

Cesare had no intention of leaving all this. He would stay until he tired of it. In Perugia he would find rooms in a good inn and go daily to the university. There would be women available to him, of that he was certain. But it would be unlikely to find such a one as Seraphina.

As for Lucrezia, he loved her still. These daily mountings with Seraphina had nothing to do with love. They were nothing but a mere clamoring of the flesh, whereas his feeling for Lucrezia was different. That feeling wounded and dazed him.

In less than two years, he thought darkly, she would be married to Don Gaspare d'Aversa. Cardinal Borgia, in casting about for a suitable political alliance, had arranged the match when Lucrezia was eleven. It would be consummated on her thirteenth birthday. Cesare had seen this pasty-faced weakling and had despised him on sight. It had taken no special gifts to see that he was a spineless weakfish who was completely unworthy of his sister.

Oh well, he thought, that was almost two years away. Right now he had something else to think about, his father's letter which had come to him only this morning, urging him to leave at once for Perugia so as to give himself plenty of time to find quarters and arrange his classes. Well, he was not leaving. He would write and say that he'd gotten involved with a woman. His father understood about women. Why, just recently, and Cesare grinned as he thought of it, he had heard of the Cardinal's latest escapade, a baptismal party from which he had barred all males save himself and a few ecclesiastical friends. One disgruntled husband was heard to remark: "My God, if every child born within the year came into the world with its father's clothes on, they would all be priests and cardinals!"

No, his father should have no serious objections to his postponing his trip for several months, just long enough for his son to enjoy himself a little.

Things might have gone as Cesare wished had he not forced his attentions on the eleven-year-old daughter of a chambermaid. When she resisted, he threw her to the ground, spread open her thighs, and raped her. When he was through, the child lay screaming and writhing in pain until two gardeners who were working nearby came running to her aid. Afraid to touch her, they summoned Dr. Sciopine. But the girl suffered for three weeks and then died in the most horrible agony.

Ludovico, when he heard of it, was furious. "That is no simple trick!" he shouted at Cesare.

The boy flushed. "The next one won't be so choosy."

34

Ludovico had the child placed in the cemetery he reserved for his own family, and stood at her graveside with bowed head until the coffin was lowered. He ordered Cesare to give twenty pieces of gold as atonement to the poor bereaved mother.

"I won't," Cesare shouted hotly. "Not even if she were the best harlot alive!"

Ludovico looked at him coldly. "You will do exactly as I say, because if you don't I will see to it that you leave this place at once and never see your sister again."

Cesare averted his face, his ears flaming.

"Furthermore," Ludovico continued, "you will beg the woman's pardon and kiss the hem of her gown."

"But she is nothing but a common chambermaid!" Cesare exploded.

Ludovico regarded him coolly. "It is meet then, for you are not even that much."

CHAPTER 6

Lucrezia was growing impatient. Time hung heavy on her hands. In a few months Cesare would be gone to his studies in Perugia. She thought of that with sadness, even though she was piqued with him now, ever since she had found out about his carryings-on with Seraphina, that and the chambermaid's little girl. There was really no end to his mischief, but only she realized how driven and tortured he was, how terribly unhappy inside. After all, hadn't he come to her more than once, laying his head against her and crying his heart out with deep, wracking sobs for no reason, except perhaps that someone had insulted him or not shown him proper respect.

The first time he had done this, she was horrified. She'd just sat woodenly as he dug his head into her breasts, the most awful sounds choking out of his throat, like an animal. And then had come the hot, pelting tears, running down the cleft of her breasts. She had sat there for the better part of an hour, numb but afraid to move lest she waken him. Poor Cesare, she thought, he was so hard on himself and on everyone else but her. How many times had she heard her father admonish him: "Go slowly, my son," pausing briefly as he always did before the word "son." "Go slowly lest you tear yourself to pieces or else someone does it for you."

And ever since she had heard her father say that, she had been plagued by an awful recurrent dream. Cesare stood in the midst of a large empty plain, on horseback. All at once, from every direction, mounted soldiers rode in with halberds and swords, hacking away at his body until he fell naked from his horse, his clothing in shreds, bleeding from a thousand wounds and dying like an animal on the hard-packed ground.

The first time she dreamed this, she had awakened screaming, and her nurse, Maria, had come running in from the alcove where she slept, to see what was wrong. When she told Cesare, he had only laughed. "What a magnificent way to die!" he had exclaimed. He still teased her about it, saying every so often, "And one day, when I am lying in a field, broken by the swords of my enemies, will you be there to comfort me?" But even so, the dream exerted a numbing horror. She would come awake moaning, her face wet with tears, filled with a hollow dread that left her sick with fear. At such times she would get out of bed and wash her hair. She always washed her hair when she was troubled and didn't know what else to do.

"So much soap and water," Maria would scold, "it will loosen the roots of your hair!"

Lucrezia would pull just to make sure, but her hair remained anchored as firmly as ever to her head.

She moved slowly across the room. Bars of yellow sunlight slanted in through the deep casement windows, but the sun was not warm. It was a thin lemony yellow that seemed to trickle rather than beam. The air out-side was crisp, the ground hard with cold. Abruptly she turned and shivered, looking away from that bleak landscape. She did not like this time of year. It made her feel shrunken and sad. The trees raised bare skeleton arms. The grass turned an ugly shade of brown. It was as though everything had sickened and died. Beneath the hard ground, she knew, were flowers waiting for the spring, just as she was waiting. She thought of them with sadness. Did they feel as badly as she? In the winter months she was fretful and cried easily. Just the other day she had found a bird with a broken wing. She had carried it to her room, placing it gently on a nest of crushed velvet and feeding it with her fingers. But it would not eat, and the next day she found it lying on its back, its claws bent to the air. This had occasioned such a paroxysm of grief that Maria had threatened to spank her if she didn't stop. She had cried for hours, for the bird was somehow mixed up with her feelings for Carlos and Cesare's departure for Perugia, and the fact that she herself someday would die. Would it be, she wondered, on a cold wintry day such as this when she would no longer, like the bird, have the spirit or the strength to draw another breath?

The air in the room was cold, even with the fire burning in the hearth. She had been reluctant to leave the warmth of her bed this morning, anticipating the cold shock of air against her body. Her clothing lay across a bench in front of the fire. The heat had warmed them and she donned them eagerly, not both-ering to change her undergarments. In the winter months she rarely bathed. Now that she had her peri-ods, she would have to wash down there, but she wouldn't have to bathe.

"Water will ruin your skin," Maria advised her re-peatedly, anointing her instead with warm fragrant olive oil. Her hair was a different thing altogether. It had to be washed several times a week or else she felt peculiar. And when she was nervous or upset, she washed it oftener. Heavy and thick as it was, it seemed fashioned of beaten gold. She did not tie it, but let it fall heavily against her neck and shoulders, keeping a strand in her hand and twining it through her fingers, as if to reassure herself that it was really there. When she was perplexed, she sucked it. When this happened at her lessons, Carlos would ask, "What is it that you don't understand, Lucrezia?"

Dear Carlos, she thought, climbing into the dress that Maria held for her. In less than an hour she would see him. She stood quietly while Maria did the hooks for her. "Perhaps I should wash my hair," she said, pulling out a strand and smelling it.

"You will catch your death," Maria said. "We will brush it clean instead."

Lucrezia sat beneath the brush, enjoying the rough animal feel of the bristles against her scalp. She loved being cared for. She could sit for hours, her head moving with the brush without any will of its own. Maria had to remind her to hold it up lest it fall off altogether into her lap. The only thing better was when Maria rubbed her with oil. She loved the feel of hands on her body, even her own. In cold weather Lucrezia complained constantly of aches and pains in her back and shoulders and Maria would apply a compress of heated lamb fat to the afflicted areas, after which she would massage more oil in deeply until her own poor fingers were numb.

"Lucrece!" Maria's voice cut across her musings. "Stiffen your neck before your head rolls off!"

Lucrezia dug her fingers into one of the fresh hot rolls that Maria had brought in a napkin, pulling out the snowy white softness and leaving the crust, which was too much trouble to chew. She ate the insides of three rolls and washed them down with some watered wine. She hoped she would not get gas, for she could not expel it in front of Carlos. Last week she had had to sit through her lessons in the most awful agony, her stomach knotted with cramps that she could not relieve. When her lessons had ended, she had grabbed her books and fled without even saying good-bye, her outraged stomach horribly distended. Perhaps if she ate slowly . . . but it was too late for that. She had already wolfed down the hot dough, gulping the wine down on top of it, and even now she could feel the bread start to ferment. With Cesare, she thought, there was no such problem, for the two of them expelled gas in one another's presence constantly. In fact, it had once been a game between them to see who could do it the loudest and longest . . . Cesare of course had won.

Maria came over to her with a strip of rough linen. "Here, open your mouth. If I left it to you, all your teeth would fall on the floor."

Lucrezia could not help smiling, for Maria did not have her own full share of teeth and was obliged to soak her rolls in wine before she ate them. Her gums, she announced proudly, were as tough as wood, but unfortunately not sharp.

"Rub," Maria insisted. "Rub hard!"

Lucrezia rinsed out her mouth in the copper basin that stood by her bed.

Maria handed her a pinch of anise. "That will settle your stomach," she said with a wink.

Lucrezia took a moment to look in the glass. "Maria, do you think I should wear my hair coiled? Perhaps it will make me look older."

Maria took the strip of linen and spread it out to dry before the fire. "Isn't that the way Signora Adriana wears her hair?"

Lucrezia shrugged. "I've never noticed."

Maria smiled. "I have it that she is with child. The laundress told me herself. There were no rags to wash this month."

Lucrezia stopped pinching her cheeks with her fingers. She ran over to the large leather trunk that stood at the foot of her bed. Perhaps she should change her dress. Perhaps she should wear her light blue silk instead of the thick plum worsted. The blue silk was very becoming. It made her eyes look almost blue.

Maria watched her. "What are you doing? Those are summer things."

Lucrezia threw open the heavy lid and started spewing things onto the floor.

Maria stood with her arms folded as Lucrezia drew out the blue silk. "You can't wear that now. You'll catch your death!"

"Please, Maria. If you argue I'll be late!"

Maria remained impassive. "Put the dress back. If you leave now, you'll be on time."

"Please, Maria. I'll cry."

"Then cry," Maria said, "but your eyes will be swollen and red."

"Maria," she screamed, "I hate you!"

Maria smiled. "Go on, Lucrece," she said gently. "You don't want to keep him waiting."

By the time Lucrezia reached the schoolroom, she'd forgotten her pique with Maria. Her feelings were always so close to the surface that one good fit of tears or anger was enough to dissipate them. By now she regretted her outburst. No matter, she thought cheerfully, when she got back she would give Maria a great hug and all would be well.

She entered the room with a light step. Carlos sat in a chair by the window, a heavy volume before him.

"You are late," he said without looking up. "Tardiness is the thief of time."

She smiled. He was always so serious. What difference did a few minutes make? After all, she was not going to be a scholar. Wasn't it enough that she could speak Spanish and Italian as well as a little French and Latin? Besides, in less than two years she would be married and what good would it do her to know that Catullus was born in Verona? She wouldn't care then and she didn't care now. She could have children just as easily, Catullus or no Catullus, and wasn't that what girls were for? She thought of her future husband with distaste. She had caught a glimpse of him some years back and she had not been pleased, for Don Gaspare, she thought, had looked like a plucked capon. True, he had had a bad cold. But all she remembered was a runny red nose set in a pale face. Cesare had taken great pleasure in pointing out his spindly calves. He had called him an ugly puke to his face, and Gaspare, who was starting adolescence, had hidden his face and sulked. Perhaps, Lucrezia thought hopefully, perhaps when the time came, her father would not insist on the match. Two years was a long way off.

"You are late," Carlos repeated, marking his place with his finger, "and you are not paying attention besides."

Lucrezia colored. How well he looked today, how very handsome. He was wearing a creamy shirt open at the throat with a simple leathern buskin. His fawn-colored tights fitted him closely down to the soft deer-skin boots, wide-cuffed at the knees. "You've let your sideburns grow," she said.

"Lucrezia," Carlos said firmly, "you must learn to be on time."

"I'm sorry, Carlos. I really am." Her eyes traveled

42

to the green beryl set in heavy gold which he wore on his forefinger. "Is that a new ring?"

"We will not speak of light things, Lucrezia, until you have had your lessons."

"I am sorry, Carlos. I try to be good, I really do. What is that book you are reading?"

Carlos smiled despite himself. "It is a book of animal stories. It is called *The Physiologus*. You like animals, don't you, Lucrezia?"

"Oh, yes," she said, settling herself down on the arm of his chair.

"Good," he said, opening the book to where his finger was. "Then listen to this: 'The lion brushes his footprints with his tail as he walks so that the hunters may not track him.' "

"Is that really true?" she broke in impatiently.

"Please, Lucrezia, you must listen and not speak. 'The unicorn cannot be taken by hunters because of his great strength, but he will allow himself to be captured by a pure virgin.' "

Lucrezia giggled. "I don't believe that, do you?"

" 'The phoenix,' " Carlos continued, " 'lives in India and every five hundred years he fills his wings with fragrant herbs and flies to Heliopolis, where he commits himself to the flames in the temple of the sun. From his ashes come a worm, on the second day a fledgling, and on the third a full-grown phoenix.' "

"How lovely," Lucrezia breathed. "I like that."

Carlos closed the book shut. He now had her full attention. "Tell me," he said, "what are the four great empires?"

"The four great empires," she repeated, still thinking of the phoenix. "The four great empires? I can't remember."

"But you studied them only yesterday," he reminded her.

"I know," she said impatiently, taking up a strand of her hair and twining it through her fingers. "But that was a long time ago and so much has happened since."

Carlos suppressed a smile. "Repeat after me: Babylonian, Macedonian, African and Roman . . . Now," he said after she had done this, "who was the last and the greatest of the Latin Fathers of the fourth and fifth centuries?"

She twirled her hair faster. "Oh, Carlos, I can't remember."

"That too was yesterday's lesson," he said reproachfully. "The answer is Augustine. Your father, I think, would like you to know that."

"Augustine," she said anxiously. "I'll try to remember that, Carlos."

"Now what is he famous for?"

She put the strand of hair in her mouth. "Famous for?" she repeated. "I don't know."

"Take your hair from your mouth, Lucrezia. Augustine completed Church doctrine for transmission."

"Yes," she said. "I'll try to remember that."

"That will be all for today," Carlos was saying.

Lucrezia was not ready to leave. "Couldn't I sit on the hassock and read? I promise to be quiet."

"What about your walk? Maria will be expecting you."

Lucrezia drew her shoulders together. "It's so cold outside. I don't really want to go."

"Nonsense." Ludovico stood in the doorway, his tall figure filling the frame. "Fresh air is good for you," he said, his eyes missing nothing. "Your cheeks are the color of chalk. What will your father say when he sees you?"

"My father?"

Ludovico smiled. "He is coming to pay us a visit. He

44

should be here tomorrow or the next day, and I can't have you looking like a consumptive."

"My father?" Lucrezia said again. "He's coming here?" All at once she was filled with gladness. Aside from Carlos and Cesare, he was the one she loved best in the whole world. She could see him arriving in the midst of an impressive entourage. He would come laden with gifts, for he knew how much she loved them. When she got him alone she would climb up onto his lap as she had always done and he would hug her and feed her sweetmeats. Perhaps then she could prevail upon him to change his mind about the marriage match. If she had to, she would even cry, for she knew how that distressed him.

She skipped from the room and smiled. He would understand perfectly when she told him that she wanted to marry Carlos.

CHAPTER 7

His Holiness did not arrive for three days. The kitchens went full blast in preparation for his arrival. Sauces were mixed and stored, haunches of venison were roasted and covered with cloths against flies and vermin, and partridge, quail, and pheasant were roasted whole and then dressed in full plumage.

Giuseppe, the custodian of the kitchen, was in such a state of nerves that he could not speak without shrieking. He would allow no one to assist him in dressing the birds which would form the centerpiece. It was he who carefully broke the necks of the birds and cut their throats, ever so carefully so that the heads still adhered to the neck skin, flaying the skin with feathers attached, drawing out the viscera to sweeten the flesh, hanging them upside down to drain them of blood, trussing and spitting them. Then when they were brown and crisp enough, he would pierce them with a fork to see whether the juice ran with blood or not, letting them cool a bit before he fastened the feathers back on and spread their tails, making them look as they looked in life.

Trenchers of bread, baked several days in advance to ensure their firmness, were waiting to sop up the sauces and juices at each place. After the meal they would be given to the poor at the gates, who would fall upon them and suck eagerly at the flavors remaining within. In addition, table loaves filled the ovens. These were delicate and fine, and the crusts were offered to the ladies to soak in their soup. Then there was the coarse-grain bread for the servants, barley bread for those who were doing penance, and a few loaves of rye for Adriana and other favorites of the court who ate it to preserve their beauty.

Some of the venison was being boiled in huge caldrons for pastries and pies. Baskets heaped with vegetables in season stood in the adjoining storeroom, all covered with garlic cloth to keep out the roaches.

Giuseppe's speciality was a macédoine of fruits which he fried like rissoles in hot fat, serving them warm with sugar and cinnamon.

The Cardinal's appetites were legend, the pleasures of the table being of no lesser importance to him than the pleasures of the bed. No matter, his stomach would not go begging.

In the dining hall Ludovico had posted the new seating arrangements. A long table would be added and placed on a dais at cross length to the already existing table. On the dais would be seated Ludovico, flanked by the Cardinal and Adriana; also Lucrezia and Cesare, the physician Sciopine, and the advisor Orvieto. Captain Capello, Seraphina, and the others were relegated below the salt, so to speak, to the lower table. Seraphina was delighted. She had no wish to sit next to her husband.

Also posted was a manual on etiquette which read:

47

AVOID QUARRELING AND MAKING GRIMACES.

DO NOT STUFF YOUR MOUTHS UNNECESSARILY.

DO NOT EAT ON BOTH SIDES OF YOUR CHEEKS, BUT CHEW ON ONE SIDE AT A TIME.

DO NOT MAKE UNNECESSARY NOISES IN SUPPING YOUR POTTAGE.

DO NOT LET YOUR FORK LIE IN YOUR FOOD. CLEAN IT PROPERLY EITHER BY LICKING IT OR RUBBING IT ON THE CLOTH.

DO NOT BITE YOUR BREAD AND LAY IT DOWN, BUT RATHER BREAK OFF WHAT YOU REQUIRE AND LEAVE THE REST FOR THE POOR.

DO NOT RECALL A DISH WHICH HAS ALREADY BEEN REMOVED.

DO NOT SCRATCH OR PLAY WITH THE DOGS AT THE TABLE.

DO NOT DRINK WITH A MOUTHFUL OF FOOD.

IF YOU MUST BLOW YOUR NOSE, CLEAN YOUR HAND AFTERWARD BY WIPING IT ON YOUR TUNIC OR PASSING IT THROUGH YOUR TIPPET.

DO NOT BLOW YOUR BREATH ON YOUR NEIGHBOR.

WHEN THE LOAF IS SERVED NEAR YOU, CUT IT IN TWO FROM BOTTOM TO TOP, DIVIDING THE TOP CRUST INTO FOUR PARTS AND THE BOTTOM CRUST INTO THREE. THEN PUT YOUR TRENCHER IN FRONT OF YOU AND WAIT QUIETLY.

IF YOU MUST EXPEL GAS, DO SO CAREFULLY SO AS NOT TO INTERFERE WITH YOUR NEIGHBOR'S APPETITE.

A staff of servants was set to polishing silver which was generally stored in the strongroom. Among the pieces was a large vase of solid silver supported by four grinning satyrs. This vessel would be filled with sweetmeats and sugarplums and would be set directly in front of the Cardinal, for his fondness for sweets was well known.

The everyday tallow dips would be discarded in favor of waxed tapers, and the candlemaker and his assistants worked day and night to supply the thousands of candles which would be needed for the Cardinal's visit.

Meanwhile, an army of servants cleaned and scrubbed. The apartment assigned to the Cardinal was completely rehung in crimson silk, that being the color of the cloth. Even Seraphina's golden swan bed had been confiscated for use, much to her chagrin, since it was the most elegant bed in the palace and had a mirrored headboard.

In the lower and upper halls, the old rushes were bundled together and the floors were swept clean of debris. The carpets were swept and laid, and where there were no carpets fresh rushes were spread with a quantity of rosemary and clove for fragrance.

Great basins of potpourri were spread throughout the lower rooms. Eucalyptus bark was collected for the hearths, and throughout the palace there ran a hum of excitement and anticipation. The only rooms that were not touched were the kitchens and the private apartments of the courtiers where the Cardinal was not expected to go.

Lucrezia climbed the winding stairs to the turret three or four times a day, looking in vain for the distant dust which would herald her father's arrival.

Cesare was less anxious. He was aware that his father had much to take him to task for, and so he was busy preparing his case, anticipating everything that would be said and forming rebuttals. When he felt he had covered everything thoroughly, he took himself off to Seraphina. In another week or so he might be gone. He would make the most of the time remaining to him.

49

On the third day Lucrezia saw a cloud of dust which announced a rider. Even as she watched, the dust disgorged a man and a horse. She clattered down the turret stairs, almost falling over the hem of her dress, which she'd forgotten to lift. By the time she reached the ground floor of the palace, the man was at the gates.

On her way down she had stopped only once, to bang on the doors of Seraphina's apartments and shout to Cesare that her father had come. Receiving no answer, she had run on her way.

Ludovico had ordered carpets to be spread over the wide staircase leading up from the main hall. They would be taken up again and stored when the Cardinal's visit was over. Now they were loosely anchored, and Lucrezia, in her haste to descend, nearly went flying into the arms of Carlos, who strolled below, book in hand. Ordinarily she would have stayed, but now she merely smiled as he steadied her and ran without pause through the heavy front doors and down the ilex-bordered path to the palace gates, where the major-domo stood waiting to receive the courier.

The man was clearly exhausted and covered with dust. "His Holiness," he panted, "will undoubtedly reach here by nightfall."

The general alarm having been sounded, everyone moved quickly. The great tables in the dining hall had been set for days. The dust covers were removed. The peacocks would be brought in last, otherwise the dogs would tear them to pieces. The great silver urn of sweetmeats was in its place before the Cardinal's setting. On either side of it were miniature silver fountains which spouted wine.

Ludovico had stripped his strongroom of at least half of its gold and silver. A good portion of his wealth sat on the table. The main part of the banquet would

50

be served on golden platters set with precious stones. The most spectacular piece of all was the nef, a vessel of solid gold and silver carved in the form of a ship with a high prow and stern. Encased within this work of art was the giant salt cellar which some laid to the hand of Michelangelo, some small towels for greasy mouths and fingers, and seldom used utensils such as forks. This vessel would be offered first to the Cardinal and then to the others in descending degree of rank.

A huge, elaborately carved drinking cup made of solid gold sat at Ludovico's right. It would be shared by the host and guest, so that there would be no question of tainted wine.

In the middle of the lower table, flanked by peacocks in full plumage, stood a multitiered silver stand piled high with pomegranates from Cyprus, almonds from Asia, lemons from Media, chestnuts from Costano, pears and apples from Greece. There were even plums from Syria, peaches from Persia, and cherries from Cerasus.

Were it summer and not this bleak time of year, flowers would have been spread in profusion. As it was, the servants contented themselves with spreading leaves. The table was a bower of greenery, leaves sprouting from under plates and trailing down to the floor in careless array. They had even arched them over windows and doorways and arranged large clumps in the corners of the room.

Lucrezia, after taking a delighted look at all this greenery, ran off at once to wash her hair. It would take at least an hour of sitting by the fire to dry. Maria would have to towel it first, rubbing the strands until they shone like gold. She would also take a bath, she decided. It had been a month since she had last removed all her clothing. Her father's visit warranted it. She shivered in anticipation of the cold air against her skin. Perhaps the huge tub could be moved next to the fire. .

When she entered her apartments, she found that Maria had made everything ready, having ordered buckets of hot water the minute the alarm was sounded. Even now the last bucket was being emptied into the tub, which Maria had placed as close to the hearth as possible. The steam from the water rose in little tendrils of vapor.

Lucrezia wriggled out of her clothing with difficulty. The woolen shift stuck to her like a second skin and Maria had to roll it off carefully.

Maria laid the shift to one side. After Lucrezia's bath, she herself would bathe so as not to waste the water. Then she would soak the shift and wash it clean. Meanwhile she sat back to watch her mistress lower herself gingerly into the hot water which she had taken such pains to procure. Only Lucrezia, Adriana, and a few others would be fortunate enough to have a bath such as this. The others of the court would go begging. The line had formed behind her as she waited. It had taken Giuseppe himself to disperse them. He had come out of the kitchens beaded with sweat, for the ovens were going full blast with preparations for the evening's feast. "There is no more room on the stoves for water!" he had thundered. They could all either anoint themselves with oil or lower themselves into an icy tub for all he cared.

Fiamina, Seraphina's maid, approached Maria. "Perhaps when you are through with the water?" she suggested.

Maria had looked through her and sniffed. Her mistress's bathwater would be used afterward to wash her clothing. After that, she said loftily, Fiamina could do whatever she liked with it, indicating that even then it would be too good for the likes of Seraphina.

She watched Lucrezia bathe. The girl's slight body was beginning to change. The boyish hips had swelled into curves. The little breasts had become firm apples. Where before there had been no waist, now it was tiny and pert. Maria smiled. Lucrezia was made for love and no doubt about that, although she was still a bit narrow for childbearing. She looked away finally from the soft golden thatch of the pubis.

Lucrezia lowered herself into the bath by degrees. The hot water grabbed at her flesh like pincers. She sank into it finally up to her chin, feeling the great good warmth of it go through her. Ah, she thought, she had not been this warm since last summer. Her eyelids drooped, her limbs softened, her mind drifted away into sleep.

Maria's voice brought her back. "If you don't get out now, your hair will never dry and you'll catch your death besides."

Lucrezia's eyes opened. She'd been dreaming of Carlos. He'd just bent over to kiss her. "Just a little while longer," she said, closing her eyes, willing Carlos to come back.

"Now," Maria said.

Lucrezia got up slowly, and as she stepped out Maria picked up the shift together with the long woolen hose and threw them into the tub. She would let them soak while she dried Lucrezia's hair. She herself would have no time for a bath. She moved the girl next to the fire, sat her down on a bench, and proceeded to rub her vigorously.

Seraphina sat in her rooms and fumed. Fiamina had been unable to procure a heated bath for her. The water in the tub was cold and uninviting. What a piss! First Ludovico had commandeered her swan bed for that fat cardinal, and now she was to be denied the comfort of a warm bath. As Orvieto's wife she was en-

53

titled to more consideration, but that miserable husband of hers had the spine of a slug and refused to intervene in her behalf. He had tried half-heartedly, at her instigation, to get her bed back and had failed at that too.

Seraphina dismissed the cold bath as entirely too astringent and wiped herself instead, paying careful attention to her privates. She and Cesare had been busy for three days without stopping.

Her hair, she noticed, was stringy and damp from all her exertions. But there was no time to bother with it, she thought irritably; the thing now was to fill the pocks in her face. "Fiamina!" She waited impatiently while the maid walked slowly in from the alcove. "Do you have the wax?" she asked sharply.

Fiamina smiled. It was she who had devised the idea of dropping a bit of melted wax into each pock hole. Since there were so many to fill, this took a long time. When she was through, she smeared them over with a thick pink paste until they were smooth. When that was dry she dusted on pulverized mother-of-pearl. The entire effect was ludicrous, rather like that of a made-up corpse, but Seraphina was enchanted by the absence of holes in her skin.

She picked up the hand mirror and help it up to her face. "What about my hair!"

"What about it?" Fiamina mocked. "Did he fuck the wrong end?"

Seraphina fought to keep some control. Let her finish her work. After that she would give her a good clout on the side of her head. "You forget where you came from" was all she said.

Fiamina laughed. "The same place as you." She took up the hot curling tongs and applied them to Seraphina's head. The result looked like snakes sticking out all over her head.

Seraphina looked in the glass. The effect was arresting; she was not entirely displeased. It would go well with the Nile green tunic and the wide girdle of gold. Orvieto, she thought happily, would pee in his pants when he saw her. "I need some more powder," she said critically.

Fiamina gathered together a bunch of pigeon feathers and dipped into the box of powder. She slapped them lightly against Seraphina's face. The result was weird, but interesting.

Seraphina peered at the pink alabaster mask, which ended at the chin and ears, leaving the rest of her skin its usual pasty color. She would outshine everyone, she thought with satisfaction. Perhaps she would not clout Fiamina after all.

CHAPTER 8

Cardinal Borgia arrived while Lucrezia was having her bath. Ludovico was similarly engaged, and so the major-domo met him at the gates and escorted him to his apartments, where a hot bath awaited him.

When he was finished with his toilet, Ludovico rapped at the Cardinal's door. He was anxious to see him and to make amends for his absence.

The Cardinal's valet came to the door, his nose sharp with suspicion. "Ah, Your Grace," he said when he saw who it was.

Cardinal Borgia, naked as a babe, sat in a large tub of steaming water.

Ludovico smiled at the spectacle before him, for His Holiness seemed to be immersed in a caldron of fire and brimstone.

The Cardinal's hawk nose and beady eyes peered out at him through the moisture. "It is hot as hell in here, perhaps hotter. One day I shall know, I warrant."

"I daresay," Ludovico agreed. "How does it go, my friend?"

The Cardinal inclined his massive head. "Not too badly. The last orgy I attended was not on a par with the others, but then one cannot expect perfection in all things." He stood up in the tub, the water sluicing from him in torrents. "I am anxious to see Lucrezia. How is she?"

"A perfect beam of sunlight," Ludovico pronounced.

"A pearl, the Cardinal replied, "a perfect pearl . . . And Cesare?"

"You have received my letters, I presume."

The Cardinal rubbed himself vigorously with the wide strip of linen his valet handed him. "Yes, well, he's always been difficult." It was clear the Cesare was not one of his favorite subjects.

"It is not merely a question of being difficult. He has caused a child's death."

The Cardinal inserted a corner of the towel in his navel, giving it a good wipe. "Yes, well, he is disgusting, like myself."

Ludovico chose to ignore that. "The boy is not bad, but he seems to have an endless capacity for cruelty."

The Cardinal, instead of answering, paid special care to his privates.

"It pains me to have to say it," Ludovico continued, "but I do not think that he is a fit companion for Lucrezia. He seems to think of nothing but the gratification of his senses."

The Cardinal, having finished with himself at last, made a reply. "I am sorry about the child. I will give the mother a purse of gold."

Ludovico waved aside the offer. "That part has been taken care of. The thing is, what do we do about Cesare?"

"Cesare?" the Cardinal repeated. "Perugia will change all that. He will have all he can do just to keep up with his studies."

57

"And what are your plans for him after Perugia?"

The Cardinal smiled. "A Pope depends a great deal for his power upon jurisprudence."

Ludovico caught his breath sharply. So now it was out in the open, the Cardinal's bid for power.

"And what about Juan?"

The Cardinal's face softened as it always did upon mention of Juan. Of his four sons, Cesare, Pedro, Juan, and Geoffrey, Juan was clearly his favorite.

"Juan will be Captain General of the Church of Rome."

"Are you so certain, then, of your election?"

The Cardinal winked. "They can do no less."

The giant hall was beginning to fill. Two hundred candles lighted the room. Torches flared in their brackets. Throughout the palace braziers burned to give additional heat.

Ludovico looked with satisfaction at the scene unfolding before him.

As the courtiers seated themselves in order of rank, a lackey approached bearing the huge nef and set it down before the Cardinal, who reached in and drew out the towels, which would then be used by the others in descending order of importance. By the time they reached the end of the bottom table, they would be black with dirt. Some refused them altogether, preferring to wipe their fingers on their clothing or the tablecloth.

Antonio, the food and wine taster, stood behind the dais. He had had nothing to eat all day but a little bread to sop up the acids in his stomach. With great gravity he reached forward and tasted the wine in the goblet that Ludovico and the Cardinal would share throughout the meal.

"Come," Cardinal Borgia said with a careless show

of bravado, "let us have none of this. It spoils my appetite."

"Stay, my friend," Ludovico said gravely. "I would not be so missed as you."

The Cardinal was pleased by this. "To put the truth squarely between us," he said modestly, "I would not be missed by many."

Ludovico smiled. There were not many who possessed Cardinal Borgia's charm. His eyes strayed from the Cardinal to his wife. Adriana looked especially lovely in a blue dress cut modestly to show the merest amount of cleavage. She met his eyes and smiled. She had not yet begun to show that she was with child.

Lucrezia was also in blue. She had prevailed upon Maria to let her wear the blue silk dress in honor of her father's visit. As soon as she had seen her father, she had run to him and jumped into his arms as though she were a child of five, hugging him and refusing to let him go. Cesare had stood diffidently off to one side, not relishing the encounter he knew would come.

Ludovico looked down the length of the other table. The Cardinal's eyes, he had noticed, kept straying to Seraphina. My God, Ludovico thought, but the woman looked even more of a fright than usual. Her ruined face glistened like a pink meringue. Her hair stood up all over her head like serpents. Orvieto, he noticed, kept his eyes studiously away from his wife.

Seraphina, aware of the Cardinal's interest, leaned across the table and shouted up to the dais, "Is it true, Your Holiness, that there are now some twenty thousand prostitutes in Rome, all of whom pay a monthly tribute to the Pope?"

The room fell into a hush as everyone waited to hear the answer. Orvieto turned a hideous shade of crimson.

The Cardinal looked down at her, taking in every

facet of her feverish face. "At the last count, my dear lady, there were only nineteen thousand. But that, of course, was last week."

A burst of laughter followed his remark.

Ludovico relaxed. Antonio stepped forward to pour the wine. Ludovico raised the goblet to his lips for the ritual courtesy sip, then handed it to the Cardinal. "May you go as far as you wish," he said softly.

Cardinal Borgia looked around at the variety and array of dishes set before him. A whole suckling pig lay on a bed of parsley, its skin crackled to a crispy brown. It would belong to him entirely, for everyone knew of his fondness for pig. From the kitchen, Giuseppe prepared to launch his masterpiece. On a bier covered with laurel leaves and supported by four lackeys lay a roasted ox. It was carried to the center of the room, complete with laurel wreath, where Giuseppe waited. From its interior he drew a roast kid, from that a roast piglet, from that a wild turkey, from that a roast capon, and from that a roast pigeon.

Cardinal Borgia led the applause, his eyes bright with anticipation. The feast had begun. The Cardinal refused nothing, heaping his plate high.

When those on the dais had been served, the waiters moved the platters to the lower table, where everyone waited hungrily.

The Cardinal ignored the fork which lay before him, preferring to use his knife and his fingers in the Roman manner. After thirty minutes of steady eating, he stopped for breath, taking up the goblet and turning it against the light. "Inside the earth," he said, "the precious metals grow, always tending toward perfection. It is also said that base metals left in the ground will improve themselves until they reach their most perfect form, which is gold."

"That may be true," Orvieto answered gloomily, trying not to look at Seraphina, "but all the same it would be better to have a philosopher's stone to speed up the process."

"There is an alchemist in Rome," Ludovico said, "who is reputed to be very successful in transforming lead into gold."

Cardinal Borgia nodded. "It was a friend of Pope Clement's who said that if all the seas were boiling quicksilver or molten lead, a handful of the philosopher's stone sprinkled over that immense quantity of liquid would transmute it into gold."

Cesare snorted, risking his father's displeasure. "If that is so, why wasn't Pope Clement wealthier?"

Cardinal Borgia looked at his son and smiled. "I was right to mark you for jurisprudence. You have a good mind."

"I put no trust in these things," Orvieto said sourly. "Those men were all rascals. It is well known that they fooled their patrons at will."

"You are forgetting the true aim of the alchemist," Sciopine broke in. "The true aim of the alchemist is to transmute man from the limited world of his senses to a superior state of being in which he is no longer the pawn of blind fate."

The Cardinal spoke softly. "I have never been limited by the world of my senses, only enlarged." Here he patted his girth and everyone laughed. The Cardinal, his eyes fastened lovingly on the suckling pig before him, reached out with his knife to hack off a last succulent morsel.

Seraphina, who felt that she had remained silent long enough, shouted up to the Cardinal. "Your Grace, do you know that they have taken away my bed and given it to you?"

His Holiness paused in the midst of transferring the piece of pig to his mouth. "Madame," he said, his eyes carefully taking in every feature of her wanton disarray, "I am forever in your debt."

Everyone laughed but Lucrezia. She did not like to see her father paying court to a woman like that. Besides, he had practically ignored her all evening. She was just about to seek his attention when Ludovico turned to the Cardinal.

"I am curious to know your opinion of the Italian peasant," he said.

The Cardinal wiped his chin of the fat which had dripped onto it. "The peasant is a pig," he pronounced, "especially when he is merry. I like him better when he weeps. It is therefore meet to keep him downtrodden at all times."

Ludovico said nothing.

The Cardinal raised a fat ringed forefinger, which he shook in the air for emphasis. "There are four things which are merciless when they gain the upper hand. They are fire, flood, pestilence, and the common folk . . . I will have some more of that," he said as the waiter prepared to remove from the table a rather large blood pudding ringed with sausage. "Their greed is infamous," he said, belching loudly. "They conceal their first fruits and pick their tithes, hiding what's best for themselves, thereby depriving the Church of its just due. Verily," he concluded, scooping up a mountain of pudding and shoving it into his mouth all at once, "they are a wretched lot."

Orvieto, anxious to distract himself from Seraphina's behavior, leaned forward. "Your Holiness's point is well taken. They do not deserve such stupendous fare as pork and geese, but should subsist on thistles and straw, thorns, beech mast and acorns, since they are not much above their own domestic beasts."

The Cardinal fixed him with a fond look. "You are a man of good parts and know what is what." He turned

62

to the others. "Do you know that the peasant women in Venice sell their own hair, on poles in the Piazza San Marco? The Venetian ladies are fond of false hair."

Carlos leaned forward at this. "It is a mark of shame to have to sell one's hair. If they do so, they do it out of desperation."

Cardinal Borgia gazed at him thoughtfully. "And who are you?"

"I am Carlos St. Angelo," the young man answered firmly.

Cesare tugged at his father's sleeve. "He is Lucrezia's tutor, the one with milk in his veins."

The Cardinal shook off Cesare's grip. "What do you believe in, sir?"

"Let me say, sir, that I do not believe in the kind of Christianity that is practiced today."

"No milksop this," the Cardinal muttered to himself. Then turning back to Carlos, he said, "It is common knowledge that the flesh of martyrs at the stake emits an odor of sanctity while the flesh of heretics when they are burned stinks like rotten flesh. How do you account for that?"

"I would venture to say," Carlos said carefully, "that martyrs and heretics smell alike when burned."

The Cardinal watched him closely. "And which, my dear sir, are you?"

"I am a tutor," Carlos answered. "Only that and nothing else."

Lucrezia sat silent, her face small and unhappy. Here were two people whom she loved, and they did not seem to like one another at all.

Ludovico picked up a large bell and rang it. A procession of servants filed in with sweetmeats and syllabubs.

The Cardinal fastened his eyes on a towering pink-

63

and-white pudding which shimmered and swayed, pyramids of little iced cakes, and tiers of glacéed fruits. His mouth watered with anticipation. He turned his attention from Carlos to happier things.

Ludovico leaned back and relaxed, watching the Cardinal sample everything in turn, his eyes shining with pleasure.

CHAPTER 9

Ludovico was not entirely satisfied with the Cardinal's visit. For after His Eminence had eaten and drunk all that he could hold, he turned his eyes toward Seraphina.

That lady played it for all it was worth, wriggling her shoulders, tossing her head, looking like nothing so much as a wild, frolicsome horse. The snakes of her hair had by now fallen into her face, which had turned such an astounding shade of pink as to be quite alarming.

It was with great difficulty that Ludovico was able to steer the Cardinal's attention from Seraphina back to the matters at hand. "If you do not separate Lucrezia and Cesare at once," he said, putting it to him bluntly, "I cannot be responsible for what may happen."

Cardinal Borgia looked at him shrewdly. "Have they been together yet?"

"I don't think so, but it is only a matter of time."

The Cardinal made a steeple of his fingers and thought. It was not unusual for brother and sister to come together, in mere animal play. They were both healthy and sensuous. However, Lucrezia, with her characteristic weakness and passivity, could easily give in just to please her brother. If that happened, she was doomed. For with a scandal like that, who would want her?

He sent for Cesare the following day. He would see to his instant departure. Indeed, he could not leave soon enough. He would make Ludovico promise that the two would not be left alone together. He looked up as Cesare came in. "Get your things together. You are leaving for Perugia tomorrow."

Cesare's face took on color. "Why?" he asked warily.

"Because, my son," the Cardinal said, pausing as he generally did over the word *son*, "I am anxious to put your talents to use."

"What is the real reason!" Cesare demanded.

The Cardinal smiled, clasping his hands. "What reason would you like?"

"I am not suited for law. Let Pedro go, or Juan, or Geoffrey."

"You have the best mind," the Cardinal said in a voice of silk. "Else I should not have chosen you."

"Why tomorrow?" he asked, his voice unnaturally high. "Why can't I have more time?"

The Cardinal softened. "All right," he said. "You may have until the day after."

The boy's face looked bewildered.

His father felt a brief stab of pity for him. "Believe me, my son, I know what is best for you."

Lucrezia sat on the floor, going over the gifts her father had brought her. Wisely enough, he had waited until Cesare left, so that they would somehow sweeten her loss. Still, she was sad. Her father had already returned to Rome, taking with him the feeling of excitement that his visit had brought.

In the grate a low fire was burning. Even so, it was chilly and damp. She looked over at Adriana, who was sitting in a chair with her needlework. "Adriana, I can't think. Please help me choose."

Adriana smiled and put her work aside. The shipment of silks had been stored in an upstairs room, as far away from the damp ground as possible, with a small fire going to dry out the moisture in the air so that molds could be kept at a minimum. There were rich brocades from the Byzantine and some lighter brocades from China, as well as the usual heavy stuff from Lucca and Venice.

Cardinal Borgia, in a quick burst of generosity, had told Adriana to choose for herself and give the rest to Lucrezia. But Adriana, knowing his sudden shifts of mood, had declined with thanks, saying that she would rather Lucrezia choose first. She would be very happy, she said, with whatever was left. Also, it would help keep Lucrezia from grieving.

"All right," she said, settling herself beside the child. "Let us see what we have here." There was some rich cloth of gold and silver seeded with tiny pearls. "This would be lovely for your wedding dress," Adriana said generously, although she would have loved it herself.

Lucrezia's eyed kindled. "But that is not for a year and a half."

Adriana smiled. "We will put it away. When the time comes, you may not be able to find anything as good." She held up one piece after another, testing them against Lucrezia's skin. In no time at all she had chosen half a dozen pieces.

Lucrezia warmed to the game. "What about this?" she asked, holding up a heavy black velvet elaborately embroidered with gold.

67

"I think that is more Seraphina's style, if you do not mind my saying so."

"I shall give it to her, then," she said impulsively, "because she makes everyone laugh."

When they were through, Adriana had chosen for her delicate shades of pale green, ivory, and peach. These colors, she felt, would not overwhelm Lucrezia's fragile beauty. She chose also a dark green velvet embroidered with lotus flowers, to be made into a dressing gown. It would be trimmed in sable.

Lucrezia's eyes were shining. "It is really not so bad to be married," she said, her small hands stroking the soft velvet.

Adriana smiled. When Lucrezia was married, she would not be so different from what she was now. She would dress up in heavy stuffs, bounce her golden ball, and run and jump with her spaniel. What would her husband think of it?

A few weeks later news came that Pope Innocent VIII was seriously ill, that his stomach could no longer retain food and it was only a matter of time. There was further news. Cardinal Borgia, it was said, was intriguing to usurp the papacy. He had given a series of dinners for the competing cardinals, several of whom died of indigestion. Rumor had it that poison was used, a kind that left no trace.

Ludovico shook his head. Cardinal Borgia was capable of anything. And Cesare was no better. He had just received a letter from the chancellor of the university, detailing the boy's outrageous behavior. Foremost among his escapades was the abduction of the wife of one of the regents of the university. He had abducted the lady and taken her to an inn, where the two of them stayed for a week, until they were discovered by a cross chambermaid who had been unable to get in to clean. The irate husband, along with twenty of his fellows, came and demanded his wife.

Cesare, looking pleasantly down from the window, inquired as to the weather outside, explaining that in the past week he had had no chance to observe it, and then in the middle of this speech he emptied a jar of slops onto their heads.

The gentlemen below drew their swords. Seeing that he was outnumbered, Cesare quickly knotted the bedsheets together, grabbed the poor woman, who was still naked, by her hair, and pushed her over to the open window, calling out to the men below that they could have her since he was through with her. She begged him to let her stay—in fact, she clung to the sill, until he finally smacked her on her bare behind, shouting loudly that she must return to her husband like a good wife, and lowered her down.

A month later Cesare was back at Monte Giordano. Upon his arrival at the palace, he had gone straight to Lucrezia's room, where he passed the remainder of the night sitting on her bed and chatting with her like a school chum.

Ludovico had written immediately to apprise the Cardinal of what had happened, but Cardinal Borgia had other things on his mind and had written back to him: "Let him stay with you until the autumn, at which time I will see to it that he continues his studies in jurisprudence at Pisa."

Ludovico sighed. A whole summer with that animal. The escapade at Perugia had taught him nothing. He went about boasting of the gratitude of married women. Well, there was nothing to do but wait, just as the Cardinal was waiting for Innocent VIII to die.

On August 6, 1492, the twenty-three cardinals entered the conclave for the election of the new Pope. It was held in the Sistine Chapel, and the Vatican palace was barricaded to enforce secrecy. The most popular candidates were Ascanio Sforza and Giuliano della Rovere.

Ludovico sat back to await the results. No one at Monte Giordano spoke of anything else. Wagers were placed. Della Rovere was the favorite, and it was rumored that Charles VIII of France had paid two thousand ducats into a Genoese bank to support him.

Cardinal Rodrigo Borgia was at the bottom of the list. He had no sponsor, and his excesses were legend. It was unthinkable that his brother cardinals would cast their votes for him.

As for Cesare, he professed not to care about the election. Out of favor with his father since his recent disgrace in Perugia, he had received a scathing letter, several pages long, from the Cardinal about his lack of discipline and control. The boy's face, after reading it, had darkened with anger. His brother Pedro, his father had written, was to be Captain General of the Church if he succeeded to the papacy. After him came his brother Juan and then his brother Geoffrey. Cesare would do well, his father concluded, to pattern himself after Pedro, who was a paragon of virtue.

Cesare thought of Lucifer. He too had been thrust from his father's bosom. And despairing of ever being loved, he had made himself hated. Well, he would do the same.

"The old goat will never be Pope," Cesare told Lucrezia one day, thinking to tease her, "for there is no tiara large enough to hide his horns!"

Lucrezia's eyes filled with tears. "You are wicked to say such a thing. Papa is good and kind."

"Good and kind to his strumpets!"

"Cesare, please don't say such things."

70

"He doesn't care about you, Lucrezia, any more than he cares about me."

Lucrezia's tears spilled over. "He is always sending me things. Would he do that if he didn't love me?"

"Why not? He takes from one and gives to another."

Lucrezia, unable to bear this any longer, gave a little cry and ran from the room.

Cesare watched her go, his heart heavy within him. Teasing her had not been fun. She was, after all, the one thing that he cared about in all the world. He saw her small white face filled with woe. He would go to her room now and tell her he was sorry. He might even tickle her; she loved to be tickled. But he stood where he was, mired in the misery he'd made for himself, for he knew he wouldn't go to her. He would go to Seraphina instead. And he'd really give it to that bitch!

On August 10, much to everyone's surprise, Cardinal Borgia was elected Pope.

"We are Pope and Vicar of Christ!" he shouted in Latin, looking about him with an expression of extreme relish.

Only Carlos was not surprised. "It is not, after all, a measure of saintliness, but of means and methods," he said to Ludovico, who seemed to be thinking of other things.

Rodrigo Borgia corroborated this by sending a courier post-haste from Rome. "The other rascals hadn't a chance," he wrote, "for I was the greater rascal."

Ludovico had smiled at this. The man's honesty was disarming.

What actually had transpired was this: Ascanio Sforza, one of the aspirants, realized that he had little chance of winning, but that he had a great deal to gain in bribes by supporting Cardinal Borgia. For Borgia, it

71

was rumored, had moved all his valuables for "safe-keeping" during the election to Ascanio's palace. There were four mules laden with gold. After that, Sforza began to work for Borgia. In securing his support, Borgia secured as well the fourteen votes that had been cast for Sforza. He now had only one vote less than the two-thirds required by law. Nobody else would vote for him. Giuliano della Rovere, the favorite, was an arch-enemy. Nobody else would accept a bribe. Borgia had a brilliant idea. He would approach Maffeo Gherardo, the Patriarch of Venice, who was ninety-six years old and in a state of senile decay. He would cajole or bribe him into giving him his vote. It worked.

Ludovico burst out laughing at Cardinal Borgia's description of how he had beguiled the old man with a promise of strumpets and wine, throwing in a quantity of gold for good measure. In the end the poor man had given in simply to get his dinner, which had been withheld from him at Borgia's instigation.

Lucrezia, upon hearing of her father's election, could scarcely contain herself. "We are all going to Rome!" she exclaimed, jumping up and down in delight.

Ludovico looked at Adriana, who was heavy with child and in no condition to travel. "Rome will be unsafe for almost a month. We will wait for the coronation."

Even now reports were filtering in of the fires and sacking that always followed an election. The city was filled with mobs who raped, drank, and looted. Raging bonfires cast a constant pall of smoke. In the midst of all this, Cardinal Borgia, who was nearly dead of exhaustion, was placed on the throne and proclaimed Pope Alexander VI. Despite his fatigue Alexander received his well-wishers effusively, dispensing the Borgia charm. Cardinal de' Medici, more glum than most at

72

the way the election had gone, was overheard to whisper to della Rovere, "We are in the jaws of the wolf."

Rome, used to all kinds of scandal, recovered slowly from the effects of the election. How had this upstart whom nobody knew managed to secure the throne? All of Venice went into mourning. The French king, who had poured endless funds into the support of della Rovere, was inconsolable, reportedly unable to take any pleasure from his bed or his table.

How, his enemies asked one another, had Borgia dared to use such bold-faced bribery? Only the King of Naples had the answer. "He was at work as we slept," he mourned. And so the ripples of dissent widened, only to flatten once again on the waters of time.

At the Vatican, Rodrigo Borgia, now Pope Alexander, according to custom, distributed his goods amongst the poor—a token gesture, since everyone knew that what he gave was merely the skin of the milk which floated on top. Still, the gesture was made, and the people of Rome cheered.

In the Orsini stronghold, only Cesare remained unmoved. His father's ascendancy to the papacy meant little or nothing to him, for he would benefit least of all the sons. Cesare clenched his fists against his anger. Never mind, he thought, someday he would have it all to himself.

CHAPTER 10

The day of the coronation emerged hot and humid. The ride to Rome had been long and dusty. Ludovico had sat opposite Lucrezia in the ducal carriage without uttering a word, his eyes on the landscape. Adriana had not felt well enough to make the journey and had stayed behind.

Lucrezia reached into her reticule and drew out the tiny miniature Adriana had given her. She turned it over; there was a little piece of Adriana's hair inside. Her eyes welled with tears. She would never find anyone as good and as kind as Adriana, never. She put the miniature back in its little box and picked up the book that Carlos had given her. It was a book of poems by Catullus, bound in rich Moroccan leather. Dear Carlos, would she ever see him again? She had begged him to come to Rome with them, but he had only smiled, saying that the climate of Rome would not agree with him. I will go back, she thought, fighting the sadness that suddenly sat upon her, I will go back soon and everything will be as it was.

Maria looked disapprovingly at the apartment that had been assigned to them in the Vatican palace. The ceilings were painted with nymphs and naked cherubs. Lucrezia ran out on the balcony, which overlooked the rose garden. "Mmmm, it smells lovely." She ran back in and looked at the bed, her eyes shining. It was hung in pale blue silk, the hangings fastened at the head by two naked, smiling cherubs. From the four corners the fabric was peaked through a golden coronet.

"I love it," Lucrezia laughed, bouncing up and down on the blue silk coverlet. "I should like to stay here forever."

Ludovico lay on his bed thinking of Adriana. He was sorry she was not able to make the journey. He would be away only for a few days, he had promised her; he would return home right after the coronation. It was just as well, though, that she had not come. The noise from below was deafening, and there was the constant clatter of footsteps. He felt that all of Rome passed beneath his window. Shouts of laughter floated up, loud and shrill. The prostitutes would do a good business.

Alexander had winked and offered a woman to go with the room. Ludovico had declined with thanks. At home Adriana had suggested some of the ladies of her court, saying that she understood, that she would not expect him to be continent for so long. Some of them had even volunteered themselves as wet nurses—to the father, they had explained prettily, offering to show him their qualifications. He had had to turn several of them out of his bed after he and Adriana had begun to sleep alone to ensure her comfort. A brazen species, women, he thought.

Here at the Vatican they were even worse, affecting the dress of the French court, displaying their breasts down to the nipples, the corsets and girdles pushing them up into everyone's faces, not even waiting for nightfall to do their hunting, brazening it out at the table, using the tips of their tongues to indicate desire. What man would not be maddened with lust? He would be glad to return home.

The day of the coronation was so hot that Lucrezia had washed her hair twice. Even so, it felt sticky. She was sorry that Cesare would not be here to witness their father's triumph. But Alexander, taking no chances, had ordered Cesare to Spoleto. That wasn't fair, she felt. He had as much right to be here as Juan and Geoffrey, with whom she had nothing in common, for they had been raised in different homes. She reached for the sponge that lay in the basin of cool water and squeezed it to her temples. Mother of God, it was hot!

"They will be fainting in the streets," Maria prophesied darkly.

Lucrezia stood quietly as Maria pulled the heavy dress down over her head.

"What a dress to wear in such weather," Maria remarked, looking at the heavy, long-sleeved white satin, all padded and sewn with pearls. "You will cook like a roast pigeon inside it."

The path that the Pope was to take had been swept clean of garbage and refuse and then watered to keep down the dust. It cut a clean swath through the filth and debris of Rome. The houses along the way were hung with banners of silk and brocade. The Borgia device, a bull grazing on a golden field, was everywhere. Huge banks of fresh flowers were massed in profusion. Outside the Palazzo San Marco was an arch which had been specially constructed with a statue of a bull spouting water from its mouth, nostrils, and ears. Engraved on the arch in gold letters was the legend:

The people of Rome went mad. Their own lives
being meager, they dearly loved a spectacle. Over everything rose the muted roar of the populace, straining
at the ropes which held them for a glimpse of the
Pope.

When he finally appeared on a white horse, looking
down his long hawk nose at them, they went mad with
delight.

"Look how well he sits his horse!" they shouted. His
every gesture brought forth a roar of approval from a
mob hungry to approve. How easily he moved, they
noted, the sun gilding his noble profile, health and
vigor bursting from him in sheer animal magnetism.
Was he not a perfect man, this Pope of theirs? They
would not have been surprised if the heavens had
opened and rained down pure gold on him.

The heat and the crowds had given Lucrezia a
headache. Beneath the prison of her heavy dress her
body was running with water which soaked through
under her arms and across the small of her back.

The procession wound on. The cardinals and dignitaries had tried to outdo one another in the splendor of
their dress, and they would not shorten the ceremony
by one jot. But this was no climate for heavy silks and
brocades, and dark splotches of moisture stained the
splendid clothing.

When the procession reached the Lateran Palace,
the Pope, half dead of heat and exhaustion, collapsed.
His loss of consciousness was taken by all to be a sign
of extreme holiness, a communing with God. Supported by two cardinals, he revived enough to make his
way to the Sanctum Sanctorum. No sooner had he sat
on the papal throne than he again fainted dead away.
Water was thrown on him until he came to, and the

77

ceremony continued. The Pope had fainted twice. A holier man was never seen!

The air in the Basilica was somewhat cooler, but the crush of bodies straining to get in soon made it hot. Lucrezia swayed dizzily, and one of the prelates pulled out a packet of cloves and held it to her nostrils. The strong, sweet odor steadied her.

The heat continued late into the afternoon, and by evening it clung to one's eyes and swelled beneath the lids. Pillars of smoke rose from the city, drifting into windows and doorways, making it difficult to breathe.

After the ceremony Lucrezia returned to her room, removing her clothes immediately. The humidity was so high that even after a cool bath the moisture clung to her body and would not dry. She looked at the heavy silk dress she was to wear that evening and wondered if she had the strength to cope with it.

She threw herself onto the bed after her bath. Although the repast after the ceremony had been light, consisting of cold meats and fowl, fruits, cheeses and wine, she had been able to eat practically nothing, looking with distaste at those whom the heat did not affect, who were eating greedily. Maria took one look at her face, which was feverish with heat, and said, "I told you so!"

Ludovico had eaten lightly. He had made his excuses and returned to his rooms to take off his clothing and rest. He closed the shutters against the heat and noise. The odor of smoke hung in the room. Christ, but he hated this place, nothing but ruins everywhere you looked, all the splendid palaces, temples, and tombs nothing but ruins. And as if that were not enough, all the porphyry and marble from these ancient buildings was being burned daily for lime. The desecration appalled him, for the modern buildings which Alexander

78

had pointed out to him were poor stuff by comparison. All of Rome's beauty lay in its ruins. The city and its filth oppressed him. How he longed to go back to Adriana and the cool fresh air of Monte Giordano. The people of Rome looked like cowherds. The simplest country peasant had more dignity than the average Roman citizen, he thought.

He sighed. The entire city stank of heat and decay. The low swamps at the city's edge lay steaming in the hot sun and giving off the miasma of rot. Those who could afford it flocked to the hills, where the air was cooler. But even so, the city was full of fever, just as it was every year at this time.

There was a sudden bombardment as the entire city exploded in an illumination of fireworks and bonfires. The people of Rome rejoiced, he thought sourly. Tomorrow there would be races and jousting and free food for the poor. In this way would the Pope win over his people.

CHAPTER 11

Lucrezia had never seen such brilliance of jewels and dress as she had at the coronation feast. Her father, the Pope, had looked magnificent in a heavy brocade surplice trimmed in summer sable. His mistress, the beautiful Giulia Farnese, had made herself inconspicuous. There would be time to flaunt her later.

Ludovico had left the very next day. Lucrezia, who had always stood somewhat in awe of him, flung herself into his arms, crying as though her heart would break. "I can't stay here," she sobbed. "I want to go home and be with you and Adriana and Carlos."

Ludovico loosed her arms gently from around his neck. "Lucrece," he said, using the name she liked best, "in less than a year you will be married, with a husband and a house of your own. Now you must stay here and learn the ways of the court."

"But everyone I love is gone," she sobbed. "There is no one here I can talk to."

"Yes, there is," Alexander interrupted smoothly, pushing Giulia forward. "There is someone who would like very much to be your friend. Wouldn't you, my dear?"

Giulia came forward shyly. "I know what it is to be lonely," she said. "I would like to be your friend."

The days at the Vatican passed slowly. With the exception of her father, there was nobody there whom she cared for. Carlos, Adriana, and Ludovico were back at Monte Giordano. Cesare was banished to Pisa, where he continued his studies in jurisprudence. Slowly she came to rely more and more on Giulia Farnese for comfort.

Giulia washed her hair almost as often as Lucrezia did. On fine days the two of them would sit in the sun, rubbing dry the golden strands. While Lucrezia's hair fell to her waist, Giulia's fell almost to her feet.

Lucrezia soon came to like her father's favorite, who was like herself a lover of fancies and trifles. The Pope, generous to a fault with those he loved, never gave a present to Giulia without also giving one to Lucrezia. The lady's boudoir, filled to bursting with baubles, looked more like a child's nursery, for here and there, scattered on tables and chairs, were all the magnificent toys she'd lacked as a little girl. Sometimes for hours on end she and Lucrezia would dress and undress the beautiful dolls, whose wardrobes, sewn by the palace seamstresses, rivaled their own. When they tired of that, they played with Giulia's little daughter Laura— who was two and was rumored to be a child between Giulia and Alexander—treating her like one of the dolls, constantly dressing and undressing her.

As for Giulia, she had never opened a book, professing a frank ignorance of Latin and the arts.

"His Holiness does not lack for good conversation around him. There are other things," she said with a smile, "which please him as much or more." It was always at times like this or when her father made a sudden appearance and Giulia gave him a look that had nothing in it for anyone else that Lucrezia, feeling left out, would long for someone of her own.

In an excess of feeling, she sent Carlos an impassioned letter, together with several volumes of poetry given to her by one of the de' Medicis.

Carlos in return sent her a carefully worded message, thanking her for the books and sending her one of his own, one which they had enjoyed together. It was the book of animal allegories.

The days stretched endlessly. Bored, she turned to petty flirtations, and it was not long before the handsome young Cardinal Giovanni de' Medici caught her eye. The look he returned was hot and full of promise. The thought of his good looks cheered her somewhat. Soon she was washing her hair and pinching her cheeks in the anticipation of seeing him.

Strolling with Giulia in the gardens one day, she caught sight of him and in a loud voice inquired of Giulia whether or not she thought there were any good-looking men at court. Giulia, with a fine nose for intrigue, saw the bold look that Giovanni threw her. Lucrezia, she realized, would have to be watched, for the Pope had great plans for his daughter.

From that time on, Giulia pampered her to distraction, fussing with her hair and clothing almost as much as she did with her own. If she detected even so much as a freckle on the tip of Lucrezia's nose, she quickly rubbed it with unguents to bleach it out. If the girl had a bad period, it was she who settled her comfortably on the couch and rubbed her stomach with hot oil to ease the cramps.

Lucrezia's devotion turned into worship. If Giulia wore a dress lined in the Neapolitan style, then Lucrezia must have one too. If Giulia affected a head-piece, then Lucrezia must do likewise.

It was about this time that Giulia became pregnant. Lucrezia watched with alarm as her beauty ripened.

"Wouldn't it be nice," she said one day over comfits and wine as she stared enviously at the other's swelling bosom. "Wouldn't it be nice if we could both have our babies together?"

Giulia repeated this conversation to Alexander, who failed to find it amusing.

"The child will do anything to emulate you," he said seriously. "She had better go to school." Accordingly he made arrangements for her at a school near the Vatican. Here, he thought, she could polish her Latin and improve her Spanish and French as well. Latin, after all, was the *lingua franca* of visiting priests of all nations and it would be nice if she were able to say a few words to them. He thought of the marriage contract with Don Gaspare d'Aversa. Perhaps he would break it. Lucrezia deserved better.

She adapted herself well to this new arrangement. Now she too, like Giulia, had something new in her life to occupy her. Besides, the school was so close to the Vatican that she could go home whenever she pleased.

When she wrote to Carlos now, she invariably wrote in Latin, the phrases stilted and stiff, sacrificing sense and interest to grammar. When she was through with one of these letters, which generally took her hours to compose, her head would ache and her fingers would be swollen and stained with ink, mute evidence of her fierce concentration and her desire to please him. Afterward, if she were at home, she would seek relief from her labors in a wild outburst of energy. Grabbing Giulia around the waist, she would dance her breathless until they sank laughing onto the floor.

Alexander, coming into the room one day after a

trying session at the Vatican, watched them from the doorway, still wearing his heavy robes of state. Lucrezia, he noticed, was fast approaching womanhood. He thought about the throne of Naples for her. No, that might be better for Cesare. He could always have Cesare, who was by now Bishop of Valencia, throw off the priesthood and marry instead into the royal family. That would make him Prince of Salerno. He paused to think awhile. He was fiercely ambitious for his children. After all, weren't they but proud extensions of himself which he had put out in the world.?

Cesare, he thought, had improved. He had seemingly given up the idea of being Captain General of the Church and had deferred to his father's wishes. Discarding his formerly surly temper, he now seemed set upon charming everyone in sight. Alexander had just received a glowing report about him from the Ferrarese ambassador, who said: "He is of a remarkably happy, cheerful temper and is always in good spirits."

Alexander Borgia had listened to this in astonishment. He had never thought of Cesare in quite those terms. "Are you certain," he'd asked guardedly, "that you do not confuse him with my other son, the Duke of Gandia?"

The Ferrarese ambassador had drawn himself up to his full height, which was not much. "Most assuredly not, Your Grace. He cuts a far better and more distinguished figure than the Duke of Gandia, who is also well endowed. And believe me, I know, for he and I are on very good terms," he finished proudly.

Alexander was confounded. Had he misjudged Cesare so? Should he have made *him* Captain General instead of Pedro? The ferret face with its angry pocks of red swam before him. If there was any kindness or humanity in that boy, he had surely missed it. Or else the Ferrarese ambassador had been in his cups.

84

Cesare, however, could wait. Lucrezia's future must be secured now, before she got any older. Disquieting reports had reached his ears regarding little flirtations with Giovanni de' Medici and others. They were probably harmless enough in themselves, but Alexander was shrewd enough to know that the same hot, impetuous Borgia blood which flowed in his own veins flowed in Lucrezia's as well. How much longer would she be content to merely lower her lashes or flutter a fan? She was closer than ever to tears and laughter all at once, a dangerous sign. And should she be so indiscreet as to take to her bed any of the handsome young men who frequented the Vatican, nobody would want her. He was forced to make a decision. Should he write to Don Gaspare and push up the date for the wedding? Or should he, as he had thought earlier, break that contract and look around for someone better for Lucrezia?

His hand was forced by Cardinal Ascanio Sforza, who had done so much to win him the election. He would be honored, the Cardinal told him, if Alexander would consider his nephew Giovanni Sforza, Lord of Pesaro, as a husband for Lucrezia. Alexander thought on it. Why not? He owed Cardinal Sforza something. He would have to pay one way or another. Giovanni was twenty-six, and his wife Maddalena had died in childbirth. He was known to be handsome and even-tempered. And his uncle was Ludovico Sforza, the Duke of Milan. The marriage would do much to strengthen his position with Milan, which had always been shaky. He would speak to Cardinal Sforza tomorrow.

CHAPTER 12

Alexander made Lucrezia a present of a dozen Circassian slaves. "They are better-looking," he said, "than the Tartars, the Turks and the Slavonians; but watch them carefully, they have no great reputation for honesty." When she was married, he reasoned, she would be entrusted with the care of a great house. Let her learn now how to handle servants. It would keep her busy.

To amuse her further while he was negotiating a proper marriage for her, he arranged a great circus in one of the piazzas, which he had closed all around with a wooden stockade. Inside the piazza were turned loose two lions, two horses, four bulls, two young buffaloes, a cow, a calf, a wild boar, a giraffe, and twenty men.

Lucrezia, soon bored by all this, let her eyes rove around the boxes which had been built for the occasion. They soon came to rest on a dark-eyed, handsome young man who seemed to be looking at her with some intensity.

She nudged Giulia, who sat next to her. "Who is that?"

Giulia smiled. "That is Giovanni Sforza. Why, do you think he is handsome?"

"Handsome enough," Lucrezia replied, pleased. He was far better-looking than Don Gaspare d'Aversa. However, when the entertainment was over he was nowhere to be seen.

Giulia watched her in amusement. She was so like a child, flushed with pleasure at pleasing, and pleased with anyone who paid attention to her. Alexander, she thought, would be happy to hear about the interest she had shown in the young man. He would be happy, too, to know that the entertainment, which had been costly, was not entirely a failure.

Lucrezia, meanwhile, kept looking around for the dark-eyed young man. When Alexander was told of this, he smiled. Giovanni Sforza had not been invited, but only told of the entertainment. He had evidently decided to come and see for himself exactly what he was getting.

A few weeks ago he had sent emissaries to the Vatican to judge the quality of the Pope's daughter. These emissaries, poor relatives of his from the provinces, were only too eager to don their best clothing and taste the delights of the Vatican court. They listened seriously to his admonition to judge well. After all, he told them, he had no intention of taking to his bed a fat ugly hairy girl, no matter who her father was.

Giulia, grooming Lucrezia for the visit, told her sternly that she must be at her best, that these men were going to carry back a report of her looks and behavior. She did want a husband, didn't she?

Lucrezia nodded unhappily. She wanted a husband, but not if it meant sucking in her breath interminably and holding her spine stiff for hours on end. If she had to do that, she would faint.

Giulia ignored this and went on with her instructions. "You must learn to walk becomingly instead of leaping about like a goat. Look straight before you and don't jump about as though you are trying to see everything all at once, and change your direction slowly as though you are engaged in serious thought. Take small steps and move about daintily. Put a pleasing expression on your face at all times. Do not laugh, chatter, or shriek. Speak softly and hesitantly and only when you are spoken to.

"At the table," she continued, "do not overeat no matter how hungry you are. Keep your hands and fingernails clean. If you are sharing a dish with the person next to you, do not pick out all the best pieces for yourself. Do not stuff your mouth with food. Wipe the grease from your chin with a napkin instead of your hand or sleeve. And do not suck your fingers, belch, or break wind."

Lucrezia's face grew longer and longer. "I don't think I want to get married after all."

"Nonsense," Giulia said sternly. "It is nice to have a man around."

Lucrezia's eyes filled with tears. "Nothing that you have mentioned is fun. Besides, I will miss seeing Papa."

"You will be too busy to miss anyone," Giulia said firmly. "Oh, yes, one thing more. You must remember to eat anise seed and fennel before you get into bed. It will sweeten your breath."

Lucrezia burst into tears.

The three emissaries from Pesaro were wrinkled and old with large liver spots on their faces and the backs of their hands. Their mouths stank; their teeth were rotten pods.

Lucrezia turned her nose away as they bent over her hand. They looked, she thought, very much like the large carp that swam in the Vatican pools.

During their visit she grew more and more emaciated. It was not like her to measure her looks and her voice, to weigh and choose each word before she spoke. But her father looked at her so fiercely the whole time they were there that she did not dare to do otherwise. Her appetite shrank. If she could not eat with her fingers and fill her mouth, she would not eat at all. The flesh fell from her bones.

The three old men looked at one another in approval. She was overly quiet, it was true, and singularly lacking in spirit, but then she was not greedy at the table either. Here indeed was a wife worthy of anyone.

Alexander in the meantime made discreet inquiries of Giovanni's behavior. Did he horsewhip his servants? How many mistresses did he have? Did he treat them well? Everything was answered to his satisfaction.

The three emissaries, stretching their visit out, left after two weeks of feasting and careful scrutiny. They took with them a glowing report as well as several bolts of fine cloth, some heavy gold chains, and several signet rings, all gifts from Alexander, who left nothing to chance. "She has golden hair," they told Giovanni, "and a brow whiter than lilies. Her eyes change color with her mood. Her nose is straight and small. Her mouth is fresh, and her teeth are even and white. Her skin is free of blemish, and her hands are small and slender. She is slim, sweet of bodice and slender of girdle. Her conduct at all times is demure. Her mien is serious but pleasant. Her manners at the table are flawless; indeed, she eats almost nothing. And her breath," they finished, fingering their new chains, "is as sweet as incense."

Giovanni took careful note of their new finery. Then he went to see for himself. As he watched her from his seat in the box, he had to admit she had a certain charm, a certain freshness of color. Her chin, however, was a trifle weak. All the women in his family had strong, jutting chins. And she did seem disposed to chatter a great deal. And her fingers did seem always to be straying toward the sweetmeat box. All in all, though, there was nothing that couldn't be corrected.

Lucrezia had looked his way then and smiled. No, he decided, the chin was really of no importance.

Alexander had made up his mind. Giovanni had made up his. Lucrezia was not consulted at all.

Giovanni took up residence in Rome to ply his suit. The girl was not without suitors, his uncle Ascanio had confided. If he were not careful, she might slip through his fingers. Ascanio of course said nothing to his nephew of the gold florins he would receive from Alexander when the marriage contract was consummated.

Giovanni found that his uncle was right. For as soon as rumor had it that the Pope was casting about for a suitable match, offers began pouring in. Giovanni, lukewarm at first, began to press his suit. He could do much worse than to marry the daughter of a Pope. And besides that, there was that smile and the lovely blond hair. Yes, he could do much worse.

Don Gaspare d'Aversa, Lucrezia's fiancé, heard rumors of the alliance and hastened to Rome at a gallop.

"I think it would be best to stay indoors until he is gone," Ascanio warned his nephew. "They say he has a nasty temper."

Don Gaspare, with his family's backing and the marriage contract in his tunic, sought an immediate audience with the Pope. His letters had gone unanswered and he had no intention of backing down gracefully, not without a struggle. His family could use the Borgia influence in their behalf, for their fortunes were failing, and the Borgia dowry would come in handy. Waving the contract in his hand, stamping up and down the Vatican halls, he shouted for admittance, to no avail. If justice was not done, he roared, if he was not heard, he would appeal to all the princes in Christendom. Furthermore, he thundered, he would see to the prospective bridegroom. For if he could not have Lucrezia, no one else would.

"Keep him out," Alexander ordered. "I have no time for him!"

Giovanni, meanwhile, stayed indoors. He spent his time lounging about in his dressing gown and drinking wine. While he waited he amused himself by talking to clothiers and jewelers, who spread their goods eagerly before him. If all went well, he thought, he would soon have more money than he had ever seen in his life. It was not too soon to start thinking of new trappings. He would outfit himself from head to toe.

Goblet in hand, he strode from bolt to bolt in his worn dressing gown. He would have that and that and that, he said, pointing to a group of rich brocades, but not right away, he added. He would need a week or two to make up his mind. Everything should be resolved by then, he thought, and he would be free to order as he chose. After all, nothing was too good for the son-in-law of the Pope. He had the jeweler put aside several heavy gold rings set with precious stones. There was also a large cabochon emerald, which would look marvelous hanging from a chain. With the wine, his spirits soared. "Come back again in two weeks," he told them. "By then I shall have made my decision."

The jeweler rolled up his goods in a velvet cloth and thrust them into a metal casket, which he locked. He was willing to wait. All of Rome knew what was going on, and the odds were with Giovanni.

Alexander could go nowhere in the Vatican without hearing about the anger of the disappointed suitor. In order to appease him, Alexander negotiated a new contract full of loopholes which gave Lucrezia a perfect out. Don Gaspare, frantic at this point and running out of steam, signed it eagerly—and unwittingly signed away his right to wed Lucrezia. For beneath the tangle of legal snares lay three thousand gold ducats with which the Pope purchased her freedom. By the time Don Gaspare was aware of this, it was too late. He had signed of his own free will and the money lay in his hand. He could do nothing now but take the money, which he was lucky to get, and go home.

Giovanni almost wept with relief when Don Gaspare departed. Jubilant at the outcome, he congratulated himself on his cleverness. After ten days of lounging around and waiting, the small white face with its frame of blond hair, the heavy brocades, the fine jewels were all his. Forgetting the Pope's part in this, he felt he had won it all by himself. He was, after all, the cock, was he not? It was he who would make that child's thin, unformed body swell up, was he not? Delighted with this new role, he walked about puffed up with importance, shouting at the servants and looking down his nose at anyone who got in his way.

He could not help but notice how everyone bowed and scraped. Through the Pope's influence he had obtained the highest-ranking post in the Milanese army, but who was to say that he did not deserve it? He had burned that shabby dressing gown of his and ordered six new ones, each in a different color. He had ordered the rings and the emerald as well. Nothing in the world was too good for someone like himself. Besides, he could not allow himself to be outdone by Lucrezia's brothers, whose taste for elegance was legend.

He rubbed his hands. He really must order an elaborate gold necklace which would give him the stamp of wealth that he wanted. He would not receive the dowry money for several months, but he could always borrow on it, once the contract was signed. He could always go to his former brother-in-law, the Marquis of Mantua, who had plenty of money. The Marquis would be delighted to accommodate him in exchange for future favors.

Giovanni was now approached by all sorts of people who had never before given him so much as a second glance. After all, was he not marrying into one of the most influential families in Rome? It was common knowledge that his future wife possessed fabulous clothes and jewelry. Her wedding dress alone was reputed to cost fifteen thousand ducats, five times the amount the Pope had given to Don Gaspare to get rid of him. It was also known that Lucrezia had the Pope's ear, and his heart as well. Doors opened to Giovanni as if by magic. If he would only be good enough to put in a word here or there . . .

Giovanni smiled and promised nothing, picking up a pelt here, a bolt there, and numerous trinkets as bribes. He was not even married yet and already he was prospering. One anxious clothier had confided to him that in exchange for the contract for Lucrezia's trousseau, Giovanni would get his own for nothing, since the honor alone would make him rich.

The ink on the contract was no sooner dry than visitors and well-wishers started plying their suits.

Lucrezia loved the excitement and the attention. She

93

had been bored to the point of tears ever since she left Monte Giordano, and now suddenly everything was happening at once. She felt she was the center of the universe. Invitations to little suppers began pouring in.

Lucrezia received visitors between the hours of ten and twelve. At first it was fun, but then it became a bother, for it necessitated her being up and dressed early in the morning so that she could be ready at ten. By noon her face ached from smiling. She had not the patience to sit and listen to the pretty little speeches which were delivered to her one after another, and there were so many cheeks to kiss that it made her weary. Most of those who came were there to curry favor. She began to fidget and yawn. It was all she could do to keep her seat.

In desperation she devised a game. She amused herself by mentally removing the clothing of all who came to call. Her sudden smiles and fresh peals of laughter were thought by all to be part of the Borgia charm.

Lucrezia, whose span of interest was very short, was soon bored with this game. She would willingly trade places, she thought wistfully, with the commonest kitchenmaid rather than go on sitting and smiling and nodding.

It was only February now, and the wedding was not to be until June. It had originally been set for April, but Alexander, fearful that there would not be enough time for all the preparations that must be got underway, had pushed it ahead two months. It was really too bad, she thought. She hated waiting for anything. She remembered suddenly the dark-eyed, handsome young man she had caught watching her at the circus. She had only seen her groom once since then. That was a week ago, when she and her friends were in the garden playing at *guilles*. Not nearly so good at the game as some of the more robust girls, she had just knocked

94

down nearly all the pins and was letting out a loud shriek, when she heard her name.

She stood there, stick in hand, her face hot, hair disheveled, as her father came forward, Giovanni at his side. Mother of God, she thought, unable to move. He looked so elegant in his heavy gold chain and his magnificent new clothes.

Giovanni, having practiced, played his part well. With no trace of expression, he had taken her hot, sticky hand and kissed it, releasing it almost immediately. He had stepped back then and smiled as though he found her and her friends amusing.

Her heart had started a slow beat. This was the man who would be her husband, the man who would lie beside her at night. Her face grew hotter than ever. In an excess of feeling, she ran over to her father and threw her arms around him.

Giovanni had watched, smiling tolerantly. And then he had gone. She had not seen him since, although little gifts had been sent as a token of his esteem. Hearing of her fondness for dolls, he had ordered some superb ones from France with hand-painted porcelain faces and elaborate wardrobes. Lucrezia opened the packages and squealed with delight. It was the sort of thing her father might have done.

The only person who was not pleased with the marriage was her brother Cesare. Aware of his insane possessiveness where Lucrezia was concerned, Alexander had taken care to tell him nothing. But Cesare was well informed. He had written to Lucrezia immediately: "Dearly beloved sister, you would do well to turn your heart and your eyes from this Giovanni Sforza, for I have it on reliable authority that he is nothing but a weakling, a strut, a rake, who loves nothing else but to dress up and mince about like a girl."

Lucrezia threw the letter aside. She could not worry

about that. She had dreamed of nothing but Giovanni since that day in the garden. Besides, Cesare was jealous. As for dressing up, la! Why not? *She* loved to dress up. The two of them would dress up together. What fun they would have!

Even now gifts were starting to pour in from every part of the Christian world. No, she would not give up Giovanni for anything. They would have a wonderful life together, she thought, not unaware that Giovanni's dark hair set off her own blond beauty to perfection. She had no time for Cesare's jealous fits. He would simply have to get over it. She was so annoyed with him that she sat down and wrote him immediately, suggesting that he put aside his malevolence and adopt the sweet, even manner of his brother Juan, whom everyone adored. She knew this would hurt him, but she didn't care. In her childish, impulsive way, she must pay spite with spite. After all, he had tried to spoil her fun, and she would allow no one to do that, no one at all.

Winter moved into spring. She and Giovanni had to be kept scrupulously apart, for any undue familiarity between them would diminish the value of the bride. With Alexander's consent, Giovanni installed two of his former emissaries at the Vatican to watch over the conduct of his future wife. The man's conceit was growing in proportion to his fortune. His bride must be blameless. His pride could accept no less.

Alexander smiled at this. Giovanni had saved him the trouble, for it was no more than he himself wanted, knowing how easily Lucrezia could be led astray.

Emboldened, Giovanni further insisted that she be examined by a physician before the wedding to be certain she was a virgin.

At this Alexander balked. If the young man was not satisfied with what he was getting, he could seek his fortune elsewhere. He would not subject his daughter to such an indignity.

Giovanni, realizing that he had gone too far, quickly retracted. He had grown too used to his new-found fortune to place it in jeopardy. Very well, he replied, he would take the Pope's word for it.

Alexander smiled. It was as he had expected. Giovanni, in trying to mask his awkwardness, had strutted about like a peacock in full plumage. Alexander had all he could do to keep a straight face.

Preparations for the wedding went along at a frantic pace. Guest lists were made and revised, menus were planned and altered. Lucrezia, unable to sleep in the midst of all this excitement, grew even more pale and thin.

Giulia gave her a smack on the behind and sent her outdoors, organizing games and outings to give her color. To these outings were invited young men and women from the best families of Rome. Through it all the two emissaries stalked Lucrezia relentlessly. She might change her plans a dozen times, and they would be there. They watched her through endless games of *guilles* and billiards. When the weather was wet, they would stay indoors and play such run-around games as blindman's bluff or hot cockles. Lucrezia's favorite was ragman's roll, in which a quantity of burlesque verses were written on little strips of parchment, wound into rolls, and tied with string. The verses were often quite coarse. All drew rolls, which they read aloud to the vast amusement of the others.

The two emissaries looked at each other and made notes. Giovanni when informed of this diversion merely shrugged. He was glad to know, he said, that his bride-to-be took an interest in such things. She would then be a willing pupil.

The evenings were devoted to backgammon, check-

ers, and dice, with some chess for those who were pa-
ient.

The young woman was fond of gambling, the two
men reported. Giovanni smiled. She could afford it.
Her father's generosity was legendary . . . Giovanni
himself had benefited handsomely. He went to the tai-
lor, the hosier, the furrier, the shoemaker, the hatter,
the glover, the beltmaker. No more, he thought with
satisfaction, would he be going to the secondhand
dealers who mended and altered old clothing or to the
cobbler who mended and resoled old footwear. None of
that ever again. Nothing was too good for the future
son-in-law of the Pope.

Work began on Lucrezia's wedding dress. Giulia had
approved the cloth of gold seeded with tiny pearls that
Adriana had chosen. The neckline would be a low
oval, cut around the shoulders. The sleeves would be
narrow to the elbow and from there would hang long
tippets reaching to the knees. The dress would be
close-fitting to below the waist, the ungirdled bodice
widening at the hips and the skirt falling tulip-like to
the floor in folds.

"Keep it simple," Giulia had advised wisely. "Else it
will overwhelm you."

Lucrezia removed her clothing and shook out her
hair before the long glass in her bedroom, looking at
each part of her body as critically as though it belonged to someone else. Her body was not as ripe as
Giulia's, but it was pleasing to look at. She hoped that
it would give Giovanni pleasure.

Men, Giulia declared, did not like their women
scrawny. After all, if they wanted boys, they knew
where to look for them. Giulia stuffed her full of rice
and pasta, none of which stuck to her delicate bones.
Giulia emphasized cleanliness, telling her she must take

special care with her toilet lest she smell like a dead carp.

She grabbed Lucrezia by the hair and turned her face to the strong light which came in through the windows. "Ah," she said, "you have not yet any need of cosmetics. But when you are eighteen or so, you will probably have to use white lead and chalk and a little kohl around the eyes. At eighteen," she added sadly, "one's beauty begins to fade." She herself, she confided, used a cream compounded of vanilla, cacao, and almond paste to whiten her skin.

Lucrezia pushed these thoughts away. At thirteen, life stretched endlessly before her and nothing bad could ever happen.

"You must lie in bed each morning," Giulia continued, "until your husband arises, for he may have need of you and it is unseemly that he should have to go searching throughout the house, carrying his need with him. At night you should dally awhile in a sheer loose-fitting gown. Contrive to have it fall from your shoulder every so often. It will increase his desire. And when he beckons you, do not be in too much of a hurry, but look a bit to the side and smile, for if you leap on him like a goat, he will think you too easy a mark and will lose interest."

Lucrezia yawned and scratched her inner thigh. Would Giulia never stop talking? It was just like school, lessons and more lessons. She had always supposed that love between a man and a woman would be a natural thing like eating, not something to be learned in a schoolroom.

She looked at herself again in the glass. She was too thin. Perhaps by June she would look different. She thought suddenly of Carlos. No wonder he had treated her as a child. Her face grew hot with shame. Would she ever feel toward Giovanni as she did toward Car-

99

los? The familiar sweetness assailed her. Dear Carlos, she thought, so kind and good and gentle. Adriana had had her baby, but it had been a stillbirth, and she was not well. Lucrezia's eyes filled wtih tears. Dear Adriana. How good they all were. What wonderful times she had had at Monte Giordano. Everything had been so safe, so good, so easy. The time ahead seemed suddenly fraught with peril. No more picnics with Adriana, no more games with Cesare, no more lessons with Carlos. She heard once again the patient drone of Latin syntax as she stared dreamily out the window, the sun-drenched air heavy with the odors of summer. How good it had been! How good everything had been, delicious cake that she had swallowed too quickly without thinking. Why had she not known that then? If only she could go back, she thought, her eyes filling with tears, she would never ask for anything else.

Giulia, looking in, found her sitting on the floor, clutching an old doll and sobbing. "Lucrece, what is it, my heart?"

Lucrezia only shook her head and clutched the doll tighter.

Giulia gathered her into her arms. "There, my little one, everything will be fine. You'll see. You will walk around all day in fine dresses and jewels and all the servants will love you. Have you seen the new gifts that came in today? The most beautiful Milanese brocades and two magnificent rings from Giovanni's family. See? They love you already." Giulia, watching closely, saw her tears start to abate. "And Giovanni's uncle, Ascanio Sforza, has sent you a beautiful credenza set in solid silver, including cups, bowls, service plates, a lovely sweetmeat dish and two goblets, one for you and one for your husband. Come," she cried, pulling Lucrezia to her feet, "look how you are filling out! Soon I will be a puny thing next to you."

Lucrezia's tears stopped. "Do you really think so?"

Giulia laughed. "Come, let us go and look at the gifts."

The room containing the wedding gifts was nearly filled, with the wedding still two months in the offing. The room was kept locked and guarded, for there was a king's ransom in silver and gold. Every monarch wished to be on the best terms with Alexander, who seemed to have everything his own way. It was a good start for any young married couple, and Giovanni, when told of what was daily arriving, had rubbed his hands and beamed.

Amongst the magnificent furs of mink and sable and ermine, the caskets of gold and silver and precious jewels, was a chest of old toys that had been sent from Monte Giordano.

Lucrezia, ignoring everything else, ran over to the chest and began pulling everything out. Soon she was seated on the floor, her eyes shining with happiness.

Giulia watched her sadly. She would have a hard time of it, she thought. She herself knew what it took to please a man, and this child who had her whole life been accustomed to being pleased by others, would be hard put to it to understand. God keep her and watch over her, she thought, crossing herself and leaving the room.

CHAPTER 13

Lucrezia scarcely had time to awaken the next morning before Giulia burst into her room. "What is it?" she asked crossly, rubbing her eyes.

"You'll never guess who is here." Giulia's smile was as bright as polished silver.

"Who?" she asked, not bothering to stifle a large yawn.

"Guess."

Lucrezia closed her eyes. "How should I know? I'm too tired to play games. Last night's wine has given me a terrible headache." She threw herself back against the pillows and made a face. *"Paugh,* what a mouth! It tastes like an old sheet. Maria," she yelled, "bring me a basin of water and some cloves!"

Giulia's smile widened. "Cesare does not care how you smell. He is notoriously lacking in nose where women are concerned."

"Cesare!" Lucrezia shrieked, throwing back the covers. "Why did you not say so?"

"Slowly," Giulia cautioned. "He is with your father

now. You will see him later, after you have cleaned yourself."

But Lucrezia had already bounded from the bed—and ran full tilt into Maria. The basin flew from the poor woman's hands and struck the floor, sending a shower of water over the carpet.

"Cara mia," the woman shouted. "Look what you have done!"

But Lucrezia, barefoot and with hair flying, ran from the room, leaving the two women to mop up after her.

The door to her father's study was closed. Lucrezia pushed it open without thinking.

Cesare's face was mottled with anger. "I do not wish to stay in the priesthood," he was shouting. "Soldiering is more to my taste."

Alexander's eyes were like steel. "I did not come to that decision lightly. Church life will gentle you, and God only knows, you need gentling. As for your brother Juan, he is already gentle enough, having been too much in the company of women who do nothing but flatter him. He is the one who needs toughening. A soldier's life will do that for him. You, my son, will fight with your mind. Believe me, I know what is best for my children."

Cesare at that moment caught sight of Lucrezia and his face softened. Before he knew it, she had thrown herself into his arms and was laughing and crying against his neck all at once.

"Cesare, is it really you?" She covered his face with kisses.

"Paugh!" he sputtered, overwhelmed with feeling. "What a mouth you have!"

"I know," she giggled. "I've missed you. There is no one here as awful as you!"

"Let me look at you," he said, his heart beating fast. "You're filling out," he told her.

She smiled happily.

She was still a child, he thought sadly, a child who would be a woman. How soft and warm she made him feel. And why could no one else do this?

One moment more and her arms were once again around his neck. "Ah, Cesare, how handsome and tall you've grown!"

Alexander watched them, his eyes narrowing. It always made him happy to see his children get along, but these two were different. He addressed himself to Lucrezia. "Go, my child, and wash and dress yourself properly."

Lucrezia loosened her hold on Cesare's neck. "I will, Papa," she said slowly, "if you promise not to send him away again."

Alexander smiled despite himself. The child was a skein of gold that twisted itself about his heart. He watched her leave, her eyes still on her brother, and then turned his attention to his son. The boy troubled him. Whereas Lucrezia was all bright sunlight, Cesare was a dark pool choked with weeds, through which no sunlight ever filtered. So unfathomable were the murky reaches of his soul that Alexander was filled with foreboding. In his mind he saw once again the pillow that Cesare had years ago held to the face of his little brother Juan. Juan, the favorite of all his sons. Alexander, tiptoeing into the boys' room as he was accustomed to doing, to view the marvel of this lovely child asleep, had sensed something amiss, something sinister in the taut line of Cesare's back. Then he had seen the pillow. He knocked it out of Cesare's hands.

But even at nine years of age Cesare showed the cool aplomb that was to characterize all his later misdeeds. "I was just trying to frighten him," he had said off-handedly. "He is such an awful baby."

Alexander, searching his face for guile, could find

104

none. A week later he had him sent away. When a cousin of his died not long after, Alexander as executor of the estate made over 50,000 ducats to his oldest son, Pedro Luis, and 35,000 to Juan. Cesare he significantly ignored. From that time on his name was purposefully omitted from all legal papers pertaining to the members of the family. Nor did he share in the various bequests that from time to time were left to Alexander's children. His younger brother Juan received all the legacies and honors that should have gone to Cesare as the older of the two.

Five years later Pedro Luis, then in his early twenties and loaded with titles and honors, returned from Spain, where he had taken part in the struggle between the Spaniards and the Moors. His gallantry in this encounter had been rewarded with no less than a dukedom. The gods smiled on this young man. With impartial idiocy, they struck him down. A few weeks later he was dead of malarial fever. His will had been made in favor of Juan, attested to and sealed by the apostolic notary, and twelve-year-old Juan suddenly found himself Duke of Gandia and heir to a vast fortune.

When he heard of it, Cesare was numb with rage. The holdings and titles which by right of primogeniture should have fallen to him had gone instead to his hated younger brother. Bright patterns of red flecked his vision and it was some time before he could speak, so great was his anger. Then he was conscious of pain. In surprise he looked at the palms of his hands. His fingernails had drawn blood. He would like to take those very fingers, he had thought, and press them tightly against his brother's throat.

Cesare's first instinct, when his rage had subsided, was a curious one. He wanted to run to his mother. Curious indeed, for he had seen Vanozza only infre-

105

quently since he was seven, when both he and Lucrezia had been sent to Monte Giordano, where Alexander felt the cultural climate was more conducive to furthering the ambitions he had for his children. How strange, Cesare thought, that he should be reminded of Vanozza now. Dim, half-forgotten feelings washed over him, the softness of her bosom, the clean smell of her skin, the odor of her hair as she held him close in her arms. He suddenly found that he wanted to cry. But that was a long time ago.

When Lucrezia left the room, Cesare turned to his father. There was no denying the shrewd eyes, the hawk nose, the folds of flesh furrowing from nose to mouth. There, locked within the reaches of that granite mind, lay his future. What a pair they would make, he and his father! For with Alexander on the Vatican throne and the Church treasury at his command, he could muster up an army that could control all the Italian states. If only his father could see that he and not Juan was capable of this. As Captain General of the Church, Juan would do no more than draw his pay and strut about in his fine uniform and sample all the brothels of Rome. Cesare choked back his anger. He would heed his father's words and start fighting with his mind.

"So," he said, "I am to shave my head and spend my time listening to complaints of all the urinary disorders of the laity."

Alexander shrugged with good humor. "It is not all that bad, my son. Who knows, one day you might even sit on the Vatican throne."

"I am more at home on a horse," Cesare replied shortly.

Alexander put on his most charming expression. "I

think you will find the Vatican bridle paths much to your liking."

Cesare smiled. He could not stay angry at this man whose mind was more than a match for his own.

"Trust me," Alexander said softly. "Trust me to know what is best for you, and say nothing to anyone of what we have said here."

"I am not a babbler," Cesare said hotly.

Alexander smiled. "That is good, for most men are babblers in one way or another. Some babble to hear themselves speak and others babble to women to swell their sense of importance. However, my boy, if you must babble, then babble to women. For although they will repeat it, no one takes much notice of what they say."

"I do not need to swell my importance with women."

Alexander hid the smile that came to his lips. "I am glad of that, my boy. And now, if there is nothing else you wish to discuss, I am due at the Consistory at eleven. It would do you no harm to be present and acquaint yourself with Vatican procedure."

"There is one thing more," Cesare said testily. "There is the business of Lucrezia's husband."

Alexander's eyes were suddenly cool. "I am not certain that that concerns you."

"It concerns me that my sister is tied to a strut, a popinjay equally at home in men's or women's clothing!"

Alexander remained imperturbable. "Giovanni's taste in clothing is no concern of yours."

Cesare's face grew hot. "I say not only am *I* concerned," he shouted, "but the whole family is concerned. We shall be the laughingstock of Rome!"

"I will be the judge of that."

"Well, don't expect me to attend that circus. I'll not be witness to such a travesty!"

Alexander's face hardened, but his words were soft as silk. "You will be there. It is fixed for the middle of June." He rose and turned to go. "I shall expect you in the Consistory at eleven."

Cesare sat and stared at the departing figure of his father. So far, his trip home had borne no fruit. Other than his having seen Lucrezia, it was a waste of time. In addition to this, he was to be cooped up in the Consistory for the better part of the day. He sighed heavily. There was not even time enough to get drunk, for he had to attend a lecture in Church procedure from that dolt Burchard, who lived for nothing else and who would not let him out of his grasp until he had bored him to death with all the petty nuances of protocol. He would probably be cooped up with him for the better part of the morning. Plague take it! Burchard's breath was notorious. In this heat it would probably be fatal. Why was it, he wondered, that all fanatics had such foul breath? A noggin of wine would not hurt. He would go to the cellar now. And on the way down it would do no harm to look in at the kitchen and see what manner of serving wenches were available. He had no sooner started down the hall than he heard his name.

"Cesare."

He made his face pleasant and turned around. His father had wasted no time in getting to Burchard, for directly in front of him stood the tall solemn German who would instruct him in Consistory procedure.

Burchard seemed very happy to see him. "I am glad to see that you are prompt, milord. Promptness bespeaks an eager spirit."

Cesare managed to keep an even expression. Pompous old fool. He would keep out of range of his breath.

"How have you been spending your time? In quiet prayer and meditation, I trust?"

Cesare smiled.

"Your Lordship is not tonsured."

Cesare coughed. "No, my head gets cold very easily."

Burchard leaned forward and the sour spume of his breath hit Cesare's nose. "But Your Lordship is a bishop. It is only fitting that you wear the holy haircut."

Cesare backed away from the odor. He would never cut off those curls which were one of his chief attractions for women. The old fool could spout like a whale for all he cared.

"Your Lordship is not only a bishop," he continued, "but Your Lordship is Primate of Spain. In view of this, milord, you should have a small tonsure at the very least, but no tonsure at all . . ."

"Yes, well, I will have to give it some thought."

"Does Your Lordship have your robes with you?"

Cesare pretended to think. The man's breath was really intolerable. "Robes? No, I'm afraid not. I left so quickly, you see."

Burchard shook his head and sighed. Never mind, he would supply the robes and anything else that was needed.

At the end of two hours Cesare was groggy and out of sorts. There was little air in the room, and what there was was fouled by the stink of Burchard's breath. The man was impossible. Vatican procedure was his whole life. Worse still, he knew his subject backward and forward and he was determined to teach his pupil all that he knew. Cesare cracked his knuckles and tried not to yawn. Where did the man get the strength?

Cesare was suddenly aware that the old fool was smiling. "We will have just enough time to make water," he was saying, "before we go on to the Consistory."

Cesare bolted down the cellar stairs. Let Burchard occupy himself with making his water. He himself would get his wine.

Ten minutes later he stood at the entrance to the side chapel, adjusting his borrowed robes. He was not prepared for the strange feeling that gripped him when he saw his father sitting on the high splendid throne, resplendent in his pontifical robes and surrounded by a red circle of cardinals. He climbed the six steps that led to the throne with shaking knees and knelt before him. With a rush of feeling that surprised him, he kissed his father's foot, his ring, and then his lips, standing quietly as his father took his face between his hands and gazed deeply into his eyes. Cesare, overwhelmed by this, restrained an impulse to throw himself into his arms. Then he saw that Alexander's eyes were blank and that he was merely acting out a part. The wine in his stomach turned sour, and he wanted to retch. Instead he backed slowly down the steps and seated himself on the low bench to the left of the throne, which Burchard had designated to him.

Alexander began to speak in that beautiful sonorous voice of his, a voice that could weave enchantments. "Heavenly Father, we have commanded our son Cesare to attend us that we may admonish him to a just life and to the service of God and of His Holy Church."

Cesare heard this with astonishment. What was his father doing?

Alexander turned his face toward him. "Cesare, we have summoned you because there are things which we would say to you in the presence of God and in the

110

presence of these our brethren. Know then, Cesare, that whilst we receive you in love, and succor and assist you in all righteous things, yet we do not propose that you will be advantaged in worldly matters by our elevation. Nor will we countenance you in any scandalous, loose, or irreligious pursuits." Here his father paused.

Cesare sat steeped in anger. Not only had Alexander announced to one and all that he would do nothing materially for his son, but he was publicly chastising him as well.

His father raised his eyes to the vaulted ceiling and continued. "We have heard good reports of your devotion, modesty, and moderation. Continue in these ways, my son, and in return we shall not withhold our love."

That was all; it was over.

Cesare sat without moving. Then as Burchard prodded him with his miter, he rose as though in a trance and kissed each cardinal. As soon as he got outside, he vomited.

When he returned to his room, his valet Agapito was unpacking his trunk and smoothing out the contents on the flat surface of the bed. "Do not bother with that," Cesare shouted. "We are leaving this place at once!"

"But milord, we have only just got here."

"Never mind. I cannot stay on in Rome after suffering a public humiliation before the entire Sacred College!"

Agapito stopped unfolding the clothes and prepared to listen. He was used to his young master's fits of rage.

Cesare spouted on, recounting each indignity and feeling a sort of release.

Agapito tried not to smile. "That was admittedly unpleasant, Your Lordship, but scarcely an excuse for leaving Rome."

111

"What do you mean?"

"Just this, milord. The revenues from Valencia to which you are entitled are sixteen thousand ducats a year. Surely for that consideration you can afford to be somewhat tolerant?"

"Not if it means shaving my head and mincing about with a bunch of fat prelates!"

"But is that not a small price to pay for such a large return?"

Cesare pretended not to hear.

Agapito held up a stained garment which he had been rubbing at vigorously with a cloth dipped in vinegar. "If I may say so, Your Lordship, you do not fully appreciate the Holy Father's position. Although he is the Supreme Pontiff and may seemingly do as he chooses, all eyes are on his every move, weighing and sorting. And so he cannot always move as quickly as he likes."

"He seemed to move quickly enough this morning," Cesare said hotly.

"So it seemed," Agapito conceded, "but that was merely a delaying action to cloak his real intent."

Cesare appeared to consider this. Then the thought of Juan made his blood rise. "I don't believe it," he said. "He can move how and when he chooses!"

Agapito, watching him closely, said, "If one wishes to know from whence the water springs, one can always go to the well."

Cesare knocked on the massive doors which opened onto his father's private apartments.

Alexander's voice bade him enter.

His father, he saw, had discarded his heavy robes and was lying naked on the bed, the powerful musculature of his body slack and loose. Even in repose,

Cesare thought grudgingly, his father was a man to be reckoned with.

"Ah, Cesare." Alexander spoke without even opening his eyes. "You carried yourself very well at the Consistory."

Cesare, still offended, burst out, "I do not enjoy public humiliation!"

Alexander opened his eyes and Cesare saw that they were filled with amusement. "I was wondering how long it would take you to come. I feel that it went very well."

"Well for whom?"

"For both of us, my boy. One must beware of pride. It tosses you up on its horns and ends by throwing you to the ground."

"I will take my chances."

Alexander smiled. "Believe me, my son, a small lesson in humility is not amiss at this time."

"What do you mean?"

Alexander looked down at his belly and grasped it between his fingers. Then he sighed. "To be forced to grovel is one thing, but to know when to speak softly, to appear to consider, to give the appearance of meekness—ah, that is another thing. One is still in command. One merely waits and bides one's time."

"What are you trying to tell me?"

"I am trying to tell you to be patient, my son. For if you are, and make no stir, it is quite possible that outside pressure will be put upon me to advance you." Alexander smiled. "And it is infinitely preferable that such pressure come from others rather than from me."

"What about Juan?" Cesare asked sarcastically.

"That is precisely what I mean," Alexander said, watching him closely. "I have already advanced Juan. Therefore, the next advancement must come from others, not from me."

"I don't see why . . ."

"Listen to me, my boy," Alexander said firmly. "I know whereof I speak. It is all right to throw out an idea, but one must let them think it's their own, for men are more prone to advance their own ideas than the ideas of others. And once they have advanced it as their own, there is no turning back for them. For it is man's nature to be as zealous at covering up his own mistakes as uncovering the mistakes of others."

Cesare remained silent as he considered his father's words. Their truth was inescapable. The man was a veritable hawk. Nothing escaped those keen eyes. He pounced upon the flaws of his enemies, playing strength against weakness and weakness against strength. This had gotten him the Vatican throne. It would get him whatever he wanted, but it would not get Cesare the Captain Generalship of the Church. That, he decided, he must get for himself and in his own way. In the meantime, he would play Alexander's game. "All right," he said grudgingly, "I will do as you say, but as Your Holiness knows, I am not well designed for waiting. And as for Your Eminence's master of ceremonies, he gives me a pain in the arse."

Alexander looked at him with eyes that missed nothing. "It would be to your advantage to study with Burchard. He understands Rome and the Romans."

"All right," Cesare conceded. "But ask him to chew some fennel. He has the breath of a hyena."

Alexander reached over to the bowl of grapes which stood by his bedside. He selected two or three of the largest blue ones and put them into his mouth. "If there is nothing else . . ."

This was Giulia's hour, Cesare knew, but he went on relentlessly. "There is still the matter of Lucrezia's husband."

114

"I have already told you that that does not concern you."

"It does concern me. I cannot stand by and see my sister married to a circus freak!"

Alexander reached over for a bunch of grapes, which he held up to the light. "Have you ever thought what a miracle a grape is? See how lightly it is fastened, yet how tightly it clings."

Cesare ignored this illusion to his slender patrimony. "I warn you, I won't attend the wedding."

Alexander plucked off a grape and let it fall to the floor. "Of course you will. Otherwise your absence might be interpreted as excessive jealousy on your part."

"There is nothing like that between Lucrezia and myself!"

His father smiled broadly. "Of course not, my boy. But try telling that to those who persist in believing otherwise. Indeed, your very denial would be an indictment."

Cesare was so choked with feeling that he could not speak.

Alexander saw this and changed the subject. "By the way, Giovanni wishes to ride a white horse at the ceremony, to match his outfit, I believe. Would you prefer to ride a white or a black one?"

"Neither!" Cesare shouted when he could speak.

Alexander smiled his most charming smile. "I think a black one would suit you best."

At this moment the door opened and Giulia came quietly in.

Alexander turned to Cesare and smiled. "I appreciate the interest you have shown in this matter. Burchard will instruct you in the proper procedures."

Cesare, too angry to speak, scarcely remembered to bow.

He ran from the room to Lucrezia's apartment and hammered on her door with both fists. Siesta or not, he must speak to her now or burst.

"What is it?" Lucrezia's voice was sleepy and cross. But as soon as she saw her brother she raised herself up and smiled. "I am so glad you have come, Cesare. I was afraid that we would have no time to talk."

Cesare gathered her into his arms, feeling the sleepy warmth of her body against his. The tension within him began to loosen. What if he were to toss everything aside and take her? What could his father do then? There would be no wedding. For one wild moment he actually considered it. He even grabbed her to him and kissed her, forcing her mouth open beneath his.

Lucrezia wrenched away, wiping her mouth with trembling fingers.

Watching her, his mind cleared. If he dared to do such a thing, he would be finished. His father would see to that. The hot tide of his blood ebbed, leaving him tired and drained. When was the last time he had slept? He could not even remember.

"Have you kissed him yet?" he demanded, tracing with his finger the stray tendril of hair that fell in front of her tiny ear.

"Of course not," she giggled. "Papa won't even let him near me."

"Do you want to marry him, Lucrezia?"

She shrugged. "I don't know. I have to marry someone."

He looked at her, at the gray-blue eyes with the tinge of amber in the iris, the fair skin, the blond hair against the high, narrow bones of her face. And the fever rose up within him. "Lucrezia, would you marry me if you could?"

A little pulse beat in the hollow of her throat. "I

116

would first marry Carlos," she said quickly, "but I would marry you next, Cesare."

He buried his face in her hair. Huge sobs shook his body. "If that idiot hurts you, I'll kill him!"

The door behind them opened so quietly that neither of them heard it. Alexander stood in the doorway, his face suffused with anger. That he had come straight from bed with Giulia was unmistakable. His dressing gown hung loosely about him. He walked over to the bed and pulled down the sheet, his hawk eyes taking in everything. Next he pulled up Lucrezia's gown to her shoulders. "Spread your legs!" he thundered. His breath soughed out in a sigh of relief.

"You will guard Giovanni until the wedding," he said to Cesare, looking carefully at a point just over his head. "Should any mishap occur, you will be solely responsible." He turned back to Lucrezia, pulling up the sheet. "As for you, my dear, you will take up residence with Giulia. It will be a little inconvenient"—he smiled thinly—"but she will better be able to instruct you in wifely behavior." He then opened the door and waited for Cesare to leave.

CHAPTER 14

As the day of the wedding drew near, Lucrezia became increasingly moody. Her normal gaiety and good spirits vanished. At mealtimes she sat and picked at her food, eating little or nothing of what was put before her.

Giulia, knowing of her love for sweets, prevailed upon the cook to prepare the things she liked best. But Lucrezia merely glanced at the chestnut torte and the almond cheesecake. When the candied blossoms were brought to the table, she fingered them absently.

Giulia turned in desperation to garlic, for its medicinal properties were well known and Lucrezia was fast losing flesh. And as men despised scrawniness in women above all things, it was imperative that something be done before Lucrezia was reduced to a pile of bones. "Everyone knows," Giulia said, sprinkling it liberally over Lucrezia's food, "that garlic provokes urine and women's flow, kills worms, cuts and voids tough phlegm, purges the mind, cures lethargy, prevents plagues and ulcers, removes spots and blemishes, eases pain, ripens and expels the accumulation of gas, and helps to prevent jaundice, falling sickness, cramps, convulsions and hemorrhoids."

"But I have none of the things you speak of," Lucrezia remonstrated.

"You can even give some to Giovanni," Giulia continued, pretending not to hear this, "for it makes cold men warm and even dissipates melancholy. However, you must not give him too much, or else it will send strange visions to his head."

"Then why are you giving me so much of it, you fool!" Lucrezia shouted, spitting out what was in her mouth.

"It only provokes visions in men. Women can eat as much of it as they like."

"Well, I have had my fill of it. You can feed the rest to the pigs!"

Giulia tried not to laugh. "What will your father say when his daughter appears in her bridal gown looking like a bag of bones?"

Lucrezia dipped her napkin in a salver of salt and rubbed it over her teeth.

Giulia continued, "What will Giovanni say when this apparition of death appears at his side?"

Lucrezia began to giggle. "He will say *paugh,* put her back in the crypt where she belongs!"

Giulia giggled with her. "It is not funny," she said, wiping her eyes. "What will you do if he refuses to take you to bed?"

Lucrezia's eyes danced. "I shall go back to Monte Giordano and stay with Carlos," she said quickly.

"Oh no you won't. Your father will quickly marry you off to some old cod. And how would you like that?"

Lucrezia's chin trembled. "Papa would never do that."

"If Giovanni refuses you, there is no telling what he will do. Now be a good girl and eat your pudding."

Lucrezia picked up her spoon and slid it into the boiled custard of rice and raisins. Very well, she would eat it. At least it was better than garlic.

Giovanni made his official entry into Rome on June 9, three days before the wedding. He arrived by the Porto del Popolo, resplendent with borrowed jewels, for his first wife's family, anxious now to be in his good graces, could not do enough for him.

Alexander had ordered the entire route to be cleared of garbage and refuse, and for days there was nothing but the rumble of wagons hauling the stuff down to the Tiber. The streets were then swept clean and watered down, and on the morning of his arrival they were scattered with the petals of fresh flowers.

Giovanni was greeted by Juan and Cesare, sitting splendid black horses, for neither of them was about to let this upstart from Pesaro put them in the shade.

Cesare in particular looked magnificent. Hearing that Lucrezia was to be dressed in black velvet despite the heat, he was dressed the same way, like her proper groom, his auburn curls ablaze with the light of the sun. Across his chest hung a heavy gold chain, at the end of which was a huge emerald.

Lucrezia, watching from a balcony, glanced from Giovanni to her brother and back again. Giovanni looked undeniably handsome. As he rode by on his white horse, he looked at her and smiled. Lucrezia's heart beat faster. Perhaps it would not be so bad after all . . . "Do you think his plumes are too high?" she whispered to Giulia anxiously.

Giulia was cautious. "They *are* a bit high," she said, looking at the profusion of white plumes which rose six inches higher than anyone else's, "but perhaps that is the fashion in Pesaro."

"Yes," Lucrezia said happily. "I'm sure you are right."

"Come, let me straighten your hair. The breeze has caught it and spread it. There," she said when she was finished, "stand off and let me look at you."

Lucrezia's thin cheeks were flushed with excitement. "Do you think he will like me?"

Giulia looked at the small figure in the black velvet gown hemmed with gold, at the gray-blue eyes that looked back at her so anxiously. "Yes," she said, fighting back the ache that rose in her throat. "Yes, I think he will like you."

The day of the wedding dawned hot. Lucrezia had slept badly, twisting and turning the entire night, trying to find a cool place on the pillow. Giulia had come to her several times during the night to ask if she wanted a drink of water or a cool cloth scented with lavender for her forehead. Lucrezia had said no, she wanted none of these things. She waited until Giulia had left. Then she got out of bed and went over to the chest that stood in the corner of the room. Throwing open the lid, she reached in and took out one by one the toys she had played with as a child in Monte Giordano. One by one she placed them on the bed. Then she lay down amongst them and fell asleep.

Adriana and Ludovico would not be in Rome for the wedding. Adriana had not sufficiently recovered from the stillbirth, and Ludovico would not leave her. Lucrezia had received a long letter together with a magnificent emerald ring which had belonged to Adriana. Adriana wanted her to have it, Ludovico had written. What he did not tell her was that Adriana had fallen into a comatose state, from which she was

121

roused with difficulty. When she was awake, she lay and stared without speaking. It was Carlos who had written Lucrezia the truth, about how he sat with her for hours reading her poetry which she did not appear to hear, how they had taken her down to dinner in the main hall, feeling that the sight of familiar faces would do her good, how she had sat for a while without eating and then taken both hands and plunged them into a pudding, so that she had had to be led away like a child.

Lucrezia could not read this part without tears. Was this the same Adriana who had taught her manners, who was always so unfailingly kind? Where had she gone? Where had everything gone? Her throat ached with sadness. Adriana, Ludovico, Carlos, would she ever see them again? Giovanni's face swam before her. She saw again the profusion of plumes rising six inches higher into the air than anyone else's. She shivered, though the air in the room was warm.

"Do not worry," Giulia had counseled her. "The height of the plumes means that he is his own man. That is a good sign, you silly goose." Giulia had then pushed into her hand a ring with a hinged top. "It is for luck," she explained, "but do not open it, for it contains the powdered jawbone of St. Sextus."

Lucrezia in her nervousness had seized it eagerly, as though it were the one thing in the world which could save her. She had put it on a chain around her neck. She could feel it now, lying between her breasts, the coolness of the metal a talisman against the hot fever of dread which pervaded her. If it worked, she thought, she would pour some of the powder into Cesare's sword hilt to protect him from his temper.

How dark his face had been when he looked at Giovanni perched high on his horse. His eyes had traveled insolently up the length of plume. Then he had

122

said, "You appear taller than the last time we met, milord. How is that possible?"

Giovanni had flushed but made no answer. But the gauntlet was thrown, for there were several snickers, although Giovanni pretended not to hear them. However, he inclined his head so that the ends of his plumes fell into Cesare's eyes. "You at least have not changed, milord," he said. "Unfortunately." He then turned to Juan and kissed the hand that was proffered him, playing up to the bad feeling which existed between the brothers. During the ride to the Vatican he favored Juan's side, praising his horse, his trappings, his dress, and saying nothing further to Cesare.

When he saw Lucrezia watching him from the balcony, his smile quickly flashed in a show of white teeth, which caused a certain amount of sighing amongst the ladies of the court. He allowed his eyes to linger on her for just the proper amount of time before he turned his attention back to Juan.

Giovanni had conducted himself properly, Lucrezia thought with relief. Cesare of course had behaved badly, as was his habit. But never mind, perhaps they would one day become friends.

Cesare, however, had continued his bad manners, leaving the cortege before it reached the Vatican, spurring his horse away suddenly so that Giovanni was left unescorted on one side. When they reached Alexander, he smoothed over the insult by bestowing upon Giovanni a dazzling smile and kissing him soundly on both cheeks.

When Lucrezia was presented to him, Giovanni did not attempt to touch her but merely bowed from the waist, giving her meantime a short fixed look to assure himself that there had been no bad dealing of any kind.

During the two days of festivities which followed his arrival, Lucrezia saw little of Giovanni, for he was either closeted with Alexander or surrounded by crowds of fawning admirers eager to take his measure. Left to herself, she sulked. After all, was it not *she* who was the Pope's daughter? So why all this fuss over Giovanni?

On the second day of his visit he favored her with a look. They were sitting together at the table in the Great Hall, when he suddenly held his goblet of wine up to the light. He pretended to admire its color, but she saw that he was looking directly through it at her. She colored instantly, her heart beating fast. Seeing that he was observed in this, he raised his glass higher, turning it into a toast. And then she saw him smile.

"Silly goose," Giulia had laughed when Lucrezia told her. "All someone has to do is smile and you fall on your face."

Never mind, she thought; the smile had warmed her. She hugged it to her now for reassurance. Soon she and Giovanni would be alone. There would be no one for him to talk to, no one for him to look at but her. What would he say, she wondered. What would he do? Would it be like when she and Cesare had one of their tumbling bouts, or would it be different? She hoped it would be as much fun. Giulia had said it would hurt, but only for a little while. Then it would start to feel good. She knew what a man looked like. After all, there was her brother Cesare, who made no secret of what lay beneath his codpiece. But she had never been pierced.

"Do not mind the blood," Giulia had told her. "It is of no real consequence."

"Since when is bleeding of no consequence?" Lucrezia had asked stoutly.

"It is not important," Giulia said airily. "It is simply the tearing aside of a curtain so that one can get to something better."

"Bleeding is bleeding," Lucrezia said, unconvinced.

"See that you don't scream," Giulia warned her. "It will only make him nervous."

"But it is I who am bleeding!"

Giulia paid no attention. "If you can manage a smile, it will put him at his ease."

At this point, Lucrezia choked with anger. "I hate him. If he comes near me, I'll kill him!"

"I was pierced when I was ten," Giulia confided. It had been one of the cardinals in the Consistory. Oh, he had not meant to pierce her, she continued, having secured Lucrezia's rapt attention, he had merely been fondling her, as she was a pretty, well-developed child. Some cardinals fondled boys and others fondled girls. This one had an appetite for little girls, none of them over twelve. He began by touching her here and there, when suddenly he opened his robes and asked her to touch him. It had been quite a sight.

"One doesn't expect to see anything like that on a cardinal, a holy man," Giulia giggled. "In fact, I had always thought that they had nothing at all down there. What a surprise it was, that big staff sticking out of his robes like that. Ah, well, I was not entirely unwilling. It was like having a new toy to play with. And so I touched him and watched it grow even larger. Then before I knew what was happening, he sat me on his lap and bounced me up and down on it. He was still not inside me, mind you. He was just working it against me and it did feel rather nice, a brand-new game, when all of a sudden he lifted me up and sat me down on top of it. Ah, Mother of God, how it hurt! It nearly split me in two. Then the poor man began to moan and take on. I was frightened out of my head. Afterward, though, he apologized, patting me on the head and stuffing me with sweetmeats to stop my crying. He was a fine one, he was. He even washed away the blood with holy water, saying that now I was pure again. Then he knelt down and said two Hail Marys, one for each of us. It was a very nice touch. After that he had me regularly, telling everyone that I was a godless creature in whom he was trying to put 'the fear of God.' " Giulia paused and laughed. "Upon my soul, I've never heard it called that before.

"One day he was riding me for all he was worth when all at once he gave a gasp and was still. He lay on top of me like a rock, his eyes bugged out and staring. When I saw the blood running out of his mouth, I tried to push him away, but I couldn't. The horror of it was such that I fainted. When I regained my senses I started screaming, and that was how your father found me. By that time the poor dead man had grown quite cold, and your father was able to pluck him off like a bug."

Lucrezia listened to this recitation with rounded eyes.

Giulia, watching her, laughed. "Don't worry, nothing untoward happened. Your father was still involved with your mother then. So he put me into a covent for safekeeping. Little girls were not to his taste. When I was fifteen, he fetched me out. He is a very patient man."

"I don't see why there must be blood," Lucrezia said crossly.

"It does not matter whether you see it or not. There will be blood. That is God's way, I suppose, of mixing the bad with the good."

"Well, then," Lucrezia said practically, "I shall wear something that I don't much care about. After all, there is no use ruining a perfectly good nightgown."

Giulia smiled. The child continually amazed her. Just when she seemed trapped in a web of her own making, she would manage to cut her way out. She was, without doubt, her father's daughter.

Lucrezia came awake slowly. She had slept so badly that there were sure to be puffy patches beneath her eyes and probably dark circles as well. She would need Giulia's pot of white lead. She kicked back the covers and lay perfectly still. Judging by the light, it could be no later than eight or nine o'clock. The air in the room was already heavy with heat. In a moment or so Giulia and the others would come to dress her. The wedding was set for noon. Meanwhile, she would lie still as long as she could. As she lay there, she let her eyes travel over her body, looking critically at what Giovanni would see. Her breasts were a bit small, it was true, but the nipples were pink and pointed. The narrow inlet of her waist and the gentle swell of hip and thigh were pleasing. Her knees were good, she thought, neither bony nor pouched, her ankles slender and well molded, the delicate arch of her foot high, her toes straight and unpinched. All in all, she concluded, it was not a bad body, with no excess hair or moles of any kind. She sighed deeply, hoping that Giovanni would not find it unpleasant. She was so absorbed in her thoughts that she did not hear Giulia come in with a basket of bread.

"No cheese and no wine this morning," Giulia announced. "It will only sour your stomach and stench your breath."

Two hours later, combed, bathed, and dressed, Lucrezia stood stiffly, waiting for her brother Juan to lead her to the altar—Alexander had taken no chances with Cesare. The cloth-of-gold dress sewn with seed pearls weighed heavily about her shoulders. The long tight sleeves scraped the delicate skin of her arms. On her hair, which had been washed and brushed until it shone, sat a tiny cap of gold netted with pearls.

She walked to the chapel in a daze. Once there, she looked about for Cesare, but he was nowhere in sight. For once she was angry with him. How could he desert her now when she needed him most? Her eyes rose in panic to the vaulted ceiling. One sardonic look, one crooked smile from him, and she would feel much better. The breathing in the room seemed hushed. Everyone looked her way.

Alexander, seated on the Vatican throne, smiled down at her benevolently. Gathered about him were the cardinals and the cream of Roman aristocracy. She counted the ten cardinals, the senators, the ambassadors, high magistrates, the friends and relatives. She did not see her mother. Vanozza, unexpectedly, had earlier insisted on walking down the aisle with her. Alexander had intervened, saying that it was not seemly, and she had refused to attend. Lucrezia felt relieved. She did not like contending with Vanozza, and they were not close.

Long shafts of light fell from the stained-glass windows high above. She walked numbly through the bars of ruby, emerald, and topaz. On the other side stood Giovanni, elegantly slim in white velvet trimmed in ermine, which set off his tanned skin and dark curls to perfection. Giovanni seemed the embodiment of young manhood, and as she reached his side she raised her eyes to his. At that moment, she fell in love.

When he slipped the ring on her finger and bent down to kiss her, she felt faint with happiness. Soon she would give him the gift of her body. Stepping down from the altar she almost tripped on the hem of her gown and would have fallen had not Giovanni instantly seized her arm and steadied her. She looked happily at the strong slim fingers that held her. Then she bent over and kissed them.

"Come, my dear." Alexander stood before her, smiling broadly. She embraced him in a rush of feeling, her face covered with tears. After all, had he not given her this perfect young man to love?

The nuptial feast was staggering, even for Alexander. Pyramids of food, interspersed with peacocks and lilies, towered on the table. Lucrezia sat in a daze, picking at everything and tasting nothing. Giovanni laughed and joked with everyone. It seemed that every voice, every smile, was directed to him. He basked, he sparkled, he shone.

Lucrezia felt quite alone. Why did he not share all of this with her? The fullness of feeling she had felt for him began ebbing away. If only Cesare were here.

At that moment Giovanni leaned over, looked into her eyes, and smiled. Between his thumb and forefinger he held a grape, which he placed between her teeth. She felt his hand search out hers beneath the table. He did care for her, after all. She returned the pressure of his hand feverishly. Dear God, she prayed, please let him love me. Please let me have someone of my own to love. If you do that, God, I shall never ask for anything more.

She forced her attention back to the banquet. Alexander had ordered fifty bowls of sweetmeats to be thrown into the laps of all the women present. "And this to the honor and the glory of Almighty God and the Church of Rome," he had said, laughing, "for what is a more glorious thing than a woman?"

Lucrezia thought about it and bit her lip. It did not seem an appropriate thing to do at her wedding, but she was not in the habit of questioning her father's motives. The talk, in fact, was so loose and scandalous that Boccaccio, the Ferrarese envoy, was moved to remark that he was glad his monarch, the King of Ferrara, was not there to hear it. Several of the ladies danced together with the lewdest of movements, then a "worthy comedy" was given, and finally the feast was over.

Alexander, who had amused himself by pinching and fondling each lady within reach, could think of nothing more to do to amuse his guests. When he saw Lucrezia and Giovanni sitting with hands entwined, he smiled and rose from the table. "Come," he shouted, "it is time to make an honest couple of them!"

Giulia, seeing Lucrezia's look of dismay, felt a twinge of pity for her. How tiny and childlike she looked in her heavy, grown-up clothing.

Giovanni kept tight hold of her hand as the procession wound its way to the nearby Palace of Santa Maria in Portico, where they would spend the night. Together they mounted the stairs to the nuptial chambers, Lucrezia's heart beating faster with each step. The chambers had been prepared for them by the Vatican court and were strewn with fresh flowers, the heavy scent of which fumed into Lucrezia's head, making her dizzy and faint. In a few moments she and Giovanni would be divested of their outer clothing, according to custom. Undressed to the waist, they would then lie on the bed, side by side. Lucrezia, dizzy from the wine, the lack of food, and the excitement, heard the heavy jesting that went the rounds of the bedchamber. In a daze she felt herself being lifted up and laid on the bed. Kneeling at her side, his face suddenly gone grave, Alexander blessed the bed and its occupants and quickly left the room, taking everyone with him.

Lucrezia lay without moving, her limbs stiff with fear.

Giovanni lay quietly beside her. At first she thought

130

he was sleeping, but then she saw that he was watching her. "If you are too tired," he began, "we can wait until morning."

She continued to look straight ahead as though she had not heard.

He smiled and reached over to the decanter of wine which stood by the side of the bed. "I think perhaps you could use some of this." He poured out a goblet of wine and pressed it into her hand.

She looked at the wine in a daze, realizing suddenly that she was naked to the waist.

Giovanni, following her eyes, pulled up the sheet and tucked it under her arms. "Drink it," he urged. "It will do you good."

She sipped at it slowly, conscious of his eyes on her all the while. As soon as she drained it, he poured her some more.

He waited for her to finish it, then he took the glass from between her fingers and set it on the table. "Now I will teach you about love."

She smiled. In a moment, she thought, in a moment he would lean over and begin to tickle her as Cesare had. She drew a deep breath and waited. She was not prepared for what happened next.

In one motion his arms went around her and his mouth covered hers. Her nose was pressed beneath his and she could scarcely breathe. When she could no longer hold her breath, she began to choke and sputter, so that he was obliged to release her.

Giovanni threw himself back against the pillow and laughed. "What a fine night this is going to be."

In the midst of all the coughing she became angry, and before she knew what she was doing, she reached over and pulled his hair.

At this he laughed even harder.

"It is not funny!" she shrieked. By this time she was

131

truly outraged. The beautiful part of her marriage, the wedding feast she had looked forward to, had been a mockery, and now this! Hammering at him with both fists, she kicked, bit, and scratched for all she was worth.

Giovanni's mood changed. A strange look came into his eyes. The corners of his mouth quivered with ecstasy. "That's it," he gasped. "Do it harder!" His breath was coming in short, quick spasms. Excitedly, he pressed her to him. She could feel the heat of him hot and hard against her. "More," he urged. "Don't stop now!"

She felt him press something against her. Then he took it in his hands and pushed it between her thighs.

"This is what you want, isn't it? Then keep on going, don't stop!"

She continued to struggle against him, spurred on by his heat and by the sudden pain that pierced her to the very core of her being. Then she was fighting for her very life. She knew she was bleeding, for she could feel the wet warmth of it running out of her. She was in a frenzy of fear now, clawing at his back and pulling at his skin with her teeth.

He shuddered against her and moaned, and then he lay perfectly still.

Her breath returned to her slowly, but she could not move, for he was still pinioned inside her and the pain was now spreading to her legs. A feeling of sickness assailed her and she closed her eyes tightly against the nausea, hoping she would not vomit. Then it ebbed away, leaving the searing hot pain and the weight of him lying against her. She thought suddenly of Giulia and the cardinal. If Giulia had been able to bear it, then so could she. After all, was she not the daughter of a Pope? She lay quietly, feeling the hot tears spring from her eyes. She could bear it, she thought, but she would not have him lying on top of her the entire night like a hippopotamus. "Get off," she screamed. "Now that you are through, get off!"

Giovanni opened one eye and smiled. Then he rolled onto his side of the bed and fell asleep.

Lucrezia lay quietly. Any movement at all was painful. She remained awake most of the night, unable to sleep, afraid to get up and wash herself, while Giovanni snored gently at her side, his face guileless and loose in sleep. She had heard of men who could perform only when beaten. Was this, then, what she had married? Cesare's words came back to her. *He is a strut, a woman in man's clothing.* No, he was not that at all. Perhaps he was simply frightened, as she was. That was it, she thought, comforted. The thought calmed and soothed her. Her body, yielding to the night's exhaustion, relaxed. She closed her eyes and slept.

When she awoke, the place beside her was empty. When she moved her legs, she felt sore. Would it never go away? She stretched slowly, moving her cramped limbs cautiously against the soreness. "Mother of God," she gasped. Then she saw the bright blood. "Maria!"

It was Giulia who came running in with a basin of warm water and cloths. "Ah, my little one, how bad was it? Tell me."

Lucrezia's throat tightened with tears.

Giulia, all business, had thrown back the sheet and was looking down at the bed. "Mother of God, you are still bleeding!"

Lucrezia squeezed back the tears that now filled her eyes. "It is only when I move."

Giulia set down the basin and went to work. "It is because you are so tiny down there. It is always the tiny ones who have the toughest hymens."

133

Lucrezia lay back weakly. She felt better now. It was nice to be cared for, and the warm water soothed the soreness. "I think I will stay in bed for a while," she sighed. "It feels good just to lie here and do nothing."

Giulia made a napkin of the clean cloth and bound it between her legs. "What did you do to Giovanni's face? His skin is hanging in ribbons."

Lucrezia smiled. She had not thought of him until now. "Where is he?" she asked.

Giulia shrugged. "Who knows? He had a whopping breakfast and then he rode out with Juan. He was all in yellow this morning," she added.

Lucrezia listened to this impassively. "And what about Cesare? Where is he?"

"That one? He could be anywhere. He told your father that he was ill and couldn't attend the wedding, but I happen to know that he has been closeted in his rooms for three days now with two of the kitchen-maids. The cook is ready to kill himself, he is so short-handed."

Giovanni did not return until late in the afternoon. He approached the bed cautiously, as though it contained a snake that might leap up and strike him. "Are you feeling better?" he inquired softly.

Lucrezia, looking at him, could not help being moved. He was dressed from head to toe in yellow suede. Over one shoulder hung a short yellow cloak trimmed in leopard and fastened with a heavy gold brooch. Standing there, hat in hand, he was the very essence of a handsome, hovering husband. "I'm sorry about your face," she said. She really was sorry.

He sat down on the edge of the bed and smiled, taking her hand in his. "Let us say we are even."

134

CHAPTER 15

Lucrezia endured two months of marriage before she started to chafe. Giovanni's habits followed a set routine. He lay in bed until noon, at which time he summoned his man Alfredo to shave him and arrange his curls. While his hair was being heated and combed, he sat in a chair before several of the new tinfoil-backed mirrors he had ordered to replace the old ones of polished metal, and clothed in one or another of his innumerable dressing gowns trimmed in squirrel, sable, or fox, searched his face anxiously for blemishes and smoothed with his fingers the lines that he imagined had sprouted overnight. The arranging of his hair sometimes took as long as an hour until he was satisfied as to the placement of each curl. He would turn his head endlessly before the five or six mirrors in front of him, unwilling to make a final judgment. He had even imported some false curls from France which the harassed Alfredo had to insert somehow in the overall arrangement.

Lucrezia, sleeping late one morning, was awakened by a high-pitched scream and the odor of burning hair.

Springing fully awake, she was treated to the sight of Giovanni leaping about in his dressing gown, his face streaming with tears. An equally tearful Alfredo tried to dodge the blows of a hairbrush, holding in one hand a curling iron and in the other a spiral of burned hair.

"Carissimo," she sighed wearily, "how can one sleep?"

Giovanni, seeing that she was awake, ran to her for comfort. "Look what he's done," he shrieked, his voice breaking with passion.

When they were first married and this sort of thing happened she had felt sorry for him, but now she was tired of it all. Whenever someone insulted him or something did not go his way, he would immediately run to her.

"Do not let it touch you so," she would say, taking him into her arms, for that was the way she had managed her spaniels. She was always able to calm him, but an hour later he would be screaming again because someone had stepped on his foot and scuffed his slipper. He always slapped the offender across the face with his glove and then ran off like a shot before he could be slapped back, and only the fact that he was Alexander's son-in-law saved him from innumerable scrapes.

That he was cordially hated by all gave him a sort of perverse, little-boy satisfaction, though in moments of pique he cried out that nobody cared whether he lived or died. He took to carrying a tiny gold dagger in a black velvet sheath, elaborately embroidered in gold. "For protection," he said loudly as he tucked it beneath his leather jerkin. With the weapon he acquired a sort of swagger. Then he took to insisting that Lucrezia taste everything first, both food and wine. No one would dare to poison the daughter of a Pope, would they?

After the copious midday meal, which he insisted she share with him, hungry or not, he usually fell into bed exhausted. If he was to look at all well in the evening, he needed plenty of rest, for any undue activity fatigued him, and he would not give his enemies the satisfaction of seeing him look poorly. He slept with his curls arranged in a sort of floating net, and the first thing he did upon awakening was to scream for Alfredo.

He took more time to dress than Lucrezia, for he could never make up his mind right away what to wear. Alfredo was obliged to fish out twenty or thirty costumes from the large chests which contained his clothing. Having spread them out all over until they covered everything in sight, he would go from one outfit to another, perspiring with indecision, with Alfredo sponging him off and Lucrezia stamping her foot at the disarray and screaming at him to make up his mind.

After he was clothed, he would look first in one glass and then another, certain that he had made the wrong choice. Cramped by his fears, he would then start to shout at the hapless Alfredo, declaring that he was the lower part of a horse and no proper valet at all. At the very end he resorted to tears, imploring Alfredo to change his costume at once.

At that point Lucrezia, worn out and tight-lipped from waiting for him, would leave the room, whereupon Giovanni, shrieking for her to wait lest he be poisoned, ran out after her.

During the first weeks of their marriage he had ridden out almost every night to make the rounds of the brothels, coming back in the early hours exhausted and full of wine, his body covered with bruises. Now he refused to leave the Vatican grounds after nightfall, saying loudly that it was unsafe, that he had no wish to be found floating in the Tiber the next morning, his face swollen and black.

Juan was the only one at court who would bother with him. "Amuse him," Alexander had told him. In the end it was Juan who was amused. "What an appetite he has for abuse," he said to Cesare, to whom he could not resist recounting their exploits. "He would be a ripe field for you to wallow in." He watched with further amusement as Cesare's face darkened. It was not often that he was able to bait his brother. "I don't know why you don't like him," he pursued. "He is not a bad sort really . . ."

Cesare's face almost burst apart at this. "He is a crotch-piece boaster, a bunghole blower, a bladder dropper, and a fool!"

Juan was careful to hide his delight. "I know, but other than that . . ."

"Other than that he is nothing!"

"Well," Juan said with a show of meekness, "Lucrezia seems to like him well enough."

Cesare's face looked so terrible then that Juan quickly excused himself.

Lucrezia spoke to no one of how she felt. She had no idea of what Giovanni was doing with his evenings until she found him fondling one of the little pages who served them. She breathed a sigh of relief. At least he would not bother her.

For almost a month he left her alone, asking her only to secure a curl or to straighten his hose. Then one night he crept into her bed smelling of wine. She edged away from him in disgust as she felt his fingers on her breasts.

"Please, I want to try it again."

She was powerless to refuse him, for he jumped on her with a little moan of passion, pressing his mouth tight against hers. With one hand he held her around

138

the neck so that she couldn't move, with the other he opened his fastenings.

He penetrated her at once, giving her no chance to respond as he moved furiously against her. He achieved a climax almost immediately, and moments later began to snore.

"Pig!" she cried angrily. "Pig, pig, pig!" That was it; there would be no more. In the morning she would press for separate apartments.

She awakened early, anxious to begin the move.

He lay where she left him, his dark curls in a tumble, framing the sweet innocence of his face.

"Pig!" she shouted. If she could have him carried out now in his sleep, she would. She got a pitcher of water and poured it over his head.

He slept on.

She leaned over and shouted into his ear. *"Pig!"*

He jumped instantly awake, his face contorted with fear.

Lucrezia smiled with satisfaction. How easy it was to frighten him. "You are moving out this morning. Alfredo will help you pack."

Sitting up in bed with his curls spilling all over his face, he looked like one of Botticelli's cherubs.

Lucrezia made her face hard.

"Moving?" he asked, scratching himself sleepily. "Moving where?"

"Out," Lucrezia said. "I want to sleep alone."

He yawned. "But I don't want to move. I like it here."

Lucrezia looked at him as though he were a roach. "You are moving out today."

Giovanni was fully awake now. "But why? Where will I go?"

"It is a big place," Lucrezia said, tying the ends of her robe. "Alfredo will find you something."

"But I want to stay here."

"No."

"But I have bad dreams sometimes."

"That is too bad. I am sick of the sight of you."

"Please, Lucrezia. How will it look?"

Lucrezia stared at him. Everything about him disgusted her. "I hate you," she said coldly. "Alfredo will help you pack."

Giovanni left for Pesaro the next morning. "I will not stay where I am not wanted," he told Juan sulkily. "Besides, she is trying to poison me."

Alexander, anxious to smooth things over, told everyone that Giovanni had left for Pesaro to put things in order for his bride, who would join him there in a few months. "After all, she is now a married woman, and they must have a place of their own."

Lucrezia awoke to a quiet room. Giovanni was gone, taking Alfredo with him. She looked over at the dressing table. Gone too were the curling irons, the pots of powder and paste, the jars of scent, the little mirrors, and the large chests holding his clothing. She drew a deep sigh of contentment and stretched the width of her bed. He had been gone almost a week and so far she did not miss him at all. It was lovely to be able to come and go as she pleased. Other than the fact that she was no longer a virgin, everything was much the same, she reflected, except that now she had her own apartments in the Santa Maria palace. That much was fun. However, she missed Giulia.

She rinsed her mouth with some wine and spit it into the basin. She reached over and dipped a corner of the sheet into the bowl of salt that stood by her bed. She rubbed the salt over her teeth and rinsed out her mouth again with wine. There, that felt much better. Now for a few seeds of anise.

Today would be a busy day. For now that Giovanni
was gone, Alexander, afraid that she might grow indo-
lent, had insisted that she take on all the duties com-
mensurate with being the mistress of a fine house. Not
only must she see to the servants and the smooth running of things, he said, but she must receive all the important visitors to Rome and learn to comport herself
with the dignity and grace of a great lady. Alexander
spoke the last sentence with the merest trace of a
smile, but his eyes remained firm.

The burden was a heavy one. She was suddenly confronted with all the grinding weariness of a formal social routine. It is not fair, she thought, hating it. First
there were school and lessons, then grooming for marriage, then Giovanni himself, and now this. To make
matters worse, who had come to Rome to pay homage
to the new Pope but Don Alphonso of Ferrara and his
formidable sister, Isabella d'Este. If only Isabella had
stayed home where she belonged. But that great lady
never stayed home. Having run her house and her husband as she pleased, she now turned to other things.
Possessing a wit as nimble as any man's, she turned to
politics and the arts, disputing and discoursing at great
length on any subject she could provoke.

Alphonso had brought Lucrezia a wedding gift from
his father, the Duke of Ferrara. There were two magnificent, deeply chased washing jugs and basins. Isabella d'Este, who had a great appetite for beautiful
things, eyed them hungrily.

Lucrezia had received the gift in silence, not daring
to meet his eyes, which were deep and piercing. She
had finally been able to murmur her thanks in some
confusion, raising her head to find his steady look upon
her. As for Isabella, she had merely looked at Lucrezia
with contempt for her lack of poise.

Alphonso's eyes followed her wherever she went.

141

She knew that look well enough, having seen it so many times in Ludovico's eyes when he looked at Adriana. The idea of a flirtation intrigued her. Anything would be more interesting than what she was doing.

She jumped out of bed. "Maria," she shouted, "I want a bath!" She would bathe and dress and then she would go to the Vatican and sit for the portrait that Alexander had commissioned. And, she hoped, she might even see Alphonso there.

Alexander had commissioned the painter Pintoricchio to cover the walls and ceilings of the Sistine Chapel with frescoes. Lucrezia would be included in one of the scenes as St. Catherine. Next he was to do Giulia and her illegitimate daughter by Alexander as the Virgin and Child. Giulia had laughed heartily at this, but Alexander would not be talked out of it. Two-year-old Laura was as blond and cherubic as any angel, he argued. In fact, he added, the two of them were a vast improvement over the originals. Pintoricchio, who had not been consulted in this, remained silent. For all he cared, the Pope could fill every room of the Vatican palace with family likenesses. It would keep him in meat and wine for the rest of his life. If he were consulted, he would make only one recommendation—that Cesare pose as Lucifer.

Lucrezia and Giulia could scarcely walk the Vatican halls without tripping over Pintoricchio and his scaffolding and paints. For that reason the Pope had shuttled some of the visiting dignitaries to Lucrezia's house, and the little Palace of Santa Maria in Portico became a miniature court bristling with intrigue. With his customary shrewdness, Alexander had billeted Don Alphonso at Santa Maria and his sister Isabella at the Vatican. Lucrezia was grateful for this, for Isabella was

142

extremely critical and Lucrezia's household was not the smoothest. Besides, since Giovanni had left there had been so many parties and receptions at Santa Maria that there was not always time to clean up properly. There were endless tiresome ceremonies which left her irritable and out of sorts, for all the foreign ambassadors and all those seeking favors who could not gain access to the Pope were now referred to Lucrezia. Every morning there were at least three or four people sleeping in the halls outside her door in addition to those who filled the lower halls.

At the end of two weeks, she had a whole chestful of appeals which she tearfully referred to her father.

"I simply can't do it, Papa. It makes me too nervous."

Alexander, watching her, smiled. "Just weigh, sift, and sort them and send me the ones that you feel have merit."

"But Papa, they are all so boring."

"You will do as I say," he said firmly. "They bore me even more than they do you."

Tonight, Lucrezia thought wearily as she bathed, there was to be a small dinner honoring Don Alphonso and Isabella d'Este. Lucrezia could already feel his eyes boring into her very bones. And that sister of his was even worse. Wearing her reputation for fashion and wit like a tiara, she made Lucrezia feel even younger than her thirteen years. She and Alexander were to sit at the head of the table flanked by Alphonso and Isabella.

Lucrezia dressed quickly for her portrait sitting. She was so nervous and irritable at the thought of the impending evening that she slapped Maria twice for pulling her hair.

Maria slapped her back. "Once perhaps," she said, "but not twice for the same thing. There, you are finished. Now go."

When she arrived at the Vatican, the halls were already full of workmen running back and forth at Pintoricchio's bidding. Her irritability increased. She did not feel like sitting, for she felt a headache coming on. And that's exactly what she would go and tell this nobody painter her father had plucked from nowhere! So thinking, she ran full tilt into one of the men in the hall. "Filthy workman," she muttered. "Why don't you look where you're going?"

"I was about to ask the same thing of you."

She looked up quickly. The face she saw was Alphonso's. She had not realized how tall he was, or how good-looking. The look he returned was cold and disapproving. Even so, she thought in confusion, there was no denying the high cheekbones, the aquiline nose, the handsome length of lip. "I'm sorry," she said. "I didn't know it was you."

His mouth turned into a humorous long line. "And if I were a filthy workman, what then? Would you still be sorry?"

There was something in him of Carlos, something teacher-like which she respected. But shyness made her rude. "I'm in a hurry. I'm late for my sitting."

He inclined his head then, standing back to let her pass.

She stood for a moment, then lifted up her skirts and ran. Why did he undo her so, she wondered, her heart beating wildly. Why, whenever she met him, was she fated to do and say the wrong thing? Never mind, she would not think about him. But she could think of nothing else. How could she face him this evening as hostess? It was clear that he thought her a dolt.

Pintoricchio was waiting impatiently. He had already mixed his colors and was anxious to begin.

She threw herself into the chair. Very well, let him paint her. She put on her most bestial expression.

Pintoricchio gazed at her for some time before he spoke. "If I may say so, milady, St. Catherine was sweet and gentle. She did not look at all like that."

For answer she bared her teeth at him.

Pintoricchio was not dismayed. "Perhaps I should do you as one of the demons in the *Temptation of St. Anthony.*"

Lucrezia burst out laughing; she could never stay cross for very long. "I can't imagine why you should want to do this at all."

Pintoricchio dabbed at his paints with his brush. "Because I have a fondness for eating."

She sat for an hour and then she could sit no more. "I'm sorry," she said, jumping up suddenly, "but I feel as though I must have a run or burst."

The young man put down his brushes. He knew better than to argue with a creature of impulse such as this one.

"All right," he said. "Tomorrow then."

But she was already out of the room. She ran out into the gardens. There would be no one here to bother her. The workmen were all inside and the gardeners were working elsewhere. She suddenly felt as carefree as she had in Monte Giordano. She ran until she was some distance from the Vatican. Then she kicked off her shoes. She would do as she pleased now. She drew off her hose. The blades of grass tickled her feet. How delicious it felt. The air was sweet and summery, the sky blue and cloudless. On an impulse she unfastened her heavy gown and flung it onto a bush. If it were only nighttime, she thought, she would undress completely and roll naked in the damp, cool grass. As it was, she was clad only in her shift, which was light and sheer.

What if she were to wade into the fish pond? Shift and all, she scrambled in up to her waist, tugging past the leathery lily pads which sought to catch her and hem her in, feeling the smooth glide of fish against her, splashing away the green patches of foam that skimmed the surface. If they could only see her now, those solemn courtiers, what would they think? She laughed aloud at the thought of Burchard, the Vatican weathercock, as Cesare called him. How boring everything was at the Vatican. How awful it was having to dress every day in that heavy clothing, receiving endless streams of people in whom she had no interest.

There was not a person at the court, with the exception of Cesare and Giulia and her father, that she cared about. She and her brother Juan had never gotten along. When he was not frequenting the brothels of Rome, he strutted about, boasting of his coming marriage to Doña Maria Enriquez of Aragon and how it would enrich his coffers. He teased her about Cesare, taking every opportunity to speak ill of him. When Giovanni's name came up, he would wink broadly. For in Lucrezia's husband he had an ally against that clever brother of his, as well as a playmate. In August, however, he was to marry Doña Maria Enriquez, and no one but Alexander would be sorry to see him go. Meanwhile he was wearing himself out with one woman after another.

As for Geoffrey, who was one year younger than she, she had no interest in him whatsoever. He was vapid and colorless. She loved Cesare, but she rarely saw him anymore, for he was closeted daily with Burchard. There was some talk of Cesare's becoming a cardinal in September, and although he chafed at his studies, he was not averse to the increased revenue his new titles

146

would bring him. That left only Giulia, whom she rarely saw now, since she, Lucrezia, was busy entertaining the constant flow of visitors to the Vatican. Not only must she receive them, but she must also receive their lengthy petitions, at which she scarcely glanced now, throwing them into the large chest for her father to look at.

The sun over the fish pond was now high in the sky. In another hour it would be time for the main meal of the day, which she would take at the Vatican. After that she would spend the afternoon resting until it was time to dress for dinner. She would do no more receiving today. She scrambled out of the pond, lifting her legs high to free them from the thick web of pads and wiping her feet on the warm grass. She could not put her clothing on over her wet shift. She would either have to remove it or let it dry on her, and there was no time for that. She made her decision quickly, tearing off the clinging chambray and reaching over to the bush for her dress. She would simply wear it with nothing on underneath. No one would every know.

It was then that she saw Don Alphonso watching her. How long had he been standing there? Anger filled her eyes. Forgetting that she was naked, she stamped her foot and screamed at him to go away. How dare he stand there and watch her like that? How dare he, how dare he, how dare he! However, he showed no sign of moving, for he stood as firm as a tree, watching her with a gaze that never wavered.

In a spasm of speechless fury, she stared back at him, letting him look as he would.

He gazed steadily at her for another moment, then he turned and walked slowly away.

All during the meal she tried to keep her eyes from him. But she needn't have bothered, for he never

147

looked at her, not once. He made a great show of conversation with Juan, to whom he had never in the past spoken more than two words. Isabella was not present. She was resting, Giulia said with a smile, which was not the case at all, for a constant stream of maids was seen going in and out of her apartment with pots of paste and unguents.

Giulia leaned forward and whispered, "She is determined to outshine you this evening, and being older, she must go to a great deal of trouble to simulate youth. Her reputation is at stake."

Lucrezia shrugged. She was not interested in competing with Isabella d'Este in looks and dress. She would be content to hold her own in conversation if she could, for that formidable lady was not only versed in politics but was well known for her patronage of artists and poets. Oh well, it was too hot to worry about things like that.

The servants removed the large platters of food and returned with bowls of fruit and sweetmeats. Alexander insisted on setting a copious table, no matter what the season.

Lucrezia's head suddenly began to throb. It was the heat, no doubt, and the wine as well, which she had drunk down too quickly.

Giulia, who had been talking to Don Alphonso, stopped talking and looked at Lucrezia. *"Cara mia,* you don't look at all well. I think you should go and rest."

Don Alphonso's eyes, which had been everywhere else, suddenly came to rest on her.

Lucrezia felt the color rise to her cheeks. This man had only to look at her, she thought angrily, and she felt weak as a fish inside. Well, she wouldn't let him see it. She rose from her chair, avoiding his gaze.

Don Alphonso's words came to her ears slowly and

distinctly. "I think a bath," he said, letting his eyes rest on her in amusement. "A cool bath might be the very thing you need. It is so very warm outside."

Giulia smiled. "Why, how very kind of you to suggest it, Your Lordship. Do you not think that a good idea, Lucrezia?"

Lucrezia's color deepened. The man's audacity knew no bounds, and what's more, she found it attractive. Why that should upset her so, she had no idea. At any rate, she couldn't go on standing indefinitely. She would have to leave. "Please excuse me," she murmured.

Once back in her apartments, her anger gave way to tears. Through no fault of hers, he had managed to see her again at her worst. What a picture of her he must carry in his head. Would he tell Isabella? Oh, what a headache she had. Everything had turned out so badly. The one person on whom she wished to make a good impression left her stupid and tongue-tied. Tonight's dinner would be a fiasco. Perhaps she could plead illness. She really did feel ill, and they were bound to remember that she had not looked well at the noon meal. Strangely enough, this solution made her feel no better. With a start of surprise, she realized that she was looking forward to seeing Don Alphonso again.

Maria, helping her to undress for her siesta, had taken one look at the naked body beneath her dress. "Where is your shift?" she demanded.

"I don't know," Lucrezia replied impatiently. "It is on a bush somewhere in the garden."

"Of course," Maria said. "Where else would it be?" She snatched the dress away then, turning it this way and that against the light, examining it for stains. Then she smoothed it away in the chest.

Lucrezia smiled against the pain in her head. Poor Maria, she took her work so seriously. "Don't worry,

Maria. One of the gardeners will find it and give it to his wife."

Maria's eyes were black and snapping. "Is that so? It so happens that I worked your initials into the cloth with gold thread. What will they think of that?"

"La, Maria, who cares what they think? They are only servants."

Maria's eyes grew blacker.

"I'm sorry, Maria. I am always saying the wrong thing somehow. You are different than they are. You know you are."

Maria remained unmoved.

Lucrezia stamped her foot in anger. "Why must everything be such a bore! Maria," she said in desperation, "if you don't behave, I shall fetch Angela in to dress me!"

With the unerring foot of a child, she had stepped on the right spot. "No one shall dress you but myself," Maria said fiercely. "It is my job!"

Lucrezia, freed of this problem, turned her attention to what she would wear. She must try to look her best and show him what she was made of. Even though the weather was hot, she would wear her grandest dress, the black velvet. After all, they would not be dining until ten or eleven, and by then the air would be cooler. She dug her way through the chest until she found it at the bottom, where Maria had stored the winter garments.

Maria stared at her in disbelief. "Are you crazy? You will die of the heat in that!"

"So what? I shall wear a wet shift. It will serve to keep me cool."

"You'll do nothing of the kind. You'll catch your death of cold!"

"Really, Maria. Would you have me die of both heat and cold all at once?" Lucrezia's eyes shone with ex-

150

citement. The dress was really beautiful. It would set off her blond hair and pale skin to perfection. She examined the gold fringe anxiously. Was it just a little tarnished? No matter. Maria would rub it with lemon and salt.

At nine o'clock the heat had still not abated. Seated before one of the small mirrors which Giovanni had forgotten to take with him, Lucrezia allowed Maria to tug her head this way and that as she brushed her hair.

"God's Blood, it is real fever weather, and you must wear black velvet. I would rather see you go in your shift!"

"Stop grumbling, Maria," Lucrezia said, looking into the glass happily. "You will give me back my headache." She was pleased at what she saw. Generally pale, her cheeks had taken on color from the heat, and her hair shone like burnished gold. The gown fell softly away from her shoulders, making her skin seem a dazzling white against the black velvet.

Maria finished the brushing. "Take my word for it, you will faint," she said, giving her head an extra knock for emphasis.

Lucrezia stuck out her tongue.

When she entered the Great Hall, the guests had already assembled. Isabella d'Este stood at the far end of the room, magnificent in emerald-green watered silk, a tiny cap of emeralds and pearls on her head. From her throat hung a large balas ruby.

Lucrezia gazed at it in envy and wonderment. As for herself, she had forgotten to put on any jewelry at all, and she suddenly felt as poor as a kitchenmaid.

Don Alphonso, staring at her from across the room, bowed. She had a sudden notion to run. Instead of that, she lifted her head and smiled. She was the

Pope's daughter. She wouldn't forget it. All eyes turned now in her direction, the ladies curtseying, the men bowing low. She had the satisfaction of seeing Isabella stop talking and curtsey, which must have caused her some annoyance. But that lady recovered herself marvelously well. In an instant she had glided forward and smiled at Lucrezia as though she were some poor child on whom she was bestowing a favor.

"Lucrezia, my dear. How well you look. Don Alphonso, does she not look well?" In those few words she had managed to convey the inference that Lucrezia generally did not look well.

Don Alphonso said nothing.

Lucrezia remained unaffected. She looked well and she knew it. Nothing else mattered.

Isabella, always anxious to turn matters to her own advantage, gave Lucrezia a little pat. "I have composed a song in your honor. With your permission . . ."

Lucrezia had no desire to hear Isabella sing, but she was not able to say so. At a wave of Isabella's hand, two lutists sprang forward. As the first few notes filled the room, it was clear to everyone that Isabella lacked a real voice of any kind, making great use of her hands and face to hide this. Everyone listened respectfully, however, and no one spoke until she was through.

Lucrezia, faint with hunger and heat, noticed that the majordomo had come into the room to announce supper and was standing deferentially to one side, waiting for Isabella to finish. Isabella, taking the polite applause for encouragement, prepared to launch into another song.

This time Alexander took matters into his own hands. Leading the applause himself, he walked up to Isabella and embraced her, saying that the nightingales themselves could take lessons from her. Then, offering her his arm, he led the way in to dinner.

152

Don Alphonso appeared suddenly on Lucrezia's right. Isabella, she noted gratefully, was seated away from her, with Alexander between them. But she was treated to the sound of Isabella's voice.

"What is your position," she asked Alexander archly, knowing full well that his son Geoffrey was secretly betrothed to King Ferrante of Naple's illegitimate granddaughter, "what is your position between Ferrante and the League of Venice?"

Alexander, aware of the interest she had in the League, which bound France, Milan, and Venice, smiled and with no change of expression said, "Your husband was kind enough to send me five hundred oysters. What is his position?"

Isabella smiled back and said nothing.

Lucrezia, listening to this, realized that she would not have known how to reply to her, for Isabella's role as political tuning fork for her husband was well known.

Francesco Gonzaga sent his wife from court to court to sound out what was happening, planning his moves accordingly. Lucrezia's marriage had afforded Isabella an excellent opportunity for a visit to the Vatican to feel out the Pope's position about the disputed succession to the throne of Naples. Charles VIII of France, the Angevin heir, was only twenty-three and could scarcely read, devoting most of his waking hours to the gratification of his senses. Vicious and gross, he saw himself as a great Crusader. He and he alone, he felt, was born to lead the Christians against the Turks. Along the way, he planned to take the kingdom of Naples for himself, encouraged in this by the Neapolitan exiles at the French court. Both he and the King of Naples relied heavily on the Pope's support. Would Geoffrey's coming marriage tip the balance in favor of the King of Naples? Nobody knew. And Alexander was not about to show his hand. Francesco Gonzaga's interest in this was perfectly natural. He did not wish to make the fatal error of committing himself to one side or the other until he knew which way Alexander would go.

The room was lighted with a thousand tapers, and Lucrezia was soon unbearably hot in the heavy velvet dress. The soft wax dripped onto the pyramids of fruit and the magnificent lace cloth from Alençon, which had taken two years to make. She drank eagerly of the wine, which had been chilled in blocks of ice carried down from the Alps. That at least was cooling, and she could refresh herself unobserved, for Alexander was busy parrying with Isabella on one side, while on the other Don Alphonso devoted himself to his food with quiet zeal.

After a few bites, Lucrezia could eat no more. Instead she drank wine, looking on the copious amounts of food with distaste. Isabella, she noticed, let nothing interfere with her appetite, eating and talking at once, tasting each dish and praising its contents, declaring all the while that she could not eat another thing. It was no wonder she was so plump, Lucrezia thought enviously.

Don Alphonso, she saw, refused most of the dishes served, devoting himself only to what he liked. Oysters, she noticed, and roast partridge and veal. Why this should have been important to her, she could not imagine. After all, his likes and dislikes were no concern of hers. But she could not help noticing how neatly he ate, how well he used his knife and fork, how often he used his napkin. Carlos had employed the same delicacy at the table, she recalled with a twinge.

Suddenly she wanted to speak to him, to have him speak to her. But at that moment silver bells rent the air, a myriad of bells that cut into the table chatter with a cool silvery sound, bringing with it the sudden fragrance of fresh flowers. Small boys in silver livery entered with silver baskets. Scattering petals right and left, the pages walked slowly around the table.

Isabella led the applause.

Lucrezia, warm with wine, found it easy enough to smile back at her.

Stewards entered the hall now, bearing silver platters of pear tarts in marzipan, fresh shelled almonds on grape leaves, milk curds with sugar, Neapolitan spice cakes, marzipan balls, and chestnuts roasted over the coals and served with sugar, salt and pepper. The pages returned with clean napkins and silver ewers filled with water.

Don Alphonso, looking at the large silver ewer which had been set before him first as a mark of honor, turned to Lucrezia and smiled. "Would Your Ladyship like to bathe first, or shall I?"

Lucrezia, giddy from the wine and the heat, made no attempt to curb her words. "If Your Excellency prefers, we can use the fountain in the garden."

Don Alphonso's eyes narrowed, but the smile on his face remained. He dipped his fingers into the ewer and wiped them with great care. Then he selected a stalk of sweet fennel from the dish before him and began to chew it slowly.

Back in her apartments, Lucrezia paced the floor. The black velvet dress lay in a sodden heap where she had thrown it after tearing it off.

Maria, saying nothing, had been about to pick it up from the floor and shake it out. But as soon as she touched it, Lucrezia had slapped her across the face and then burst into tears. Maria, her face red with anger, left the room. A few months ago they might have pulled each other's hair and then laughed together af-

155

terward. But Lucrezia was older now, married and the Lady of Pesaro, and so the slap was a heavy thing between them.

Lucrezia felt bad. The slap, instead of making her feel better, only made her feel worse. It had been a bad day from the beginning and it had gotten no better. Along with the insult of Don Alphonso's prolonged silence at supper, she had almost fainted from the heat and the wine. When supper was over, she had tried to rise, swaying unsteadily on her feet, and were it not for the fact that Don Alphonso himself had steadied her, she most certainly would have fallen. How he could have sensed this, she had no idea, for he had not addressed one word or look to her after he had eaten the fennel. As soon as she felt his arms about her waist, she had tried to shake them off, but they remained where they were. With all the strength that was left her, she had finally struggled away.

The heat rose to her cheeks in shame, for she could still feel the hot strength of his hands on her. She moved toward the balcony. The long doors stood open against the warm night. She walked naked to the balustrade, her hair hanging to her waist, and breathed in the warm petal aroma of the night.

A slight tap at the door made her turn. She smiled. So Maria had changed her mind after all. The knocking continued. "Come in, you fool!" she shouted, feeling better.

The door swung open and Don Alphonso stood framed in the doorway.

Lucrezia could only stand and stare at him.

Don Alphonso threw something lightly to her, which fell at her feet. "I believe this belongs to you."

Lucrezia looked down at the shift without moving.

Don Alphonso walked into the room then, closing the door carefully behind him. "I would have returned

156

it earlier," he said, looking at her without embarrassment, "but I thought it indiscreet. Here, why don't you put it on?" When she made no move, he bent over and picked up the shift, then drew it gently down over her head.

Lucrezia watched in amazement as he settled himself into a chair and began leisurely to finger a peach in the bowl of fruit which stood on the table beside him. "A pity," he said softly. "It is not quite ripe."

Very well, if he could be so casual, so could she. With just the merest tremor in her limbs, she walked over to the dressing table, picked up the heavy silver-backed brush that was part of her trousseau, and began brushing her hair. As always, the movement of the bristles against her hair relaxed her.

Don Alphonso laughed. "What a perfect child you are. I suppose that is what Isabella detests most about you. She was born a woman, you know."

Lucrezia brushed determinedly against the sound of his voice, her eyes fixed on an ointment pot on the dressing table. She would not allow him to annoy her any further with comparisons between his sister and herself. When she looked up at the glass, she saw that he was standing behind her, holding a strand of her hair between his fingers.

She watched without moving as his hands fell to her shoulders. Then she felt him turn her so that she was pressed against him, his eyes probing hers. She could feel him against her, vibrantly alive, and if he had chosen at that moment to take her, she would have made no protest.

As it was, he took her face in his hands, looking deeply into it, and said, "Someday we will mean much to each other, but that day is not yet come." Then he bent his head swiftly and she felt the soft warm pressure of his lips on hers.

CHAPTER 16

Lucrezia was roused the following morning by a
series of knocks. She came awake slowly. The first
thing that came to her mind was the feeling of Don Alphonso's lips on hers. She smiled. Whatever faults he
had, kissing was not one of them. The knocking continued, but she paid no heed. Why had he not stayed
with her, she wondered. She would have let him. She
had wanted him to, in fact. But after he kissed her, he
had released her, drawing away. She had sensed the
tremor within his body, but he had mastered it, saying,
"The time is not yet, little one." Then he had left her.
She had been so bewildered that she had taken up the
hairbrush and thrown it after him. But he had only
smiled and closed the door softly.

She lay quietly now, thinking about what might have
happened had he stayed with her. She would like to
know what it was like with a real man and not a jackanapes like Giovanni.

The knocking at the door grew louder. Maria, no
doubt.

"Come in, you fool!" she shouted. She was damned if she would get up to open the door. Let her open it herself. Suddenly she remembered having locked it in frustration after Don Alphonso had left. "One moment," she screamed. "I am coming!" On the way to the door she stopped to pick up a peach. Not ripe indeed! The meaning was not lost on her. Her outrage increased. With the peach in one hand, she fumbled at the lock. "Damn, damn, damn!" As soon as she got that door open, she would pull Maria's hair out, see if she didn't. "Very well, I've unlocked it, you idiot. Do you wish me to open it as well!"

When she received no answer, she broke off a few grapes. The purple juice trickled down her chin and she wiped it with her shift. What a time Maria would have getting it out. On second thought, she would smear it over her face and give the woman a real fright. Then she took the handle of the door and swung it open.

Don Alphonso stood outside.

Her first impulse was to shut the door in his face, but his foot interfered.

"I am glad to see that you have had breakfast," he said with an amused smile.

She raised her fingers and would have clawed at his face, but he pinned her arms to her side.

"Listen to me," he said, "and listen well. I am not in the habit of kissing just anyone, do you understand, you little fool?"

She nodded at him stupidly, her hair falling into her face.

"This marriage of yours, this farce, it will not last forever. I have therefore prepared a list of books for you. See that you read them. After all," he said, looking into her eyes and smiling, "we must be able to talk to one another as well."

159

Was she hearing him correctly? Was he proposing marriage between them?

Before she could think any further, he brushed her hair aside and kissed her. She found herself kissing him back eagerly.

Suddenly he pushed her away. "That's enough," he said thickly. "Happily, you are everything that Isabella is not." The next minute he was gone.

She looked at the door in a daze.

When Maria came in, she was washing her hair. "What's wrong?" Maria asked.

"Maria," she sputtered through the strands of wet hair, "you deliberately stayed away!"

Maria smiled and said nothing.

"I need some lemons for a rinse, Maria," Lucrezia said mildly, "and I've spoiled my shift. I'm sorry." Her anger had dissipated at Don Alphonso's first touch.

Lucrezia sat patiently while Maria dressed her hair. She had chosen to wear a simple dress of white lawn, and Maria was busy threading blue velvet ribbon through her curls for contrast. She was determined that Don Alphonso should see her at her best for once. Lucrezia had rubbed at the grape stains on her face until her skin shone red. Her hands strayed to the powder jar. A bit of chalk would tone down the color.

Maria slapped at her hand with the brush. "I do not think that he cares for such things. That sister of his uses enough paint to cover a wall."

"And what has that to do with me?"

Maria sighed. "If only you were not so stupid at times."

Lucrezia smiled. Maria, at least, was back to normal, and that was good. "Very well, I shall defer to you in this, since you are always right."

"Are you feeling well, little one?"

160

Lucrezia laughed. "Very well indeed. Tell me, do you think that I am as pretty as his sister Isabella?"

"Prettier, since his sister is not pretty at all."

Lucrezia, unable to contain herself at this, burst out laughing. "That is enough fiddling around. I can't sit still another moment. I feel so good, I think I shall scream."

"You will do nothing of the sort," Maria replied, "since his sister Isabella has been moved next door and she will think you quite mad."

"La, Maria, you were always one to take the joy out of things."

"Yes, and speaking of that, there is a message for you from your father. You are to spend the entire morning sitting for your portrait."

"Oh, he can paint me from memory," Lucrezia said, thinking how inconvenient it was that her father should insist upon a sitting this morning. Ah, what a nose the man had. Nothing escaped him. And why should he be so determined to hold her marriage together? Just because he wished to be on friendly terms with Giovanni's stupid uncle, the Duke of Milan? She was sick of the whole thing. She was sick of Giovanni, the Duke of Milan, and the League of Venice as well. Perhaps someday Cesare would subdue them all and then she could do as she pleased. Well, she would go and sit for her portrait. Perhaps on the way she might see Don Alphonso.

Instead of Don Alphonso, she met Cesare.

He looked at her critically, pleased by what he saw. "Why so pretty this morning? Don Alphonso has gone."

For one moment she wanted to slap him. "No, he has not," she said, her heart beating faster. "I saw him scarcely an hour ago."

"So you did. And now he has gone."

161

"Gone where?" Lucrezia asked, thinking that it was certainly too hot to hunt in all this heat.

"Ask our father, dear sister. He is God's right hand and knows everything, since he manages to arrange everything."

"What does that mean?"

"What do you think it means? It means that he does not want you to stray just yet."

Lucrezia stamped her foot. "How dare he!"

"How indeed," Cesare mused. "God dares everything, or hadn't you heard?"

"You hate Don Alphonso, don't you?"

"On the contrary. I think that he is one of the few people in this world who is not a fool."

A warm feeling rose up in her for this brother of hers who was so unhappy. "Cesare," she said gently, "don't be so angry all the time. Things will come right, you'll see."

"Yes," he said. "I shall *make* them right."

"A Church career is not so bad, Cesare. Look at Father."

"He had no right to put Juan before me and make him Duke of Gandia. That title should have been mine."

"Cesare," she said, taking his sleeve, "what if Father is planning that you should succeed him? What then?"

Her brother looked at her in disbelief. "Lucrezia, how can you be such a fool? Don't you know how many enemies he has in the Sacred College? If anything happened to him, they would cut me down. Or else they would relegate me to some obscure little post in the provinces. I would rather be cut down like a dog than have that happen. No, the only real power lies with the Captain General of the Church, and he has given it to that idiot Juan!"

"We must trust Papa," she said, her voice faltering. "He knows what he is doing."

"Does he?" he asked coldly, his eyes blazing. "Is that why he has made my stupid younger brother second in rank only to himself? Is that why Juan takes precedence over me at all official functions?"

Cesare's face was so livid that Lucrezia was sick with pity for him. "Promise me you won't do anything rash. Your chance will come, you'll see."

"Poor Lucrece," he said, stroking her hair. "You will do anything he says, even marry a fool."

"Giovanni is not a fool," she said without conviction.

"Is he not?" Cesare asked, resting his cheek against hers.

"Yes, he is a fool," she whispered. "But please don't tell Papa."

"Dear Lucrece," he said then, looking earnestly into her eyes, "I am the man you should marry, and Father knows that as well as I. Perhaps that is why he has not made me Captain General. For then he could not control me."

That made her sad. She had no desire to marry Cesare, for she did not love him like that. But she would never tell him so—she would never tell him that the violence in him terrified her, that she preferred a man of quiet strength coupled with gentleness, like Carlos, like Don Alphonso. Instead of freedom, she thought, marriage had brought her chains.

Cesare was right about Juan, though. Not only had he been given Cesare's birthright, but he had been given Cesare's intended fiancée as well, for now that Cesare belonged to the Church, he could not marry. Lucrezia could understand her father's preference for Juan. Unlike Cesare, he did as he was told, which pleased Alexander's vanity enormously. "Juan is a good boy," he told everyone. "He listens to me because he loves me." That was not true, she thought. He listened because he was afraid. It was too bad that Cesare and his father were so much alike, circling one another like two wary dogs.

Juan was not a good soldier. He enjoyed his comforts and his women. He was inordinately vain. He loved to parade about in fine clothes and imagine that every eye was on him. If he could not perform on the battlefield, at least he could perform in bed. It was no wonder that Cesare detested him, Lucrezia thought. She herself did not care for him either. As a child he had been a whiner, always seeking his father's ear against the others. And now he was a big show-off. When his marriage to the Spanish princess Maria Enriquez was arranged, Alexander commissioned the Vatican jewelers to make him an endless array of jewelry. The artisans lived for months at the Vatican, doing nothing but setting precious stones in rings and necklaces. Juan, knowing Lucrezia's fondness for such things, lost no time in showing her everything. There were great lustrous pearls, marvelous rubies, diamonds and emeralds and heavy gold chains. Lucrezia, who had practically nothing compared to this, looked at these things with tears in her eyes. Juan took as much pleasure in her reactions as he did in the jewels themselves.

Juan and Maria Enriquez were finally married with much pomp and ceremony, and were to leave for Spain by ship immediately after the wedding. Alexander, who was anxious to make this political marriage work, trusted to luck in nothing. Accompanying the bride and groom were two valued advisors whose function it was to watch Juan by day and night and keep him out of mischief. They were ordered to send back daily reports, for Alexander was not entirely blind to the faults.

164

of the son he loved so well. He had issued orders to Juan himself that he was not to go out at night unattended, not to gamble, not to dip into the revenues of his duchy without his father's consent, and that he was to treat his new wife with respect and consideration at all times. Juan had no sooner taken leave of his father, bearing all these injunctions, when he was overtaken by a papal messenger bearing further instructions. He took the new orders and later, when no one was about, threw them overboard.

In fact, no sooner had they reached Barcelona, where he was at a safe distance from the father he feared so much, than he proceeded to go his own way. First of all, he was not pleased with the choice of his wife. It was an inescapable fact that she was far from pretty, and therefore he had no interest in her. Not only did he not consummate the marriage, but he had ignored her completely from the moment they boarded the ship. The poor girl broke out in a rash and stayed in her room and cried. Instead of sympathizing with her, Juan told her how ugly she was, saying that if she did not believe him, she had only to look into her mirror for the truth.

Once settled in their own home, Juan proceeded to prowl about Barcelona on his own, taking up with the low women of the town since he could not very well approach anyone of good family. He gambled prodigiously, and in two months had dissipated twenty-six hundred gold ducats. He was just about to dip into the revenues of his duchy when news of this reached his father.

Alexander was beside himself. For a moment he was tempted to punish the boy by transferring his goods and titles to Cesare. Then reason prevailed. No matter how profligate Juan had become, he was still less of a threat to him than Cesare. Accordingly he wrote to Juan, upbraiding him bitterly for his bad behavior.

Juan, frightened by his father's letter, answered with a long list of excuses. His bride, he wrote, was so homely that not even the stoutest-hearted man could make love to her without quailing. Indeed, in order to make love to her at all, it would first be necessary to put a sack over her head. Also, she was as bony as a crab, all sharp points and angles. It would be impossible, he wrote, to embrace her without impaling himself on one of her bones. Also, she was rashy and covered with pimples.

As for the reports of his wenching and gambling, they were flagrantly untrue. He was both hurt and shocked that Alexander should give credence to the "sinister reports written by malicious people without proper regard for the truth." That his father should in any way attach him with blame caused him "the greatest anguish he had ever suffered." As to the reports that he prowled around at night, all he had ever done was to stroll the promenade in the company of the King of Spain, who dearly loved to walk.

Alexander, cutting through this with his usual keenness of mind, choked with laughter. He did not believe any of it, but it did not matter. He had made his point, and he had discovered a resourcefulness in Juan which he had never suspected. When at last he received a letter from Juan saying that his wife was pregnant, he breathed a sigh of relief. For despite Juan's protests, the marriage had been consummated.

Meanwhile, Cesare chafed at the religious life he was forced to lead.

Alexander, in order to bolster his self-esteem, dropped all sorts of briefs and proclamations at his door for perusal. "Because I value your opinion, my son," he explained glibly.

166

Cesare saw through this easily. It was but another way of throwing Church work on him and keeping him out of mischief. It was with increasing difficulty that he wore the charming exterior of which the Ferrarese ambassador had written so glowingly to Alexander. It was but a cloak to hide his despair and his discontent. And the cloak was quickly growing thin.

Lucrezia sighed. The tight, stiff pose that Pintoricchio had set her in was beginning to tire her.

"That's enough," she said, stretching and yawning. "I really cannot sit any longer."

The painter began to clean his brushes. By now accustomed to the caprices of this child, he knew it would be pointless to argue. Besides, he thought with satisfaction, he had gotten in a good two hours of work. It was more than he had expected, since Lucrezia rarely sat for more than thirty minutes without fidgeting. "Until tomorrow," he said.

"Tomorrow," a voice echoed. Alexander, who had been standing in the doorway, came forward. "You have captured her very well," he said, patting the artist on the shoulder. "And you, my dear," he said to Lucrezia, "have been a very patient subject. And because of that I have a surprise for you."

"What is it, Papa?" she asked with some misgiving.

Alexander's eyes sparkled. "I have written to Giovanni and asked him to come back to Rome."

Lucrezia tried to hide her disappointment. "Perhaps he is happier where he is."

"Nonsense," Alexander said firmly. "A bridegroom is never happy away from his bride."

"But it is plague season," Lucrezia said in desperation, "and he has vowed not to return until it is over."

Alexander smiled. "I think he has changed his mind. I have just received a letter from him requesting five

167

thousand gold ducats. It seems the poor boy is being pressed by his creditors."

"What are you going to do, Papa?" she asked quietly.

"I have already written to suggest that he return to Rome in mid-October when the weather is cooler, at which time I will not only pay off his creditors but will give him thirty thousand ducats to play with."

Lucrezia's eyes filled with tears. "But Papa, could you not pay off his creditors and let him stay in Pesaro?"

"I had not thought of that," Alexander lied. "Besides, it does not look well for you. A wife belongs with her husband."

Lucrezia turned away so that he could not see her tears.

"Also, my pet, I have regards for you from Don Alphonso. He regrets that he was unable to see you before being called away."

Lucrezia's tears turned to anger. "Called away where?"

Alexander smiled. "Why, on a diplomatic mission, I believe."

"Very well then, I shall write to him."

"I would not advise that, my pet."

"And why not?" she asked stoutly.

"Because, my sweet, you are a married woman, and he is a married man. A letter from you might be misconstrued."

Lucrezia's anger burst forth. "Surely there is nothing to be construed from a mere letter!"

Alexander put the ends of his fingers together with care. "Nothing and everything. Believe me, my dear, I know what is best for you. He will visit again sometime, and you and your husband will receive him together. In the meantime, you can get to know his dear sister, Isabella."

Lucrezia felt her anger becoming a hard knot. "Thank you, Papa, but I think I know her well enough already."

Isabella stayed on for another month. During that time Lucrezia was rarely away from the sound of her voice, for Alexander had asked her to take Lucrezia under her wing—"to teach her all that you know, if that is possible," he had added in his silkiest voice. Isabella had lowered her eyes against his flattery so that he would not see how pleased she was.

She had immediately given Lucrezia a book list made out in her own exacting hand. Lucrezia, comparing it to the one Don Alphonso had given her, laughed to herself. It was one and the same.

"She is an apt pupil," Isabella reported later.

"She has an excellent teacher," Alexander replied.

Neither of them, however, was aware of the source of her zeal.

Lucrezia generally spent the morning at her studies, using this as an excuse to beg off from the tedious portrait sittings. Pintoricchio, glad to be rid of such a difficult subject, declared that he could paint her from memory.

At the midday meal Isabella contrived to converse with her pupil in loud, learned tones so that Alexander would be certain to hear.

At one such meal Alexander leaned toward them. "Your pupil does you credit," he said, and handed her a small casket.

Isabella, opening it, gasped with delight, for lying before her on a swatch of black velvet lay four perfect Oriental pearls.

"When your course of instruction is finished,"

169

Alexander informed her, knowing her passion for such things, "I shall give you the rest of them."

Lucrezia pretended not to notice.

From that day forth Isabella redoubled her efforts. She even shared Lucrezia's siesta period, determined to earn the rest of the pearls as soon as possible, discoursing endlessly on poetry and philosophy even though Lucrezia generally fell asleep.

"As for art," she finished when the month was up, "you must develop your own taste by exposing yourself to it."

Lucrezia wearily assured her that she would try.

"Perhaps," Isabella continued with an arch look at Alexander, "Lucrezia can come to Mantua to visit with Francesco and myself. We have an extensive collection." It was the first reference she had made to her husband in all the time she'd been gone.

On the day of her departure for Mantua, Alexander handed her a casket containing the rest of the pearls. There were forty-six in all, twelve millimeters across, and each one evenly matched.

Isabella scooped them up lovingly, letting them run between her fingers. Then she tied the casket with cord and locked it in her chest. "I shall be happy to instruct Lucrezia whenever Your Excellency should require it," she said, taking the key and thrusting it into her bosom.

It was not until after Isabella left that Lucrezia found out that her father had bribed her not only to give her lessons but to confiscate any letters which Don Alphonso should send in her care.

In early November Giovanni, convinced that the plague threat was over and pressed beyond endurance

170

by his creditors, returned to Rome with his new valet, Giacomino.

Lucrezia was asleep when he arrived. She was awakened by his servant unpacking the endless jars of unguents and scents.

"Who is it?" she asked sharply, sitting up in bed.

Giacomino smiled and bowed and continued his unpacking.

She jumped from the bed, putting on the long dressing gown which lay at its foot, tying it about her quickly. Back or not, Giovanni would not sleep in her bed. She would see to that. "Maria!" she shouted.

Giovanni stood in the doorway, resplendent in canary-yellow velvet trimmed in sable. "Ah, my beautiful wife."

She took one look at him and all her former revulsion returned. "Get out of here!"

Giovanni smiled, showing perfect teeth. "Papa says that I am to sleep with you, my darling."

"How dare you call him Papa? He is *my* Papa, not yours. Now get out!"

"Lucrezia, my dear," Alexander said, coming into the room. "Giovanni has missed you so much that he could not stay away any longer. Is that not true, my boy?"

Giovanni nodded and continued to smile fixedly.

"He has finally come home, my dear, to claim his conjugal rights."

"A plague on him!" she burst out.

Giovanni paled. "You said the plague was over."

"And so it is," Alexander said soothingly. "There is practically no danger, my boy. Take my word for it."

Lucrezia was thinking fast. "Papa, I am not feeling very well. It is probably nothing, only a touch of fever, but perhaps we should use a bolster to keep Giovanni on his side of the bed."

Giovanni's face went white. "It's the plague," he cried. "I know it. I've seen that look before!"

Lucrezia smiled and stretched out her arms. *"Caro mio,* give me a kiss!"

Giovanni gasped and ran from the room.

He stayed away from her for two weeks. It would take at least that long, he declared, for any of the plague symptoms to manifest themselves. During that time he busied himself with ordering a new wardrobe. Giacomino had moved his master's things into the apartment vacated by Isabella. There Giovanni set up court for the tailors, hatters, furriers, and jewelers who passed through his rooms in a steady stream. In no time at all he had spent most of the thirty thousand gold ducats that Alexander had given him.

Lucrezia for her part was delighted. She gave Maria explicit instructions to keep the doors to her apartment locked at all times. Alexander for once let her alone, and she passed the time as she chose, rising late, dressing or not dressing, doing whatever she pleased, even taking her books and picnicking on the banks of the Tiber or just frolicking in the grass with her spaniel. This state of grace lasted for exactly two weeks.

At the end of that time, having bought everything he could lay his hands on, Giovanni was bored. "That was a nasty trick you played on me," he said, coming up to her from behind as she sat reading.

Lucrezia smiled sweetly. "Take your hands off me!"

"Why, you're my wife, aren't you?"

"No," she said through clenched teeth. "I am not!"

"Very well then, I shall tell Papa."

"My father," Lucrezia said loftily, "has other things to do than listen to your tiresome little tales."

"He'll listen," Giovanni said confidently.

"You leave him alone!"

"I wouldn't bother him at all," he said, running his fingers over her arms, "if you were nice to me."

"Oh, all right. But if you do one thing that I don't like, I shall tell Cesare."

"You will have no cause to be displeased. I've been practicing."

The prospect of spending the night with Giovanni weighed on her like a stone. She had put it off as long as possible, and her father's displeasure was always more than she could bear. If only Juan were not in Gandia, awaiting the arrival of an heir. He would have kept Giovanni busy at the brothels, for they were two of a kind, living only for the pleasure of the moment. Juan would busy himself with the women of Rome while Giovanni would amuse himself with the young boys. If she asked Cesare, she thought, he might be able to arrange something . . . No, Cesare detested him even more than she did. And although she did not relish Giovanni as a marriage partner, she was unwilling to see any harm come to him. There was nothing to do but give in.

After Giovanni had left Rome, Lucrezia had had her apartments redecorated to her own taste. She had ripped down the dull red draperies and bed hangings and had them done over in a pale yellow silk which had come from Canton. She loved yellow. It was the color of sunshine, and even on a cold gray day the room would look warm and cheerful. The walls were hung in the same fabric, and she had given orders that the vases be kept filled with fresh flowers in varying hues of yellow and orange. Lucrezia had ordered several dressing gowns in yellow, and Maria was kept busy stitching yellow silk pillows to be scattered in careless disarray. Giulia, upon seeing the room for the first time, clapped her hands in delight. "It is like living inside a sunbeam!"

173

Lucrezia lay now on the yellow satin sheets waiting for Giovanni to come to her. Perhaps he might forget or be too tired, she thought hopefully. But no, the anxious bridegroom was already at the door, locking it carefully behind him.

"You won't be sorry," he whispered, sliding into bed beside her.

She lay taut, letting him touch her where he would. Against her will, her body responded, her nipples growing hard beneath his fingers. She felt her breath coming in hot little gasps. Suddenly she wanted to feel the heat and the strength of him. With frantic fingers she found his hardness and guided it in.

Giovanni, anxious to please, managed to control himself. He lay quiet, letting her move against him, pressing her to stop only when he felt he could no longer hold back.

The fever within her mounted higher and higher, taking her with it until, in a sudden gasp of pleasure and surprise, she felt it lift her and take her completely. Delighted, she finally lay back, letting the feeling spread, savoring the sweetness in her thighs.

"There, did I not tell you?" Giovanni said proudly, after he had satisfied himself as well. "Did I not tell you you would not be sorry?"

Lucrezia smiled and fell asleep.

Alexander, seeing her at the midday meal the next day, appeared pleased. "I have told Giacomino to move Giovanni's things. After all, the apartment is large enough for both of you, is it not, my dear?"

"Yes, Papa," Lucrezia answered.

The days passed peacefully, and the nights too. Giovanni amused himself by initiating Lucrezia in all sorts of little tricks. After a while his innovations did not bother her anymore. But she still preferred having him inside her. "It feels better that way," she said.

174

"I have an idea," he said eagerly.

His tongue was so hot and quick, her feeling of pleasure so intense that she nearly fainted. "I think we should alternate," she said when she could speak. "Next time you'll go inside me."

Giovanni had other ideas. "Do you not like it this way?"

"It isn't that," Lucrezia said in some embarrassment. "It's just that it feels so empty there with nothing inside me."

"It is all in your head," he answered.

"Why don't you want to put it in me?" she asked him several nights later.

"Because," he said sharply, "it does not feel good to me that way."

"I don't want to do it the other way anymore."

"Why not?"

"Because it is not the right way."

"Don't you know, you little fool," he cried, "that *any* way is the right way!" Then he said, "Open your mouth."

"If I open my mouth, it will be to scream," she shouted.

"Go ahead. You scream so much that nobody listens anymore." As he spoke he dug his fingers into the tender flesh of her throat.

"Why are you doing this?" she whispered, her eyes swimming in tears.

"Because, dear wife, you are longing for something inside you, and that you are going to get now, one way or another!"

"What is this?" Alexander said, coming into her room the next day. "Giovanni says that you threatened him and that he wants to go back to Pesaro."

175

"Let him go," Lucrezia said wearily. "He's a madman. I wish to have nothing to do with him."

"I am not ready to let him go just yet," Alexander said evenly. "When I am ready, I shall let you know." Then, gently, he said, "Are you feeling all right?"

Lucrezia began to cry. "Oh, Papa, if you only knew what he made me do."

Alexander patted her head and looked away. "Give it a year," he said softly. "By then we will no longer need him."

"But Papa, do you know what he did?"

"Never mind," Alexander said. "You'll soon feel better. Look, I have brought you something nice."

Lucrezia looked silently at the small silver casket he had set on the coverlet.

"Open it."

"I don't want it, Papa."

"Open it." Alexander's voice was firm. Then he added, "I have told Giacomino to remove Giovanni's things. I will also cut off his allowance."

Lucrezia opened the box, but the emerald that lay within, one of the finest she'd ever seen, was blurred by tears.

Two weeks after Giovanni's eviction his uncle Ludovico Sforza, the Duke of Milan, invited King Charles VIII of France to invade Italy and Naples, pledging his support. Alexander was furious when he heard of it. "Just because I would not grant him a certain favor! It is nothing but spite!" Up to that time, and because of Lucrezia's marriage to Giovanni, Alexander had thrown in his political lot with Milan and Venice. And now Ludovico had turned traitor. Alexander went to King Ferrante of Naples. Giovanni was a nuisance, he told him, and added that he was looking for an excuse to be rid of him and to extricate himself from the Milan and Venice League. To show that he was sincere, Alexander signed a marriage contract between his son Geoffrey and Sancia of Naples. "I give you my son and my word," he told King Ferrante.

When Giovanni found out, he was sick with fear. What would happen to him and his family now that the Pope had changed sides? He bit his nails, he lost weight, he became hysterical. Finally he went to Lucrezia. "Have you heard what your father and Cesare are planning now?" he cried. "How can they do this to me?"

Lucrezia looked up from her needlepoint and smiled. "I know, my love. And they have promised to give me your scrotum as a souvenir."

Giovanni clapped his hands over his crotch. "Rotten bitch!" he shrieked.

He stationed himself outside the Pope's door, pouncing on him the first thing in the morning.

Alexander merely smiled. "Patience, my boy," he said, and turned to Cesare, who joined him in the hall.

But Giovanni would not be put off. With boldness born of fear, he trailed at his father-in-law's heels and whined about his position.

"That is enough!" Alexander exploded finally. "What would you have me do, foretell the future?"

"No," Giovanni said quickly. "It is just that I feel so useless not knowing anything. I should like to be able to do some good."

"That is fine, my boy. You can do the most good by staying out of my way." Alexander turned abruptly and went to his breakfast.

Cesare laughed in his face. "Do you think my father has nothing better to do than to think about an idiot like you!"

Giovanni let this pass. "Speak to him," he pleaded. "Ask him what's going to happen."

Cesare pretended to consider. "If I were you," he said at last, "I should enter a convent."

In desperation Giovanni tried a new approach. The people of Pesaro, he told the Pope later that morning, had never seen their countess. Would His Excellency allow them that small pleasure? Giovanni neither ate nor slept while Alexander considered.

It was really not a bad idea, Alexander thought. It would get his stupid son-in-law out of his way while he was negotiating with Naples. Besides, the plague was getting bad again and he had considered sending Lucrezia and Giovanni into the country anyway.

Late in May they left Rome for the duchy of Pesaro.

CHAPTER 17

No sooner had Lucrezia and Giovanni left for Pesaro than Alexander regretted his decision. The French situation was worsening. That idiot Charles VIII, stunted in mind as well as stature, actually believed himself capable of leading an army into Italy.

Alexander shrugged. The man was a fool. But even a fool has to do something to feel less foolish, he thought, even if it meant invading Italy. He did not blame Charles. He blamed the men who had his ear, the men in Milan and Venice. He could see Ludovico Sforza, whom everyone called "il Moro"—the Moor—behind his back, strutting about and telling Charles what a great king he was.

Alexander laughed. Great indeed. The little king needed three special steps just to climb up into his bed at night. But that was not what nettled him. What nettled him was the idea of Sforza filling Charles's head with stories of corruption in the Vatican and inflaming the monarch until he believed that he was both Jesus Christ and St. Paul and that it was his duty to lead a crusade against the Pope and his supporters. Il Moro had done his job well.

It was too bad, Alexander thought, that he had let Giovanni go back to Pesaro. He would have made an admirable hostage to the French. Ah well, he would get him back later.

Cesare was less confident. "That freak will never show his face here again. He is lucky to have escaped at all and he knows it."

Alexander disagreed. "As long as he does not lose his taste for expensive things, we have nothing to worry about."

It had been no easy matter to persuade Lucrezia to leave the city for Pesaro. Alexander had finally had to take her down to the charnel house to view the plague victims, black and swollen in their shrouds, before she would consent to go.

"I have no wish to see you like that," Alexander had said, watching her.

"All right, Papa," she sighed. "I will go." They had left their nose cloths at the door, but even out in the street the stench was so great that Lucrezia vomited at once.

A picture is worth a thousand words, Alexander had reflected later in his study.

Now that they were gone, there was nothing to do but wait for Charles to make his move. In the meantime, Alexander decided, he would strengthen his position against Milan. He wrote to Lucrezia suggesting that Giovanni quit his service in Milan, which paid him practically nothing, and accept instead the command of a Neapolitan brigade for better pay. "After all," he wrote, "they are angry at him in Milan anyway since I broke off relations with them." Alexander neglected to mention that Giovanni's new pact would strengthen his own position with the Neapolitans.

When Giovanni read the letter that Lucrezia handed him, he had a prompt attack of nerves. If he broke his ties with Milan, he would be completely at the mercy of the Borgias. "I would rather be eaten by wolves!" he cried.

Lucrezia looked at him with contempt. "Do as you like. I have a fitting."

For one week Giovanni bit his nails and broke out in a rash. Lucrezia refused to speak to him.

The court at Pesaro was a far cry from the luxurious magnificence of the Vatican palace. The whole place had fallen into disrepair, for the funds which Alexander had given Giovanni for its refurbishment, Giovanni put on his back. The roofs leaked, the walls sweated with damp, the hangings grew mold. Lucrezia was forced to have her clothing brushed and aired constantly. Only the principal rooms were furnished and kept up decently. The rest of the place was as cold and dank as a tomb. The courtiers, all of whom Lucrezia found unbearably provincial, walked about swathed in layers of woolen clothing.

"They look like peasants and they smell like tallow," Lucrezia complained. "What is the fun of giving parties when everyone looks such a fright?"

When she wrote to her father about how gloomy and dreary Pesaro was, Alexander promptly sent her chestfuls of brocades and hangings, along with the suggestion that she keep after Giovanni about the Neapolitan post.

After weeks of nagging, Giovanni made his decision. He would keep his ties in Milan and accept the Neapolitan post as well. However, he said nothing of this to Lucrezia, or to anyone else for that matter. To Lucrezia he said only that he was accepting her father's offer.

She smiled and said nothing.

This done, Giovanni sat down and wrote the Milanese envoy, telling him that he was accepting the Neapolitan post only because it would enable him to keep Milan better informed as to Alexander's movements. The fact that he was committing treason by doing this occurred to him, but his position frightened him so much that he refused to think about it. After all, what else could he do? He could not run the risk of offending the Milanese. They were his only ally. Nor could he risk offending his father-in-law. Later perhaps, when Charles had ousted Alexander from the Vatican, then he would have his fun. In the meantime, he would accept money from Naples and money from the Milanese for spying.

He allowed his mind to float. How sweet it would be to be able to humiliate the Borgias—Cesare especially. He would ask il Moro to have Cesare thrown into prison so that he could go and taunt him. He might even take a supply of rotten vegetables and fruits to pelt him with.

Unfortunately, he had neither the wit nor the cool hand necessary for double-dealing. The whole thing was making him so nervous that he could not sleep. He trembled and shook at every sound.

In a matter of weeks he was in such a state of nerves that he wrote to Ludovico Sforza saying that if even one shred of the information that he was sending to him leaked out, he, Giovanni, would be a dead man. The Duke replied by sending him a set of superbly matched sables and a huge cabochon emerald set in heavy gold, which Giovanni immediately had made into a ring.

As for Alexander, who was never in the dark about anything for very long, he chose to remain silent for the moment, saying nothing about the treachery to

Cesare. His main concern was the approach of the French army.

For three months Alexander waited for Charles to move. Finally, toward the end of summer, Alexander wrote to Lucrezia and Giovanni to return to Rome. The palace was lonely without his children, he wrote. He needed them to cheer him up in his hour of difficulty.

"I won't go," Giovanni sobbed. "It is some sort of trick—I know it."

"My father has better things to do with his time," Lucrezia said, starting to pack. The sooner she left this place of decay, the better. The winter damp had given way to summer humidity, and the walls which had formerly run with cold now sweated with heat. Once she returned to Rome she would get rid of her clothing, which was falling to pieces from mildew. In fact, she would not even bother taking many of her things with her. She would take what she needed to travel in and nothing more, nothing to remind her of her unpleasant stay in Pesaro.

"I won't go," Giovanni repeated, watching her pack. "It's not only your father and Cesare. There's the plague as well."

Lucrezia smiled. "On the whole, I prefer the plague to Pesaro."

But Giovanni refused to leave, and Lucrezia, as his wife, was forced to remain with him.

In Rome, Alexander paced and fretted. Lucrezia had been gone three months now, and although he had the French invasion hanging over him, he was provoked that his daughter was not with him to lighten his mood. Alexander sent off a letter to Lucrezia and Giovanni, berating them for staying so long.

Giovanni read the letter and threw it at Lucrezia in

183

fright, forgetting that it was he who insisted on staying. "Look what you have done now. He'll blame it all on me."

"What do you mean by that?"

"Nothing!" he shrieked. "Nothing! Write to him at once and explain that I had nothing to do with it. Hurry up and do it now. The messenger can take it back with him!"

"All right," Lucrezia said wearily. She would do anything to quiet him. His constant screeching and jumping about were working on her nerves.

When Alexander received her letter, he repented his harsh tone with her. She was a child, after all, and married to a fool.

On August 4 Charles crossed the Alps with a huge army traveling in his wake and a formidable supply of artillery. He met with no resistance.

Cesare was livid. "Does Your Excellency realize that he can invade us? With an army like ours, it is child's play. We have nothing but a bunch of mercenaries under condottieri, who are afraid to risk losing them in battle, who simply feed and clothe them for the sake of having them around so that they can collect their protection money."

"Tut-tut," Alexander soothed. "How often are we invaded?"

"Now!"

"Never mind, I am taking care of it."

"How?" Cesare shouted. "With pen and paper?"

Alexander smiled. "Yes."

"It is not enough. We need men and arms. We need an army, an army so great that no one will ever dare to think of invading us again!"

"Ah, yes. Well, that is very nice, Cesare, but I have some letters to write."

"While you are at it," Cesare shouted, "write to Charles and tell him to go back to France!"

Alexander balanced his pen between his fingers. "Tell me, Cesare. If you were Captain General, what would you do?"

"I would fashion an army recruited from the provinces. Men fighting on their home ground have more to lose than mere mercenaries from other countries."

Alexander considered. "That is very interesting. What else?"

"I would have light siege artillery, and in addition to that I would have light brass field guns to keep up a rapid fire of iron balls like the French have. Our guns are too heavy and too slow."

"And who would teach these country louts how to use them?"

Cesare thought of Gian Capello, the Sicilian captain at arms at Monte Giordano. "I have the man," he said. "Together we could recruit and train your country bumpkins."

Alexander lowered his pen and started writing. "Yes, well, it is too late now. Perhaps next time . . ."

"Next time?" Cesare exploded. "It is now or never!"

"You are very like your mother," Alexander remarked. "Easy to anger and slow to judge."

By December the situation was desperate. Cesare, bursting into Alexander's apartments, found his father kneeling at his prie-dieu.

"Your Holiness!" he burst out.

Alexander finished his prayers and then turned slowly around. "Well?" he asked.

"They say that the French are within fifty miles of Rome!"

"Thirty," Alexander corrected him calmly.

"What are you going to do?"

185

"Do?" Alexander climbed ponderously to his feet. "Why, I am going to give Charles a reception."

"A reception?"

"Why, yes. I believe it is customary for a man in my position to receive a visiting monarch."

"Visiting?"

"Yes."

"Then you will not offer any resistance?"

Alexander seemed shocked. "Why should I offer resistance, particularly when he has twenty-five thousand men with him?"

On December 31, 1494, the French army entered Rome amidst a volley of cheers from the populace. All around them rang shouts of *Francia! Colonna! Vincoli!,* the last being a salutation to the hated della Rovere, who was Cardinal of San Pietro in Vincoli.

"Do you know why those idiots are cheering?" Cesare remarked sarcastically from the balcony where they watched. "It is so they will not be sacked, burned, or murdered. The fools! Don't they know it will happen anyway?"

"Yes, they know it will happen," Alexander said quietly, "but they also hope that it won't. In the meantime," he added, "it might be best if you stayed in your rooms for a while. You will not find your incarceration unpleasant."

This much accomplished, Alexander sat back to wait. There was unfortunately nothing he could do to prevent the sacking and burning of his city. The French were simply behaving like soldiers, pillaging, robbing, and raping. Were they not engaged in this, they might do worse, Alexander thought, thinking of the Vatican and all its treasures. No, he would not interfere.

By January 6 the situation had worsened. The smoke in the city was so thick that the citizens who walked the streets were obliged to hold wet cloths to their faces in order to breathe. By day the air was rent with shrieks of torment. At night no one ventured out.

Only Cesare had a pleasant time of it, for Alexander had sent him two of Rome's most talented young prostitutes. When he tired of the usual things, he amused himself by suggesting to them every indignity he could think of. "Consider yourself fortunate, my dear," he said to the plump dark-haired girl as he rode her around the room like a mule, whip in hand. "Consider yourself fortunate that you are here with me instead of at the mercy of the French."

"There is nothing left for them to do," she gasped.

Cesare had just about run out of ideas when his father entered the room.

Alexander, looking about him, could scarcely believe the wild state of disarray before him. Food and clothing were scattered everywhere. Without realizing it, he had trod on a bunch of grapes which had carelessly been thrown on the floor. "What happened to the other girl?" He asked, seeing only the one that Cesare sat astride.

Cesare pointed to the ceiling with his whip. Suspended from a hook by an ingenious system of wires and pulleys hung a girl with flowing red tresses. "It is very simple, Your Holiness. You see, I launch myself from here . . ."

"Cut her down," Alexander said quietly.

"Just as you say, Your Saintliness. It was beginning to be a bit of a bore anyway."

That night Cesare and his father crept from the Vatican through the underground passage leading to the fortress of Castel Sant'Angelo. Once there, Alexander relaxed completely.

187

"How can you eat like that with the French army all about us?" Cesare fretted.

Alexander raised a pear with his knife and peeled the skin with care. "What would you suggest I do? Starve?"

"They could be at the gates at any moment!"

"Let me know as soon as it happens," Alexander said, rising from the table and belching. "I am going to sleep now."

Cesare paced nervously for three days, watching in disgust as Alexander consumed great quantities of food and joked with the castle guards. Finally he could take it no longer. "Do you realize," he shouted, bursting into Alexander's room as he slept, "do you realize that we are sitting here waiting to be slaughtered like hogs by those miserable French!"

"Oh, it is you again," Alexander said, sitting up in bed and yawning. "I wish you would not use the word 'hogs.' Sheep are more to my liking." With that he fell back against the pillows and resumed his nap.

On the fourth day it was Alexander's turn to awaken Cesare.

"What is it? What's happened?"

Alexander smiled and scratched himself. "Tonight I am meeting with Charles."

"What!"

"You may come along if you wish, but you must take good care to hide yourself."

Cesare grinned.

"I knew you would be pleased. I know your love of subterfuge. However, I must insist that you remain here until I send for you."

Cesare paced the floor. At seven o'clock there was a knock on his door. "What is it?"

"Open it."

Cesare recognized the voice of Ludo Sange, one of his father's secretaries, and opened the door cautiously.

The other man smiled. "Come with me," he said. The two men crept down the underground passage, back to the Vatican palace.

"Where are we going?" Cesare asked, expecting to be taken to one of the reception rooms.

"Shhh!" Ludo answered.

Cesare followed him out of the passage and into a pleached alley paved with stones. A spicy fragrance filled the air. The herb garden, Cesare thought, feeling the thick rimming of herbs between the paving stones. It was a favorite trysting place of his father's.

"Why here?" Cesare whispered.

"Shhh!" Ludo warned him, pointing to a place behind some bushes where there stood a chair and a table of sweetmeats.

Cesare, not knowing what else to do, sat in the chair.

The night was warm for January. A pale moon hung in the sky, partly obscured by smoke, making the garden luminous and gilding the edges of the evergreen hedges. Here the smell of smoke was not unpleasant. Cesare settled in the chair more comfortably and listened to the sounds of the night. The darkness wrapped about him like a cloak. Cesare felt himself come alive. He was, after all, a creature of the night, thirsting after black things.

Suddenly he heard footsteps along the path. His hand crept toward his dagger, his eyes peered through the darkness. It was a man, that much was certain, a little man with a large nose and a hump on one shoulder. Then it hit him. The ugly little man was Charles.

At the same time, Alexander entered the path from a door in the wall. Cesare could just make out his white alb and girdle. Strangely enough, he seemed totally unaware of the man on the path before him.

Charles, plainly unsettled by this lack of recognition, started forward. "Holy Father," he said tentatively.

Alexander seemed deaf as well as blind.

Cesare chafed. What could his father be thinking of to treat the King of France in such a fashion?

Alexander continued to walk on his way.

Charles began to twitch. "H-holy F-father," he stammered.

Alexander noticed him as for the first time. He paused in his walk and knelt suddenly.

Charles, completely agitated by now, put out a hand to restrain him. "N-no, Your H-holiness, it is I w-who sh-should kneel . . ."

"What did you say?" Alexander asked loudly, affecting not to hear.

"I-it is not p-proper," Charles stuttered.

Cesare stifled the laughter that rose in his throat.

"Proper?" Alexander boomed, still on his knees. "Surely it is proper that I kneel to the King of France? For after all"—he smiled, rising to his full height, which was considerably above that of the little man who stood on the path before him—"after all, if I were not merely Rodrigo Borgia but Pope Alexander VI, Christ's Vicar on Earth, then surely my son the King of France would have instead knelt to me?"

Charles stood speechless, trying to decide what to do, the muscles of his face working furiously.

It was then that Alexander chose to hold out his hand.

Charles, who was waiting for some such sign, fell on his knees and kissed the hem of Alexander's robe.

Cesare, watching from his chair, could scarcely believe what he saw. Who but his father would have thought of such a trick as that? He continued to watch, stunned, as his father, having made the sign of the cross over Charles's misshapen back, turned on his heel and walked off, with the little monarch limping uncertainly after him.

Cesare remained in his seat until the pathway was clear. Then he got up to leave. The moon had slipped behind a cloud and it was more difficult to see. At that moment his father's secretary stepped from behind the bushes. "You are to wait for His Holiness in the sacristy," he whispered.

Then it was not only the birds he had heard in the bushes, Cesare mused; it was his father's secretary making certain that he did not leave his post.

Cesare waited in the sacristy for over an hour.

Alexander walked in slowly, seemingly unaware of him. That was all right for the King of France, Cesare thought angrily, but to treat his own son in such a manner was something else entirely. He watched in silence as his father knelt on the prie-dieu and bent his head. Really, Cesare thought, there was no one else in the room but himself; the old fool didn't have to bother impressing him.

Alexander remained kneeling with bent head for ten minutes.

"Your Holiness," Cesare began, realizing how much like Charles he sounded.

Alexander appeared not to have heard.

"Your Holiness," Cesare repeated louder.

Alexander turned slowly, seeming to come from a great distance. "Ah, Cesare," he said in surprise. "I was hoping you would come."

"Hoping?" Cesare repeated. As though the old fool had not brought him here purposely.

Alexander rose to his feet with some difficulty and settled himself comfortably in the pontifical chair. "I have been speaking to the King of France," he said conversationally, as though Cesare were not already aware of it, "and in exchange for crowning him King of Naples and a few other things, he has agreed to withdraw his troops."

"What other things?" Cesare asked guardedly.

"Well, for one thing," Alexander said, reaching over to the bowl of plums which stood next to his chair, "you are to accompany him to Naples."

"Why me?"

Alexander examined the plum he was about to eat and smiled. "Well, for another thing, it is high time that you had some diplomatic experience."

"Experience as a hostage, you mean."

Alexander waved his hand. "Do not concern yourself with that, my son."

"Why not?" Cesare asked hotly. "Since it already concerns me whether I like it or not!"

"It is really of no consequence," Alexander said. "Believe me."

"If it is of no consequence, then I shall not go."

"You will go," Alexander said quietly. "You will go."

Cesare rode with Charles for three days before he deserted. He returned to the Vatican to find his mother closeted with Alexander. Before he had time to withdraw, he heard Vanozza's voice raised in anger.

"They have taken everything," she cried. "They have torn down the tapestries, broken the windows, and trampled my gardens to bits!"

Cesare remained where he was, listening. His mother was no doubt carrying on about the damage done by the French.

"Yes, that is very unfortunate," Alexander said.

"Unfortunate!" Vanozza's voice was as cold as the grave. "Is that all you have to say?"

"Please, madam. I have fifty petitions to study and a High Mass to celebrate."

"Is that all you have to say to me, the mother of your children?"

Alexander looked up from the papers he was studying. "No, I have this to say: all cardinals should remain celibate. Now go home."

Vanozza's venom spread. "You can say that to me after all that has happened!"

"For God's sake, woman! All that trash will be replaced."

Cesare quietly moved close to the door and watched in amusement as Vanozza said, "And my dignity? What of that!"

"What of it?" Alexander inquired.

"I want you to summon Charles back to Rome and insist that he apologize for all the inconvenience he has caused me!"

"Are you mad? I have just had one hell of a time getting him out of Rome!" At that point his eyes fell on Cesare. "What are you doing here!"

"I got tired of watching Charles drool all over himself. He is rather disgusting, you know," Cesare replied easily, not bothering to acknowledge his mother, who was not one of his favorites.

"You are your mother's monster!" Alexander exploded. "Two of a kind and no doubt of it. And what am I to tell Charles, pray?"

"You don't have to tell him anything. I think he was glad to see me go."

"And why is that?" Alexander demanded.

"Oh, nothing," Cesare said innocently. "When the minstrels came in during supper and compared him to St. Paul and Jesus Christ, I think I laughed."

"I see," Alexander said, and smiled.

CHAPTER 18

In the spring of the year, the French having gone, Alexander sent an escort to Pesaro for Lucrezia and Giovanni.

Giovanni was not happy about going. "I am better off staying where I am," he said in a pout to Lucrezia. "Your father does not respect me, and Cesare does nothing but throw insults. At least here in my own duchy I am looked up to."

"Do as you like," Lucrezia said, busy with her packing. "I don't care whether you go or stay." Living with Giovanni had become unbearable. He had now resorted to wearing makeup, and there were so many false curls sticking out from under his hats that Lucrezia swore he looked like one of her ladies-in-waiting.

A week later Lucrezia handed Giovanni a letter.

"You open it," he said nervously, his fingers busy with the frills about his wrist, the newest thing from the French court. "His letters always disturb me so."

For answer Lucrezia handed him the letter stamped with the Fisherman's seal.

Giovanni broke the seal with hands that trembled. "I won't go!" he screamed even while he was reading it. "He can't force me!"

"You had better do as he says," Lucrezia said, watching him in amusement. "You see, he knows all about that treasonous business of yours with the Duke of Milan."

"Oh my God! It is all over with me. If he does not have me killed, that brother of yours will!"

"Nonsense," Lucrezia said firmly. Alexander had written to her privately, stating that Giovanni must accompany her back to Rome at all costs and that he was holding her personally responsible for his return. "They will do no such thing. After all, if Papa wanted you dead, he could just as well have you killed here and save himself the trouble and expense of outfitting you for the journey."

"Outfitting?" Giovanni inquired.

"Why, yes," Lucrezia said, handing him a page of the letter her father had sent to her.

Giovanni's mouth moved as he read. "My dear daughter, I know of Giovanni's pact with the Duke of Milan, but all that is over and done with. He is still your husband and my son, and so I forgive him and enclose herein as proof of my good feeling a letter of credit in the amount of ten thousand gold ducats to be spent by him as he pleases in preparation for the journey to Rome . . ."

In the end Giovanni succumbed to the ten thousand ducats, just as Alexander had known he would. "It is not the money," he said, reaching out his hand for the letter of credit. "It is only that I wish to please you in this."

Lucrezia smiled and said nothing.

It was a warm spring day. Cesare, with his usual superabundant energy, was working out in the bullring. "It is a far better sport than jousting," he had said to Alexander in trying to persuade him to import the bulls from Spain. "And besides, it is less crippling."

Alexander agreed, as it was his policy to agree with all things in which he was not personally concerned.

Alexander watched while Cesare wiped his dripping face and neck with a length of linen, then poured a gourd of water over his head and shook himself like a dog. He was really rather splendid-looking, yet what was there about the boy that frightened him as he stood there so handsome and full of health in the strong sunlight?

He made his smile wide. "You did very well, my boy."

Cesare flushed with pleasure at his father's compliment, until the older man added, "By the way, Lucrezia is here."

Something in Cesare's eyes shifted and came alive. "Why was I not notified?"

"They came in late," Alexander said lightly. "I did not want to disturb you."

"You could have disturbed me for that. How is she?"

"Tired," Alexander said shortly.

"And that donkey her husband?"

"You will see for yourself."

"Indeed, I cannot wait."

"By the way, your brother Geoffrey and his wife Sancia are coming home to live."

"And why is that?"

"Because," Alexander said carefully, "I like having my children around me."

"Between Geoffrey and Giovanni, you will have nothing but a stable of donkeys."

"That is no way to speak of your brother," Alexander said sharply.

"A donkey is a donkey. And as for that wife of his, you may not know it, but she is a devout eater of men."

"I had hoped," Alexander said, making his face solemn, "that we might all live together like a family. It is a long time since we have all been together."

Cesare wiped his neck and grinned.

"I am not joking," Alexander said sternly. "It is not good to show a disunited front."

"Ah," Cesare said softly, "so it is *the appearance of a real family* that concerns you. In that case, I suggest that you marry off your children more carefully."

So preoccupied were the two men in their verbal jousting that they neither saw nor heard Lucrezia approaching.

"Cesare!" she shrieked, throwing her arms about him and kissing him wildly. "I could not sleep. I simply had to come and see you!"

Cesare held her close, breathing in the sweet scent of her skin and hair. "Well, that husband of yours has taught you nothing of kissing. There," he said, kissing her full on the mouth, "that's better. Now let me look at you."

Alexander smiled at Lucrezia's shyness. That was as it should be.

"I do not look very well, do I, Cesare?"

He looked at her thinness and at the dark circles under her eyes and bit his lips in anger. "I have seen you look better," he said quietly. "What has that donkey put you through?"

"Nothing," she said quickly. "It is only that I have been homesick."

"What has he done to you?" Cesare insisted.

"He has done nothing," Alexander interposed quickly. "You heard the child. She was homesick."

"Why must you always speak for everyone?" Cesare said impatiently. "Look at her face. It speaks for itself."

At that moment a shrill cry rent the air. "Lucrezia, you promised to wait for me!"

Cesare turned slowly. "What is that!" he gasped in amazement.

Giovanni, in honor of the occasion, was wearing a cloth-of-gold suit which fit him like a second skin. Glittering in the sunlight, his curls sprinkled with gold dust and brilliants, he was dazzling to behold.

Alexander raised his brows in disbelief.

"Can you see now what a circus he is, what an ass?" Cesare hissed through clenched teeth. "He will make us the laughing-stock of Rome with his antics!"

Alexander, ignoring this, smiled thinly and held out his hand for his son-in-law to kiss. "Ah, my boy, I see that you have put my gold to good use."

Giovanni blushed like a girl. "I hope that Your Holiness is not disappointed."

"No," Alexander said carefully. "I am not disappointed. Are you disappointed?" he asked, turning to Cesare.

"No," Cesare said shortly. "It is fully as I expected."

"He has not greeted me." Giovanni pouted and pointed a heavily ringed finger in Cesare's direction.

"I am not in the habit of conversing with donkeys," Cesare said.

"Let's not quarrel," Alexander admonished. "We are a family, are we not? Lucrezia, your brother Geoffrey and his wife Sancia are coming home. You will do everything in your power to make her stay a pleasant one, will you not, my child?"

"Yes, Papa, I shall be happy to."

"If I may say so," Cesare interrupted, "I do not consider Sancia a fit companion for her."

"You may not say so," Alexander said sternly.

"Is she beautiful?" Lucrezia inquired uneasily.

"She is evil," Cesare said. "She is a fit companion for me, but not for you."

"My boy," Alexander said, examining his nails with care, "do you not have something else to occupy you at this moment?"

"Yes, my sister's welfare."

"Suppose you leave that to me."

"I have," Cesare said, with a glance at Giovanni. "And look what happened."

"He is nasty," Giovanni burst out. "He is just as nasty as ever!"

"Papa," Lucrezia said, ignoring the outburst, "when is Sancia coming?"

"In two weeks, my child."

"That is good," she sighed. "Perhaps by then I will have my looks back."

Lucrezia entered into an orgy of preparation for her meeting with Sancia. She was, after all, the daughter of the house, and she did not wish to be found lacking in looks or in anything else. The trip from Pesaro had so tired her that she felt at least twenty years old, which was almost middle-aged. "You must try to find out all about her," she instructed Maria. "Some of the servants must know . . ."

Meanwhile she washed her hair daily, rinsing it with lemon and egg to make it shine, and spent a great deal of time lying in bed with her head hanging down to pull the blood into her face.

Maria came to her one day with glum news. Sancia was not only beautiful, having high color and dark

199

Spanish good looks, but she had the most stunning wardrobe one could imagine.

"She has only one flaw," Maria reported. "She has a bosom which looks as though it has been run over by a chariot."

Lucrezia brightened. Her own breasts were none too large, but at least they were firm and high.

On the day of Sancia's arrival, Lucrezia rose early. There was scarcely any trace of the blue shadows beneath her eyes, but she had Maria rub in some white lead just to make certain.

"How do I look?" she asked anxiously, pinching her cheeks to give them added color.

"Bellissima!" Maria exclaimed.

"That is good, for she will always remember how I looked when she first met me."

Maria had blinked at the black dress she had chosen to wear, but when she saw it on Lucrezia, with her skin so pink and white and her hair a mantle of gold, she agreed that the dress was right after all. The child looked like a doll, she thought, in the low-cut dress with its large billowing sleeves.

"I want her to know," Lucrezia confided, "that I do not come from the country."

"And what is wrong with that?" Maria demanded, since she herself came from an obscure province.

"Must you choose this time to argue?" Lucrezia asked crossly. "You know that there is no time, and besides, it makes lines."

Lucrezia arrived on a magnificent parade horse caparisoned in alternating bands of black velvet and satin. Waiting in the courtyard were all the members of the palace, the palace guards, and the Italian and foreign ambassadors.

The two young women met and embraced solemnly,

200

taking one another's measure. Sancia, Lucrezia was pleased to note, was wearing entirely too much rouge. Her black eyes were thickly ringed with kohl, and the corners were already sprouting crow's-feet.

"My sister," Lucrezia murmured sweetly.

Sancia narrowed her eyes, taking in the other's fresh young skin, the burnished gold of her hair. She nodded curtly.

Geoffrey rode ahead with a flourish, and a smile for Giovanni, who wore silver and black plumes fully a foot higher than anyone else's. A black patch cut in the shape of a star covered a blemish on his cheek.

Sancia rode between Lucrezia and the Spanish ambassador, her hot eyes heavy on Giovanni.

Lucrezia suppressed a smile. If Sancia expected anything from that quarter, she would be doomed to disappointment. From a distance Sancia's heavy makeup gave the look of glowing good health. She was attractive, Lucrezia conceded, in the Spanish manner.

Cesare, sitting near his father, and clad in simple black like Lucrezia, watched over the entire spectacle with an expression of amused tolerance, but in his eyes lurked the anger that he was careful to keep in check.

His brother Geoffrey, bronzed by the Spanish sun and the sea, was the only one who looked really happy, Cesare reflected bitterly. His glance traveled to Giovanni and hardened. Somehow he would have to find a way of disposing of that jackass. He robbed the family of dignity.

Two days later on Whitsunday the Pope, his court of cardinals, and all the women of the court, led by Lucrezia and Sancia, assembled at St. Peter's to listen to the Prelate of Spain preach of Christ. He was so long-winded that the only person present who was not bored was Burchard. Even Alexander fidgeted.

201

Lucrezia and Sancia looked at one another solemnly. Lucrezia giggled first, Sancia followed suit. "Come," Lucrezia whispered, taking her by the hand. Together they clambered up to the stalls reserved for the canons of St. Peter's for the singing of the gospel. The other women of the court scampered after them, glad of an excuse to leave. Once they were all upstairs there was a lively exchange of whispers and looks as they settled their skirts and smoothed their hair.

Lucrezia, catching sight of Alexander's disapproving eyes from below, quickly looked away and whispered something to Sancia.

Ah well, Alexander conceded, watching them, the prelate was a bore. Perhaps the two women would become friends.

There followed a succession of balls and concerts for which both women had a fine time ordering gowns. Each was good-naturedly determined to outdo the other. When at one party they appeared in almost identical gowns, they burst out laughing and really became friends. There was nothing to fear, Lucrezia felt, from this bold, audacious girl who dared everything and therefore longed for nothing.

In an excess of good feeling one day, Sancia took off her own perfect pearls and put them around Lucrezia's neck. "There, my sister," she said, her white smile flashing in her dark face. "Now you see that I love you." Lucrezia, unable to say a word, hugged her tightly.

Lucrezia had an idea, of course, that Sancia's real life began after the parties were over. She became aware of it one night when she couldn't sleep. It would be fun, she decided, to visit Sancia's apartment so that the two of them could talk over the evening's festivities. They might even visit the palace kitchen and fix themselves something to eat. She padded down the hall in bare feet, full of anticipation. She knocked softly at the door, for she did not want to awaken Geoffrey. When she received no answer, she turned the handle.

She was not prepared for what she saw. There in the center of the bed, naked, lay Cesare. Astride him sat Sancia, her hair flying, her small breasts jiggling. Lucrezia, watching them for a moment, could not help thinking how lovely she looked.

Sancia saw her and laughed. "Come in, little one. There is always room for one more."

Cesare scowled and said nothing as his sister turned and fled.

Going back to her own bed, Lucrezia felt tears of anger and disappointment come to her eyes. Then knowledge burst like a flood. She would like to be like Sancia!

As Sancia's escapades increased, so did Lucrezia's devotion.

"I know she does not always behave as she should," Lucrezia confided to Maria, "but she is such fun and she is so honest about everything."

"As though she could hide it," Maria muttered.

It was in Sancia's apartment one rainy summer afternoon that the two girls were amusing themselves. They had escaped from the other women of the court, whom Sancia pronounced boring. The air rolled in from the Tiber hot and sticky, and all morning long there had been distant sounds of thunder. It was really too hot for cards or anagrams, and Sancia, leaning over to Lucrezia as they sat at the midday meal, had whispered something in her ear. Not long afterward the two young women had strolled off arm in arm.

"They seem to be getting on well together," Alexander said to Cesare, watching them go.

Cesare belched and said nothing.

Giovanni's high voice broke in. "That Sancia's a lousy rotten bitch!"

Cesare smiled. "So she found out about you, did she?"

Once in her apartment, Sancia removed her clothing. "It is much cooler like this. Why don't you take yours off?"

"I'm comfortable, really I am," Lucrezia said, staring at her. She had the body of a young boy.

Sancia looked at her and laughed. "Come on, my little pagan, let me look at you."

Lucrezia felt a feeling of excitement rise up within her. "No, it's not right."

Sancia's brows rose like wings. "Why not?"

Lucrezia, confused by her feelings, said nothing.

Sancia sat down beside her. "Didn't anyone ever tell you, little one, that anything you enjoy is right? Come on," she insisted when Lucrezia made no answer, "undo your dress, and I'll brush your hair."

Wordlessly, as though her fingers were not her own, Lucrezia undid the fastenings of her dress . . .

When Lucrezia thought about that afternoon, she was filled with shame. She was uncomfortably aware of the fact that the episode was common court knowledge, for Sancia, with her customary lack of scruple, had not hesitated to inform everyone who would listen. She had had no less than the Pope's daughter, she boasted. "I have had the whole family," Lucrezia could hear her saying, "except for the Fisherman himself." Perhaps she had had her father as well. Lucrezia shrugged. Alexander's sleeping arrangements had never concerned her; she was on the best of terms with her father's mistress, Giulia. The only thing that bothered her, strangely enough, was the thought that Don Alphonso might find out. What would he think? Gossip like that never stopped short of the palace doors. She had not thought of Don Alphonso in a long time. Why should she think of him now? She resolved to see less of Sancia. She would be perfectly cordial, but she would make certain never to be alone with her.

Then something happened which was to change the entire course of their lives. Alexander, remembering the French invasion, determined never to be caught short again. He wrote his son Juan a letter, recalling him home from Spain. Cesare's idea of an army was not a bad one, he mused, but it would be headed by Juan, not by Cesare. This army would cut its teeth on the wealthy land barons. Italy was made up of petty states, and each state was ruled by a prince or duke who lived off the people of his land. These nobles were independently wealthy, and wealth meant power which could be used against the Church at any time. He would reduce that power.

"Where is the money to come from?" Cesare demanded sourly. He was furious with his father, for not only was he using his idea, but he was making Juan Captain General of the Church.

"Never mind, I will take care of it."

Cesare had no doubts as to how his father would take care of it. He would probably stage a banquet to which several wealthy and unpopular cardinals would be invited. Several days later they would complain of feeling ill. Shortly after that they would die, leaving their holdings to the Church, represented by Alexander. Cesare had heard of an alchemist who had devised a poison that was odorless and tasteless and that worked so slowly it sometimes took as much as a week or a month to kill its victim. Alexander would be long vindicated by then. Oh well, it was no concern of his how his father obtained his revenue.

The army, it seemed, was not his concern either. But Lucrezia's husband—now that was another thing entirely. He could concern himself with that, with getting rid of a jackanapes who was an embarrassment to the entire family.

"That fop is a blot on our name!" Cesare had burst out to Alexander.

His father sat sorting endless papers, as was his custom when he did not wish to discuss something.

"Will you kindly listen to me!" Cesare shouted. "Are you aware of the fact that my sister is obliged to sit idly by while he and that idiot servant of his have a go at one another!"

"Yes," Alexander sighed. "Well, Charles VIII still sleeps with his nurse on occasion, and no one thinks any the worse of him for it. But," he added blandly, "he is not our problem, is he?"

"No, but that gnat-brained brother-in-law of mine is!"

"Only if you make it so. Now run along, Cesare. I have work to do."

"I won't leave until you promise me you'll do something."

"All right. I'll take it under consideration."

"Yes, and perhaps you had also better take under consideration the fact that Juan hasn't a chance of winning against the land barons!"

"Suppose you leave that to me," Alexander said shortly without looking up from his papers.

On August 10 Juan and his wife Doña Maria Enriquez reached Rome, and Lucrezia found herself with yet another sister-in-law. Alexander, doing things in his usual fashion, decreed that the entire Vatican court should go to the Porta Pertusa to meet them. Cesare, he announced, as Cardinal of Valencia, would lead the procession.

"It is only meet," Alexander told him. "After all, you are next in line."

Cesare bit his lip and said nothing.

Lucrezia, watching him on his black horse with its black and silver trappings, thought how handsome he was. Dressed entirely in black as was his custom, Cesare looked proud and angry. His eyes flashed fire and his auburn curls glinted like metal in the sun. If only they had not chosen to come on such a hot day, Lucrezia thought, wiping her neck and brow with the strip of chambray she had taken from her bodice.

She craned her neck for a glimpse of her new sister-in-law. When she finally caught sight of her, she was pleased by what she saw. There was no beauty there. Doña Maria's skin was the color of tallow. Her dark hair was worn plain and unbecomingly. As for her eyes, they looked like two black holes stuck in her face.

Lucrezia and Sancia turned to one another and smiled. They had the same thought. She would not be a rival. As for Juan, Lucrezia had never really cared for him. He did not have Cesare's magnificent physique or bearing. Women and wine had softened him. He had always been morally weak, and like many such people, he was cruel as well. Cesare was right. He would be no match for the powerful land barons like the Orsinis and the Colonnas.

She herself had no heart for what was going to happen. "You cannot do this to the Orsinis, Papa," she had begged, remembering Adriana. "They have always taken care of me."

Alexander had brushed this aside lightly. "I must do what is best for the Church."

As Cesare urged his horse forward, the cortege followed suit and soon the two brothers were face to face. Cesare, looking down at Juan, smiled, his eyes still. "It is good to greet you, my brother, and to greet your wife as well."

Juan nodded, his face as remote as Cesare's. He did not return the greeting. What Doña Maria thought can only be imagined, for she never raised her eyes.

"It was an insult," Cesare told Lucrezia later.

"I think he is jealous. After all, Papa has made you a cardinal as well as Duke of Valencia, and it is no secret that you have more money and holdings than all the rest of the cardinals put together."

"It is also no secret that he is going to be Captain General of the Church. Nothing that I have compares to that!"

Sancia was not shy. She immediately set her cap for Juan, enjoying Cesare's discomfiture. "Why is Doña Maria so pale?" she asked Juan over the risotto at dinner that night. "She is the color of a bad cheese. I hope she smells better than she looks."

Juan nearly choked on his food, but he looked at Sancia with interest.

Lucrezia kept her distance. She knew what Sancia was up to, and she wanted nothing to do with it. She felt sorry for Doña Maria, and resolved to be kind to her. The next day she fell into step with her in the garden and began by praising her nose, which was long and sharp.

"I do not have a good nose, and I know it," Doña Maria said firmly.

"It is not so bad," Lucrezia said at once, ashamed of her insincerity.

"I do not have a good nose, and neither do I have good eyes, a good mouth, or good skin."

"You have nice ankles," Lucrezia offered.

208

Doña Maria smiled, bent over and kissed her, and the two women were friends.

Since Sancia was now busy with Juan, the two of them spent much of their time together.

"I know what she is up to," Doña Maria said one morning as they walked in the palace rose garden.

"Who?" Lucrezia asked artlessly, sniffing one of the late blooms.

"You know very well who I mean. Don't try to spare my feelings."

"She doesn't mean anything by it. It is simply her way."

"She is a whore!" Doña Maria said vehemently. "She even sleeps with some of the guards."

"I don't believe that," Lucrezia lied.

Doña Maria looked at her closely. "Don't you? Well, I do. I have heard some very strange stories."

Lucrezia blushed. She would have to speak to Sancia as soon as possible.

"Doña Maria is unhappy," she said when she saw Sancia. "Leave Juan alone."

"Why should I?"

"Please, Sancia. You don't need him. You have more than enough men to choose from."

"So? One more is always nice. You wouldn't be jealous, little one . . ."

Lucrezia looked away and said nothing.

"If you only knew, little sister, how happy I make him. He has never had anyone like me before."

"But you don't need him," Lucrezia repeated, not knowing what else to say.

"And that cock of his, it is grateful too. It goes right up in the air for me. He cannot get it up for her at all."

"Please don't tell me about those things. I don't want to hear them."

"Of course you do," Sancia laughed. "I shall tell you

what. If you are very good I will let you watch. All right?"

"No!" Lucrezia shouted. "No!"

From then on, whenever Sancia saw her she would sidle up to her and grin. "Would you like to watch, little one?"

"She has had Cesare too," Doña Maria told her, her face twisted with woe, "and perhaps even Giovanni."

"She is welcome to Giovanni," Lucrezia said, hoping that she had heard nothing more.

"I will be glad when Juan goes off to fight against the Orsinis," Doña Maria said with tight lips. "Then at least she will not be able to have him."

As soon as Alexander became aware of what was going on, he made Juan Captain General of the pontifical forces and sent him off to the wars. It was only the end of October, and he had planned to wait until spring, but perhaps it was just as well, he told himself.

"I hope he doesn't come back," Doña Maria confided to Lucrezia. "Then she will never be able to get her hands on him again."

Three months later, ignominiously beaten, and wounded in the face, Juan fled back to Rome.

Cesare was jubilant. "I told you he was no soldier," he said to Alexander.

His father, preoccupied as usual with his papers, did not answer. A moment later he said to Cesare, "I am through with Giovanni, that idiot son-in-law of mine. You may do as you like with him."

"Do you mean that?"

Alexander looked up from his desk. "I always mean what I say. However, I do not wish to find him floating in the Tiber. Be discreet."

"Leave it to me," Cesare said quickly. "I will think of something."

Alexander smiled. "I'm certain you will." The fact that Giovanni Sforza was of no further political use to the Borgia family was common knowledge. The House of Sforza had lost its prestige. Lucrezia could now be married off more advantageously.

"May I ask a question?" Cesare said curiously.

"Go ahead," Alexander sighed. "You will in any case, whether I say yea or nay."

"Why are you now allowing me to do this?"

"Because," Alexander said, looking for some papers he had misplaced, "I suggested that he dissolve the marriage and return to Pesaro, and he was loath to do so."

"And who is my sister to marry next?"

"That is not for you to know just now."

"Don Alphonso of Ferrara, perhaps?"

Alexander said nothing.

Cesare was probing a raw spot and he knew it, for Don Alphonso still had a wife, whom Alexander could not remove without issuing a decree of annulment. Such a decree could be issued only if the marriage were not consummated.

"Why not invite her to dinner?" Cesare suggested. The inference was clear. Where others guessed about the occasionally fatal Borgia feasts, Cesare knew for sure.

Alexander looked at him through lowered brows. "If you have nothing else to say, I have work to do."

When Cesare told Lucrezia what Alexander had said about Giovanni, she looked at him and bit her lip.

"I cannot allow you to do him any harm."

"Why not?" Cesare wanted to know. "It would be no worse than the killing of a peacock on the palace grounds, for that is what he is."

"That is not true. He is a human being, and I will not see him harmed."

211

Cesare lost patience. "Has he ever brought you one moment's happiness?"

Lucrezia did not answer.

"Perhaps you should know that Father is considering Don Alphonso. You would like that, wouldn't you?"

Lucrezia's cheeks colored. "I simply cannot look away while you harm another human being, Cesare."

"If I urge him to, Father might grant Don Alphonso a special dispensation so that he can divorce his wife and marry you. It was a loveless marriage, even Giulia told you so."

"I think you are stupid," Sancia said to her later. "What do you care what happens to a strut like Giovanni?"

"I don't know," Lucrezia answered. "I just know that I cannot do him any harm."

Alexander, anxious as always to keep up appearances until the end, gave Giovanni his official place of honor during the Easter ceremonies in St. Peter's and handed him, with a smile of benediction, the Easter palm.

Lucrezia, watching this bit of treachery, came to a decision. "I have an idea," she said to Cesare. "Why don't we simply frighten him and perhaps he'll go home?"

"That shouldn't be too difficult," Cesare answered. "What do you suggest?"

"I was thinking, perhaps if he overheard you plotting to kill him . . ."

"It would be much easier to just kill him and get it over with."

"No, Cesare," she said firmly. "If you did that, I should never forgive you."

Several days later she made the first try. "Giovanni,"

212

she said, watching him as he adjusted his false curls, "I think it might be better if you went home for a while. Cesare is out to do you some harm."

To her surprise, he appeared unmoved.

"Did you hear what I said, Giovanni?"

He gave his curls a final pat. "He would not do anything so foolish as that, Lucrezia. Your father would not permit it."

"I do not think that Papa cares anymore, Giovanni. Nor does he care anymore about the Milan Treaty. I think you should go back to Pesaro where you're safe."

"I am very comfortable where I am," he replied, pulling down the sleeve of his new suit. "Besides, I know what they are up to. As soon as I leave they will try to annul the marriage, and they will tell everyone that I am impotent."

"What makes you think so?"

"Never mind. I have my sources."

"Giovanni," Lucrezia said softly, "would you rather be called impotent or dead?"

"Neither!" Giovanni shouted, adjusting a ruffle. "I am your husband and the Lord of Pesaro, and no one will unseat me in either!"

When Lucrezia repeated this conversation to Cesare, he looked thoughtful. "Well, I will simply have to take care of it in my own way."

"Please, Cesare. Couldn't we keep trying to frighten him?"

"No, for as you can see, he is too stupid for that."

"What if he were to overhear something? Quite by accident, of course. What then?"

"Ah, Lucrezia, how soft and tender you are. What would you suggest?"

"Leave it to me. I have an idea. It should be very amusing."

That evening Lucrezia summoned the servant Giacomino to her apartments. "I feel you should know," she said, looking at his thick lips with distaste, "that your master is in great danger. My brother wants to kill him. My father refuses to interfere." Lucrezia watched his face grow pale as pork.

"Have you told him of this?" the servant gasped.

"I have tried to," Lucrezia said, looking with satisfaction at the drops of sweat that sprouted on his forehead. "But he wouldn't listen."

"That is strange," Giacomino said, beginning to shake.

"Shhh," Lucrezia warned. "I think I hear someone coming. Quick, jump behind that screen!" The poor man had no sooner hidden himself than Cesare strode into the room.

"Well," he said loudly, "I have finally decided what to do about that stupid husband of yours."

"And what is that?" Lucrezia asked, trying not to laugh, for they had already rehearsed their play.

"Never mind. I have given certain orders to certain people. After tonight there should be one less bore at the table."

"Cesare," she implored, covering her mouth with her fingers, "can't you think of some other way?"

"There is no other way. I have men digging now in the forest. There will be room enough for that valet of his as well."

"Cesare," she sputtered, "if only there was some other way."

Giacomino, shaking with fright, interpreted her laughter as hysteria. Then forgetting his hiding place, forgetting everything but the danger to himself and Giovanni, he jumped from behind the screen, knocking it over in his haste to leave the room.

Cesare and Lucrezia fell to the floor, rolling with laughter.

When Giovanni heard from Giacomino what had happened, his face turned ashen. Not even pausing to pack, he leaped on a Turkish horse and spurred him all the way to Pesaro, stirrups hanging, where the poor animal dropped dead of exhaustion.

"All right," Alexander said some days later, looking pleased. "We have gotten rid of him. Now what?"

"Now we sue for divorce," Cesare said grimly.

"You know, of course, that the only grounds recognized by the Church is impotence."

"Of course," Cesare said shortly. "He will be publicly branded impotent."

"And just how do you intend to accomplish that?" Alexander asked with interest.

"It is simple. The marriage was never consummated."

"I couldn't say anything like that," Lucrezia stammered.

"You won't have to say anything," Cesare assured her. "All you have to do is nod at the right time."

The following week, when Cesare put the case in the hands of a special commission headed by two friendly cardinals and they asked her formally whether her marriage with Giovanni Sforza was never fully consummated, she looked away and nodded.

Giovanni, back in Pesaro, refused to plead guilty. With the Borgias at a safe distance, he felt he could afford to avenge himself. Not only had their marriage been consummated, he shouted in court, but they went at it day and night, for Lucrezia suffered from a lust that was insatiable. It might have killed an ordinary man, but fortunately, he had been up to it.

Lucrezia, hearing this, blushed with shame. Her first thought was, What would Don Alphonso think?

"I knew I should have killed him when I had the

215

chance!" Cesare fumed. "Never mind, I'll take care of it now!"

"No violence," Alexander insisted.

Cesare rolled his eyes heavenward. "He is besmirching our good name and all you can say is 'no violence.' Since when are you so squeamish?"

Alexander looked away and said nothing.

Giovanni's next step was to turn to his uncle Ludovico il Moro, Duke of Milan, for support. "They have insulted me," he shouted. "They have insulted all of us!"

The Duke looked at his nephew's painted face and said nothing.

Cesare meanwhile went to work on Cardinal Ascanio Sforza, who, ashamed of his former treachery in supporting Charles against the Pope, was anxious to make amends. Knowing that everything he said to Cardinal Sforza would be repeated to Ludovico il Moro, and knowing too that if il Moro had to choose now between his nephew and the Vatican, he would choose the latter, Cesare flattered the Cardinal to the top of his tonsured head. As far as influence went, he said, Giovanni Sforza was a "dead man" at court, and nobody in his right mind would put ducats on a dead man. "But you," he said to the Cardinal, "have your whole future before you. His Holiness has forgiven you for your past indiscretions and wishes only to be allowed to show the nature of his forgiveness."

When Cardinal Sforza repeated this bit of information to il Moro, the Duke urged him to go to Rome and kiss the Pope's feet. "It will not hurt either of us," he added.

To his nephew Giovanni, il Moro had two suggestions to make: first that he wash his face, and then that he prove his prowess as a male in front of the papal legate and two sworn witnesses.

"What!" Giovanni shrieked. "How do you expect me to get it up in a situation like that!"

Il Moro smiled and said nothing.

"I will not be humiliated!" Giovanni cried.

Il Moro again made no answer.

In the end, with no help forthcoming from any side, Giovanni was obliged to state that Lucrezia had been his in name only. No sooner had he spoken the words than he was sorry. "They have robbed me of my manhood," he wept. "None of it is true!"

Only Lucrezia felt sorry for him. "I wish that there had been some other way."

"There was," Cesare replied. "It is still not to late to silence him."

"No," she said. "Leave him alone. He has suffered enough."

Giovanni, however, having found his voice, would not be quiet. "I have possessed her *infinite volte!*" he told all who would listen. And when he tired of that, "She is a whore, all cunt and nothing else, a real Messalina who has had her father, her brother, and all of Rome besides!"

Giovanni's impact was heavier than ever he had hoped. Rome, always attuned to scandal, had pricked up its ears ever since Giovanni's flight to Pesara. Now, anxious to know the real story behind it all, tongues wagged without cease. In the baths Roman matrons whispered into one another's ears. In the hovels and in the marketplace the people spoke of nothing else.

The Vatican palace housed a family of demons, it was said. Horrible specters were seen lurking at night beneath its walls. During a service given by Alexander a sudden gust of wind had sprung up from nowhere and blown out all the candles on the main altar. A monstrous creature covered with scales and talons had dropped from Lucrezia's womb and was pounded to

217

powder by her brother Cesare in a giant mortar, after which it was scattered around the rose bushes in the Vatican gardens, giving rise to black roses with giant thorns.

Fear was everywhere, intensified by the growing numbers of plague and famine victims. God was displeased with the papal family and now He would punish everyone for its sins.

The final sign was a dark cloud which had hung over the Tiber for days and which slowly assumed the shape of Lucifer.

The peasants in the field grumbled. Someone cried that there would be another flood like the one which had occurred in the autumn of the previous year when the Tiber had overflowed its banks and engulfed half the city.

There was no flood, and the dark cloud over the Tiber slowly disappeared.

Lucrezia had been severely shaken by all the gossip. "I think I would like to enter the Convent of San Sisto for a while," she said to Alexander.

Alexander looked at her in bewilderment. "Why? Are you not happy here?"

"It is not that, Papa," she answered in some confusion. "It is just that everything seems so strange now. People look at me differently. I want to go away and think for a while."

Alexander, noticing for the first time the extreme pallor of her cheeks and the dark circles beneath her eyes, gave his consent.

Lucrezia stayed for six days, eating nothing but a little bread and cheese. She was so light-headed from hunger that she began to see visions.

When Alexander heard of this, he became concerned. What would everyone think of this? They might think her mad, and then he would never be able to arrange a proper marriage for her. As it was, rumor had it that she had entered the convent to have an illegitimate child. No, he was in no position to humor her any further, and sent a group of men together with a sheriff to escort her home.

Lucrezia was heartbroken. She had come to love the gentle, clear-eyed nuns, who had also come to love her. She had asked for and received a small volume of poems which she had remembered reading with Carlos in the far-off days of Monte Giordano. She had even started to sketch, shyly asking several of the nuns to sit for her. On soap- and candlemaking days she rolled her sleeves up to the elbows and plunged in with joy, happy to be busy finally at something useful. In the midst of all this, the sheriff and his men arrived.

"Don't let them take me back," Lucrezia begged the prioress tearfully. It was the only peace she had known in years.

The prioress was touched, for Lucrezia during her stay at the convent had asked for nothing more than the others, only shelter and food. This she could not deny her. "Be of good cheer, my child. You shall stay if it is at all possible."

The nuns fled to their cells as the men beat on the doors. But the prioress was a stout-hearted woman. Admitting no one into the courtyard, she herself stepped outside and talked to the sheriff. It was never known what she said to him. She was absent some twenty minutes. When she returned she said, "They have gone."

Lucrezia dropped to her knees and kissed the hem of her gown. Then she ran to the nuns to tell them the good news. "I would like to stay here always," she said in an excess of feeling, really believing her own words. "I never want to go home again."

CHAPTER 19

For the time being Alexander allowed Lucrezia to remain at San Sisto. He had other matters to occupy him now. King Ferrante, the fat King of Naples, died suddenly of a clot on the brain, and he was succeeded by his uncle Federigo, who had not bothered to secure official sanction of his title from the Church of Rome. This, Alexander decided, would never do. Accordingly Federigo was informed that papal recognition would not be forthcoming without a substantial tithe from the Neapolitan treasury.

That could be arranged, Federigo wrote swiftly.

Alexander had no real objection to Federigo but he was not about to offer official sanction without the customary tithes or to extend the credit already owed. Negotiations went back and forth until the Consistory at Alexander's urging appointed Cesare as cardinal legate to Federigo's coronation.

"You see, my son," Alexander said to him, "I have the greatest confidence in you."

Cesare said nothing. It was but a ruse to get rid of

him while Alexander worked out the details of the Captain Generalship with Juan.

"Perhaps if you gave him a farewell dinner it might make him feel more important," Alexander suggested to Cesare's mother.

Vanozza, never one to spend money without a good reason, demurred. A party would be too costly. She did not care for Cesare any more than he cared for her, and besides, Alexander had never really replaced the things she had lost in the French invasion with things she really liked. In fact, she would be ashamed to use the poor stuff she had.

"All right," Alexander said wearily. "What do you want?"

That was all he had to say. Vanozza went through the palace making a clean sweep. Before she was finished she had collected nearly a third of the Vatican dishes and silver.

"But you are not having that many people," Alexander protested.

Vanozza looked at him in mock horror. "What? You would not have me change dishes after each course?"

Alexander sighed. "Take what you will," he said. "But mind you, return it."

Vanozza smiled. She had no intention of returning anything, and well he knew it.

She planned the dinner for June 14, the evening of Cesare's departure. Alexander did not plan to be present. It would not be wise to call attention to the nature of his past relationship with this woman. Besides, Giulia was still his mistress, and she did not want him to go. And Vanozza did not press it. She invited Cesare and Juan and several of their friends. Cesare grumbled, but he went. He and his mother had never been close. He could count on the fingers of one

221

hand the times he had been to visit her at her villa in the Trastevere on the slopes of the Esquilino.

It was getting toward dusk when Cesare and his friends arrived at the villa to find his brother Juan already there with an unknown man whose face was covered by a mask. Cesare, aware of his brother's strange bed habits, asked no questions, nor did Juan make any attempt to introduce his companion.

The day had been warm and the table was set beneath a vine-covered pergola hung with grapes. It was still early in the summer and the grapes, small and tight in their skins, gave forth a sour-sweet odor. Vanozza had used on her table none of the service she had confiscated from the palace, all of which was locked up in chests in the cellar of her house.

Cesare looked at the table with amusement. "Well, Mother, and what have you done with the things that you sacked from the Vatican?"

Vanozza looked at this strong, brash son of hers with thinly veiled dislike. "I do not think that those things are well suited to dining out-of-doors."

Whatever Vanozza lacked in table service she had made up for in food. There was more to eat than their small party could consume in one night.

Cesare and Juan found little to say to each other. Juan directed his conversation to the masked man at his side, who either grunted or else spoke in monosyllables.

Cesare, watching them, laughed. "What have you there, a man or a monkey?"

"You'll find out," Juan said, flushing darkly.

The man in the mask said nothing, but bent his face toward his food. The others made desultory conversation. It was Vanozza who kept up a steady stream of chatter. The evening air was soft and warm, and the sounds from the valley below drifted lazily up the vine-covered slopes, carrying the voices of the peasants in the fields and the ringing of the bells for the evening vespers.

"It is pleasant up here," Cesare said, reaching up and cutting off a bunch of grapes which hung over the table.

Vanozza looked with narrowed eyes at this son whom she feared and disliked. "If that is so, then why is it I see you so seldom?"

"That," Cesare said, peeling a grape and eating it with relish, "is what makes it so pleasant."

Vanozza said nothing. With Juan she could move this way and that, but Cesare offered her no more than a blank wall to maneuver against.

"Are you looking forward to going to Naples, dear brother?" Juan asked with a smirk.

"As much as you are looking forward to assuming the Captain Generalship," Cesare answered.

"How nice it is," Vanozza interrupted them tactfully, to have my sons about me again."

"Stop pretending, Mother," Cesare said coldly. "Pretense ill becomes you."

Vanozza crumbled a piece of bread between her fingers and said nothing more.

It was midnight when Cesare finally arose from the table and stretched. "Well, I for one have had enough of listening to crickets and frogs."

"Really?" Juan said, flushing. "And which one, pray, am I?"

"Whichever one you prefer," Cesare said shortly.

"I don't see why you two cannot get along," Vanozza said crossly.

"If you do not see that, Mother dear, then you cannot see at all." Cesare turned to the others. "By the way, I suggest that we all leave together. It is a lonely and dangerous road down to the bottom, and there are

223

undoubtedly creatures lurking in the bushes which are simply longing to pounce on flesh as soft as yours," he said, looking directly at Juan.

"My flesh is as hard as any man's!" Juan said angrily.

"Perhaps," Cesare said lightly. "In any case, we'll not put it to the test tonight. Shall we go?"

The man in the mask stood up first, the others following suit.

Vanozza put her arms around Juan, for he was her favorite. "Go with God," she said. To Cesare she said nothing.

"And have you no words for me?" he asked.

"I have words," Vanozza said, "but they are not meant for other ears."

Cesare laughed thinly and urged his horse down the slopes, with Juan and the others in pursuit.

"Goodnight, Mother," Cesare called out. "Have us again when you are next in need of more palace plate and silver!"

The night was dark, for the moon was sickled and gave little light to the horses and riders picking their way down the rocky slopes. Cesare noted with contempt how hard Juan had to work to keep his horse from slipping. They rode together until they reached the Sforza Palace at the bottom, in the Ponte quarter.

It was then that Juan grew braver. "I am not going back now. I have something else to do." With that he turned his horse into one of the alleys leading toward the Piazza degli Ebrei, which was the Jewish quarter of the town, the masked man in close pursuit.

Cesare snorted in contempt. "Let him go to the herring-eaters. Each to his own taste."

The rest of the party continued along the bridge of Sant'Angelo to the palace.

It was midnorning when Cesare, lying in bed, blinked at the sudden light stabbing his eyes. Someone had thrown open the shutters. He blinked again. Alexander stood looking down at him with a face that was awful to behold.

"Where is your brother?" he asked harshly.

"Where?" Cesare repeated, struggling to come fully awake. "Why, he is probably in the arms of some Hebrew whore. Why do you ask?"

"Why? Because Doña Maria reports that he did not come home last night."

"Well, if that's all," Cesare answered, stiffling a yawn, "you have no real cause for alarm."

"Do not trifle with me," Alexander snapped. "I have an ominous feeling in this."

Cesare reached over and took a swallow of wine, running it around inside his mouth and spitting it out in the bowl beside the carafe. "I do not share my brother's enthusiasm for kosher meat," Cesare said, throwing the sheet away from him.

Alexander, looking at the long, lithe, muscular body, felt a grudging admiration for this strong young son. "You will delay your trip to Naples until your brother is found," he said.

"With pleasure," Cesare said, throwing himself back against the pillows. "I am not anxious to make this journey, as Your Holiness well knows."

"In the meantime," Alexander said, searching his face, "you may put on your clothing and help look for Juan."

"I'd rather not," Cesare said, settling himself more comfortably. "I do not like the smell of Jews in warm weather."

By nightfall the palace was in an uproar. Juan had still not returned, and Alexander had ordered every

225

palace guard to join the search. Doña Maria sat in her room weeping.

Cesare alone remained calm. "He will either come, or he will not come," he said aloud, holding his goblet of wine up to the light and studying its ruby depths. "In any case, what does it matter?"

The only ones who mourned Juan's absence, it seemed, were Alexander, who had remained at prayer all day, and Doña Maria. Her eyes, swollen and red from crying, made her nose look longer than ever.

Cesare looked at her with contempt. "If you are lucky," he said, "you will never see him again."

At midnight Cesare was awakened by Sanseverino, one of his father's secretaries. "His Holiness wishes to see you at once."

Cesare threw on a dressing gown. "Where is he?"

"He is still at his prie-dieu in the sacristy."

Cesare on entering the room saw an old man in place of his father, for in twenty-four hours Alexander had aged. His eyes had sunken into his head from lack of sleep, and the slack folds of his face were covered with gray stubble.

"Go bring your brother home," Alexander said, looking at him with hollow eyes. "He has just been plucked from the river, and the fishes have had their way with him."

Cesare followed Sanseverino and Savelli to the banks of the Tiber. There on the grass lay something covered with canvas. At Cesare's approach the guards pulled back the cloth and lowered their torches. The soft jelly of his eyes had been eaten away, Cesare saw, as had his lips and the fleshy part of his nose. His glance fell to the thighs and to what was left of the genitals. "It is Juan," he whispered. "Cover him."

The guards were holding a man with a stained yellow beard—a rough sort of boatman, by the look of him.

"What is it?" Cesare asked sharply.

The yellow-bearded one shook, but his voice was strong and steady. "I was in my boat when I saw them, and it was not yet morning. There were two horsemen, and they came out from the street near the Hospital of San Girolamo on the road from the castle to Santa Maria del Popolo."

Cesare shook his head impatiently. "Go on," he ordered.

"There were two of them," the boatman repeated, "and they looked around as though they had something to hide. Then one of them came forward and he had something slung across his saddle. He rode over to where they empty the dung carts. Then the two of them took it, whatever it was, by its hands and feet, and they threw it into the river. Then one of them said, 'Wait, what is that?' and the other one said, 'It is only his mantle.' And they pelted it with stones until it sank."

"Did you see their faces?" Cesare asked.

"In that light?" the old man said.

"And their voices? What were their voices like?"

The old man dropped his eyes. "I don't know about their voices, but one of them addressed the other as 'milord.'"

"Very well," Cesare said. "That is enough. You would do well to forget what you have seen and heard."

"Yes, milord. But there was one more thing, milord. The light was not good, it is true, but I believe that one of the horses was white and the other one was black."

"That is enough," Cesare said quickly. "You may go now."

Once again the thing in the canvas was stretched across the saddle, its mouth and nose spouting water.

When Cesare returned to the palace he found Alexander still on the prie-dieu. "You may as well get off, Father," he said angrily. "Nothing can help him now."

"I am not praying for him," Alexander said quietly. "I am praying for you."

"You don't think that *I* . . ."

"One of the horses was black," Alexander said.

"It could have been Juan's," Cesare said quickly, wondering how he knew. "And anyway, the light was poor."

"Juan's horse has not been found," Alexander said, looking at him steadily. "And I do not think, *I know.*"

"Do you wish to see him?" Cesare asked.

"No," Alexander murmured. "I want to remember him as he was."

Alexander had just enough strength to arrange the funeral before he collapsed. Although Juan had been far from popular, Alexander eulogized him as though he had been a saint. The body of his son was encased in fresh flowers, cunningly arranged to hide the parts which had been eaten away, and placed on a black velvet catafalque with holy icons at its head and feet. The entire arrangement was then placed on a barge, painted in black and gold for the occasion, and floated down the Tiber, preceded by two hundred boats lighting the way with torches.

The following day Doña Maria left for Spain, and Alexander took to his bed. For seven days he did nothing but sigh deeply as though trying to rid himself of an unbearable heaviness. On the eighth day he convened a Consistory and announced that his son Cesare was to be made Captain General of the Church of Rome. From that day on he never spoke of Juan again.

Alexander's next act was to cast about for a new husband for Lucrezia. His first choice, of course, was Don Alphonso d'Este, but Alphonso was still a married man and he saw no feasible way of breaking the bonds of matrimony.

"But his wife is not a problem," Cesare suggested. "At least she is not a problem that cannot be resolved."

"There will be no more bloodshed," Alexander said with something strange in his eyes.

"There wouldn't be any blood necessarily," Cesare said with a little thrill of power, for he realized that the thing he'd seen in Alexander's eyes was fear.

A week later Alexander decided on Alfonso d'Aragon, Duke of Bisceglie. Alfonso was Sancia's brother, and like her was tall, dark, and pleasing to the eye, all of which he thought Lucrezia would not mind, and furthermore, he and Lucrezia were both about the same age, as he was eighteen or thereabouts. Lucrezia would be informed of these plans at the proper time.

But now there was a more pressing problem—that damned monk, Savonarola, who for years had inveighed against the Borgias, calling them "Spanish upstarts" and "spawn of the Devil." Now he was ranting and raving about Juan's death and Cesare's probable part in it. He would have to be silenced. Otherwise it might be difficult to find anyone willing to become a member of the Borgia family.

"If you are so keen on drawing blood," Alexander said to Cesare, "you may go to work on Savonarola," Cesare smiled. "With pleasure."

For years the Dominican monk had been preaching against the excesses of the Borgias. "The Devil himself is sitting on the Vatican throne," he proclaimed to all who would listen. He had completely won over the Florentines with his preachings, and with the fall from power of the Medicis in Florence he was in a position to do the Borgias great harm. Alexander so far had done nothing to stop him, biding his time with characteristic patience until he had the proper cards to move against him, and now that time had come. For Savonarola had recently fallen in popularity.

"Mind you, not with your hands, but with your mind," Alexander said, tapping his head for emphasis. "Never do with your hands what you can accomplish with your mind."

"It is not the same thing," Cesare said disappointedly.

"All the same, it is better. Now here is what you are to do. I want you to spread word that he is anti-Church, since he regards his own preachings as dogmas. This will set everyone against him. They dislike him anyway, but if they are made to dislike him enough, then they will do our work for us."

"There is no sport in that," Cesare grumbled.

Alexander smiled thinly. "If it is sport enough for the gods, then there should be sport enough for you."

With Cesare's help, the Franciscans challenged Savonarola to an ordeal by fire. The foolish monk accepted it.

"I knew it," Alexander said, rubbing his hands. "There are some people who are placed on this earth only to die. And Savonarola is one of them."

Having set the top spinning, Alexander sat back to wait. He was not to wait long. "Would His Holiness please be good enough to send a panel of judges to try this thorn in our flesh?" the Florentines pleaded. Alexander could and would. The judges Alexander sent had implicit instructions. Savonarola was in no way to be allowed to escape the flames.

Alexander listened to an account of his burning with

great satisfaction. "He went like a spitted calf," he said to Cesare at dinner, spearing a piece of roasted meat and putting it thoughtfully into his mouth. "Who knows, he finally might have had an orgasm."

Meanwhile, Lucrezia came home from her stay at the convent, rested and refreshed. She had nothing to say about Juan's death. She, like Cesare, had never cared much for him, but she did pray for the repose of his soul nonetheless.

Now that Savonarola was out of the way, Alexander felt free to negotiate the marriage contract. Federigo, a notorious bargainer, insisted on a dowry of forty thousand ducats for Alfonso. Alexander pretended to chafe while he considered. He would really be paying only ten, for he had gotten back the thirty thousand ducats from Lucrezia's marriage to Giovanni Sforza. However, he made Federigo agree to give Alfonso the cities of Biselli and Ondrata with all the tithes and revenues, together with the title of Prince of Biselli, before he signed his daughter over.

CHAPTER 20

When Alexander advised Lucrezia of the impending marriage, she stamped her foot and shouted, "I won't marry him. I married one buffoon, and I won't do it again!"

When Alexander gave no sign of having heard her, she burst into tears. Through all of this he sat unmoved. She was even at eighteen still a child, and could not be expected to know who or what was good for her. He waited until she had cried herself out, then he took her in his arms and rocked her like a baby.

"I know how you feel about Alphonso d'Este," he said softly, smoothing the damp tendrils away from her face as he used to do when she was small. "But he still has a wife, and there is nothing we can do about that right now."

"But he doesn't love her," she said brokenly. "He loves me."

"Perhaps, my child, but love is a luxury that we Borgias cannot always afford, at least not now."

"Later?" she whispered, taking in the warmth and comfort of her father's arms.

"Perhaps," he said softly. "We'll see."

The wedding was set for the following July. Lucrezia, never one to grieve very long over things she could not control, set about ordering her trousseau. It was to be far more splendid than the last one; her father had promised her that much. She read once again the letters and poetry which Alphonso d'Este had managed to send her after Isabella had left. Then she put them carefully away.

Cesare meanwhile prepared to go to Naples to attend the coronation of Federigo, which Juan's death had interrupted. It was now fixed for August 10, 1497, and he would have to leave at once. After Juan's death he had thrown himself into an orgy of women, taking on the highest and the lowest, as though to remind himself that he was at least still alive. After amusing himself in this fashion for several weeks, he was now ready to attend to business.

"Remember," Alexander said sternly, "you are representing the Vatican, the highest throne in Christendom. Do not do anything to discredit it, for it will be your last commission as a cardinal."

"Thank God for that!" Cesare said fervently.

When he reached Capua on August 1 he began to feel unwell. The meeting with Federigo came off badly, for he had such severe nausea and headache that he could scarcely remain upright. Instead of feeling better, he began to feel worse, until finally he was forced to take to his bed. On August 5 he had need of a physician, for he was feeling so poorly that he thought he might die.

Gaspare Torella, the Spanish physician who examined him, took one look at his genitals, which were bright red and covered with pustules, and announced, "You have the French disease, my son." He then proceeded to treat him with gold and silver, for it was well known that this disease responded to the application of precious metals. "It is necessary that you remain quietly in bed for at least three days, so as not to activate the pustules. After that, God willing, you will feel better."

Cesare did as he was told, although he complained bitterly that it was dull stuff indeed to be in bed for such a length of time without a woman to keep him company. After the third day, whether from the metals or his own iron constitution, he began to feel better. Federigo breathed a sigh of relief. It would have gone badly for him, he felt certain, had the Pope's son not recovered his health.

As for Cesare, he sailed through the coronation with style and wit, receiving with every show of humility a magnificent sword engraved with the words *Cum numine Caesaris amen* and *Caesaris Borgia Cardinalis Valentianus*. In addition to the motto the sword was engraved with various battle scenes depicting great feats of heroism, ostensibly his. Thinking of his future role as Captain General of the Church of Rome, Cesare smiled and bowed his head, murmuring his thanks.

It was at the banquet following the coronation that he noticed a tall dark youth who kept glancing his way.

"It is only proper that you should meet," Federigo said, introducing them, "for you will one day soon be brothers."

So this was Alfonso, Duke of Bisceglie, Lucrezia's future husband. He was almost too comely for a man, Cesare thought grudgingly, yet there was nothing femine about him.

Alfonso smiled with white even teeth, his dark-gray

eyes lighting up with pleasure. "Well met, brother," he said, clasping Cesare's hand.

No, Cesare could find nothing amiss with this one. He would make Lucrezia an admirable husband; he was certain of it. Why, then, did he feel such a stirring of dislike inside him? Was it the total lack of guile in this man which disturbed him, a thing of which he himself was full? Or was it the sense of a man at peace with himself? Whatever it was, it made his bowels writhe.

"Brother," he said thinly, barely bothering to veil his contempt for this youth on whom fortune and family had always smiled.

When the festivities were over, Cesare leaned toward Alfonso. "What does one do here to amuse oneself?"

The smile that Alfonso turned on him was warm and friendly. "There is the hunt," he said. "We have some very good birds here."

"That is very interesting," Cesare said, turning to the flagon of wine nearest his plate. "What about women?"

The smile on Alfonso's face remained unchanged. "We have those, too."

"Yes, I thought that you might," Cesare said, draining the flask. He was in a mood now to enjoy himself. His father had sent him to Capua with three thousand ducats and an entourage that included seven hundred horsemen and a score of attendants. Upon his arrival he had found the Aragon palace shabby and in disrepair. Even the Byzantine trappings which had been hastily thrown up could not hide the shabbiness of the place. He was impatient of poverty; it depressed him. Furthermore, he had been two whole weeks without a woman, and now that he was over his sickness he intended to indulge himself to the fullest. Accordingly he ordered clothing and costly jewels for those women of

235

the court he found most attractive. To placate his restless entourage, who found their quarters far from ideal, he ordered clothing and jewelry for them as well. In no time at all his money was gone and he was forced to dip into the meager Neapolitan treasury.

"If he does not leave soon," Federigo said worriedly, "we shall be bankrupt."

Fortunately for Naples, Cesare soon tired of his amusements. "I am sorry to have to tell you this," he said to Federigo at dinner one night, "but I feel that I must return to Rome."

Federigo bowed his head to hide his pleasure. "I hope that your stay here has been a pleasant one."

Cesare smiled. "Very pleasant. But you see, I miss my dear father. I can only be parted from his company for so long."

During his stay he had said no more than a few words to the handsome youth who was to become his brother-in-law. He turned to Alfonso now. "We in Rome shall look forward to your visit. We have both birds *and* women there."

As soon as he returned to Rome he hurried to the Vatican palace. First he would see his father and then he would tell Lucrezia all about her intended bridegroom.

"Did you have a good visit?" Alexander asked him, having taken care to hide the report which he had received of his son's visit.

"Good enough."

"I certainly hope so, for I have received a bill from Federigo for twenty thousand ducats."

"It was not that good," Cesare said.

"What about Alfonso?"

"Why do you ask questions to which you already know the answer?" Cesare asked wearily. "You have outdone yourself this time."

236

Alexander looked at him shrewdly, then put the points of his fingers together. "I think it advisable that you do not see Lucrezia right away. I have finally got her in the proper frame of mind about her marriage, and I should like to keep her there."

Lucrezia's days passed pleasantly enough. She always enjoyed ordering clothes and making plans, and besides, Sancia talked about nothing but her brother Alfonso and how handsome he was. At one point she showed Lucrezia a miniature of him which she kept in her jewel box.

Lucrezia looked searchingly at the pale handsome face framed in thick black curls. "What color are his eyes? I can't make them out."

"They are dark gray," Sancia said, watching her. "La, I think that you are falling in love already."

"What is he like?"

"He is not like me at all. He is very nice."

"Do you think," she asked, running her finger slowly over the smooth surface of the miniature, "do you think that he will like me?"

Sancia stopped her bantering. Her eyes grew suddenly soft. "I think that he will love you, little one. You are very much alike."

"It is strange that Cesare has not spoken of him."

"It is not strange at all," Sancia said. "We always hate what we cannot be."

To please his daughter, Alexander had summoned tailors, coatmakers, shoemakers, furriers, capmakers, glovers, and wreathmakers, to the Vatican. They came in droves. The empty apartments in the palace overflowed with bolts of material. There were Spanish and Italian velvets, Flemish cloth from Brussels, fine linens from Bavaria, furs from Poland, brocades and silks from China. For her wedding dress she selected cloth of gold over which hung a finely woven netting of gold thread strung with Oriental pearls. A tiny cap of gold netting also strung with pearls completed the outfit. For her feet the shoemakers were fashioning thin golden slippers. Yes, this trousseau would be far more splendid than the last one.

In the midst of all this, Sancia kept giving instructions. Alfonso would like this, he would not care for that, and so on. "He is not like that monkey, Giovanni," she said. "He is addicted to simplicity in dress and in all other things."

"And what about women?" Lucrezia wondered. "What is his taste in women?"

Sancia smiled. "You will do. He will love you to distraction."

"I know I am foolish to feel this way, but I am afraid to think of sleeping with a man again. I am so used to sleeping alone."

"Nonsense. If you could sleep with Giovanni, then you can sleep with anyone! Besides, Alfonso is different, as you'll see."

"How do you know?" Lucrezia asked suspiciously.

"La, never you mind."

"If you have had him," Lucrezia asked with growing irritation, "then I don't want him at all!"

Sancia laughed at this. "I haven't had him since he was twelve. I am certain that he is a lot different now. But even then he was not bad."

"Is there anyone at all you haven't slept with?" Lucrezia burst out.

Sancia considered the question as she studied the sketch of a dress which had been left for Lucrezia's approval. "Very few," she answered. "Now, the question of sleeves . . ." Sancia had decided that Lucrezia should have narrow sleeves with high armpits and trumpet-shaped cuffs broadening down to the palm of her hand. "That will suit you the best," she said, narrowing her eyes. "You have the shoulders and arms of a child, thin and narrow."

"And what does that mean?"

"It means that large puffy sleeves are fine for a strumpet like me, but not for you."

Lucrezia, looking at the wide sleeves of Sancia's dress gathered together into a band at the elbow and continuing down narrow to the wrist, could not help but agree with her.

"By the way," Sancia said, trying to soften the other's mood, "did you know that your brother Cesare has asked for my cousin's hand in marriage?"

The effect on Lucrezia was more than she'd hoped for. "How do you know?"

"He told me the last time we slept together."

"Really, you are disgusting! I don't believe it."

"Well, it's true," Sancia said, adjusting one of her sleeves which had become twisted.

"Charlotte of Aragon?" Lucrezia whispered at though to herself. "That would make him King of Naples, wouldn't it?"

"That is the general idea," Sancia said, kissing her on the cheek.

Lucrezia smiled shyly. It was difficult to reject Sancia. She simply would not stay rejected.

"Of course," Sancia added, "she has not accepted him yet."

"She will," Lucrezia said confidently, liking the idea. "She will."

The marriage preparations went along smoothly. Alexander had resolved to deny Lucrezia nothing. Even now the carpenters, painters, and drapers were busy refurbishing the apartments the young couple would occupy.

Lucrezia wanted nothing around to remind her of

239

the travesty with Giovanni. The yellow hangings were torn down and in their place were installed silks of Venetian red. Borgia red, Lucrezia explained; the color of blood. Alexander coughed and said nothing. The mirrors were regilded and brushed with Venetian red as were several pieces of furniture, and whatever was not gilded was lacquered in black or red.

"It is really quite wicked-looking," Lucrezia said doubtfully. "Do you think that Don Alfonso will like it?"

"Perhaps not," Sancia admitted, "but I do. It is a courtesan's dream."

As for Alexander, he was wise enough to pay the bills and say nothing.

One evening when Lucrezia and Sancia had nothing better to do, they curled up before the massive stone fireplace in the Venetian-red apartment. Lucrezia had washed her hair for the tenth time that week over Maria's strenuous objections, for she declared that by the time Lucrezia got married she would be lucky if she had one hair left on her head.

"Brush it for me, please. I love the way you do it," Lucrezia said, handing Sancia one of the massive silver-backed brushes which were a part of her trousseau.

"All right, but only for a little while. I want to save myself for later."

"I don't know where you get the strength," Lucrezia said wonderingly.

Sancia strung out the long golden strands so that they shone like metal in the firelight. "What foolishness. Do you need strength to eat, to breathe?"

"Is Alfonso like that also?" Lucrezia asked shyly.

"Probably. In any case, you had better rest up."

Lucrezia blushed. "Tell me again what he is like."

"What can I tell you—that he is one of the most charming and most handsome men in all of Italy? Well, he is. As to the other thing, I have already told you, I don't know. I haven't slept with him since we were children."

Alfonso arrived in Rome on June 15. Lucrezia was so nervous that she could not go to greet him.

She confided her fears to Sancia. "I don't know what to say to him."

"Say *buon giorno*," Sancia suggested.

"Naturally, but after that . . ."

"After that," Sancia said, looking at the blue-gray eyes luminous with excitement, at the cheeks stained with color, at the gold sifting of hair, "after that will take care of itself."

Lucrezia dressed for dinner with care. For the first meeting she had chosen a simple gown of sky-blue silk with matching slippers. Blue was his favorite color, Sancia had told her. Her hair, freshly washed, hung loose to her waist. She looked in the glass and pinched her cheeks until they flamed in protest.

"There is no need to do that," Maria told her. "Unless it is your wish to look like an Indian."

"I do not wish to look like an Indian," Lucrezia screamed. "Nor do I wish to look like a lump of tallow."

"An Indian now, a lump of tallow later. What is the difference?"

Lucrezia, her nerves snapping, delivered her a stinging slap—then ran back and kissed her. "Forgive me, Maria, but I am so frightened. What if I wet myself?"

Maria stood with folded arms. "Then you had better wear black," she said unforgivingly.

Lucrezia uttered one last scream and left the room. She descended the grand staircase slowly, for it was early. At the foot of the stairs a young man waited. She found herself looking into a face that was almost like Sancia's, a face alight with gray eyes and framed in dark curls. And when he smiled at her with those white even teeth she thought she had never seen anyone so handsome.

"Buon giorno," she managed.

"Buona sera," he corrected softly.

For one brief moment she thought of Don Alphonso d'Este. What would it be like, what would happen if the other Alphonso were standing beside her now instead of this one? A feeling of wild confusion spread through her. The color in her cheeks heightened. If he were here now, she thought, she would throw herself at him like an animal and never let him go. Of that much she was certain.

"My sister has scarcely done you justice." Alfonso was smiling, looking at her flaming cheeks.

"Why, what has she said?" Lucrezia asked sharply, Alphonso d'Este suddenly gone from her mind.

"Well, she said that you are too pale, for one thing."

"What else?" she demanded.

"What else?" he repeated, looking her over carefully. "Well, she said that you are also too thin."

"Yes, well, to a cow a calf is thin. What else!"

"What else? Let me think."

By now Lucrezia's cheeks were on fire, her eyes flashing sparks. "There must be something else, too pale, too thin—what else!"

"She said that you scream a great deal," he said, trying not to laugh, "and that you have a terrible temper."

Lucrezia's voice rose to an awful pitch. "Your sister has the disposition of a goat, and she smells besides!"

"I do not think," he said, trying to keep his voice even, "that you are too pale or too thin."

"That is good to know," Lucrezia shouted, "but per-

242

haps I should tell you here and now that I do not care a fig what you think!"

By now he could not contain the laughter that rose in his throat.

Lucrezia, the short fuse of her patience at an end, lifted her shirts and kicked him with the sharp toe of her slipper. "There, now you may laugh about that as well!"

"Hoyden," he said, pulling her to him. "You are a hoyden, just as she said you were."

"Did she really say that?" Lucrezia asked, forgetting her pique.

"Yes," he said, holding her fast. "She said you were a thin, pale hoyden."

By now she was thoroughly confused. She could feel the warmth of his breath on her face and smell the freshness of his skin. She could feel too the press of his body against hers, and to her surprise, the feeling was pleasant. In a panic, she searched for dignity. "I don't enjoy being teased by someone I scarcely know."

"Really?" he asked, without releasing his hold on her. "Would you rather be kissed instead?"

"I don't know," she said, resorting to candor as she generally did when confused.

The press of his mouth came swiftly. It was not hard, but soft and warm, seeking to know the shape and taste of her. It was, she thought with a thrill of joy, exactly the way that Alphonso d'Este would have kissed her if he were here.

CHAPTER 21

The day of the wedding dawned bright and clear. In a nervous frenzy, Lucrezia had washed her hair before breakfast, and now it was so damp and limp that Maria declared that nothing in the world would dry it in time for the ceremony.

"Sit in the sun," she admonished, bringing the morning meal out on the balcony.

Lucrezia looked at the platter of cold meat and cheese and at the flask of watered wine. "I have no stomach for anything," she said nervously, "and the sun is bad for my skin. Would you have me go down the aisle looking like one of your relatives?"

Maria said nothing. Instead she took up the heavy silver brush. Lucrezia's nerves had been in a sorry state for three days now. After the wedding everything would be different, either better or worse. It was difficult to tell.

At the first brush stroke Lucrezia screamed. "Damn you, you are killing me!"

"That is a good idea," Maria said. "I hadn't thought of it."

Lucrezia picked up a piece of meat and let it fall back on the plate. "It is sour. I won't eat it!"

"Suit yourself," Maria answered with a shrug.

Lucrezia broke off a piece of the freshly baked loaf and stuffed it into her mouth.

"Bread without meat will fill you with gas," Maria observed. "You will explode in his arms."

"I will not eat the meat!"

"You are wise," Maria agreed. "The meat would only fill you with venery. Never mind, he will find other qualities to admire in you, your needlework for one thing . . ."

"I do not like needlework," Lucrezia said rudely, picking up a piece of meat. "As you well know."

"Ah yes, I had forgotten that," Maria said, trying not to smile. "Now then, if you wash your hair once more, I will not answer for the result."

The ceremony was to be celebrated in the Borgia apartments at the Vatican. Alexander himself had seen to everything. The nuptials would be simple, nothing too ostentatious to show up the court of the King of Naples.

A wedding aisle had been created, cordoned by red velvet ropes and garlanded with fresh flowers. Two large baskets of flowers stood on the altar. Lucrezia appeared in the archway on the arm of her father, and her pale loveliness lighted the room. Alexander, with his usual love of stagecraft, had engineered the aisle so that its path caught the colored shafts of light that streamed from the great stained-glass window above. Lucrezia, resplendent in the cloth-of-gold gown, her golden hair loosely restrained beneath its delicate fillet of Oriental pearls strung together with golden threads,

245

seemed to float in space amid a shower of golden motes. Before her waited Alfonso in a cloth-of-gold doublet trimmed in summer sable, his long shapely legs sheathed in cloth-of-gold tights, his gray eyes gleaming with anticipation.

"They look like the god and goddess of love," Sancia murmured to Cesare mischievously.

. Cesare affected not to hear. His brother-in-law was far too good-looking for a mere man. As for Lucrezia, she looked radiant. And when she reached Alfonso's side, the look of love and tenderness that she turned on him shriveled Cesare's heart.

Alfonso reached out and took her hand, holding it throughout the entire ceremony. When it was over, he drew her to him and kissed her gently on the lips, releasing her only to look in her eyes and murmur, "I will make you happy." Lucrezia thought again of Alphonso d'Este. Her feeling for him blurred and merged and became love for her new husband.

No sooner had Lucrezia and Alfonso become man and wife than Alexander held up his arms to announce dinner. Everyone trooped into the long banqueting hall with keen appetite. Here the Pope had spared no expense. Down the long T-shaped table ran fresh garlands of flowers and leaves interspersed with golden fountains spouting wine into golden basins. Alexander had gone into the Vatican vaults for the gold service and chalices set at each place. In between the fountains rose tall pyramids of fresh fruits and flowers.

Lucrezia and Alfonso sat at the head of the table and looked only at each other. All around them reigned unbridled merriment. Bearers in gold uniforms marched in to a fanfare of bugles, bearing large platters of game birds in full plumage, whole fish in aspic, their tails curled between their teeth, and skylarks roasted on the spit, their tongues sliced and laid over them.

246

Toward the end of the meal two pages brought in an enormous pie and set it down before Lucrezia and Alfonso. Another page handed Lucrezia a gold knife. With a smile Lucrezia stood and cut out a wedge of the pie. As she did, two doves flew out to symbolize love and harmony.

Alexander leaned over to Cesare. "When you marry Charlotte of Aragon, I will give you as good a feast or better."

Cesare broke his bread into crumbs and said nothing.

After the main meal, after the toothpicks served from golden dishes filled with rosewater and the ewers of clean water together with fresh napkins were passed around, came the sweets and confections. When everyone was comfortably full and relaxed in their chairs, Alexander stood up to salute the newlyweds. All who could manage to stand rose with him.

"A long and happy life," Alexander toasted, "and good digestion."

With bursts of laughter the entire party quitted the hall for the ballroom, where there would be dancing and theatricals. Cesare, appearing on stage dressed as a unicorn, the symbol of purity and chastity, drew a large round of laughter, to which he responded by bowing low.

No one saw the young couple slip away, hands joined, to their new apartments. Maria had drawn the coverlet of the bed and laid out their nightclothes, seeing to it also that a fire, seasoned with cinnamon and clove, was laid for cheer and warmth. A large flagon of wine and two silver cups stood on the table by the bed, along with a large bowl of fresh cherries.

Lucrezia nervously seized a cherry and popped it into her mouth.

Alfonso took her hands and drew her slowly to him.

247

"You have no need for cherries now, nor of anything else but me."

Lucrezia reddened. "Where is Maria? She promised that she would be here."

"You have no need of Maria either. I can do everything that must be done." He unfastened her dress slowly and let it slip to the floor in a ripple of gold. Then he undid her shift, stepping back afterward to look at her. Somehow she managed to look back at him. Then he was at her side, his mouth on hers, his hands busy with his clothing. When he was done, they stood looking at one another in wonderment.

"You look like a child," he said softly.

A feeling of weakness enveloped her, and she felt she might fall. His arms reached out and caught her, bearing her down in front of the fire. "I am not going to take you yet. I want to know you first." His fingers touched her eyes, traced the planes of her face, the hollow of her neck. When he reached her breasts, he ran his lips lightly over the nipples. Her groin felt sweet and hot. He kissed the soft golden down of her belly and buried his face in the golden thicket between her legs.

She reached out for him then, wanting to feel the strength of him between her fingers.

He raised his face and looked at her. "We will play afterward, but now I want to be serious." He entered her gently, so that his flesh became slowly her own. "Tell me if I am hurting you."

"No," she gasped. "No." She moved with him as though she had known him always.

"Let me know when you are ready."

". . . Ready. Oh my God . . . Now!"

He pressed her to him then as though he would never let her go. When they were lying quietly together, he turned to her and smiled. "Next time wait a little longer, and you'll see that it will feel even better."

When she awakened during the night, he was still holding her close. She moved against him and felt him grow. She loved feeling his hardness. She moved some more. He grabbed her about the waist with both hands. She felt the heat of his mouth on her neck. He entered her gently. "Slowly," he murmured. "Slowly." His thrusts became longer and deeper and just when she thought she could bear it no longer, he whispered, "Now!"

When she awakened next it was morning. Alfonso was propped up on one arm, eating cherries and watching her.

Lucrezia looked at him shyly. This was her husband.

Alfonso smiled. "You sleep with your mouth open like a child."

"I'll try to remember not to."

He reached out and touched her face gently. "I like it. It makes you look so innocent."

"Am I innocent, do you think?"

"Compared to Sancia, you are."

"I don't want to be compared to Sancia."

"Why not? She is very good in bed, I am told."

Lucrezia, forgetting that she was naked, stood up and hit him on the head with her pillow. "Is that so? Then why aren't you sleeping with *her?*"

Alfonso reached out and grabbed her ankles, causing her to fall. Then he pinned her arms to her sides. "Because," he said, "this week I am sleeping with you."

"I don't think that is very funny," Lucrezia said, her eyes filling with tears.

Alfonso kissed her on the nose. "I'm sorry. Sancia said that she had told you something about us as children. I just wanted to tease you. Do you mean to say that you have never experimented with Cesare?"

"That is none of your business, and besides, we were very young."

Alfonso choked with laughter. "What a funny girl you are. Come and get dressed. I am hungry."

"You must kiss me first."

"Where?" he queried.

"Wherever you like."

He kissed her again on the nose, then he turned her over and smacked her on the behind. "Hurry and dress. I am ravenous."

They sat on the balcony, which Maria had banked with fresh flowers.

Lucrezia sat watching him eat. "If you really loved me, you would not be able to eat so much."

Alfonso continued peeling a peach, which he ate from the point of a knife, turning it as he ate. "That is not so. Love always gives one an appetite. It is only unrequited love that makes one sicken and fade."

"But you have eaten ten figs," Lucrezia said reproachfully.

"Twelve," Alfonso corrected. "You should pay more heed."

Lucrezia sighed and drummed with her fingers on a large round melon. "It is boring to have to sit so long and watch someone eat on and on."

"I can assure you," Alfonso said earnestly, "that if our positions were reversed, I should watch each mouthful that you took with the utmost reverence and devotion."

Lucrezia could not help laughing. How amusing he was, and how good to look at. He was as bright as Cesare and much better-humored. Pride of possession rose in her like a song, and she reached out and took his hand, stroking it against the side of her face.

250

Alfonso looked at her and smiled. "You are such a child."

"But we are both the same age," she said quickly.

"Yes, I know," he said, taking her hand in his. "Except that you are still a child."

CHAPTER 22

Now that Alexander had gotten Lucrezia safely married, he turned his attention to Cesare. After all, Lucrezia's marriage had been arranged in the first place to cement ties with Naples so that Cesare might sue for Charlotte's hand. It was unthinkable that Cesare, in his present position as Captain General, should marry anyone who was not of royal blood. Alexander had considered carefully before he finally settled on Charlotte, the pretty daughter of King Federigo of Naples, whose treasury was practically bankrupt.

But although King Federigo's throne was shaky and his kingdom was crumbling about him, his pride was still very much intact. No commoner would be allowed to sully his daughter's Aragon blood. However, he was not unmindful of the Pope's power, and anxious not to offend him entirely, he had offered to transfer the late Juan's estate in Naples to Cesare, and the title of Duke of Gandia as well. Surely that expressed his good will adequately, he thought with relief.

Alexander was undaunted. He saw his course

clearly. Since Charlotte was staying at the French court, he would petition Charles VIII to espouse his cause.

Charles, easily influenced, promised to do whatever he could. But neither he nor Alexander could possibly have foreseen the circumstances that would prevent him from doing so.

During the spring of the year, Charles went to Amboise to supervise the restoration of his favorite château. There, with all his artisans busily at work around him, he struck his poor oversized head on a beam as he was escorting the Queen to a game of lawn tennis. At eleven o'clock that night he was dead.

Alexander was sitting at his desk going over some of Lucrezia's bills when he received the news. He brushed the courier aside and sent for Cesare. "The twelve-toed king is dead. It looks as though we must now do business with his cousin Louis."

Cesare said nothing.

Alexander looked at him with narrowed eyes. "If you are to woo Charlotte, you must leave the Church at once."

Cesare smiled.

"In a way," Alexander reflected, "it will be much easier doing business with Louis. He has far more sense than Charles had."

Cesare shrugged. "A lemming has more sense than Charles had."

"At least he had the good sense to die." With that Alexander took up his quill and quickly wrote on a page of parchment. "There," he said when he had sanded and sealed it, "we have cast our bread upon the waters. Let us now see what comes back to us."

The answer was not long in coming. Louis would do all that he could to advance Cesare's cause with Charlotte. Indeed, he would be only too happy to oblige,

253

provided that Alexander do three small favors for him—only three. Number one, he wished to divorce his present wife, Jeanne de Barry. He wished instead to marry Charles's widow, the lovely Anne of Brittany, who brought with her a vast duchy. Secondly, Alexander was to divest himself of his ties with Naples so that Louis could invade Lombardy. And thirdly, Louis wanted a cardinal's hat for Georges d'Amboise.

Alexander looked up from the parchment before him. "This is even better than I expected," he said to Cesare. "But that is not all. He has proposed to send to us one thousand of his soldiers and to defend the Vatican against any usurpation of its authority."

"A thousand soldiers sounds to me like an invasion with your consent," Cesare interrupted.

Alexander raised his hand. "Patience, my son. We have larger fish to fry at the moment. In the meantime, I think it might be best for you to resign your hat in Avignon."

It took Cesare two months to prepare for his trip to France. Alexander himself combed the Italian peninsula in order to outfit his son properly. By the end of September there was not a valuable piece of jewelry left in all the shops of Rome.

When Alexander beheld Cesare in all his splendor on the morning of October 1, his heart swelled within him. Whatever their differences, Alexander could not help feeling a surge of pride and love for his handsome son.

Alexander blessed him and looked quickly away. Of all his children, Cesare was the one most like himself. Perhaps that was why he was never very easy with him.

"You look away so soon, Father. Are you so glad to see me go?"

Alexander brought his eyes back to his son. "I am glad to see you go, but only for your sake."

Cesare scanned the heads of the crowd. "And Lucrezia, I suppose she is too busy with that husband of hers to come and bid me farewell?"

"Ah, Lucrezia," Alexander suddenly remembered. He reached into the folds of his cassock. "She has asked me to give you this."

Cesare reached down and took a small pincushion embroidered with a heart and a tear. "My tender-hearted sister," he murmured, tucking it carefully into his doublet. He bowed stiffly to Alexander. Then he turned his horse abruptly and rode down to the sea.

Alexander mounted the steps of Castel Sant'Angelo, watching from the parapet until Cesare and his retinue faded into the horizon.

On October 3 Cesare set sail aboard the *Louise*. With him he took a secret dispensation from the Pope allowing Louis to marry Anne at once, as well as a cardinal's hat for d'Amboise, Bishop of Rouen, and a letter from Alexander introducing "our nostrum, our beloved son, Duke of Valence, dearer to us than all else."

Cesare landed at Marseilles on October 12 and traveled to Avignon, and from there proceeded slowly through the provinces to the French court at Chinon. He lingered at Valence, his new duchy, modestly declining all the honors bestowed upon him as Duke and thus alienating the French nobles, who saw his refusal as haughtiness and nothing more. Louis, anxious not to create a rift, arranged to meet him informally just outside of Valence, as though by accident. Cesare, who loved nothing better than intrigue, was charmed.

With his usual flair for drama, Cesare hid himself and his men in a thicket until Louis's retinue appeared. He allowed them a quarter-hour of impatient pawing and snorting. Then, just as they were about to to ride off in disgust, he charged through the bushes and landed in their midst.

Louis was visibly shaken but managed to recover. "You startled us," he reproached, and smiled thinly.

Cesare dismounted and bowed. "I did not intend that, Your Majesty."

Louis looked at Cesare, bemused. "I daresay. At any rate, everything is fixed between us. How are you at the hunt?"

Cesare smiled, genuinely charmed by Louis's easy air of familiarity. "I am very good, Your Highness."

Louis laughed outright. "I like a man who knows his own worth. Mind you are not lying to me now?"

"Not now, Your Highness."

Louis looked at him keenly. "Not now, but later perhaps?"

Cesare grinned. He had never felt so much at his ease. "Perhaps."

"You are your father's son. I see that. We will get along, you and I. You may come to court whenever you like now."

Cesare bowed.

"You will, I suppose, want to make your own arrangements as to entry."

"With Your Majesty's leave."

Louis nodded. "Something original, no doubt. I shall be looking forward to it." With that he turned his horse and was gone, his men clattering after him.

Cesare's entry into Chinon was not so original as it was spectacular. In a never-ending procession came dozens of mules carrying chests and coffers, caparisoned in red covers emblazoned with the arms of the Duke of Valence. After them came eighteen pages mounted on splendid chargers, the nature of their finery causing much speculation as to their identity.

Cesare himself sat astride a magnificently caparisoned courser, dressed in a suit of red satin striped with gold and encrusted with pearls and precious stones. He wore a large crushed hat of the same material, which was liberally sprinkled with enormous rubies. In the middle of the hat was a pearl the size of a large walnut. Even his boots were edged with gold cord trimmed with pearls. His horse was shod with silver, as were the other horses in the suite. But Cesare's horse was further decorated with precious stones. On the crupper sat a pearl as big as a pomegranate. The bodice of Cesare's doublet was encrusted with diamonds that flashed and blazed with light.

Louis, watching it all from a window of the palace, turned to his courtiers and sighed. "At least this is better than having him leap out of the bushes at us."

Cesare entered the large hall, bowing from the waist as he did so, and pausing in the middle of the hall to bow again.

Louis raised his hand, beckoning him on. The King was to remark later to some of his gentlemen that anyone would have known how to behave with more dignity, that Cesare had shown his lack of breeding with his absurd behavior.

CHAPTER 23

Although Louis laughed at Cesare behind his back, he was scrupulously polite to his face, asking anxiously whether his accommodations were to his liking or if there was anything he lacked. Cesare just as politely assured him that all his needs were answered most excellently, as indeed they were. Louis showed him every consideration as a guest at his court, even supplying him with his own personal guard and treating him in general as he would an equal. The only thing he did not do was the thing that Cesare wanted most, to further his suit with Charlotte.

The days passed pleasantly enough. There was always the hunt, at which Cesare excelled, and jousting enough to test his skill, which was considerable, but still nothing was mentioned about Charlotte.

Louis, although he said nothing of it to Cesare, was having his own problems with that. Charlotte's father, King Federigo of Naples, simply would not have the Pope's bastard for his daughter. On that subject he was vehement. As for Charlotte, she raised her pretty eyebrows whenever Cesare's name was mentioned, saying wittily that she was disinclined to gain the title of La Cardinala.

Louis could do nothing with either of them. In desperation he planned a dinner and sat Charlotte next to Cesare, hoping that some good would come of it.

Charlotte took one look at Cesare, Duke of Valence, and raised her nose, remarking to all within range of her voice that she found the condition of his skin deplorable, especially at dinner.

From that moment Cesare's suit ceased. He stormed into the King's presence the very next day, saying he wished to return to Rome.

Louis, genuinely alarmed, attempted to calm him. He did not wish to antagonize the Pope just now, as he planned an attack against Venice and needed his support. "In truth," he said soothingly, "the lady finds you most attractive, but she loves another. You know how these things are . . ."

Cesare turned his back and said nothing.

"It has nothing to do with you, my friend. Nothing at all. As I say, she finds you most attractive, but her heart is otherwise engaged. You would not want to possess a woman like that. She would give you no satisfaction."

Cesare merely grunted.

Louis tried another tack. "Let us forget her. Now what about Charlotte d'Albret, sister to the King of Navarre? She is high-born, and to tell the truth, she is much better-looking than the other Charlotte, who, between you and me, has a bad color. No, I would not like to have to look at her before my morning wine."

Cesare turned around in interest. "This other Charlotte, what does she look like?"

The King smiled to show his enthusiasm. "Well, as I

259

have said, she has very good color without being ruddy like the English, neither too red nor too pale."

"What else?"

Louis stroked his chin deliberately. "Her hair springs thickly from her head, and her teeth are even and white."

"Yes, go on."

"She is beautiful, lively and charming, and has a ready wit."

"What else?"

"What else? What else could you ask for?"

"What about her figure?" Cesare persisted. "What sort of figure has she?"

Louis smiled broadly. "She is proportioned to suit the severest critic. In fact, were it not for several important political considerations, I would have chosen her over Anne."

Cesare mulled this over. It was well known that Louis's alliance with Anne was designed to promote an alliance with Brittany. "Very well. When may I see her?"

"Tut-tut." Louis shook a finger. "Not so fast, my friend. I must first inform her estimable father, and then we will see."

"That old goat," Cesare snorted. "He doesn't know one of his parts from another!"

"His knowledge of anatomy is not relevant to your suit," the King said severely.

"Very well," Cesare decided. "I will postpone my departure until you hear from him."

"One other thing," Louis said. "I wish that you would write to your father and assure him that everything possible is being done to forward a suit for you. He seems to have gotten some notion that I am not fulfilling my promise in this respect."

"Really," Cesare murmured, remembering the angry

260

letter he had written Alexander concerning Louis and the French court. "I cannot think how he came by such a notion."

"No," Louis said dryly. "Neither can I."

When Cesare returned to his quarters, he found Agapito packing his things. "Never mind that. We are not leaving after all."

"But we are, milord. The King has given orders. You are to be moved to larger quarters in the royal palace."

Cesare had difficulty hiding his pleasure.

"Also," Agapito reminded him, "he has favored you with the protection of his own guard."

Cesare thought of that. If Louis was granting him honors on the one hand, he was depriving him of his freedom on the other. "It sounds as though we are to be prisoners."

Agapito shrugged and went on packing.

The new apartments were splendid, almost as splendid as those of the King. As he entered, Cesare saw a large sword lying on the table. It was encased in a magnificently worked scabbard. Next to it lay a small dagger, similarly encased. He drew out the sword. The blade was of the finest tempered German steel. The handle was worked in onyx inlaid with silver and had come from one of the finest masters in Florence. Set in the pommel was a large cabochon ruby. The dagger was a perfect match. Cesare plucked a hair from his head and swiped at in with the sword. The blade cut it neatly in half. This time he did not even try to conceal his pleasure. He slid the sword reverently into its scabbard. The dagger he fastened to his side. "Well," he said to Agapito, who stood watching, "at least the King has issued the prisoner arms."

Louis did his best to amuse Cesare while he waited for Alain d'Albret's answer. It was not long in coming.

The King of Navarre regretted that he could not give so lovely a pearl as his sister to a bastard of the Pope's. Louis thought on this. King Federigo's refusal of Cesare's suit for Charlotte's hand had obviously prompted Alain d'Albret to refuse also. News of Cesare's malady had no doubt reached his ears. The other Charlotte had told everyone who would listen that Cesare's complexion was a fright. As a matter of fact, Cesare's face was healing as the disease moved deeper inside him.

What would it take to make him change his mind, Louis wrote to d'Albret, reminding him shrewdly that he was indebted to Louis for most of his holdings and tenures.

The King of Navarre wrote back quickly that perhaps his decision had been too hastily made, and that if the dowry were raised to one hundred and twenty thousand gold ducats instead of the one hundred thousand livres that Louis had offered, and if Louis would add thirty thousand livres to that, then arrangements could be made.

Louis smiled. He did not intend to turn over a penny of this money. But that would come later, after the marriage was consummated. In the end it was agreed that Cesare's duchy of Valence was to be settled on his wife and that Charlotte's brother Amanieu would be made a cardinal. Cesare signed the contract at Blois, with Agapito and his faithful secretary Ramiro de Lorqua looking on.

When the arrangements were finally concluded, Louis heaved a great sigh. The proceedings had taken almost three months to negotiate and he was heartily glad to be done with it. Also, Cesare, with his boundless capacity for insolence, had managed to antagonize almost every noble at court. It was not enough that he had bested them at jousting and the hunt and every other sport imaginable, but he did not bother to conceal his contempt for them and he was really only pleasant to the ladies—which was another problem altogether. Louis would have been only too glad to get rid of him and restore peace among his noblemen, except that he needed him to go along as the Pope's emissary when he entered Milan. For his own part, he had become truly attached to Cesare. He admired his strength and his courage, and he enjoyed the mental jousting at which Cesare excelled. His own courtiers stood in awe of their king and could rarely bring themselves to break the French tradition of deferential restraint.

Cesare once more felt himself in a position to bargain. Louis had already shown his wish to please him by securing him a princess. But Cesare had no intention of settling down to a domestic routine. He still saw himself as Captain General of the Church, and he saw Louis's invasion of Milan as a way of attaining his ends. He put it to Louis one afternoon as they rode back from a particularly good day's hunting.

"This business in Milan, what is my part in all this?"

Louis smiled. Another joust was in the making. "What part would you like?"

Cesare shrugged. "I was thinking of a command, one that I could keep."

The first thrust had been made. Louis countered. "I don't think I understand you."

"It is really very simple. We are having a great deal of trouble collecting tributes from the provinces. If you were to give us six hundred lances with six men to a lance and artillery and foot soldiers, it would make our collections much easier."

"I see," Louis said. "And who would maintain this army of yours?"

"You would," Cesare said without hesitation.

263

Louis laughed out loud.

"The idea amuses you?"

"Amuses me?" Louis choked, his eyes filling with tears. "Yes, it amuses me."

"Well, may I have it?" Cesare asked seriously.

"Tell me," Louis said, wiping his eyes with a piece of fine chambray which he pulled from his sleeve, "if I refused you in this, would you then be reluctant to serve with me in Milan?"

"Very reluctant," Cesare agreed.

"That's what I thought. Very well then, you may have them."

"My father will be very pleased," Cesare said, unwilling to show his own pleasure in this.

"I daresay," Louis replied dryly. "And I hope that it pleases you as well."

Cesare's marriage to Charlotte d'Albret took place on May 12, 1499. Cesare, looking speculatively at his chestnut-haired bride, was not without pride in her. Louis had not lied about her looks. She was fresh and glowing with large brown eyes and very fair skin. Also, there was a certain shyness and reticence about her which pleased him. He had had his share of bold women and would again, no doubt, but boldness was not a quality to be much admired in a wife.

When at the ceremony he was called upon to take her hand in his, he felt it tremble. He thought of Lucrezia and resolved that he would try to be gentle with this girl, as gentle as he could be. After all, he could always visit a courtesan afterward if it was necessary. At the end of the ceremony he bent down to kiss her, and she looked into his eyes as he did so and did not pull away. He felt extremely aware of the blotches on his face, which he had taken care to cover with heavy powder, but she seemed not to care or even to notice them.

Louis accompanied them to the bridal chamber as an act of courtesy. Then he kissed the bride and looked at Cesare as though he were about to say something. But he thought better of it and left without speaking. Cesare thought of his father and smiled. If Alexander were here, they would not be able to get rid of him so easily as that. He would expect to fondle and kiss the bride and then he would make broad jokes and stay to see that they went about it in the right way. It was fortunate that he was not here now to instruct the bride in her duties, although it seemed to Cesare that instruction might serve her well, for she had retired to the alcove to undress and half an hour later still had not returned.

Cesare, finally impatient, strode in to find her sitting in her linen undergarments, her hands folded in her lap. Looking at her pale face and bitten lips, he was suddenly sorry for her. "If you wish, madam, I can find solace elsewhere."

She raised her eyes to his. He saw the fear in her face, but he saw something else as well.

"Come," he said, taking both her hands in his. "I am not so very bad, am I?"

"They say that you are very rough with women," she said in a small voice.

"Not with princesses."

She smiled a little at that. "I am afraid," she confided.

Cesare bent down and lifted her in his arms. He had never treated a woman in this fashion, but then most of his women had been experienced. He lifted her easily and carried her over to the bed, letting his silk dressing gown slip to the floor. The warmth of her body against

265

his had had its effect on him, and he stood before her so that she could see it.

She looked at his lithe, muscular body. Then she began unworking the fastenings of her shift.

In the morning Cesare reached for her again.

"I am still sore from last night," she whispered shyly.

"That is because you need practice," he said, kissing her lightly.

Getting married was not as bad as he had thought it would be, Cesare reflected at the morning meal with Charlotte sitting opposite him. He was pleased with his bride, and aware that she was not displeased with him. He enjoyed watching her delight at the gifts he had brought her from Rome—three chests filled with gold, silver plate, and countless jewels. To show her gratitude, Charlotte wrote her new father-in-law a charming letter in which she praised Cesare as a husband and expressed a wish to visit Alexander in Rome.

Louis had sent Alexander one hundred casks of Burgundy as proof of the good will he bore him, and to confirm his approval of the match, himself bestowed upon Cesare the Order of St. Michael, which was the highest honor in the kingdom. When Alexander heard of this, he roared his delight, ordering fireworks and bonfires to mark the occasion. Then he dug deeply into the Vatican treasury and sent Cesare every last ducat he could spare. When that was done he publicly announced the Vatican's allegiance to France, proclaiming further that the Sforzas must be expelled from Milan. Louis had played his hand cunningly.

CHAPTER 24

As soon as Lucrezia's husband heard of the Pope's alliance with France and his negation of the Naples-Milan treaty, he turned to her and said, "I am a dead man."

Lucrezia, who was six months pregnant and showed it, shook her head. "Papa loves you," she said stubbornly. "He would never let anything bad happen to you."

Alfonso smiled at her, but the worry in his eyes remained. "He has already banished my sister Sancia. I'd be a fool not to follow her home."

"Really, Alfonso, the only reason Papa asked her to leave was because of the way she behaved. She slept with everyone but Burchard. Everyone in Rome was talking about it."

"That was simply an excuse, Lucrece. She behaved no differently than she ever has."

Lucrezia's hands flew to her hair. "You can't go, Alfonso. Now not, when I'm like this. And besides, what has Milan to do with us?"

"Dear child, don't you see? First it will be Milan, and then it will be Naples. That will leave me clinging to a falling limb."

"But everyone knows that you don't care about politics."

Alfonso took her hands in his and kissed them. "You are such a child, my dearest. The people you love can do no wrong. If you want a father for your child, try to understand that what I am doing is best for both of us."

In the end it was Alexander himself who warned Alfonso to leave. "It will only be for a little while, my son. Just until everything blows over."

"What about Lucrezia?"

"Ah yes, Lucrezia." Alexander scratched his chin reflectively. "It might be best after all if you left while she's at her siesta. Leave it to me, my son. I will tell her."

"And when will I see her again?"

"When? Ah yes, when . . . Don't worry, my boy. I'll send her to you as soon as possible."

When Lucrezia awoke the afternoon sun was slanting through the shutters. Alexander sat in a chair, his hands folded, staring at the opposite wall. Lucrezia stretched. When she saw her father, her body shrank with fear. "What are you doing here, Papa? Where is Alfonso?"

Alexander got up and sat down beside her. "He is gone, my child. I sent him on an important mission. He asked me to give you this."

Lucrezia took the note and read it. "But that is not his writing, Papa, and there is no signature."

"Yes, well, he did not have the time, my pet."

Lucrezia uttered a piercing cry. "He's gone. I'll never see him again!"

Alexander gathered her in his arms. "There, my

flower, there." Her cries and the shuddering of her body were more than he could bear. What if she should lose the child through grief? "Look, my angel, I have an idea. How would you like to be the Governor of Spoleto?"

Lucrezia's cries grew more frenzied. "I want Alfonso. Alfonso!"

"Yes, my angel, I know. But in the meantime, while you are waiting for him to return, you and your brother Geoffrey can go to Spoleto. It will be much gayer there for you. After all, Sancia is gone and there is really nothing here for you to do. In Spoleto you will have the entire town at your feet and you will learn the principles of government, so that when Alfonso has his own duchy one day you will be able to assist him."

"I don't want to go with Geoffrey. I would rather be with Cesare."

Alexander tried to be patient. "Cesare is with Charlotte. You cannot expect him to leave his bride, can you?"

"Oh, Papa, why did you have to send Alfonso away? Why couldn't you have sent someone else?"

There was no one else I could trust, my child. Believe me." Alexander held her to him until her weeping stopped. Then he stroked her hair and kissed her. Of all his children, she was the most innocent, the most absent of guile, and so he loved her the most.

A week later everything was in order and on the morning of August 8 Lucrezia and Geoffrey were ready to leave. Alexander, anxious to make Lucrezia happy, had organized a magnificent cortege including forty-three coaches, most of which were filled with Lucrezia's things. Along with Maria, Alexander had included in the party a number of young people for gaiety, ladies-in-waiting, attendants, and soldiers for protection.

The cortege left from the Palace of Santa Maria in Portico. Alexander watched from the benediction loggia. He raised his hand and blessed them three times, looking after them until they were gone from view. Then he sighed and went inside. He was truly fond of his son-in-law, and he hated having had to send him away. But what else could he do? And now Lucrezia was gone also. Ah well, he would have to dance to the French tune for a while, and after that he would see . . .

Lucrezia chattered incessantly along the way to keep up her spirits, first with the Neapolitan ambassador, whom Alexander had persuaded to ride along as far as the Castel Sant'Angelo in exchange for his own safe conduct home. There the good man looked at her sadly and bade her adieu, adding that he hoped it would not be too long before the atmosphere in Rome changed back to happier times. Lucrezia clung to him and wept as though she were saying good-bye to Alfonso himself instead of to one of his ambassadors. Then she turned back to the others in her suite and smiled. After all, she was in charge now and had a role to play. And she was determined to assume her new position of responsibility no matter how low her mood.

Even had she been prone to sulk, the landscape and the weather would have lifted her up, for she responded as readily as a child to her new surroundings. The road took them through fields and meadows dotted with grazing sheep and then just as suddenly through woods of dappled chestnut and rippling streams. All this was so delightful in aspect that she felt her cares drift from her, and when she saw the Castle of Spoleto high on its green promontory she felt nothing but keen anticipation.

They stopped for lunch just outside Spoleto at the Castle of Porcaria. No sooner had they stopped than they were greeted by four commissioners followed by four hundred infantry, bidding Lucrezia welcome as Governor of Spoleto in behalf of the city. After lunch they continued on their way, reaching Spoleto at about two in the afternoon. There Lucrezia was transferred to a golden litter so that she could ride in state.

The town was decked with flowers and flags for her arrival, and the faces of the citizens who turned out to see the Pope's daughter were friendly and curious.

Lucrezia smiled her sweetest smile. When they saw her gray-blue eyes as clear as a child's and the spun gold of her hair, they were charmed. Alexander could not be so bad after all, they told one another; look at his daughter. They cheered her wildly, glad to have a celebrity in their midst and to have an excuse to keep them from their work. Completely intoxicated by her reception, Lucrezia ordered free wine and roasted oxen for the entire town, declaring aloud that the Pope would be proud of such loyal subjects.

By the time all the magistrates had made their speeches, the sun was low in the sky. Lucrezia, who had been traveling since early morning, was beginning to feel the effects of her journey. But the sound of her name ringing in her ears was like music.

Finally it was over and the cortege passed under the archway of the castle and into the sumptuous Court of Honor with its magnificent arcades. Lucrezia, still playing her role, reached into the folds of her dress and drew out the Vatican briefs, handing them over to the Chief Magistrate, who smiled and bowed.

When she was finally alone with Maria in the quarters which had been done over for her in Borgia red, she looked about in delight and flopped on the bed.

"Pig!" Maria reproached. "Take off that dirty dress!"

Lucrezia lay on her back, her eyes shining. "Did you see how much they loved me? Did you hear how they shouted my name over and over?"

Maria sniffed. "They would have shouted the Devil's name for the sake of free meat and wine."

Lucrezia lay rapt, unhearing.

"The dress," Maria repeated. "Take off that stinking dress!"

Lucrezia smiled and closed her eyes. "You take it off. I am going to sleep."

When she awakened in the morning, she scarcely knew where she was. The sun crept in through the shutters, making strange patterns on the walls. At home her bedchamber would still be dark, for the sun did not reach it until afternoon. Maria had somehow managed to remove the dress without waking her; she was lying in her shift. She raised her arms and stretched, and surveyed her new surroundings. Then she threw off the covering, feeling suddenly gritty and dirty. "Maria!" she shouted. She would not put in an appearance until Maria had bathed her and washed her hair.

The apartment approximated as closely as possible the decorations of her own apartment in Rome. Lucrezia smiled. Alexander had seen to every comfort. Her father, she thought snugly, would always see to her wants. And Alfonso and Cesare as well. She felt a sudden surge of confidence. There was really no cause for worry, no cause at all. And in the meantime, she would show her father that she could govern and govern well.

"Maria!" she screamed again. She wanted to be clean and she wanted her morning meal. She had been too excited and too tired to eat very much the day before and now she was hungry.

272

Before she could scream for her again, Maria entered the room with a tray. Lucrezia took one look at the cold roast chicken, the goat's cheese wrapped in chestnut leaves, and the pyramid of fresh figs, and tore off a chicken leg, stuffing it greedily into her mouth. "Bread," she mumbled with her mouth full. "Where is the bread?"

Maria pulled a fresh loaf from under a linen napkin. "If those people could only see you now, they would put you out to feed with the pigs."

"Be careful how you speak to me, Maria, or I will put you in the dungeon."

"Is that so? And who would wash your hair for you then?"

"That is no problem," Lucrezia said, wiping her fingers on her shift, "I can always get a handsome boy from the village. Why is there no wine?"

"There is water there," Maria said, motioning to a silver pitcher beside the bed. "It has been there all night."

"I do not want stale water," Lucrezia cried. "I want fresh wine!"

"Sit in your bath meanwhile and drink some of the water, and I will go to the cellar and draw you a pitcher from our own casks."

Maria returned a quarter of an hour later. Lucrezia grabbed the pitcher and swallowed deeply.

"Ah, if they could see you now, those good people."

Lucrezia tilted the pitcher more, letting her throat fill with wine.

"It is not watered," Maria shouted. "You will fall off the Council chair onto your head!"

At ten o'clock, her cheeks slightly flushed with wine, Lucrezia entered the Court of Honor, picking her way slowly to her chair, which was on a dais. The magistrates, who had been waiting for three-quarters of an hour, were in a sour mood.

The Chief Magistrate rose and bowed. The rest of the Council followed suit. Lucrezia, suddenly nervous, giggled. The magistrates looked at one another in consternation. Was Alexander mad sending them this lightheaded daughter of his to govern them?

Lucrezia, aghast at her own behavior, rose from her seat. "Milords," she began, uncertain of what she would say, but knowing she must say something, "you must forgive me my bad manners. I meant no disrespect toward you. It is only that I am unused to this, and being apprehensive about my role here, I indulged in too much wine to give me courage. It gave me none. That being a mistake, forgive me. It will not happen again." She looked around at the impassive faces. "I know not what else to say milords, and so let us begin," she faltered.

Lucrezia's words, so lacking in guile, had their effect. The faces around her softened.

The Chief Magistrate stepped forward. "The Council wishes to welcome you, milady. It wishes to state further that it will be of help to you in any way it can." The Chief Magistrate almost smiled. "Do not be afraid of us. We mean you no harm."

Lucrezia drew a deep breath. She had made a bad start, but she was determined to do better. "We may, if you like, proceed to the business of the day."

The Chief Magistrate nodded. "We have read the briefs from Rome. Pope Alexander has suggested to the Council that since he has given us something of value, it is therefore incumbent upon us to do the same. And so the Council has proposed that in addition to the present tributes which we send to Rome, we add one-quarter of our yearly production of wine, olives, and oil plus a yearly tithe of oxen, cattle, and

274

sheep to be used at His Holiness's discretion. Does Your Grace find that agreeable?"

Lucrezia, who was listening closely, nodded. How very like her father to trade on his children whenever possible. "It is agreeable," Lucrezia said uncomfortably, wishing that Alexander had not sent the briefs. She would write to him later. Perhaps he would withdraw them.

"Milady . . ."

Lucrezia found herself looking into a pair of handsome brown eyes.

"Milady, I have here a petition which might interest you."

The Chief Magistrate rose. "All petitions must be addressed to me first."

"It is all right," Lucrezia said kindly. "What is it?"

The man who addressed her was young and well formed and appeared to be in his mid-twenties. "If you will, Milady, my name is Ascanio Descanso."

Lucrezia's eyes took in the form-fitting fawn tunic and tights, the thick cluster of dark curls which framed his face.

"Yes, go on."

"I have addressed several petitions to this court, but they have never been heard."

"You will be heard now," Lucrezia said, her heart warming to this handsome stranger.

Descanso nodded to the Chief Magistrate. "If it please Your Honor . . ."

The Chief Magistrate looked away sourly.

"Well, a client of mine, a young girl by the name of Angela Ortello, was indecently assaulted by a member of this court one day as she was making up the beds in his house. Nine months to the day of the assault on this child, who was only eleven years of age at the time, she was delivered of a boy child. When the mas-

ter of the house was apprised of this, he turned out
both mother and baby into the streets without so much
as a florin or a loaf of bread. As it was winter and very
cold, the baby caught pneumonia and died. As for the
girl, she had been disgraced, and so no one would take
her in and she was forced to go on the streets in order
to live. Then, because of her wracking ordeal and the
nature of the life she was forced to live, her lungs went
bad and now she can no longer support herself. I con-
tend that she is entitled to payment for the indignities
suffered by her at the hands of this person and com-
pensation for the fact that she cannot now lead a normal life and may never enjoy the position of wife and
mother, a position which is the birthright of every girl
born of God."

Lucrezia, listening to this, could not help thinking of
her own child which lay inside her now. "The gentleman you speak of," she said slowly, "is he in this court
today?"

"He is, milady."

"And what is his name?"

"His name is Stefano Segretti, and he is a magistrate
of this court."

Lucrezia nodded to the Chief Magistrate.

"Will the petitioned please stand?" he asked. For a
moment there was no movement as everyone waited.
Then finally, at the back of the hall, a large man rose
to his feet. He reminded her of Alexander because of
his size, and that somehow made her unhappy.

"Signor Segretti," the Chief Magistrate asked, "are
the facts in this petition well taken?"

The large man cleared his throat of phlegm. "If by
that you mean was I first, I was not. That one had
been at it since she was an infant."

"Were you the father of her child?" the Chief
Magistrate persisted.

"What if I was? If I were to support all the bastards I've fathered, I'd not have an ounce of gold to my name."

Lucrezia was confused and upset by the feelings which rose inside her. "Signor Segretti," she said unsteadily, trying to choke down the anger which threatened to overwhelm her and tangle her speech, "are you a bastard?"

"I am, Your Grace."

"And did your father support you?"

"He did."

"That is a pity," Lucrezia said slowly. "For if he had not, then perhaps you would not have survived to perpetrate such mischief on an innocent child."

The man's face was suffused with blood. "I do not understand," he choked. "This petition has been presented before, but it has never been heard. Why now?"

Lucrezia smiled sweetly. "Perhaps because it was never presented to a woman. I respectfully suggest to the court that this man pay the sum of five hundred gold ducats to the girl for her injury and one hundred gold ducats a year for the support of her child."

"But the child is dead, Your Grace!" the man gasped.

"So it is," Lucrezia said evenly. "The one hundred gold ducats a year will go to support the grief caused by the loss of the child."

The Chief Magistrate rose hastily. "Are there any objections from the court?"

Lucrezia waited, her body beginning to tremble. There were none.

When she walked out into the paved courtyard, she felt grateful for the warmth of the sun, for the atmosphere in the hall after the verdict was delivered had been stern and cold. Although no one said a word, she sensed the hostility around her. As soon as the court convened, the men waited respectfully for her to leave and then formed into tight little groups around the defendant. At first her ears had strained for their words and then, ashamed of this, she had walked quickly out. Her eyes filled with tears. Never had she felt so completely alone. More than ever she longed for Alfonso and the warmth and comfort of his love.

"You are very brave," Ascanio Descanso fell into step with her.

"I am afraid I have done nothing but make enemies," she said, turning her face away so that he could not see her tears. "That is not what my father sent me here for."

Ascanio Descanso took her hands in his and kissed them. "You need not be ashamed of kindness, milady."

The touch of his lips, the warmth of his skin on hers, so overwhelmed her that she almost shook. Was this what happened when you were deprived of the one you loved? One more moment and she might have done something foolish. "It was nothing," she said, holding her arms to keep herself from trembling. "Send the girl to me. I will make a place for her. And now I must go. Please excuse me."

Ascanio stood looking after her. What was wrong? Was she ashamed of what she had done? Well, no matter. At least Angela was assured of a place in the world. He had seen to that. As for the new governor, with her golden hair and her look of fragility, she was something to think about.

The others were waiting for her in the dining hall.

"Well, you made a thorough fool of yourself," Geoffrey said, raising his wine. "Wait until Father hears of it."

Lucrezia sat down and said nothing.

"Do you know what they said about you in the Council after you left? They said, 'Alexander has given us the least and taken the most.' That is how they rate you as Governor."

"I would like some wine, please," Lucrezia said evenly.

"What right have you," Geoffrey persisted, ignoring her request for wine, "to go about changing things? What about the *droit du seigneur*, the Rights of Lords?"

"What about the rights of that child?" Lucrezia asked severely.

"That child is nothing. She has no rights."

"As long as I am Governor here, everyone will have rights."

"Governor!" Geoffrey choked on his wine. "You are no more a governor than I am! Father merely wanted to give you something to do so that you would not keep whining to him about Alfonso. It is merely another form of needlework. You are expected to sit still and say nothing."

Lucrezia's fury worked its way into her hands. She took up her trencher of bread and hit Geoffrey over the head with it. "I am here to govern, and I shall govern. And if you expect to pull any of the tricks here that you pull in Rome, you'll answer to me for them!"

Geoffrey's laughter was edged with scorn. "My dear sister," he announced to the company at large, "is going very holy on us. One hundred gold ducats to the man who can get her on her back. There is enough to go around, I'll warrant!"

Lucrezia's eyes forged themselves into steel. "Listen to me, you fool. If you or any of your company dares to touch me or any woman here against her will, I will deal with them as I would with the meanest criminal. And now you may pour me some wine!"

CHAPTER 25

The following morning as Maria was dressing her hair, there was a knock at Lucrezia's door. The morning bells had just sounded nine o'clock.

"See who it is," Lucrezia said, taking up a mirror.

Ascanio Descanso's voice came from the doorway. "Please tell Her Grace that I have brought Angela Ortello to her."

Lucrezia began pinching her cheeks to give them color. "You may come in, Signor Descanso," she called out. Why should he not come in? She looked especially well this morning in her pale-blue silk dressing gown—and besides, the presence of a handsome young man was not unwelcome at any time. Alfonso's absence made a mild flirtation almost mandatory.

Lucrezia's good looks were not lost on Descanso. His eyes warmed as he took in the silk dressing gown and the long golden hair. "You are too kind, Your Grace. Please allow me to present Angela Ortello. She will serve you well."

Lucrezia found herself looking at a child no more

than eleven or twelve years of age, all sharpness and bones, whose face bore an extreme pallor. Lucrezia took her hands and looked into her face, then looked away in pity from the sunken eyes. "You are going to be all right now. We will take care of you. And when you are well and strong, then you will help me to take care of my baby."

The sunken eyes came to life then. "A baby?" Angela kissed the hands that held hers.

"Take her to the kitchen and feed her," Lucrezia said to Maria. "And then put her to bed."

"Come along," Maria said reluctantly. "A skeleton for a nurse; my God!"

Lucrezia, whose world had been so sheltered, had never seen anyone like Angela. How many others were there like her, she wondered.

Ascanio seemed to read her thoughts. "There are many unfortunates in this world. Happily Your Grace knows little of that. In my work as notary I am faced with many such people. Angela is just one of them."

"I do not understand why there was no one to take her in," Lucrezia said.

Ascanio shrugged. "Her mother was a whore, one of the thousand or so who work the streets of Rome. She could not care for her, so she sent her into the country, where she ended up as a maid in the Segretti household. Had she not been forced to take to the streets in order to eat, some kindly housewife might have taken her in, but no one wants such a person about with husbands and sons in the house. I myself did not learn of her plight until I saw her lying in a doorway several months ago, more dead than alive."

"But surely the nuns in the convent . . ."

"They have their quotas. There was simply no room for her and not enough food."

Lucrezia twisted her fingers nervously. "If Papa

281

knew about things like this, I'm certain he would do something to help. I will write to him and tell him. I know that he will do what he can."

Ascanio looked away.

"I will write to him today," Lucrezia continued, "and ask him to release Spoleto from tributes so that Angela and others like her can be helped."

"It is not just the money," Ascanio said. "It is the law which needs changing. As long as the *droit du seigneur* exists, injustices like this will continue. After all, it is only human nature to take advantage of situations, and if one knows that he can get away with it . . ."

"That is wrong."

"Yes," Ascanio said gently. "It is wrong."

"The two of us," Lucrezia began slowly, not certain of what she would say, but certain that she did not want to see him leave just yet, "perhaps we can change things."

Ascanio smiled. "We can try."

"Will you stay and take midday meal with us?"

"No, I had better not. There is enough talk about this already. I don't wish to add to it."

"But that's stupid!" Lucrezia burst out. "All I have done is to try to help someone."

"That's so," Ascanio admitted. "But you have gone against the order of things. That is what they don't like."

"Can we not see one another at all, then?"

He smiled. "Of course we can. I will come to get news of Angela, and when I come, perhaps Your Grace will be good enough to chat with me."

"When will you come?" she demanded.

"I will come," he said, looking into her eyes. "Believe me."

She held out her hand and he took it and kissed it.

On his way out he almost collided with Geoffrey, who stood looking after him.

"That hot Borgia blood of yours is going to get you into trouble yet," he said with a leer at his sister.

"What do you want, Geoffrey?"

"Want? I waited outside so as not to interfere with anything. I didn't, did I?"

"You could have saved yourself the trouble." she said irritably. "There is nothing between us but Angela."

"What a pity," he said. "I'm certain you would have it otherwise if you could."

"Look, Geoffrey, I'm in no mood for your nonsense. What is it you want?"

"It's the Council," he said, looking at her curiously. "They have commissioned me to ask you to change your mind."

"About what?" she snapped.

"About the girl. They do not care that you have taken her into your house, but they do not wish to set a precedent by levying a fine against Signor Segretti."

"Is that so? And why have they not approached me themselves? Why have they sent you?"

Geoffrey examined his fingernails with care. "It was a question of delicacy. We Borgias seem to have engendered a certain reputation. And so they feel that your decision might have been prompted by Ascanio's good looks rather than by any concern for the girl herself."

"I see. And what did you say to that?"

"I agreed."

Lucrezia's color mounted.

Geoffrey smiled at her discomfiture. "They suspect that if Ascanio were possessed of a hump on his back or a crooked nose, you would have heard the petition differently. And so," he said with a show of modesty,

283

"they have asked me to see what I could do to change your mind."

"Is that so? Well, you may go back to them and say that you can do nothing. Tell them that I do not listen to drifters and mountebanks such as you. After that, you may tell them nothing!"

Geoffrey's nostrils pinched in anger. "Papa will hear of this. He will have you thrown out of office!"

"Indeed he will hear of it. I will write to him with my own hands. And now," she said, trying to keep her temper, "you may leave!"

Lucrezia, watching the door close behind him, began to shake with anger. There was no one in the entire Roman faction who sided with her. They had all sided with Geoffrey to curry favor, since they felt that he wielded more influence at home. "She is more willow than oak," they had said of her. Very well, she would show them differently.

After a few weeks of rest and food, Angela was beginning to put on flesh. For the first few days all she did was cry weakly, and even Maria, whose heart had been hardened toward her, softened.

"Perhaps it will turn out all right," she said to Lucrezia after a month had passed. "She is not a bad girl."

Lucrezia, who was going over some papers at her desk, smiled. Everything seemed to be working out after all. The Council was cold, but it did not openly oppose her. As for Geoffrey and his friends, they slept late and pursued their own pleasures, taking care to keep out of her way.

Were it not for Alfonso's continued absence, she would have been perfectly happy. They had been apart now for over a month. She had received only one letter from him. In it he had likened his love for her to that of the mistle thrush who pines for the juniper and the hazel tuft, adding that he pined for her no less and that he longed to be her husband again in all ways.

Lucrezia had read this with damp eyes. Then she had tucked the letter carefully away in her desk, resolving that if they could not be together, then at least she would pass the time in trying to make him proud of her.

Ascanio, she found out, had been coming to see Angela, but he had not tried to see her. It was probably for the best, she thought; it was difficult to keep her heart from leaping at the sight of him. And yet it had nothing at all to do with her love for Alfonso, which was real and constant. The child which was growing within her seemed to increase the appetites of her body. She wanted desperately to lie beside a man and to feel his hardness within her. She lay awake at night for hours thinking of Alfonso and imagining him near her. Sometimes she thought of Ascanio as well.

It was in this frame of mind that she rode forth one morning just as the mists were rising from the castle walls. Her mind and her heart were restless, but more than that, her body's fierce insistence was more than she could bear. Maria had packed her a lunch of cold chicken, cheese, and fresh fruit and had given her a flask of cool wine, expecting to go along with her.

"No." Lucrezia was firm. "I must be by myself and think my own thoughts for a change."

She would ride as far as the next convent and visit the nuns there. Perhaps their serenity and tranquility would spill over onto her.

Half an hour later, Maria set out after her. If anything were to happen to Lucrezia in her present state, Alexander would never forgive her. And what's more, she would never forgive herself.

Lucrezia looked with pleasure on the surrounding

countryside. She could almost feel the push of green shoots through the soil, likening it to the growth of the child inside her. She looked at the fields on either side of her and at the peasants in their coarse linen tunics, their faces and arms browned by the sun. She smiled to the peasants and waved. They leaned on their hoes and watched her, their young at their sides or underfoot, since there was nobody at home to care for them.

Lucrezia felt a sudden surge of love for these people who made such a pleasant picture at their work. Farther down the road near the vineyards some children sat weaving horsehair snares to keep the grapes safe from the birds. The sounds of their laughter drifted to her over the golden air.

The vineyards gave way suddenly to green meadows dotted with sheep, the lambs frolicking beside them. Then came a cluster of houses that marked the village, and then the village square with its fountain and trough. A group of women stood by the well, gathering water and gossiping. As Lucrezia rode by they smiled and waved, for she was held in good esteem ever since it was known that her sympathies lay with the poor.

Lucrezia blew them lighthearted kisses and then looked toward the building that housed the notary, half hoping to see Ascanio standing in the doorway, but there was no one. She guided her horse slowly through the center of town, past the cathedral with its bells and spire, past the wooden shed where the blacksmith worked at his forge, past the stalls where the open market was held, and then the fields took over again, this time ridged with furrows. The convent was only half an hour's ride from here, but instead of following the road she plunged off into the woods that had sprung up on either side of her. She had never really meant to go to the convent; she knew that now. She had only meant to ride by the notary's house in the hope of seeing Ascanio.

The forest was thick with a green glaze of leaves, with the sun filtering through and dappling the ground beneath her. She could hear the sound of water trickling over some rocks. The trees were alive with birds that rustled and sang. She would rest awhile and enjoy the woods. She dismounted slowly and tethered her horse to a tree. Then she unstrapped the carpet Maria had provided and spread it out on the bank of the stream. She was not yet ready to eat. Perhaps she would just remove her shoes and hose and bathe her feet. The water felt good, and so she lifted her skirts and waded out to the middle.

Her horse snorted. There was a rustling of leaves.

"Who is it?" she called, frightened.

Ascanio came into view, his dark green tunic almost indistinguishable from the forest. "Do not be afraid. It is only me."

Fear gave way to relief and then pleasure at seeing him. "You frightened me. How did you know I was here?"

"I saw you ride through, and I followed. You shouldn't be riding alone like this." He reached out a hand to her, and she moved toward the bank.

"I was hoping I might see you," she said honestly.

"I have been waiting for you to come. I couldn't go to you. You know that, don't you?"

She lifted her face to his and he drew her close, then his lips were on her, tasting her neck, her eyes, her mouth.

"God only knows how I've wanted you," he told her. "You've wanted me too, haven't you?"

"Yes," she said. "Yes." Her breath was coming in short gasps.

His hands were busy with her clothing. "You are

wearing enough garments for a nun." His fingers found her breasts. He pushed aside her dress and kissed them. "How long has it been," he whispered, "Since you have had a man?"

She pressed herself against him for answer.

When it was over, they both lay panting and spent.

"We will never do this again," she said, turning her face away from him.

"I know," he said soberly.

Maria was waiting for them by the side of the road. "I will ride back with you," she said to Lucrezia, ignoring Ascanio's presence altogether. "It will look better that way."

CHAPTER 26

Two weeks later Alexander sent an emissary to King Federigo of Naples to negotiate for the return of Lucrezia's husband. If he did not do something soon, there would be no more tributes to the Vatican from Spoleto, for the officials there were outraged by Lucrezia's policies. It seemed that no man who molested a woman against her will was safe from her wrath. Every kitchenmaid, every field hand, had her ear and her sympathy. No longer could a nobleman mount a peasant woman with impunity in Spoleto.

Alexander shook his head and smiled. When he appointed Lucrezia to the office he had had no idea that she would take her duties so seriously. He had expected her to dally there much as she had dallied at home. Furthermore, it was rumored that she was carrying on a liaison with a young notary from the village. Well, she was not a nun. How long was she expected to do without a man? Yes, if Alexander knew what was good for him, he would get Alfonso back home as quickly as possible.

After many guarantees for Alfonso's safety, Federigo agreed to send him back to Rome. Alexander heaved a great sigh. If Federigo had not agreed, there was no telling what might have happened. Of course, if it had come to that, Alexander would have been forced to fall back on his own resources and have Alfonso abducted. But that would not have looked too well, and he thanked heaven it had not been necessary.

He knew Cesare would not be pleased by this turn of events. Cesare had never approved of the Aragon-Naples faction. It stood in the way of his designs against the Italian states. But Cesare was with the French forces in Milan for the time being, serving his apprenticeship under Louis before he struck out on his own. Cesare had chafed when Louis put the command of the forces in the able hands of the famous Captain Gian Giacomo Trivulzio, for he himself yearned to command. But as Louis had told him, patting him easily on the back, he was still young and his time would come.

Alfonso arrived at Spoleto late one evening in mid-September. The villagers had been harvesting their crops for the past month. The grape harvest had been left for last so that the grapes could store up sugar under the hot sun. The feet of the peasants were stained purple and would remain so until mid-winter for lack of washing. The air rang with their shouts and their laughter. Lucrezia had ordered fresh oxen to be killed and roasted each day that the harvest lasted. At first Lucrezia and Geoffrey and the entire contingent from Rome had joined in the festivities that marked the close of each day, but the Roman gentlemen, now unable to have their way with the simple country girls, soon tired of it all and returned to their hunting and falconry.

Lucrezia had seen Ascanio twice since the episode in

the forest, but they had not been alone together. She had seen the fever of possession in his eyes, though, and that haunted her, especially at night when she tossed and turned in her warm bed, feeling once again the touch of his skin on hers. Oh, but she would like to be able to leave this place now. It was not her home and never would be. She was homesick for the familiar sights of Rome, forgetting in her loneliness its rancid odors, its late-summer miasmas, the thick fetid smoke that rose from the pyres of burning garbage along the Tiber.

The day had been very hot, and the heat of the sun still lingered in the evening air, leaving long fingers of red against the sky. Lucrezia had washed her hair twice against the heat of the day and it lay damp and cool against her neck. Maria had flung open the shutters to let in whatever breeze there was. The odor of roasted oxen still hung in the air. There was the sound of evening bells from the village and then a clatter of hooves in the courtyard below. Perhaps a courier, a message from Alfonso, she thought wearily. She was too tired to stir. Whatever it was, Maria would let her know . . . Minutes later the door to her room was flung open and Alfonso ran to her side.

Lucrezia's first reaction was complete disbelief, then joy. The strength of his arms, the warmth of his face against hers, was no illusion. Overcome with love, she began to cry, the pent-up emotions of the last months coming through at last.

Later, as they lay side by side, she traced the contours of his body with her fingers. "That spot," she said, pointing to a birthmark on his shoulder. "I don't remember seeing that before."

He smiled gently. "Two months is a long time."

"You've heard about Ascanio, haven't you," she guessed.

"Yes, I've heard."

"Are you angry with me?" she asked in a small voice.

"Yes, I am angry."

"I'm glad," she said with relief. "I would not like it if you didn't care."

"How many times were you with him?"

"Once," she answered firmly. "Only once."

He held her close and squeezed her to him.

"What about you?" she asked anxiously. "Did you find someone too?"

"No," he whispered. "I waited for you."

In the morning he reached for her again. "How was it with him? As good as with me?"

"I don't remember," she lied.

"Good," he said soberly. "We will start all over again as though nothing has happened."

She kissed his neck, his ears, his eyes. "Promise," she whispered, "that you will never leave me again."

"I promise," he said, stroking the curve of her cheek. "But only because I see you cannot be trusted."

They had their breakfast on a table in front of the open doors leading out to the balcony. Maria had provided cold pheasant, a fresh loaf and honey in the comb, and a basket of fresh green figs.

Lucrezia peeled several figs and handed them to Alfonso, who took her fingers instead, kissing them and curling them into his own. After breakfast they strolled out onto the balcony and stood looking down at the rolling Umbrian countryside dotted with sheep and red-tiled roofs. The sound of bells drifted lazily up from the cathedral.

"The noonday bells," Lucrezia murmured. "Half the day is gone and I have done almost nothing."

"Half the day is gone and you have done almost everything," Alfonso said, watching her. "And now if you

292

don't mind, you may take that big belly of yours back to bed, as I have not quite finished with you."

"I have not bathed since last week," Lucrezia protested.

"I know," Alfonso said happily. "You smell like a warm cheese. But when you begin to smell like spoiled fish, I will let you know."

Lucrezia and Alfonso made their appearance at Sunday Mass at the cathedral fronting the Piazza del Duomo. Alfonso, to the amusement and cheers of the villagers, carried his pregnant wife up the soaring flight of steps, setting her down carefully at the top step and kissing her in front of everyone. The people went wild. They followed the young couple to the door of the cathedral with cries of *"Bravo! Bravissimo!"* Lucrezia, entranced, ordained another day of feasting.

"And who is to pay for all of this?" Alfonso asked her seriously.

"Why, Papa, of course," Lucrezia replied. "Who else?"

The warm days of autumn passed in leisurely splendor. Together they explored the countryside, riding out each day to a different place, a wicker basket of delicacies strapped to one of the horses. To Lucrezia, who had never been happier, the air seemed drenched in a golden haze which fell softly over the green rolling Umbrian hills, the groves of olive trees and the vineyards, the meadows dotted now with mounds of hay and grazing sheep. The only place they had not yet visited was the woods where Lucrezia had been with Ascanio.

Alfonso led the horses there now. But the place seemed different, almost alien somehow. The sun, at a lower angle now, bent its rays through the leafy arches, sending thick shafts of light through the trees, leaving the rest of the forest in darkness. When they came to the stream, Alfonso reined in the horses and stopped. "This seems a pleasant enough place. We will picnic here."

Lucrezia's face went white. "It is sunnier farther on."

"But there is water here and the horses can drink. Come, I'll help you down."

At lunch Lucrezia said little and ate almost nothing.

Alfonso watched her. Then he said, "Is this the place?"

Lucrezia nodded.

They passed some minutes in silence.

Alfonso broke off a blade of grass and chewed it thoughtfully. Then he gave her his hand. "Come, we will go."

On the way to the horses, she tripped over a root and nearly fell. As she tried to keep herself from falling, she reached out to the trunk of a tree. Growing in the shadow of the oak was the ghostly white outline of a parsley flower.

Alfonso, hearing her cry out, was concerned. "Have you hurt yourself?"

"No," she said, squeezing her eyes shut and crossing herself against this awful symbol of death. "But please take me home. I am cold."

Back in Rome, Alexander set about extricating Lucrezia from her role as Governor. "Your daughter," the Spoleto councilmen had written, "who is a pearl of goodness and tenderhearted in the extreme, champions the cause of every wayward girl. No man is safe from her wrath. No longer may the nobles dally, as is their wont and their right, with the maidens of the village. There is some talk of stopping Your Holiness's tributes, which come in the main, as you yourself

294

know, from the nobility themselves. We earnestly entreat Your Holiness to take this matter in hand."

Alexander set the letter aside and pondered. Now that Alfonso had returned, there was no longer any need for Lucrezia to remain in Spoleto. Also, in another month her child would be born and he wished to make certain it would be born on Roman soil. He took pen in hand and wrote.

Lucrezia waved the letter from Alexander in the air. Alfonso, who sat reading the poems of Catullus, looked up. "Papa wants us to come home now. I want to go. I am so tired of it here."

"I don't know," he said seriously, closing his book. "It is quiet here, and safe."

"Why, what do you mean? You know very well that Papa has made peace with everyone. There is nothing at all to worry about."

Alfonso took her hands and drew her onto his lap. How could he tell her that Alexander and Cesare were guilty of "kind words and hostile deeds"? Such was the talk going the rounds, since Cesare, who had finished up his term with Louis in Milan, made no secret of his plans to conquer the petty principalities of the Romagna and take them one by one for the Church of Rome.

Alexander, to clear the way, had drawn up proclamations stating that the lords of Pesaro, Imola, Faenza, Forlì, and Urbino had forfeited all their lands and titles since they had been delinquent in their tithes to the Church. No sooner was this accomplished than Cesare, who had been waiting impatiently, gathered together his army and marched on the Romagna.

Naples and Aragon were scandalized. Alfonso was uneasy. Who knew what Cesare might do next? This, then, was the situation they would be going home to.

"All right," he said reluctantly. "If you want to go home, we will go."

Lucrezia's eyes took on added sparkle. "When?"

"Whenever you like."

"Tomorrow?" she asked anxiously.

"Silly child, you know we cannot leave as soon as that."

A week later they entered Rome. Alexander, who had really missed them, blessed them both with tears in his eyes. Alfonso was reassured. Perhaps things were not as bad as he had imagined.

Their apartments in the Palace of Santa Maria in Portico had been freshened and aired, and Lucrezia returned to them joyfully, taking up and putting down each little trinket as though seeing it for the first time.

Even Geoffrey was glad to be back. The moral climate of Spoleto had stifled his worst impulses. He went immediately to the Street of the Prostitutes and was not seen for a week.

Alexander had arranged a surprise for his daughter. He clapped his hands and a great cradle was wheeled in. It was covered in gold leaf and canopied in white damask with the crests of the house of Borgia and the House of Aragon intertwined. At the head of the cradle Botticelli had painted some of his famous angels against a sky of azure.

Lucrezia touched it and smiled. "It is fit for a prince, Papa."

Two weeks later the child was born. Lucrezia was in the garden gathering herbs for a poultice when she felt the kick. The force of it nearly threw her down. "Maria?" she screamed.

Maria, who was instructing Angela in the manufacture of a pessary concocted of wild cucumber and breast milk to induce menstruation, came running. Together she and Angela lifted her to her feet. It was then that Lucrezia felt something warm sliding down her legs.

"I can't look," she screamed. "It's blood!"

"You have broken your water," Maria soothed. "That is all."

They carried her up to her bedchamber and laid her on the bed. A servant was sent to summon Alexander and another rode out after Alfonso, who had gone hunting. Hot water was ordered from the kitchen below.

Maria tied an apron around Angela and one around herself. "Do not worry," she said to Lucrezia, who was writhing in pain. "Your child simply wants to be born, that is all." She told Angela to fetch a basket of juniper berries and throw them on the fire to ward off any evil spirits which might be hovering over the birthing, waiting to enter the child. To Lucrezia she gave a thick length of hempen rope, directing her to bite it and pull on it.

"Please," Lucrezia begged, her eyes filling with tears. "Please get Alfonso!"

Maria administered a cup of thick brownish liquid. "They have gone to fetch him. Here, drink this. It will hasten the birth."

Lucrezia tasted it and gagged.

Maria meanwhile was carefully ripping Lucrezia's dress at the seams, so that it could be removed and later resewn. When she had removed the dress and the undergarments, she peered between Lucrezia's legs. The head had not yet appeared. An hour passed and still there was no child.

"He is a stubborn one," Maria muttered, putting some red pepper on a feather and shoving it under Lucrezia's nose. "Here, breathe it in."

Lucrezia breathed in and sneezed.

"Breathe again," Maria ordered her. "It will sneeze him out."

Alexander burst into the room. "And how is my grandson doing?" he demanded.

"Not well," Maria told him. "Perhaps we should send for your physician."

"You know very well that he will not assist at births. That is women's work. Now if she runs a fever afterward or hemorrhages, that is something else again."

"Papa!" Lucrezia screamed, her eyes rolling in pain. "Get Alfonso, please!" She shrieked as another pain tore into her.

"I don't think I can stand much more of this," Alexander said nervously. "I will wait out in the corridor." As he left the room, he almost collided with Alfonso. "Take care of her, my son. She needs you," he admonished him.

Lucrezia's son was born an hour later. It took Alfonso and Angela both to hold her down while Maria pulled the child out.

There was a copper basin of water in front of the fire. Maria carried the child over and sponged him clean. Then she rubbed him with warm olive oil and wrapped him in clean linen before placing him in a basket, where he promptly went to sleep. Next she tended Lucrezia. Dipping strips of linen into a basin of hot water and wringing them out, she washed away the blood. Then she sponged her face with a clean cloth and rolled the dirty sheets out from under her. Together she and Angela remade the bed with fresh linen, rolling Lucrezia gently onto the clean sheets.

"Make her drink this," Maria said to Alfonso, handing him a silver goblet of hot spiced wine and mare's milk. "It will bring forth the afterbirth."

Alfonso looked at his young wife. She seemed more

dead than alive. Her skin had the pallor of chalk. Her closed lids were veined with blue and her golden hair spread damp and lank against the pillow. He bent over her and kissed her softly. She had given him a son.

Alexander, hearing no more screams, tiptoed in. "Is it over?" he inquired.

"She has given you a fine grandson," Alfonso said proudly.

Alexander bent over the infant and unwrapped his bindings. "Well, he has everything he should have, but he is a bit on the puny side, is he not?"

"He is fine," Maria said stoutly. "As soon as we are through with Lucrezia, we will purge him with honey and then we will put him to the breast."

When Lucrezia awakened the room was dark except for the fire in the grate and the dim glow from a small oil lamp which hung by the side of her bed.

"I have been waiting all this time for you to get up," Maria grumbled, handing her the infant. "He is as hungry as a hound!"

"He is so tiny," Lucrezia said weakly. "Is he all right?"

"He is just as he should be," Maria said gruffly, rubbing her nipple with honey and putting him to the breast.

"Where is Alfonso?" Lucrezia asked.

"He is at supper with your father and Geoffrey. He was here through the birth, and he stayed until you fell asleep."

"I am still asleep," Lucrezia said drowsily. "Wake me when Alfonso comes back."

"I wish he weren't so funny-looking," Lucrezia said fretfully to Alfonso the following day.

"He is not at all funny-looking. He is my son."

"But he is," she said, tears of weariness sliding down

299

her cheeks. "His face is all wrinkled and red and his nose is pushed in." She began to weep loudly. "If he had sores, he would look like Orvieto."

Alfonso laughed. "Orvieto never looked that good in his life. When the milk comes, you will feel better."

Alfonso was worried, but he tried not to show it. So far nothing had come from her breasts but a thin watery fluid which, Maria said, would only give the baby colic if he drank it. If nothing happened soon, they would be obliged to engage a wet nurse. Maria had even tried rubbing Lucrezia's back with an ointment compounded of eels, but so far nothing had happened.

"It is because you will not eat," Maria said crossly. "How can you make food for an infant from nothing?"

"I am not hungry," Lucrezia said weakly."

Two weeks later, as Lucrezia watched from her bed, the child was baptised. The entire household had been preparing for this event ever since the birth. Floors were scrubbed, stairs were swept, new rushes were laid in the dining hall. In the kitchens and pantries the activity approached pandemonium. Great tubs of honey and olives and great casks of wine and oil were brought up from the cellars. Baskets of game and tubs of fish lay everywhere. The ovens and spits went day and night and through all the confusion the cooks and kitchenmaids ran back and forth, tripping over one another in their haste. Extra gold and silver service was brought over from the Vatican vaults, along with extra help to take care of all the guests and foreign dignitaries who were expected to attend the christening.

Through all of this Lucrezia lay, trying to nurse her child. On the day of the baptism, when all the carpets and tapestries had been swept and aired and everything was in order, Maria and Angela brought the infant from the wet nurse to his mother for another try at the breast. To everyone's astonishment, the milk gushed forth. Lucrezia, watching the miracle at her breast, was oblivious to everything but the sucking child.

When Maria came to wash her hair for the ceremony, Lucrezia refused to let the baby go. "He will drown," Maria said firmly, removing him with force. After she had washed Lucrezia's hair, she took a sponge and bathed the upper portion of her body. "The rest will have to wait until you are healed," she said. Over her head she pulled a gold brocade dressing gown with long flowing sleeves. "There," she said proudly, "you look like an angel. Now let us hope that no one looks under the sheets."

Lucrezia studied herself in the silver hand mirror. "I look as pale as a corpse." she complained. "Perhaps some of Sancia's rouge . . ."

Maria refused. "You are a mother, not a whore."

When the time came for the baptism, Lucrezia sat waiting, propped up on a mass of pillows against a backdrop of blue velvet. One by one the visitors filed past her bed. Lucrezia smiled wanly at them all and thanked them for coming. Soon, she thought gratefully, it would be all over. Everyone would go in to the feast, and she would have the infant to nurse again.

In the Sistine Chapel Cardinal Cosenza christened the baby Rodrigo after the Pope and then handed him over to Paolo Orsini as proof of Alexander's good will toward the Orsini family. The infant, who was full of milk, immediately made water and began to howl. A bad omen, Burchard decided. Paolo Orsini made light of it, looking at his hands and laughing. The rest of the company laughed along with him. Then little Rodrigo was restored at last to Lucrezia's waiting arms.

CHAPTER 27

Cesare returned to Rome a week later and went immediately to see Lucrezia. He found his sister in bed, propped up against the pillows, her golden hair falling about her shoulders, the baby Rodrigo at her breast.

"Is he not beautiful?" she asked him at once. "Do you not think he resembles Alfonso?"

"No," he said sourly. "He looks like you."

"I am so glad you are here," she said happily. "Now everything is perfect."

Watching her with her child, Cesare thought he had never seen anything so beautiful. Why, then, did he feel as though his heart were pricked with needles? "I have brought you something," he said, taking out a small leather box. "I hope you like it." He opened the box at her delighted request and drew out a cabochon ruby brooch set with diamonds.

"Cesare," she exclaimed, "it's beautiful. Pin it on me, please."

"It is from Charlotte and me," he said, fastening it

302

to her wrapper and trying not to notice the small rosy breast at which the child sucked.

"How is Charlotte?"

"She is with child," he answered shortly. "At least that is what she says."

"When will you see her again?"

"I don't know," he replied indifferently. "When I am through campaigning, I suppose."

"Do you not miss her?" she asked seriously.

"Miss her?" he repeated. "Why, no, I do not think so. My head is full of other things."

At that point Alfonso walked into the room. The two men looked at one another and said nothing. Finally Cesare bowed. Alfonso bowed back.

"You are to be congratulated," Cesare said. "You have a fine son."

"Yes," Alfonso said modestly. "And he has a fine mother."

Lucrezia, looking happily from one to the other, interrupted. "Alfonso, look at what Cesare has brought me from France. Is it not beautiful?"

Alfonso bent to kiss his wife. "It is beautiful. Almost as beautiful as you."

Cesare, watching, felt the needles prick him anew. "I must go," he said, bending over to kiss Lucrezia on the cheek. "I have not yet seen my father." He nodded to Alfonso and left.

When Cesare entered Alexander's study, his father rose and clasped him eagerly, kissing him on both cheeks. "It is good to see you," he said, holding him away and looking at him. "You seem taller than when we last met."

"I am the same, Father." He paused a moment, then asked abruptly, "What are we going to do about Alfonso?"

"What do you mean?" Alexander said, taken aback. "I thought we had settled all that."

"We have settled nothing."

"I do not think I understand," Alexander said uncomfortably. "Your sister has a child."

"Yes, and the child has a father."

"Well, and what is so unusual about that?"

"Nothing," Cesare snapped, "except that he is a political embarrassment. Either send him home and dissolve the marriage or else get rid of him."

"I will do nothing of the kind," Alexander replied firmly, for he was genuinely fond of his son-in-law. "I fail to see why you cannot get along with him. He troubles no one. His only interests are his wife, his child, and his books."

"It is what he represents. The Naples faction will never go along with our consolidation of the Italian states. They see it as a threat. It would make things much easier, Father, if Alfonso were in Naples where he belongs."

"And what about your sister?"

"She will get used to it."

"No," Alexander said firmly. "I will not go through that particular thing again. Now let us talk about your plans."

"By all means," Cesare said. "And while we are doing that, allow me to inform you that Louis plans to take Naples. Not only is he relying upon me for assistance in this, but he has made it a condition of his support."

"All right," Alexander said wearily. "We will deal with it when we have to, but not now."

Cesare smiled. At least he had set the stage. The rest would follow. He could wait until the battle at Forlì was over.

As the weeks passed, reports began filtering back from the battlefields. Cesare had won stunning victories at Imola and Forlì. He had completely subjugated the ferocious amazon Caterina Sforza, who had ruled those provinces with an iron hand and who, it was rumored, was hung with the genitals of all her past husbands and lovers. Not only had he subdued her, but he incarcerated her in a cage like an animal and marched her through the town so that her former subjects could jeer and poke at her. She had not been a popular ruler. She had overtaxed her people to the point of poverty, earning herself the title both at home and abroad of "Amazon, Devil Incarnate."

Alexander was jubilant. "Cesare was born to rule. The people love him."

Lucrezia too was proud of him. "Just think," she said to Alfonso, "he has returned two of the Italian states to the Church. Geoffrey could never have done that!"

Alfonso looked distracted.

Lucrezia caught up the infant Rodrigo and held him to her. "There will be lots of parties," she said, her eyes shining with happiness. "I'll have to have some dresses made, and I'll need some shoes to go with them. Oh, it's been so dull around here. Perhaps Charlotte will come and visit now. I would so like to meet her."

Alfonso bent over and kissed her lightly. She was such a child. Then he went to his study and wrote to the Neapolitan ambassador, suggesting that he and Lucrezia visit Naples with their infant son.

Meanwhile Alexander made extravagant plans for Cesare's triumphal entry into Rome. It was the year 1500, the occasion of a fiftieth jubilee. He planned to celebrate the two events together, thereby giving Cesare's accomplishment added glory. Carpenters were ordered to build reviewing stands along the newly constructed Via di Borgo Nuovo which led to St. Peter's Square. Jewelers and goldsmiths were commissioned to fashion medallions commemorating the occasion. Seamstresses and tailors were kept busy making new clothes and repairing old. There was not a family in Rome who did not attend to its wardrobe in anticipation of the coming festivities.

A week before the event Alfonso entered Alexander's study. "I have decided to go home for a little visit," he said. "I would like to take Lucrezia and Rodrigo with me. My family has never seen them."

Alexander looked up from the speech he was writing. "When would you like to go?"

"As soon as possible," Alfonso said firmly, showing him a letter from the Neapolitan ambassador. "My mother is not well, and one never knows what will happen in such cases. I would like her to see her grandchild."

Alexander looked at the letter briefly and handed it back. "If you leave now, everyone will think that you have something to fear. Believe me, my son, no one wishes to harm you."

"Then you will not give me permission to leave?"

Alexander squirmed uncomfortably. "How can I? If you leave before Cesare returns, everyone will say that you are afraid, and that would look bad for us. If you leave afterward, they will say the same thing."

"I do not care what they say," Alfonso replied. "I simply wish to live in peace with my wife and my son."

Alexander leaned forward and grasped Alfonso's hands in his own. "I give you my word that no one shall harm you, for if they did, they would be harming me. I think of you as my own son. You know that, do you not?"

Alfonso looked away. "Unfortunately Cesare does not feel as you do."

Alexander waved that off. "Cesare has other things to think about, as you know. No more of this nonsense, my boy. By the way, I had almost forgotten," he said, reaching across his desk and picking up a small metal casket. "I have something for you." Alexander opened the casket and drew out a heavy gold chain and medallion. He placed it around Alfonso's neck. "There, my son. I had one made for each of my children. Wear it in good health, and may God bless you and keep you."

The medallion, Alfonso noticed, was an exact replica of his own profile. He was moved by this. All at once he felt ashamed that he had ever doubted Alexander's word. "I will treasure this always," he said quietly. "As you know, I have no quarrel with you. You have been like a father to me. It is only that I feel my position here may become untenable as a result of your consolidation of the Italian states."

"Nonsense, my boy. Everything that we do is for the family, of which you are now a member. So put all such thoughts away from you. They have no place in your head now or ever."

"You see," Lucrezia said happily when Alfonso showed her the medallion. "I told you there was nothing to worry about."

"I hope you are right," he said, fingering the heavy chain thoughtfully.

But Lucrezia was already out of the room and running to her painting lesson, which her father's new artist, Filippino Lippi, was conducting for some of the high-born ladies in one of the salons on the main floor.

This day, however, no one was paying any attention. Instead they sat in groups and chattered, discussing what they would wear at all the parties. Her handsome brother was coming home a hero, and Lucrezia, looking at the ladies of the court, knew what would happen. They would all, married or not, do their best to flirt with Cesare. Some of them would no doubt end up in bed with him. The others would simply have a good time. She smiled. It was nice to be able to think of something pleasant for a change.

Cesare entered Rome on a cold, wintry day to the wild clanging of bells. Alexander had decreed that every church in the city ring out its welcome. The entire pupulace had turned out to greet him, thronging forward, anxious to catch a glimpse of a real hero, a thing wondrous and rare.

Cesare had dressed down for the occasion, wearing a simple suit of black velvet, adorned only with the Order of St. Michael. The noble ladies of Rome nearly swooned at the sight of him.

Cesare rode between Cardinal Orsini and Cardinal Farnese. Directly behind him, at Alexander's insistence, rode Lucrezia's husband, Alfonso, Duke of Bisceglie. Behind him rode Geoffrey, looking arrogant and puffed up with pride. Last of all came one hundred men armed with clubs to beat off the mob should it become necessary.

Alexander, who had been waiting impatiently on the loggia to catch a glimpse of his son, felt his eyes brim with tears when Cesare finally knelt before him. He blessed him and bade him rise. Then pandemonium broke loose and Cesare was besieged on all sides by the cardinals, bishops, and ambassadors of the court, all anxious to pay homage to this new warrior. The ladies watched, and waited their turn.

Cesare was at his best now. Always the consummate actor, he smiled and bowed modestly, charming everyone.

"You see," one of the cardinals said to Burchard,

who was watching from the sidelines. "He is not as bad as we thought."

"No," Burchard replied. "He is worse."

"What do you mean?" the poor man asked, flustered.

"Unlike the hyena, who begins to feed at once, *he* first takes the trouble to smile and adjust his napkin."

At the banquet that night Lucrezia wore a white velvet dress trimmed in sable and cut low to show her breasts, which were still full from nursing.

Alexander had organized all sorts of events for the following day. "We will given them their money's worth," he said to Cesare. "It will sweeten the tax raise." Accordingly he staged horse and chariot races that recalled the glories of ancient Rome, as well as pageants and plays. Bonfires and fireworks lit the city at night. People thronged by the thousands to the Piazza Navona, transported from their ordinary selves into something grander. He was all right, that Pope of theirs, they told one another, and that son of his, he was a handsome dog who had brought new glory to Rome.

On Sunday, March 29, everything was in readiness for the jubilee. Between shafts of light Cesare walked with measured steps down the nave and across the transept where Alexander was to crown him Gonfalonier of the Church. Alexander waited in the choir surrounded by the entire Sacred College and members of the court. After he invoked a blessing, Burchard removed Cesare's brocade gown. Alexander then placed the mantle of the Gonfalonier around him, saying, "May the Lord endow you with this cloak of salvation and place around you the garment of joyousness, in the name of the Father, the Son and the Holy Ghost. Amen."

The choir burst into song, puffs of incense filled the

air, and myriad candles sent points of flame ceiling-ward. Then Alexander, canny enough to merge his son's elevation to Gonfalonier with the jubilee celebration, watched as pilgrims from all over the world paid homage. The gold from their purses, he thought, would more than make up for the deficits in the treasury incurred by Cesare's campaigns in Forlì and Imola. After Louis withdrew his support, Alexander had sold benefices, confiscated properties, and levied higher taxes. The jubilee, which brought thousands of people into Rome, was one more source of revenue, and Alexander was determined to milk it for all it was worth. He taxed the houses of prostitution and the merchants impartially, knowing that they would both do a thriving business. There was no reason why the Borgia family should not benefit from both religion and sin, Alexander reasoned.

The streets of Rome were teeming with people day and night, for the inns, filled to capacity, could hold no more.

Lucrezia had no taste for the crowds. She busied herself instead with her accounts, her needlework, and little Rodrigo. Occasionally she would interrupt Alfonso in a historical project he was working on for Alexander. Several of her interruptions had resulted in their making love on the floor of the study amidst the books, papers, and quills. Afterward Alfonso would kiss her and go back to his books, where he was entirely at home.

CHAPTER 28

In the spring of the year the Borgia star was riding high. The pilgrims had finally returned to their homes, leaving Rome a shambles. Refuse was piled into heaps and burned. The daily bonfires cast a pall of smoke over the city, creating a constant stink. The weather had turned uncomfortably warm, promising the threat of Roman fever in the heat of summer. "All we need now," Alexander said, "is an outbreak of plague."

His exchequer was kept busy counting the gold coins which kept pouring in. Everyone, it seemed, even those who had not made the pilgrimage to Rome, wished to be absolved of something.

"Thank God for sin," Alexander commented happily.

Between the jubilee and all the benefices he was selling, Cesare would have more than enough money to continue his campaign in the Romagna, with or without Louis.

"It would be nice," Alexander said, "to have Louis

on our side, but if he won't come over to us, we can always appeal to Spain for support."

Cesare, aware of his father's weakness for his Spanish heritage, felt otherwise. His own ties were in France. He had just received word that Charlotte had been delivered of a baby girl, whom she called Luisa. "I would rather have Louis than Spain," he said firmly.

In the end it was Niccolò Machiavelli, now at the French court, who prevailed upon Louis to throw in his lot with Cesare once more. A loyal Italian patriot, Machiavelli realized that Italy's only chance to be strong lay in unification, and that this could be accomplished only by someone with a strong hand, someone who could subjugate and unify all the bickering Italian states into one cohesive force. Cesare, he believed, could do it.

"But what do we do about Venice?" Louis asked. "They are our allies."

Machiavelli smiled. "We shall remain allies up to a point. However, you need Rome to get to Naples, and Rome needs you to help in the unification of her states."

"What about Lucrezia and Alfonso? You cannot expect the Pope to cast out his own son-in-law."

"He will not have to," Machiavelli said carefully. "I understand that there is no love lost between Cesare and his brother-in-law."

Louis's assistance came just in time, for Cesare knew that he was not yet strong enough to stand alone. He could not rely forever upon Alexander. He was seventy years of age, and he was beginning to show it. Although he was healthy and vigorous enough, he could not be expected to continue this way indefinitely. This was brought home to Cesare by a series of disturbing events.

Alexander was working in his study on a warm June

day when suddenly, without warning, the heavy plaster ceiling fell on him, burying him almost totally. Were it not for the cloth-of-gold canopy over his lectern, which broke the fall of the ceiling, he might have been killed.

Lucrezia had just organized a musicale for that evening and was in the midst of arranging for refreshments when one of the Vatican guards rushed in. She and Alfonso went immediately to the Vatican. Gaspare de Torre was cauterizing the wound in Alexander's head. Several attendants stood about with basins and cloths.

Lucrezia rushed to her father's side. The sudden appearance of frailty appalled her. "Papa," she said, "I will take care of you myself. Alfonso and I will move in next door with the baby. Alfonso, please have Maria and Angela bring Rodrigo and cancel the musicians. There will be no musicale tonight."

With Maria's help, they set up a kitchen in the alcove of his apartment. Alexander, who normally trusted no one, now feared even more for his life. It was not uncommon to try to unseat a man when he was down. He would not eat anything except what Lucrezia prepared for him with her own hands. After a week of convalescence he grew more confident, and finally his fears dissipated. But for the first time in his long life, Alexander had been confronted with his own mortality. He realized now that his children must be protected beyond his own lifetime. For at his death, he would not be able to prevent the run on the treasury that always followed the death of a Pope.

His first act of business as soon as he was well enough was to issue a decree that cardinals' hats would henceforth be given only to those favorably disposed to Cesare and his policy of confederation. He did the same thing with benefices. Next he acquired for Lucrezia the city of Sermoneta together with the castle

313

and the grounds, which had recently been taken away from the Caetani family, who had had the bad sense to sympathize with Aragon. Her holdings now included the duchies of Bisceglie, Nepi, and Sermoneta, in addition to Spoleto, which she had governed briefly.

Cesare through all of this was busy charming the people of Rome. Whenever he rode by with his personal guard, everyone rushed out to see him. He had formally affected black as his daily wear, and he was a striking figure on his black charger, his auburn curls framing his handsome face. The zenith of his popularity was reached one hot summer's day when he rode into the bullring and, armed only with a sword, jumped from his horse and beheaded with one stroke an enormous bull which had just been let loose. The entire arena went mad. *"Il Duce!"* they shouted with one throat. *"Il Duce!"* Soon all of Rome was at his feet, shouting his name whenever he appeared.

His reputation traveled all the way to France. Louis, hearing of his latest exploits, smiled. "It will be good to see him again, the devil. There is no one else like him."

All the old and best families of Italy, who had hitherto stood off from the Borgia clan, now made advances. Foremost amongst these were Isabella d'Este and her husband, Francesco Gonzaga. Isabella had tutored Lucrezia before her marriage to Giovanni Sforza, and these two, Francesco and Isabella, notoriously turned with every wind that blew. They went so far as to ask Cesare to be godfather to their newborn child.

Amidst all this furor Cesare kept his head. He would need it, he reasoned, for the coming campaign in Faenza in the fall. As for Charlotte and his child, he had heard that the baby Luisa was hideously ugly, and he did not wish to see her. He sent Charlotte a letter of congratulations on the birth of his daughter, together

314

with a gift of some spices and oranges and twenty yards of cloth so that she could have some dresses made. To the child he sent nothing.

Lucrezia remonstrated with him. "You should send for Charlotte and Luisa. Now that Giulia has gone to live with her family, I have no one close, no one I can really talk to. Charlotte and I could be friends."

"She is happy where she is," Cesare said.

When Charlotte received his letter, she wept. She truly loved her husband, and she had hoped that the birth of their child might bring him back to her.

As for Lucrezia, she moved even closer to Alfonso, taking on some of his interests and presiding over a small salon which included all the literary lights of Rome. Alfonso, always bookish, had taken on a tutor. Not to be outdone, Lucrezia sponsored a poet, Vincenzo Calmeta, a man whose verse was well received throughout Italy. At Lucrezia's request Alexander settled upon him a good income and a fine house, and he was constantly in their company. Lucrezia had taken to carrying about with her a little red-leather volume of Petrarch. His love poems appealed to her now as much as they had all those years ago at Monte Giordano, when Carlos had first introduced her to them. She still thought of Carlos with affection. He had become a model to her of all that was good and desirable in a man. It was strange how much Alfonso resembled him in both looks and temperament.

As for painters, there were always Lippi, and Pintoricchio, who had covered the walls of the Sistine Chapel with paintings depicting the various members of the Borgia family as saints and madonnas. She had prevailed upon Lippi to paint a portrait of Alfonso, as she had only a miniature of him. There was Michelangelo, but he was moody and tense. He hated gatherings of

315

any kind and was really interested only in his work and his young boys.

Alfonso's portrait was almost finished when Alexander became ill with Roman fever.

"Papa wants us to stay at the Vatican," Lucrezia said to Alfonso. "It is just until he is better. Then we can go home."

Lucrezia saw to Alexander's diet and to his comfort, again allowing nothing to touch his lips except that which she and Maria had prepared. For the most part, she just sat in the airless room with him and waited until he needed her. Alexander would not permit them to open the windows. "The air will do me in," he fretted.

In his delirium he muttered constantly, as though carrying on a conversation with someone he knew. At one point he screamed and made a horrible face.

"He is speaking with the Devil," Maria said, crossing herself.

Two days later, at four in the morning, he groaned and sat up. "Bring me something to eat. I am hungry!"

Lucrezia was fast asleep, but his voice brought her fully awake. "Maria," she called, "make some broth!" The two of them sat on either side of him, Lucrezia feeding him and Maria wiping his chin.

"Cesare has been here every day, asking for you," Lucrezia told him.

Alexander shivered. "I saw your brother Juan. He said that Cesare murdered him."

"Papa, you were out of your head with fever," Lucrezia reproached him.

"He was all in white," Alexander continued, as if he hadn't heard her. "Half eaten away by fishes, that beautiful boy. Juan, my favorite son." Tears began to slip from his eyes. "Ah, this fever has made an old man of me," he said, wiping his eyes with a corner of the sheet.

Maria brought a basin of warm water and began to shave him. Alexander winced at the razor's touch, for his skin was still sensitive from the fever.

"You must promise not to leave me alone in the room with Cesare," he said after he was shaved.

"All right, Papa. I promise," Lucrezia answered. She helped him to a chair so that she and Maria could remove the fever-soaked sheets and lay fresh ones.

"Where is Alfonso?" Alexander asked when he was back in his bed. "I want to speak to him."

"I'll get him," Lucrezia said, "if you promise to rest."

"I will rest after I speak to him," Alexander said stubbornly. He lay against the pillows, refusing to close his eyes until his son-in-law came. When Alfonso entered the room, he reached out to him. "Come close, my boy. It is good to see you again."

"Thank you, Your Holiness," Alfonso said, pleased by Alexander's greeting.

"I want you to go to Naples and visit your family. And you must take Lucrezia and Rodrigo with you."

"That is very good of you, Your Grace, but we cannot think of leaving until you are entirely well."

"I am well," Alexander said firmly. "Believe me, I am well. See if there is not a ship leaving this week. If there is, take it."

"There is no hurry. We can just as well wait." Alfonso was at a loss to understand Alexander's sudden change of heart.

"No!" Alexander almost shouted. "You must listen to me in this, I beg of you!"

"All right," Alfonso said, looking across the room at Lucrezia. "If it brings you peace, we will go."

Alexander, looking past them, suddenly appeared terrified, his eyes starting from his head. They turned to see what had frightened him.

Cesare had entered the room unannounced and stood smiling at them from the doorway. "Why was I not told that you were holding court, Father?"

Alexander's voice was unsteady. "I still have some fever. I did not wish to contaminate you."

"But my dear sister is here, and her dear husband . . . Are you not afraid of contaminating *them?*"

"You cannot afford to become ill, Cesare. You have too much ahead of you."

"Is that really so, Father? Well, I am glad that you think so. And how are you, my dear brother?" he asked, extending his smile to Alfonso.

Alfonso nodded briefly. "I am quite well, thank you."

"I could not help overhearing. Are you planning a little trip?"

"I am not certain yet." Alfonso looked at Alexander, who had turned white.

"In any case," Cesare said pleasantly, "if you are finished with your visit, I should like a few words with His Holiness in private."

Alfonso nodded. "Come, Lucrezia."

"What, no kiss for your dear brother?" Cesare said to her in mock dismay.

Lucrezia looked at him sternly. "You are agitating Papa, and he is still very weak. Do you want me to stay?" she asked her father.

"No," he said wearily. "It is all right. You may go."

"If you need anything, just ring," Lucrezia said, pointing to the bell rope at the side of the bed.

"Why should he need anything," Cesare asked, "as long as I am here?"

When the door closed behind them, he went over and sat down on Alexander's bed. "Are you entirely mad? How can you think of allowing him to leave Rome?"

318

"Why not?" Alexander asked weakly.

"Why not? You can ask why not, after all the plans I have made? You know how Louis feels about him, how he feels about Naples. And you are going to let him go home so he can babble about everything that goes on here?"

Alexander sighed. "He will not babble. If he wishes to babble, he can always do so in a letter."

"That is not likely," Cesare said. "He must be aware that his mail is being intercepted."

"By whom?" Alexander asked.

"That is not the point. The point is that he is now an embarrassment to us politically."

"If that is true," Alexander said quietly, "then let him go home in peace."

"It is said that you look upon him as your own son."

Alexander said nothing.

"And how do you look upon me?"

"I should like to sleep now," Alexander said wearily. "I am suddenly very tired."

"First it was Juan," Cesare muttered, "and now it is Alfonso. Why can it not be me, your own son? Can you not see how far above him I stand? In everything?"

Alexander looked at him, his eyes filled with pity. "You are Lucifer," he whispered, "fallen from grace. God help you, my son. God help you."

Lucrezia stayed on at the Vatican with her father for a few more days.

Alfonso went back and forth between the Vatican and the Santa Maria Palace. He had secured passage on a ship to Naples, preparing to go home.

It was a warm summer evening in July. He had just finished dining with Lucrezia and Alexander at the Vatican when Alexander grabbed his hand suddenly and raised himself up from the pillows. "Be careful to trust no one, my son. Have a hundred eyes in your head, like Argus."

"I am careful," Alfonso said simply. "Goodnight, Your Holiness." He kissed Lucrezia and went out into the night with his companion, Tommaso Albanese, and his master of the horse. The air was warm and fragrant with the scent of shrubs and flowers. Alfonso sniffed appreciatively and looked at the moon which sat like a silver sauceboat in the sky. "It will be fine tomorrow," he said to Tommaso. "I hope the weather holds until we sail."

They quitted the Vatican grounds, saluting the guards who let them out of the gate, and turned into St. Peter's Square, the sound of their boots on the paving stones echoing in the clear air.

Suddenly there was a movement from one of the archways and several men rushed forward with drawn swords. The night rang with the clash of steel on steel.

"Look to yourselves!" Alfonso shouted to his escort. "It is me they want!"

His two men stood by him, fighting furiously. Alfonso fought well, but he was no match for the hired assassins. One sword thrust got him in the shoulder, another in the arm. He would have fought on but for a blow to his head, which knocked him to the ground. His companions, although themselves wounded, immediately began dragging him back toward the Vatican and shouting for help. There was a sudden stream of light as the Vatican gates opened and the papal guards rushed out. The attackers took to their horses and galloped off into the night.

They carried Alfonso bleeding into the Borgia apartments, where Lucrezia was getting ready for bed. At the sight of her husband, his head spouting blood, she fell senseless to the floor.

320

Maria ran forward and began tearing off his doublet and shirt, pressing them to his head to stanch the bleeding. "Get de Torre," she ordered, and then, noticing the way his eyes rolled back in his head, she screamed for a priest to administer last rites.

Angela, who had been sleeping in the alcove with the infant Rodrigo, looked white-faced at the bleeding man, whose lips were already turning blue.

"Attend to Madonna Lucrezia," Maria shouted at her. "Slap her wrists and her face!"

As Lucrezia came to, they were lifting Alfonso gently onto the bed. She saw nothing but the priest bending over him and she began to scream.

Gaspare de Torre turned to silence her. "Be quiet," he ordered her sternly. "He is not dead yet! Cut away the undergarments," he directed Maria.

She drew a pair of shears from a nearby chest, but the blood quickly glutted the blades. In desperation she took the fabric between her fingers and tore it in two.

"Warm water and bindings!" de Torre shouted.

Lucrezia, looking at the mass of blood spreading over the sheets, fell to her knees and began praying.

Alexander's massive body filled the doorway, his face turning to ashes. "What has happened?" he asked hollowly.

Tommaso Albanese, his doublet cut to shreds, blood running down his face, came forward. "It happened as we were leaving the Vatican, Your Holiness, at the foot of St. Peter's Square. Several men came out of the shadows and attacked us. When they saw the guards, they jumped on their horses and rode off."

"Who were they?" Alexander asked steadily. "Did you see their faces?"

"It was too dark."

Alexander nodded thoughtfully. Then he went over to Lucrezia and took her into his arms. "There, my child," he said, rocking her back and forth. "My poor little girl. Try to compose yourself. He must not see you in tears, he must not."

"Some coarse salt," de Torre was saying. "We must apply it to the wounds to cleanse them."

There was a low moan from the bed.

"Thirty thousand gold ducats if you pull him through!" Alexander shouted to the doctor.

De Torre shrugged. "It is out of my hands entirely."

"Thirty thousand ducats," Alexander repeated. "You must save him!"

"I will do everything. Your Grace. Everything within my power."

Alexander looked down at Alfonso's battered head and looked away. "Whoever has done this will pay!"

"If I am not needed," Tommaso said, "I should like to go. I can stay with Vincenzo Calmeta. We are friends."

"Yes," Alexander said absently. "God go with you."

Lucrezia, who was slowly gaining back her composure, came forward and kissed Tommaso's hand. "God bless you," she said. "And you as well," she added, turning to the master of the horse. "Without your help he might already be dead."

Alexander looked at his daughter, pride welling up within him. She was far stronger than she seemed, thank heaven. Now he must deal with Cesare.

"I hope you realize," Cesare said as he was ushered into Alexander's room, "that you have taken me away from a very delightful evening. I hope it is important."

"Why did you do it!" Alexander demanded tersely. "Why could you not let him go in peace?"

"I am not certain I know what you are talking about," Cesare said mildly.

"And I am certain that you know exactly," Alexan-

der retorted sharply. "Alfonso has been severely wounded, and I am laying it at your door."

"Is that so?" Cesare said, making a great show of
surprise. "How can that be? Everyone here loves him
so."

"Your hand in this thing was not seen," Alexander
said, "but I'm certain that it was there."

"My dear father," Cesare said solicitously, "I'm
afraid the fever has affected your mind."

"My mind was never clearer."

Cesare's voice rose sharply. "I will not be accused
every time some faint-hearted fool falls in the streets!"

"Alfonso is neither faint-hearted nor a fool. Neither
did he fall. He was felled."

"What I cannot understand," Cesare said stubbornly, "is why you should take his part against me,
your own son."

"My own son," Alexander repeated. "I cannot understand that either."

"Look, Father, you have been ill and it is late.
Things may look different in the light of day. For my
part, I will station my own personal guard before Alfonso's door to see that he is not molested any further,
and I will do everything in my power to apprehend his
assassins."

Cesare's ploy was clear. He had eased himself out of
it, and he invited Alexander to do the same. It would
simplify matters for both of them. Alexander had no
real proof. Perhaps Cesare had had nothing to do with
it, after all. Dear God, if only that were so . . .

"Look at me," he entreated Cesare. "Look at me
and tell me that you had nothing to do with it."

Cesare fastened his eyes on his father and with an
unflinching gaze said, "I had nothing to do with it, so
help me God!"

Alexander dropped his eyes wearily. "So be it. In

323

the morning, it might look better for all of us if you were to personally issue an edict posting a reward for the apprehension of the assassins."

"Of course, Father. Whatever you think best," Cesare said, attempting to embrace him.

Alexander held up his hand. "I am too tired for that. I am going to bed."

By morning Alfonso's condition had not changed.

"He will get better," Lucrezia said firmly. "I know that he will, with God's help."

Toward noon Alfonso opened his eyes. The first person he saw was Lucrezia.

"Caro mio," she said, attempting to smile. "Do not try to speak, my dear one. Rest."

"Another pillow," de Torre ordered, "to ease the congestion. And bring some more salt to cleanse the wounds. Are you in pain?" he asked him.

Alfonso nodded weakly.

De Torre opened his bag and extracted a vial of belladonna. He poured some into a goblet and added wine. "Drink this," he said, pressing it against Alfonso's lips.

Alfonso tried to swallow, but the liquid made him choke, and ran out the corners of his mouth.

"Try not to cough," de Torre said. "It will open the wound."

With the doctor's help, Alfonso was able to swallow half the contents of the goblet before he fell back weakly against the pillows.

The next morning they moved him to Alexander's private wing for greater comfort and security. The rooms were large and light. Into these had been brought furniture in vermilion leather from Aragon, which the Pope thought would make Alfonso feel at home. As an added precaution Lucrezia and Maria would supervise the preparation of all his food.

Alexander dispatched a courier to King Federigo, asking him to send his own personal physician and surgeon. "Do not dally," he had written. "Send them quickly." In case Alfonso did not recover, he did not want the King of Naples to cry that his nephew had succumbed to inexpert medicine.

The room resembled a large camp. Lucrezia had ordered a cot brought to the foot of Alfonso's bed for herself. Maria and Angela lay on pallets in the alcove, next to Rodrigo's cradle. Cardinal Corletti, who was afraid to leave lest he be suddenly needed to administer last rites, snoozed in a large chair. De Torre rested on a rug beside Alfonso's bed.

The room was hot and airless. De Torre ordered the women to open the windows and shutters and to snuff out the candles. "They create too much heat," he said. "We do not want him to sweat into his wounds."

Two weeks later King Federigo's personal physician and surgeon arrived, together with Alfonso's sister Sancia. When Lucrezia saw her, she broke down and cried.

"It is all right, my heart," Sancia said, kissing her gently. "We who love him will make him well, you'll see."

Signors Clemente and Galeano, Federigo's men, approached the bed and examined the patient. They tasted, probed, and sniffed. The fever had gone, but the head wound was still serious. They applied balms, poultices, and leeches while de Torre looked sourly on.

"Be of good cheer, my man," Alexander said to him, taking him aside. "You are still entitled to the thirty thousand, and I will see that you receive it."

A week later Alfonso was sitting up in bed and taking nourishment. Maria had boiled him a chicken with some cloves and tarragon. The physicians insisted that she add some carrot and onion, to keep his bowels open. Lucrezia sat beside him feeding him the broth together with some pieces of white meat. Little Rodrigo was allowed to sit on the bed and was given a drumstick to gum. He banged it against his mouth and crowed, looking around for approval.

Alfonso looked at him and smiled. "Well, he still has a father, it seems."

"And I have a husband," Lucrezia said, bending over and kissing his cheek.

Alexander, considerably cheered by the way things were going, resumed his Vatican duties. The Neapolitan ambassador looked in once or twice a day. Lucrezia and Sancia sewed and chatted in a sunny corner. And Vincenzo Calmeta, the court poet, at whose home Tommaso was recuperating, wrote to King Federigo that all suspicion pointed to Cesare, but that "the wounds are not fatal if they are not added to."

The poet was assured of immunity from Cesare's wrath by virtue of his prodigious correspondence with nobility throughout the world. "They would be stupid to attack my house," he said when he invited Tommaso to stay with him for safety's sake. "If they did that, the whole world would know it." Vincenzo Calmeta kept in touch with Lucrezia, and during the last weeks of Alfonso's convalescence he came to visit, bringing with him a much-prized copy of Dante's poems. In parting he said to Alfonso, "They say that the face of your would-be assassin is as familiar to you as your own. Take care and trust no one." To Federigo he wrote that Alfonso would set sail for home as soon as his health permitted and before anyone had a chance to finish the job.

Another week passed, and Alfonso improved so much that he was allowed out of bed for short periods.

Sancia was delighted. "There is no reason why we cannot go home in another week or two."

Alexander agreed. He booked passage for them on a ship that was sailing in two weeks' time, adding, "By then he will be as fit as a flea."

A week before they were to sail, Cesare paid a visit unexpectedly. Sancia was sitting with a piece of needlework on her lap. With her left foot, she rocked the cradle.

"Ah, my dear sister-in-law." His voice caught her by surprise. "I had heard that you were here, and since you did not come to see me, I have come to see you, and Alfonso too, of course," he added, nodding to his brother-in-law, who looked at him stonily from the bed.

Lucrezia came from the alcove, where she had been heating some broth, and stared at him without speaking.

He went over and kissed her on the cheek, eliciting no response. "I have brought a basket of cherries," he said. "The last of the season. They are perfectly good, never fear." He took one and put it in his mouth.

It was Sancia who spoke. "We do not want any cherries from you, nor anything else for that matter."

Cesare chose to ignore this. He set the basket on a table and turning to Lucrezia said, "I have heard such glowing reports of Alfonso's progress, due of course to your expert nursing, that I have come to see for myself. It is indeed a miracle. Perhaps someday I can count on such care from you for myself, should it ever be necessary . . . Who knows," he added, shrugging, "what the future has in store for us."

The two women did not reply. Alfonso stared straight ahead.

"Well," Cesare said, settling himself comfortably into a chair, "tell me, dear Sancia, what sort of scandalous behavior have you been engaged in since I last saw you?"

"Nothing that would interest you," she said shortly. "Why don't you leave? You are not welcome here."

"But I've only just arrived. As I said, I had to see this miraculous recovery for myself. Tell me," he said, looking directly at Alfonso, "do you attribute this recovery of yours to prayer or to plain good fortune?"

"I attribute it to your absence," Alfonso said firmly. "And now I should like you to leave."

Cesare flushed and then paled. "Well, what was not done at supper might still be done at breakfast," he said, rising, "so I suggest that you take care."

Alfonso said nothing.

A few days later, on August 18, 1500, Alfonso was lying on his bed resting. Lucrezia and Sancia were dozing in chairs by the window, for the afternoon was warm. Clemente and Galeano were conferring in a corner about further treatment, when the door burst open and in rushed Don Michelotto, Cesare's lieutenant at arms, with several of his men.

"Clemente and Galeano are under arrest!" he shouted.

"On what charge?" Lucrezia demanded.

"Treason," Michelotto replied promptly. "They were heard conspiring against His Holiness."

Lucrezia's face flushed with anger. "That is preposterous!"

"What is it?" Alfonso wanted to know, waking from his nap.

"It is nothing," Lucrezia said. "I will take care of it.

328

You wait here," she said to Michelotto, "and do nothing until I return. I am going to talk to His Holiness himself about this. Come, Sancia." The two women left the room.

No sooner had they gone than Don Michelotto had his guards remove the two physicians, who were plainly terrified and offered no resistance. Then he approached the bed where Alfonso lay, grabbed a pillow, and pressed it into his face.

Alfonso's hands went up in a gesture of supplication.

Michelotto held the pillow to his face until Alfonso's hands dropped limply to the bed.

When Lucrezia and Sancia returned a few minutes later without finding Alexander, Michelotto's men were guarding the door. The Vatican guards were gone.

Lucrezia, fearing the worst, screamed and sank to the floor.

Sancia flailed at the men with her arms, kicked them, and screamed for help.

The door to Alfonso's apartment opened and Don Michelotto stood framed in the doorway. "I think that you had better send for a physician," he said gravely. "His Highness seems to have suffered a hemorrhage."

CHAPTER 29

For two days Lucrezia lay prostrate with grief, unable to eat, to wash, to do any of the ordinary things that are part of the day-by-day process of living.

Alexander, relieved at not having to see her just yet, gave orders to Gaspare de Torre to dose her with belladonna. "It will keep her quiet," he added, "and the rest will be good for her right now."

Alfonso's body was buried the very night he died. Lighted by torches and followed by several friars mumbling prayers for the dead, he was interred without pomp in the yard of the little Church of Santa Maria delle Febbri near St. Peter's. The gravediggers worked quickly and well, and in no time at all the hastily constructed pine box was lowered into the grave and covered with dirt. The gravediggers snuffed out their lanterns and left, their pockets bulging with gold coins.

Vincenzo Calmeta, who was horrified by the entire proceedings, wrote to the King of Naples expressing his sorrow and his wrath at what had happened. "Lucrezia's real drama," he wrote, "lay not so much in weakness, but in her tactic of ignoring what was going on around her, and never being able to make a judgment on her father's and brother's behavior, has resulted in a real tragedy."

When Lucrezia was at last able to rouse herself from her lethargy, it was all over. Alfonso had been buried, Sancia had been sent home, and Alexander was unwilling to discuss it. To all her tears and recriminations he turned a deaf ear.

"What would you like me to do?" he said at last. "Bring him back? I cannot, as you well know. You must occupy yourself now with other things."

"And what about Cesare?" she asked quietly. "Is he to go free?"

Alexander looked at her sternly. "Cesare's part in this has never been established. Do not even allow yourself to think such thoughts."

Lucrezia's eyes filled with tears. "But everyone is saying such dreadful things."

Alexander put his hands on her shoulders and looked into her eyes. "Believe nothing of what you hear, my child. It is all a bundle of lies. As long as we rule, we will be in men's mouths. Simply try," he repeated, "to occupy yourself with other things."

Lucrezia continued to mourn, her very tears and grief the only way she could revolt against what had happened. Alexander could no longer look at her. He could not bear the sight of her red eyes and long face. Finally he removed himself from her altogether, telling her that if she did not improve he did not want to see her at all.

She grieved for a time in private, visiting Alfonso's grave secretly and covering the headstone with hot tears. Then, all at once, she had had enough of crying. Something within her hardened. The sights and sounds of Rome oppressed her. She could not bear the sight of

331

the servants with their evasive eyes, nor could she bear the sight of her friends, who were unable to give her solace with their empty phrases and hollow platitudes. The halls of the Vatican palace filled her with a slow, creeping horror. She decided to retire to her estate in Nepi.

Alexander was greatly relieved by the news. "It is a fine idea," he said. "The cool mountain air will do you good. You should come back greatly refreshed."

Lucrezia bit her lip and said nothing.

Alexander, anxious to do something to please her, organized an entourage of six hundred horsemen to accompany her on her journey. When Cesare attempted to see her before she left, she was adamant; she would not see him. She absolutely refused, and then burst into tears. To try to smooth things over, Cesare sent her a bolt of scarlet Florentine brocade woven with peacocks and tigers, which he had been planning to send to Charlotte. Lucrezia fingered it absently. Then she put in away in a chest and locked it.

A week later she was in Nepi, writing to Alexander for some warm clothing for little Rodrigo, for the weather was cool. As far as she was concerned, her life was over, buried in the churchyard with Alfonso. She wrote to her friend Vincenzo Calmeta. "All that I have ever loved or hoped for is lost. My flesh melts away with weeping."

In Rome, Alexander was casting about for a third husband for Lucrezia, one who would be a good political match. Proposals were already pouring in. Among those suing for her hand was Louis de Ligny, a cousin to the King of France, and one of his favorites. Naturally Cesare favored this alliance, as it strengthened his bonds with Louis. The Italian court felt otherwise. Cesare might favor the French for his own ends, but the court distrusted France. Let Lucrezia find an Italian husband, they agreed. The next suitor to apply for her hand was Francesco Orsini, Duke of Gravina, who had just broken with his beautiful young mistress. The Duke was a widower in his middle years with two sons. He professed great love for Lucrezia, whom he had never met but who, he insisted, had visited him in his dreams.

Alexander snorted and put this proposal with the others.

"It is a large wonder," Burchard said, sorting the papers, "that anyone should apply, considering the short history of her other marriages."

Alexander ignored this and went on to a proposal by a Spanish count. "It is a possibility," Alexander said, tapping the parchment against his teeth. His own Spanish blood would be reinforced by such a union.

In Nepi, Lucrezia received a letter from Alphonso d'Este expressing his sympathy and offering his condolences at Alfonso's death. He had lost his wife, Anna, several years earlier in childbirth. And although it was not a happy marriage, he was said to have mourned her loss.

"Dear Madonna Lucrezia," he wrote, "please accept my sympathy at the death of your husband, Alfonso. I know that there are no magic words to ease your pain, but I offer these in the faint hope that they may help. From one who has thought of you very often, Alphonso d'Este of Ferrara."

Lucrezia folded the letter and tucked it under the lining of her sewing basket. Every day she took it out and read it for solace, thinking sadly back to Alphonso d'Este's visit to Rome. She had been so young then, so carefree, and he had seemed so intriguing. Would she ever be happy again?

In Rome, Cesare was gathering his forces for an assault on Faenza. Alfonso's death had strengthened his alliances with France and Venice, both of which planned to march on Naples when the fight in the Romagna was over. It was all working out just as he had planned.

Alexander opposed him in nothing now. This son of his completely overwhelmed him with his brilliance and boldness. The ripples caused by Alfonso's death were dying down now, just as Cesare had said they would. What mattered now was seizing the moment for their own ends. Alfonso's name was never again mentioned between them.

The money from the jubilee was still pouring in. Alexander, rubbing his hands over Burchard's figures, declared that it was the most successful year they had ever had.

Cesare smiled. Most of the money would go to finance his campaign. It was sorely needed, for his army was soaking up money at an alarming rate, just sitting around and waiting.

A few days later Cesare gathered together the whole of his army in St. Peter's Square and watched with the people of Rome as eight hundred fierce-looking Spanish soldiers went through their paces.

On October 2, 1500, Cesare and his staff left to join up with the French regiments which Louis had finally dispatched. The Roman hills were turning brown and gold with autumn's touch. The air was crisp with a foretaste of winter, and Cesare was anxious to be gone.

Alexander saw him leave with mixed feelings. In Cesare he now saw his greatest hope for achievement. How strange, he thought to himself, that the son whom he had loved the least should be such a source of pride to him now. He watched from the loggia as Cesare rode out, escorted part of the way by the heads of the noblest families of Rome.

Two days later Cesare stopped at Nepi to visit his sister.

Lucrezia, who had not expected him, was stupefied. "I will not see him!" she told her master at arms.

"He will not leave," that gentleman replied.

"Where is he?" she asked uneasily, all sorts of emotions rising within her.

"He has quartered his horses in the stables. His men are camped outside the grounds."

"And where is *he?*" she repeated.

"His Lordship is making himself comfortable in the west wing and requests the pleasure of your company."

"He *what?*" Lucrezia exploded. "How dare he! We will see about that!" She gathered up her skirts and hurried down the long halls, expletives fast-forming in her head. Not bothering to knock, she burst into his apartment and surprised her brother in the act of taking a bath.

He was seated before the fire in a copper tub, up to his waist in water. "My dear sister," he said, rising to greet her.

Lucrezia looked at him in stunned silence, staring at the well-muscled body, the wide shoulders tapering down to narrow waist and lean flanks, the knotted thighs thinning down to well-turned calves. Then she lifted her eyes and shouted, "How dare you come here like this!"

Cesare smiled and motioned to Agapito for a towel, which he draped around his waist. "The warmth of your welcome overwhelms me, my dear Lucrece. Are you not, then, glad to see me?"

"I have not been glad since Alfonso was murdered in his bed."

"Ah, yes," he sighed, beginning to dry himself. "I have wanted many times to speak to you of that, but I have been told that you would not see me, and as it is not my custom to push myself where I am not wanted . . ."

"And since when has that become your custom?"

"Why, always," he replied, dropping the towel and allowing himself to be enveloped in a heavy robe.

"Then why are you here?"

"Why?" he asked, pushing his feet into thick brocaded slippers. "Because I have heard that you blame me for what has happened, and I do not wish to go into battle with that between us. I want your blessing."

"I cannot give it," she said, turning away.

"Lucrece," he said, grasping her firmly by the shoulders, "you must believe that I had nothing to do with what happeneed. Nothing at all."

"And what of Don Michelotto?"

"He was simply there when Alfonso hemorrhaged."

"Alfonso did not hemorrhage," she said firmly. "He was murdered."

"There is no proof of that."

"Then why was Michelotto there?"

"He was there because we had received word that the physicians from Naples were spies. Don Michelotto had orders to arrest them."

"Then why did he not arrest them and be done with it?" she asked, her voice rising in anger.

"Because," Cesare said with care, "you and Sancia interferred. Don Michelotto told me that after you left the room Alfonso seemed very agitated and then he seemed to faint and give way altogether. There was nothing he could do to revive him."

Lucrezia stood without speaking. The earnestness of his tone troubled her. She wanted to believe him.

As though he could read her thoughts, he took her

face between his hands. "You must believe me, Lucrece, in God's name, if I mean anything to you at all."

She moved toward him then and burst into tears. "Do you know what it's like," she sobbed, "to know that your heart's love lies beneath a heap of stones?"

He drew her close, murmuring softly, brokenly, "Lucrece, my sweet, my own little girl."

She stayed close to him, drawing in warmth and comfort as a plant draws in the sun. She had no one now, no one but him and Alexander and little Rodrigo.

"Cesare," she whispered, "I'm so afraid and so lonely." She felt his body tremble.

His arms drew her so close that she could feel the beat of his heart. They stood without moving, one locked against the other. Then Cesare, his face flushed, his eyes bright, looked at her and stroked her hair. "I wish we were children again," he said softly.

Cesare stayed with her for two days. He had brought with him his chiefs of staff and some nobles from the leading houses of Rome. The castle was filled with movement and laughter, and Lucrezia felt her spirits lift like mists warmed by the sun.

As though she were his wife, Cesare told her of all his hopes, all that he planned to do. She listened to him half-heartedly at first, then with growing interest as he described how he would conquer and unite all of Italy in the name of the Holy Roman Church.

She listened to him with shining eyes, glorying in his strength and his wisdom. Then she said shyly, "Alphonso d'Este has written to me. I think that he likes me still."

Cesare looked at her closely. He had not wanted to think of her marrying again, even though he knew that she must. "I think that you could do worse," he said slowly, watching the firelight flicker against the small oval of her face.

"No," she said. "It is too soon."

That evening Cesare wrote Alexander a letter. The Este family was one of the oldest and most powerful in Italy. Isabella d'Este Gonzaga, Alphonso's sister, had already shown favor to Cesare by making him godfather of her and Francesco's child, together with the Emperor Maximilian. An alliance with a family such as theirs would be invaluable to Cesare. Also, the duchy of Ferrara was large and fertile and strategically situated. "Our father," he wrote, "would do well to look in that direction for a husband for Lucrezia."

Dinner on Cesare's last night at Nepi was gay and boisterous. Cesare and his staff were in good spirits. They would be moving on to Faenza in the morning, but now they lived for the moment. Lucrezia's ladies-in-waiting, delighted by the presence of so many good-looking men, did their best to please.

Cesare looked at Lucrezia and raised his wineglass. "To the most beautiful woman in all of Italy," he said softly, "and perhaps the entire world."

In the morning Lucrezia rose to bid him good-bye. The air was gray and damp. A heavy rain was falling, and the mountains were obscured by mist. As she stood under the portico in the paved courtyard, the leaves dripping moisture, her spirits sank as low as the wet paving stones beneath her feet. Cesare was leaving, taking with him the only warmth and cheer she'd known since Alfonso's death. She clung to him closely. "God bless you and keep you," she whispered.

Cesare looked at her strangely for a moment, as though there was something he wanted to say. Then he turned away abruptly, leaped on his horse, and was gone.

In Rome, Alexander was composing a letter to Ercole d'Este, Alphonso's father. "It is perhaps meet," he wrote, "that two proud and powerful families such

338

as ours should unite through an alliance with our children, Lucrezia and Alphonso, whom God has seen fit to widow." He went on to list the advantages of such a union, feeling certain that the crafty old Duke would seize an opportunity that was to his advantage. He took great care to list Cesare's accomplishments in the Romagna, stressing the importance of having the Borgia protection for Ferrara.

When Ercole told his daughter Isabella of the Pope's letter, she sniffed contemptuously. "We do not want any Spanish upstarts in the family."

"You thought sufficiently well of them," the old Duke reminded her, "to name Cesare one of the godfathers of your child."

"Yes, well, that was something else again. It did not gain him admittance into the family," she retorted. "Besides, everyone is laughing at them. They are saying that the Fisherman is spreading his nets and anyone unlucky enough to fall into them will be Lucrezia's next husband."

"That is unkind of you, Isabella," the Duke said severely. The idea of the union appealed to him. He knew also that Alphonso was favorably disposed toward Lucrezia. He would see about striking the best bargain he could.

In Nepi, Lucrezia was finally bored. Her routine was rustic and simple. She could either take her afternoon ride through the woods or she could walk through the village. Fortunately she had brought to Nepi some of the books that Don Alphonso had long ago recommended to her, as well as the poems of Petrarch and Catullus. But that only made her long for the sprightly conversations of the salon. She missed Vincenzo Calmeta and the round of court painters and musicians.

She missed the sophistication of Rome. She found the daily routine at Nepi tedious to distraction.

After a month she left for Rome. Alexander was glad to see her. He fussed over her like a hen, asking her anxiously if there was not something that she wanted.

Lucrezia smiled and pressed his hand. He seemed older and frailer than when she had seen him last. "I am all right, Papa," she said softly. "I really am."

She unlocked the chests where she had stored her bolts and drew out the brocade that Cesare had given her. She held it against her and looked in the glass. It was so vivid that it blotted her out completely. She suddenly wished that it were some other color. She sighed. Alfonso had not liked her in red. But then, she thought sadly, he would not be here to see it, and ordered a dress made of it.

She wore it to the first musicale, which Vincenzo had arranged. Bernardo Accolti, a new poet, sat at her feet like a spaniel.

Tommaso Albanese, who had recovered from his wounds, pledged her his protection and followed her everywhere. Alexander had granted him a house and a nice income for the services he had rendered Alfonso, and he felt bound to Lucrezia as well.

Lucrezia moved through the evening as though locked in a dream. Nothing seemed real. Everyone seemed to speak hollow phrases, with the exception of Vincenzo Calmeta and Tommaso Albanese. She wondered how she was going to spin out her days in the company of these people. When she reached the quiet of her apartments, she looked about her, grateful for the absence of voices grating in her ears. She felt under the lining of her sewing basket and took out Don Alphonso d'Este's letter to her, drawing comfort from the strong, slanted hand. Then she put it back carefully and closed the basket.

Alexander came to her the following day. "I do not quite know how to say this," he began awkwardly, "but it is not too soon to begin thinking about your future."

"What future, Papa? I do not have a future."

"You are only twenty, my child. You should have a husband."

She shook her head sadly. "No one would want me, Papa. My husbands have been too unlucky."

Alexander cleared his throat. "You are wrong, my child. I have several suits for your hand. Here is one from Louis de Ligny, cousin to the King of France."

Lucrezia picked up the letter and read it. "I don't wish to live in France," she said listlessly.

"He will live here," Alexander said quickly. He had not yet heard from the old duke Ercole, and he did not want to pass anything up.

"He is too compliant," Lucrezia said. "I should not be happy with a husband like that."

"Here is one from the Duke of Gravina," Alexander continued, handing her another letter.

Lucrezia turned away. "The Duke of Gravina is a fool. I do not wish to repeat an earlier mistake."

"Well," Alexander said slowly, "I have written Ercole d'Este, suggesting a match between yourself and Don Alphonso, but I suppose that you would not like that either."

Lucrezia's heart skipped a beat. Alphonso d'Este . . . she could still feel his kiss and the intensity of his look. She was immediately shaken by the force of her feelings. How could she feel at all, so soon after Alfonso's death? "I am ashamed," she said to Alexander, "ashamed to be thinking of anyone else for a husband."

Alexander's glance was kindly. "Nonsense, you are a

young healthy woman who needs a man to love. There is no shame in that, God knows."

A week later Alexander received word from Ferrara. Don Alphonso, it seemed, was willing to marry Lucrezia, and would himself address a letter to Alexander, asking him formally for Lucrezia's hand in marriage. However, the old Duke continued, determined to gain the best settlement obtainable for himself and his son, there were certain conditions. Lucrezia's dowry was to consist of two hundred thousand gold ducats and the castles and estates of Cento and Pieve, which were now a part of the Bolognese duchy. Also, Alexander was to supply her with clothing and jewelry and art objects in the value of seventy-five gold ducats. In addition to this, the old Duke asked for a reduction of his yearly tithes to the Vatican. Instead of paying four thousand ducats a year, he would pay only one hundred.

Alexander blanched at this but read on. The male issue of the union would inherit the duchy of Ferrara. The Duke's son Cardinal Ippolito d'Este would succeed to the title of Arch-Priest of St. Peter's with all the benefits accruing thereto. As for Lucrezia, she would get Don Alphonso and with him the illustrious position of Marchioness of Ferrara.

Shortly thereafter a formal suit from Don Alphonso himself arrived. Lucrezia, weary to death of her life in Rome, urged Alexander to accept it for her. Vincenzo Calmeta, writing of the negotiations to the King of Naples, said: "Lucrezia is frantic to leave her family and Rome. She is anxious to exchange her role of Borgia pawn for Este respectability. She seems afraid, indeed almost frantic to get away. What will happen, God only knows. But I think she at last realizes what deception her family is capable of and she wishes to place herself as far from them as she can."

Tales of Cesare and his exploits filtered back to Rome. His attack on Faenza had been repulsed and he was waiting out the winter in comfort and luxury, employing jewelers and armorers the while to keep himself amused. An Eastern potentate lived no more lavishly, and a steady stream of women filtered through the camp. Alexander chafed at all the expenditure. He was sending Cesare one thousand gold ducats a day.

Toward the end of April, 1501, Alexander happily informed the court that Cesare had taken Faenza.

Lucrezia shivered. If she were lucky, she would be gone from Rome by the time he returned. Meanwhile, Don Alphonso had sent her a few little gifts, together with a note. "I hope that you remember the book list," he wrote. "You should have had time by now to read everything. And what else do you remember?" he had ended. She smiled, remembering her impromptu bath in the pond in the Vatican gardens and the way he had stood watching her. She couldn't have been much to look at then, at thirteen. But he had not seemed to mind. And then he had kissed her, twice. She remembered that very well. She brushed her lips with her fingers. Alfonso had been dead almost ten months now. Alexander was right. She had the need of a man to love her. "That hot Borgia blood runs in your veins as well as mine," he was fond of saying.

The wedding arrangements were not concluded until five months later, in early September. Don Alphonso would not come to Rome. The old Duke was adamant on that. He would not see his son go the way of Lucrezia's former husband. The wedding would take place on December 13 by proxy. Alphonso's younger brother Don Ferrante would stand in his place.

Alexander demurred. What show of trust was that?

343

"Please, Papa," Lucrezia pleaded, almost in tears. "Let us do as they say."

Alexander, seeing what a state she was in and fearing a breakdown, acquiesced. He issued a public proclamation and ordered fireworks to celebrate.

Lucrezia, going on her knees before the altar in the Church of Santa Maria del Popolo, heard the fireworks and felt they were the sounds of her deliverance.

CHAPTER 30

Once more Lucrezia put together a trousseau. This one, she decided, would have to be even more splendid than the others, for she would now be forced to compete with Don Alphonso's sister, Isabella d'Este Gonzaga, whose appetite for beautiful things was insatiable.

Alexander, anxious to please this child who had been through so much, informed Lucrezia that she might have whatever she wanted, no matter what the cost. From Cesare she received a vermilion leather casket bordered with a narrow gilt band from France. When she opened it, she found that it contained emeralds, pearls, and rubies, some as big as walnuts. Accompanying it was a note: "Your sweet features will always stay in my memory . . . Bend your eyes in pity to my lament, since fortune wills you not to yield consent." The jewels were lovely, but she had no heart for them. She put the note in the casket and locked it away in a cupboard, resolving never to wear them.

In the middle of all the preparations Cesare returned to Rome, bearing more gifts. He was delighted with the

Este alliance and took no trouble to hide it. "Isabella is a bit difficult," he told Lucrezia, "but she can be brought to bay. As for her brother, Don Alphonso, I understand that he is cold." He looked at her speculatively, but she said nothing. "The old Duke Ercole," he continued, "is as stingy a man as you'll find anywhere. But never mind, if there is ever anything you need, we'll supply it." Then he uncovered the things he had brought her from Venice, adding that he had sent a duplicate package to Charlotte. There were beautifully molded wax tapers and procelain figures, fine sugars and syrups, heavy brocades, Oriental spices, fine leather gloves, and twenty barrels of wine from France.

"You are not wearing the ruby brooch I gave you," he said.

"No," she replied evenly. "I do not wear as much jewelry as I used to."

The following week he gave a magnificent dinner for her. For entertainment afterward, there were stallions and mares which mated amid much laughter. Lucrezia stayed for five minutes and then rose to leave. "I have a headache," she explained.

Cesare looked after her and said nothing.

The following day he stood before her in the herb garden of the Vatican as she was gathering some herbs for a *tisane*. "What do you want?" he asked at last. "What will make you happy?"

"I do not expect to be happy," she said slowly. "My happiness lies under a stone in the churchyard of Santa Maria."

On December 15 two envoys, Gerardo Saraceni and Ettore Bellingeri, arrived from Ferrara, bringing with them a miniature of Don Alphonso for Lucrezia.

She received them at the Palace of Santa Maria in Portico and shyly thanked them for the gift. Wearing a plain, unadorned dress for the occasion, she told them sweetly that they should consider Santa Maria their home while in Rome, adding that if they lacked for anything, they had merely to ask for it. The two men were charmed by her simplicity. They had expected to find a decadent woman of the world, and were confronted instead by this lovely young creature barely out of her teens, whose face shone with goodness. They reported to Ercole: "Far from being the divorced, besmirched and widowed Messalina she is rumored to be, she is no more than a good simple girl who wants very much to be liked."

The old Duke read this with satisfaction to Isabella. "You see, just because she is a Borgia does not mean that she is bad."

"No," Isabella replied. "But neither does it mean that she is good."

Lucrezia studied the miniature. She could only dimly recall Alphonso's appearance. She could remember more clearly the look in his eyes as he had watched her and the touch of his lips on hers. His face in the portrait appeared stern and ungiving, his mouth a thin line, his eyes inscrutable.

The envoys, who had come to settle the business of the marriage contract, were obliged to wait for Giuliano della Rovere, the Archbishop whose consent was necessary before Alexander could transfer the two Bolognese properties promised to Ercole. As della Rovere was in transit somewhere between Milan and France, the two envoys settled in to wait, occupying themselves with observing Lucrezia and her family. They saw a devoted, dutiful daughter, for each day, accompanied by her court, she journeyed from her palace to the Vatican to take her accustomed place near the Vatican throne for the purpose of reviewing marriage contracts. She did this meticulously and well, giving each pro-

347

posal her conscientious attention, and each suitor the benefit of a gracious smile. At home she paid great care to the keeping of her house and the comfort of her staff. The envoys wrote again: "She is in truth an angel, a sweet child who is concerned for the welfare of all. And this is not merely for our benefit alone, for everyone here speaks well of her."

Lucrezia spent her time getting her trousseau in order and in reading. She did not want to go to Alphonso unversed. But the delay in settling the last few details of the marriage so unnerved her that she neither ate nor slept.

"Don Alphonso does not want a skeleton for a wife," Maria informed her, adding that if that were his desire, he could satisfy himself very well at the family crypt.

Lucrezia fretted about leaving Rodrigo behind in Rome, but Alexander insisted. Don Alphonso, he told her, did not want a child; he wanted her. Alexander would see to the child himself, and Angela would stay behind to take care of him. Then later perhaps, when the marriage was older, they would see . . .

Finally della Rovere returned to Rome and gave his consent. Everything was settled. Lucrezia breathed a sigh of relief.

Two days before Christmas Don Alphonso's three brothers arrived from Ferrara. There was Don Ferrante, who was to act as proxy, Cardinal Ippolito, and Don Sigismondo, accompanied by a large suite of retainers. They were welcomed while they were still some distance outside the city gates by Cesare, who, instead of wearing his customary black, was elegantly clad in cloth of gold. With him were the French ambassador and two thousand horsemen. At the moment of meeting and again as they passed through the city gates on their way to the Vatican, the air was rent with church bells and cannon salutes. The people of Rome, who had lined the streets to watch, roared out their approval. The Pope's daughter would no longer sleep alone.

The three brothers were greatly pleased with such a reception and impressed with Cesare's good looks and bearing. "He carries himself like a prince," they wrote to their father, adding that "Lucrezia is as good and as beautiful as any princess in the kingdom, if not the world."

Isabella, hearing of this, sniffed and said nothing.

Alexander had taken great care that the Estes should see Lucrezia at her best. On the night of the formal reception, he arranged that she would descend the staircase of the palace on Cesare's arm, since the two of them looked so well together. She appeared in a white dress bordered in gold, her lovely hair encased in a golden fillet strung with pearls. Flushed with excitement, her eyes shining, her small oval face seemed beautiful. When Cesare asked her to dance, all eyes turned their way. "It is easy to believe the rumors about them," Cardinal Ippolito whispered to Don Ferrante.

On December 30, the day of the wedding. Lucrezia arose while it was still dark and sat by the fire biting her nails. The day that she had so anxiously awaited was here. She felt completely helpless, unable to move or to dress herself.

"What is wrong with you?" Maria asked sharply.

"I don't know," Lucrezia said, beginning to tremble. "I feel as though I am going into a thick forest and will never come out again."

"Don't be foolish," Maria said more gently. "You will be starting a new life, one that will make you happy. Isn't that what you want?"

"Not without Rodrigo," she quavered.

"Angela will take good care of him," Maria said firmly. "And there will be other babies."

When her hair was dry, Maria pulled the crimson velvet and gold brocade dress over Lucrezia's head and fastened it. It was lined with ermine to keep out the cold. Maria caught her hair up in a simple black ribbon. Over her shoulders she threw an ermine cape.

Downstairs Don Ferrante and Don Sigismondo were waiting for her, together with the members of her court. The procession moved on to the Vatican, where Alexander and the others waited. As Lucrezia entered the chapel, the sound of trumpets filled the air.

The marriage ceremony was performed with Don Ferrante speaking for Don Alphonso. When it was Lucrezia's turn to speak, she spoke in such a low voice that the bishop had to lean over to hear her words. Alexander, realizing the strain she was under, cut the ceremony short with a wave of his hand. Don Ferrante offered her the ring. Lucrezia smiled nervously and accepted it.

Cesare, who was strangely quiet, escorted her to the celebration in St. Peter's Square. "Do not allow the Estes to look down their noses at you," he said finally. "Their family abounds in bastards."

Lucrezia was touched by his concern for her. Actually the Este family history was almost as bloody as that of the Borgias, Cesare reminded her, adding that the old Duke, apprised of a nephew's treason, had had him decapitated with no hesitation whatsoever.

"I will be all right," she said quietly.

On January 6, 1502, Lucrezia said good-bye to Alexander. Although he tried to put on a good face, he was downcast at her leaving. When she finally embraced him for the last time, his eyes filled with tears at the thought that he might never see her again. Then he brushed them aside and laughed foolishly. "It is not

350

as though you are going to the ends of the earth, after all." Then, pressing her hands to his heart, he drew her to him and held her as though he would never let her go, admonishing Don Ferrante to treat her with care and saying loudly, so that all could hear, that if she were not well treated he would be certain to hear of it.

Cesare, Ferrante, and Cardinal Ippolito escorted her out of Rome and into the open countryside. When it was time for Cesare to take his leave, he wheeled in his horse, took Lucrezia's hand, and raised it to his lips. Then he removed from his finger the gold ring that Anne of Cleves had given him and put it on her finger, saying, "If you ever need me, for anything at all, simply send me this ring and I will come." Then he turned his horse and was gone.

Lucrezia sat and looked after him, her eyes beginning to fill with tears. Then the new Marchioness of Ferrara, accompanied by Don Ferrante, Don Sigismondo, bishops, ambassadors, prelates, ladies-in-waiting, noblemen, soldiers, knights and grooms, and 150 coaches, went on her way to her new home in Ferrara.

CHAPTER 31

In Ferrara there was a frenzy of preparation for the formal wedding, which was set for the day after Lucrezia's arrival. The old Duke, who was devoted to letters and the arts, had an overriding passion for the theater. Although thrifty in most things, he did not mind spending endless sums of money sponsoring repertory companies that performed classical dramas and original plays commissioned by him.

Ercole was not a promiscuous man. The duchy of Ferrara had had its bastards. Unwilling to sully the House of Este with any more, he had married Eleanora, the beautiful daughter of King Ferrante of Naples. They had lived happily together until her death seven years ago. During their marriage she had given him six children, Isabella, Beatrice, Alphonso, Ippolito, Ferrante, and Sigismondo. Of all their children Isabella was the most like her father, inheriting his love of letters and politics. Unlike her father, she was snobbish in the extreme, and she cultivated no one whom she did not consider her intellectual equal. Had she been a man, she would have been a tremendous force in politics. As it was, her husband, Francesco de Gonzaga of Mantua, used her as a sounding board, sending her from court to court that she might ferret out his neighbors' intentions. When she was not engaged in politics, she spent her time studying Greek and Latin, corresponding with all the literary lights of the day, and designing unusual costumes and fabrics for herself so that she might look different from everyone else.

When she found that there was nothing she could do to keep Lucrezia from coming into the family, she set about to learn her strengths and weaknesses so that she could best her in everything. She knew that she herself was not beautiful. She tended to flesh, and being short, looked stocky. But she arranged her hair so cleverly and arrayed herself so exotically that she impressed everyone with her looks. She enjoyed music, and loved to sing.

Isabella wrote to Vincenzo Calmeta, with whom she corresponded occasionally, asking him for an analysis of Lucrezia's character. Vincenzo, aware of the rivalry, wrote back: "Madonna Lucrezia is simple and good. She has no wish to compete intellectually, nor has she any ambition to rule. She simply wishes to be happy, and like the child she is, desires only that everyone like her."

Isabella, reading this, was skeptical. Either Vincenzo was hiding something, or the girl was a ninny. Who could believe that Lucrezia, who had always been given everything she wanted, could be satisfied with so little.

Her father, the duke Ercole, had sent a wedding invitation to her only, adding that Francesco should stay at home in Mantua to protect his frontiers, since it would not be unlike Cesare Borgia to use the wedding as a diversionary tactic and attack the castle in the owner's absence. "You know," the old Duke wrote to Isabella, "the Borgias are not to be trusted. His Holiness gives with one hand and takes away with the other." Isabella, who obeyed her father in everything, left her husband at home.

As for Don Alphonso, he was as unlike his father as possible. Good-looking and well made, he had an eye for a pretty woman. After his wife's death he had found plenty of consolation. But he had not fallen in love. Far from sharing his father's reverence for the arts, his taste ran to weapons and warfare. Growing up as he did during the war between Ferrara and Venice, and remembering with bitterness the loss of valuable lands, he attached great importance to strength and was constantly after his father to build an army.

Ercole, bitterly disappointed that his son did not share his taste in art and music, replied that Alphonso could go into battle naked if he wished, but that he would not spend one gold piece to outfit him or his men. Alphonso, who was then much younger, had appeared in the piazza the next day naked and waving a sword. The people of the town, used by now to his peccadilloes, smiled and went about the business of locking up their daughters. They were regularly treated to the sight of Alphonso and his brother Ippolito beating up one another in the main square, urged on by their respective households.

Lucrezia, naturally curious about her new husband, questioned his brothers while they traveled. Wisely enough, they told her very little, saying only that they felt certain he would like her and that if he did not, they knew others who would.

Lucrezia traveled slowly, stopping to rest at Spoleto, where she had served as governor. She stood for a time on the turrets of the castle, thinking once again of the golden month she had spent there with Alfonso. She

354

saw Ascanio's face in the crowd that welcomed her, but he did not attempt to step forward. She smiled and nodded and made conversation with her hosts, but feelings from the past engulfed her, and she wanted to cry out and rush backward into time where she might find Alfonso. She cried herself to sleep that night. In the morning they left for Urbino.

In Urbino she was welcomed by Elizabetta Gonzaga, the Duchess of Urbino, who was also Isabella's sister-in-law. Lucrezia, aware that she was being scrutinized and that Isabella would get a full report, was on her best behavior. She was so charming that Elizabetta was forced to write to Isabella that "she is truly good and gives offense to no one, wanting only everyone's good will," adding that "she is beguiling to look at, with a sweet expression, and dresses in the latest fashion, wearing nothing twice."

Lucrezia could not help wishing that Isabella were as pleasant as Elizabetta. The journey was nearing an end, and she was becoming increasingly nervous.

They had just quitted Bologna when Don Alphonso, impatient to see his bride, surprised them. They had been riding for an hour or two when they saw a tall figure on horseback approaching them, followed by a small entourage of riders.

Lucrezia, taken completely unaware, found herself looking across at a handsome man who sat his horse very well. There was no mistaking the eyes and the thin lips. It was Don Alphonso.

He doffed his hat, looking at her steadily, then smiled. "You look better than when I last saw you."

Lucrezia, for some reason feeling entirely at her ease, was able to reply in kind. "Had I known you were coming, Sire, I should have rubbed my face with fruit."

He burst out laughing at that and she joined in.

355

They rode together for a time, chatting pleasantly. Then he made his good-byes. "No one else knows that I am here," he told her. "My father is intent on welcoming you himself. I shall see you later." He raised her hand to his lips, looking at her all the while. Then he turned about and was gone, taking his party with him.

Lucrezia's blood quickened within her. She liked boldness in a man, and the unexpectedness of his visit thrilled her and gave her heart. She had more courage now for the meeting with the old Duke and reunion with his daughter Isabella.

She and her retinue boarded a barge now for the next part of their journey. Lucrezia stood on deck, anxiously scanning the shore until she caught sight of the Duke and his party waiting for her on the bank. When the barge was tied up she gathered up her skirts, stepped lightly ashore and ran to her new father-in-law, kneeling at his feet and kissing his hand in respect.

Ercole, completely disarmed, lifted her up and hugged her roundly while Isabella looked on in disapproval. "We are happy that you are finally here," he said, looking into her eyes and smiling. Then he took her by the hand and led her to Isabella.

"I am very happy to see you again," Lucrezia said clearly.

"Yes," Isabella said, her face still unsmiling.

The Duke led Lucrezia away, after first giving Isabella a stern look, and introduced her to the other members of the court, repairing at last to a great golden galley which would take them on the last leg of the trip. She was given first place, between the French and Venetian ambassadors. Isabella, who was unused to second place, was plainly annoyed.

"Don Alphonso is anxious to see you," the Duke teased, "but I told him that an old man's pleasures are few, and that greeting you first was one of them."

Lucrezia smiled and nodded.

Isabella occupied herself with finding fault with Lucrezia's costume. She had to concede the girl's fresh skin and shining hair, but the sweetness of expression which had so captivated her sister-in-law, Isabella found vapid. Even so, one would have to be blind not to see how much attention she was getting. The French ambassador, all charm and chivalry, kept up a steady stream of conversation with her. On her other side, the Venetian ambassador tried to get a word in when he could. Isabella stood alone, completely ignored by everyone, her jaw stiff with resentment.

As the galley neared Ferrara, cannon boomed forth in greeting. Don Alphonso waited on the bank in a specially constructed stand, surrounded by his trumpeters and crossbowmen. The galley touched the bank, and Don Alphonso moved forward to greet her. He did not embrace her, but took her hands in his own and raised them to his lips. He accompanied her as far as the Este villa, where she was to spend the night. He would not enjoy her as his wife until tomorrow, after the formal wedding.

Ercole saw her comfortably deposited in her apartments. "My son is very impatient, but it is better that way," he said with a smile.

"Oh, my God!" Lucrezia said when she and Maria were finally alone. She had dismissed the ladies-in-waiting and then collapsed on the red and gold canopied bed, her arms and legs flung out in every direction. "I don't know when I have been so tired. My face is going to crack from smiling so much. Please, Maria, draw me a bath. And also, I must wash my hair."

"Naturally," Maria replied sourly. "You have not washed it since this morning."

Lucrezia made no answer. She was already asleep.

Maria awakened her early the next morning.

Lucrezia woke up red-eyed and cross, uncertain of where she was. "Why did you let me sleep?" she demanded angrily. "Now there is no time to do anything!"

Maria, knowing how dangerous it was to argue with her when she was in this frame of mind, said nothing. Instead she helped her to undress.

Lucrezia stepped into the warm tub and, holding her nose, sank under the water, her hair fanning out like seaweed. Soothed by the warm water and Maria's ministrations with the cloth, she was soon ready to dress, and rose from the tub. She did not hear the door to the apartment open and close, and so when she saw Don Alphonso standing there staring at her, she was too startled to move.

It was Maria who finally came to her senses and threw a towel around her.

"Milord," Lucrezia said angrily, "I did not hear you knock."

"I am sorry," Alphonso said. "I merely wanted to see you once more before the ceremony."

"Well, milord, you have seen me. I hope that I am to your liking."

Alphonso's eyes remained inscrutable, but there was a hint of a smile about his lips.

As soon as he left the room, Lucrezia burst into tears. "Each time he sees me I look worse than the last. I hate him!"

"Dry your eyes," Maria said, rubbing her head furiously with a towel, "or you'll look like a wall-eyed pike."

At the end of an hour, hot and flushed from the fire, her hair glistening like glass, Lucrezia stood in her wedding dress of crushed gold satin.

Maria, settling the golden cloak carefully about her shoulders, looked at her with satisfaction. The Este

358

rubies and diamonds sparkled at her throat and in her hair.

"I am absolutely beautiful," Lucrezia exulted. "Do you think he will think so?"

"If he can think at all," Maria replied, folding the damp towels and throwing them into a basket. "That sister of his, though, she'll fall over in a dead faint when she sees you."

In the courtyard of the villa stood a gray stallion, part of the waiting procession. It was hung with crimson velvet. Lucrezia mounted the steps and was lifted on. At the head of the procession rode the Duke, followed by the nobles of Ferrara, then the Duchess of Urbino's noblewomen and finally Don Alphonso himself, all in beige. Behind him rode the Spanish and Roman nobles, dressed in somber black, followed by five bishops and twelve ambassadors. Alphonso's crossbowmen came last.

"Damn their hides," the old Duke muttered. "He's not fighting a war, he's getting married."

Lucrezia, sitting her horse stiffly with a set smile upon her face, looked like a toy doll propped up on a huge stallion.

"She is completely overdone," Isabella remarked sourly to her sister-in-law Elizabetta.

When the fireworks began, Lucrezia's horse trembled and reared. Alphonso urged his horse forward. In a daze she felt herself being lifted off the stallion and sharing the saddle with Alphonso. The old Duke drew up on the other side of her, and together they entered the city of Ferrara, the streets thronged with people shouting her name.

Lucrezia, looking at the crowd which filled the roofs, balconies, and windows, smiled and waved, blowing kisses. The crowd roared back its approval.

"Such a fuss," Isabella remarked. "After all, she is not the Queen of France."

"No," her brother Don Sigismondo reminded her maliciously, "But she *is* the Marchioness of Ferrara, and she is young and beautiful besides."

When they reached the Piazza del Duomo, Ercole had arranged for two acrobats to throw themselves at her feet in homage. Lucrezia, delighted with this, blew them kisses. Everyone laughed and applauded.

"Really," Isabella exclaimed, "it is like a bad play!" As Lucrezia approached her, she arranged her features into the semblance of a smile. "My sister," she said mockingly.

Lucrezia, looking at the bizarrely painted face, smiled briefly and passed into the reception hall, which had been decorated for the occasion in gold and silver tapestries and hung with silk.

Alphonso, who was directly behind her, muttered under his breath. If he had had a hand in it, the place would not be cluttered up with finery and glitter. There would be horses prancing to martial music and battalions of soldiers stepping smartly. But then he was not paying for this. It was the old Duke's show entirely.

It was finally over. The old Duke moved forward to escort Lucrezia to the nuptial chamber. Isabella followed with the ladies-in-waiting. Lucrezia would have preferred that Maria remove her clothing, but Maria had demurred, saying that it was their right, not hers.

Lucrezia stood numbly as they drew off her dress and all her finery. She was suddenly aware that Isabella was waiting to see her without her shift. She stepped out of it lightly.

Isabella stood staring at the firm high breasts, the narrow waist, the golden crest. "Madame," she said stiffly. Then she turned and left, leaving the ladies to dress Lucrezia for her husband.

"She is scrawny as a chicken," she was to say later on, trying to rid her mind of the soft rosy flesh. "I only hope that Alphonso is not too disappointed."

Lucrezia sat in the bed and waited. She was grateful that the Duke had barred the members of the court from attending, to make certain that Alphonso did his duty by her. If he did not come soon, she thought sleepily, she would not be able to stay awake.

She was fast asleep when he entered the room, closing the door softly behind him. A series of small noises made her come awake. She opened her eyes slightly and watched him undress. He folded his clothing neatly and stretched. He was too large for her, she thought fearfully, and he wasn't even erect. A feeling of fright took hold of her. If only she could leave now. She would give anything to be back in Rome, in the safety of her own bed. She made a little sound like a moan.

He stood looking down at her. "You needn't worry," he said. "I have just come from a woman."

She sat up, speechless with fury. "You dared," she sputtered, "you dared to do that!"

"I thought it best, under the circumstances," he said, sitting down on the edge of the bed. "So much time has passed since we knew one another."

"You are not used to women like me, are you?"

"No," he said, taking her hand in his. "I'm not."

"They will know," she said slowly. "When they see the linen in the morning, they'll know that we did nothing."

"I can always scatter my seed."

"You would prefer that to me?" she asked wonderingly. "Why did we ever marry?"

"Because our fathers thought it prudent."

She lay staring up at the ceiling, feeling the tears

361

gather. No man had ever rejected her before. Her throat filled with anger. She made a little strangled cry. Before she knew what she was doing, she had dug her nails into his back.

He was at her instantly, his mouth seeking hers, his harsh breathing filling her ears. "Is this what you want?" he whispered hoarsely. "All right then, you'll get it!" He entered her so suddenly that her body flinched. He held her in an iron grip, so that she had no freedom of movement, his face and mouth riveted to hers. He stayed inside her for what seemed an eternity before he finally came.

When it was over she lay there, her body rigid with pain, her mind numb with outrage, listening to him breathe, until at last she fell asleep.

When she awakened in the morning, he was gone. She raised herself on one elbow and looked around the room. Slowly she remembered the night before. He had behaved like an animal, it was true. But at least he had not ignored her. She reached over and pulled at the bell rope. "What time is it?" she asked when Maria appeared.

"It is ten o'clock," Maria replied, eyeing her curiously. "Are you hungry?"

"Yes."

Maria uncovered the tray that stood by the side of the bed. Lucrezia looked at the ripe pear and the slab of cheese. She broke apart the fresh loaf and stuffed a piece of it into her mouth, chewing ferociously. "I'd like some wine, please."

When she had finished eating, she fell back against the pillows, feeling more relaxed. "I think I will go back to sleep now. I'm tired."

Maria's impatience grew. "What will they think of you, lying in bed until noon like a slattern!"

"I don't care what they think." In another few minutes, she had fallen asleep.

The bells were pealing out the noon hour when Alphonso returned from hunting to find his sister with the ladies of her court, tapping her foot impatiently. "Your bride is still sleeping," she said, her voice dripping acid. "You must have worn her out."

Alphonso removed his gauntlets and smiled. "She is obviously unaware that her dear sister-in-law is so impatient to see her."

Isabella ignored this. "She is obviously unaware of our customs. We have been denied access to her entirely."

Alphonso cleared his throat. "Perhaps she is used to more privacy."

"Privacy is but another word for rudeness. It is merely her way of keeping us at arm's length."

"Still and all, the custom may be different in Rome," Alphonso persisted.

"Nonsense, there is no difference of custom. One awakens in the morning and is attended by one's ladies-in-waiting. It is a snub, make no mistake!" Isabella said sharply.

Lucrezia lay in a warm bath, easing her body's soreness and going over and over again in her mind the events of the night before. She was disappointed, but she would not show it. She would not even tell Maria.

There was someone moving in the next room. "Maria," she called, "I am not in to anyone." When she looked up, Alphonso stood before her, his leather jerkin stained with sweat. She looked at him, uncertain of what to say.

"I am sorry about last night," he said finally. Then he turned on his heel and was gone.

Later that morning she was sitting at the little desk in her dressing gown, writing to Alexander, when the

363

door to the suite opened. Alphonso came in, still wearing his hunting clothes. He came over and stood by her chair.

"What are you writing?" he asked.

"You may read it when I am through," she replied. She wrote a few more words and then handed him the parchment.

He read it and put it down slowly. "You made no mention of last night."

"No," she said. "I did not think it would be right, and I did not want my father to worry."

He put his hands on her shoulders, feeling the soft skin beneath her gown. "Let us set matters right," he said, drawing her to him roughly.

She stood with her face pressed against his chest. She did not find the sweaty leather unpleasing.

"Don't be so stiff," he murmured against her ear. "I will not hurt you this time, I promise." His hands were already busy with his fastenings. He stood before her, tall and muscular. He undid the tie of her dressing gown and pushed it back on her shoulders so that it slid to the floor. Then he clasped her to him, the heat of their bodies mingling. His mouth pressed hers, his fingers sought her breasts. With a moan he caught her up and carried her to the bed. His mouth traveled her face, her neck, her ears. His hands were all over her. In a frenzy she turned and let him have her. He entered her slowly, almost hesitantly, letting his body move with hers, their breaths mingling, until with a sharp cry she moved against him and came. He let her move, achieving his orgasm in his own time. She reached for him then, her face against his. They lay looking at one another, filling their eyes. Then they fell asleep in one another's arms. When they awakened, they made love again. Afterward they had Maria fill the tub, and they lay together in the warm water.

Lucrezia did not put in an appearance until the following day. Conscious of the figure she was expected to cut as the new Marchioness, she took great pains with her toilet. She chose a lilac-colored dress bordered in violet and gold and trimmed with pearls and amethysts.

Isabella, who had been kept waiting for two days now, was barely civil until Alphonso hissed in her ear that she could either show Lucrezia the respect due her as Marchioness of Ferrara or else she could go and join her husband in Mantua. Isabella looked at him in surprise. After that she made a great show of cordiality, which made Lucrezia feel more uncomfortable than ever.

To celebrate Don Alphonso's marriage to Lucrezia, the old Duke arranged an elaborate reception, complete with theatricals. It was an occasion, he decided, worthy of his best efforts.

Lucrezia entered the Great Hall on the arm of the French ambassador, who complimented her on her dress. Alphonso was waiting for her under the gold canopy that the Duke had erected for her and her court. His eyes held hers for so long that she finally looked away in confusion. At the first sound of music, Lucrezia's foot began to tap. The French ambassador stood up and asked her to dance.

Ercole slapped his son on the back. "She is a real beauty," he said appreciatively. "Is she any good at all in bed?"

Alphonso, who was watching Lucrezia, made no answer. Instead, he rose to his feet and divested the ambassador of his partner.

Lucrezia, dancing with her husband, felt the thrill of possession that comes with being loved. Then it was Ercole's turn, and he proved to be a better dancer than all of them, holding her firmly but lightly, bending now and again to whisper pleasantries in her ear.

After a flourish of trumpets, the entire company moved to the theater to watch a series of plays which the Duke had chosen for presentation.

Seated on gold brocade cushions with the Este family, Lucrezia felt a glow of happiness. Her eyes lighted excitedly on the stage, which held a hundred or more actors. In Rome they had staged small theatricals, but nothing so grand as this. Impulsively she turned to her father-in-law and kissed him on the cheek, her eyes shining wth anticipation. "Your Highness is to be commended for such a production. I have never seen anything so beautiful!"

The old Duke, pleased, squeezed her hand and smiled.

The next morning, Saturday, Lucrezia slept late. Alphonso had made love to her twice during the night. The first time she had participated wildly. The second time she had been half asleep, but he had not seemed to mind.

She dawdled over breakfast. Maria, seeing this, smiled. "Your sister-in-law, the Duchess of Mantua, has been here twice. I told her that you were sleeping."

"I am still sleeping," Lucrezia said between yawns.

"She is up at dawn, I am told."

Lucrezia shrugged. "Perhaps there is nothing to keep her in bed."

Lucrezia did not make an appearance until the afternoon. She walked into the salon in black silk muslin, her hair shining and caught up beneath a black lace mantilla. The only jewel she wore was a magnificent cabochon emerald which had belonged to Alphonso's mother. She pinned it to the cleavage of her dress, where it drew all eyes. Lucrezia and her entire court wore black to celebrate the sabbath. The effect was at once somber and elegant.

"They look positively funereal!" Isabella said contemptuously. The thing that bothered her most was Lucrezia's strict insistence on privacy and the way she protected her privacy by using her own attendants in preference to the Ferrarese attendants presented to her. After all, Isabella had chosen them with an eye to spying and was now thwarted.

Two weeks later the wedding guests started to leave. The Duke breathed a sigh of relief. There were still almost five hundred people and as many horses to be housed and fed. Chafing at the expenses incurred by the hangers-on, he found excuses for dismissing them. He wrote to Alexander, complaining that "the noble-women accompanying Lucrezia have so many cavaliers, grooms and servants that the burden of providing hospitality for them grows too heavy for me. After all," he added, "I have not your treasury at my disposal."

"His is the tightest purse in the empire," Alexander said after reading the letter.

Isabella was as anxious to return home, but before she left, she made one more attempt at creating trouble for Lucrezia. Knowing that her father deplored the heavy expenses, she spread the rumor that Lucrezia was going to dismiss all the Ferrarese attendants in favor of her own. When the Duke was informed that the ladies-in-awaiting personally selected by him and Isabella were to be dismissed, he ordered all of her retinue save Maria to return to Rome immediately.

Lucrezia burst into tears when she heard this. "Why is he doing it? I have shown nothing but respect for his wishes up to now."

Alphonso sympathized with her. "It sounds like some of Isabella's work."

"Talk to him," Lucrezia pleaded. "I cannot stay here without any friends."

Alphonso returned from a visit to his father's study. "There is no changing his mind. He is simply using it as an excuse to pare expenses."

"Is there nothing at all you can do?"

Alphonso's thin lips tightened. "I can antagonize him into making one of my brothers his heir, but I don't think it is worth it."

When Isabella said good-bye, she looked at Lucrezia with a hint of malice. "I hope that we will truly be sisters," she said sweetly, "especially as your own people will soon be leaving . . ."

Lucrezia looked back at her and said nothing.

A week later the old Duke summoned Lucrezia to his study. A sparse fire glowed on the hearth. The Duke, bundled up to his chin, did not believe in wasting wood, or anything else for that matter. Lucrezia drew her cloak about her against the cold.

Ercole, tapping his quill against his lips, said, "I have been going over my accounts, and I find that the twelve thousand ducats yearly allowance provided for you in your dowry is excessive. Eight thousand is quite enough. The difference will be used to defray the cost of running my court."

"It is not enough for me," Lucrezia said boldly.

The old Duke looked at her quizzically. "If Isabella can run her house on eight thousand a year, so can you."

Lucrezia bit her lip against the tears of anger. He would not have the satisfaction of seeing her cry. She turned on her heel and left.

CHAPTER 32

In March, Lucrezia found out that she was pregnant. She told Alphonso the next morning at breakfast. "I am not feeling too well," she began.

Alphonso, who was thinking of other things, did not immediately understand. "Then why are you eating?" he asked, his mind on the mock battle he had set up on the board in his study.

"Because, idiot," she said, "one should always eat when one is expecting. How else is the child to grow?"

Delighted by the news, he took her hands in his and smiled. "Father will be pleased, I know. He might even decide to increase your allowance."

Lucrezia spread some of the creamy goat cheese on a piece of bread. "It is the least he can do. After all, he has sent away nearly all my attendants, and so he is saving there."

"We'll see," he said, taking her into his arms.

"We have just eaten," she reminded him.

"What has one thing to do with another?" He picked her up in his arms and carried her over to the bed.

When he left her for the toy soldiers in the study, she leaned over the chamber pot and was sick. This had not happened with her last pregnancy. I hope it is not a bad omen, she thought, crossing herself.

She and Alphonso had moved at her request from the ducal palace occupied by the old Duke into a large square castle built by Niccolò III. "We will have more privacy," she had said, playing with a lock of his hair. Now she was sorry. It was a dreary old place surrounded by a moat of stagnant water, and the furnishings were abominable. Each room was done in a different color, and her own room, which fortunately opened out into a sort of garden, was done entirely in gold satin, which was all wrong for her.

"It is so ugly," she told Alphonso. "The whole place depresses me."

Alphonso tried to talk to his father into redecorating Lucrezia's quarters, but the old man was adamant. "She is spoiled," he said. "Nothing is good enough for her. She will have to make the best of it."

"He will do nothing," Alphonso had to tell her. "Nothing at all."

Lucrezia had burst into tears. She cried very easily now. "He does not want me to be happy; he *doesn't*. First he sends away everyone I care about, then he withholds the allowance which my father meant me to have from the dowry, and now, knowing my state of mind, he will not do the slightest thing to make me happy."

Alphonso had been distinctly uncomfortable. "He will not live forever, you know. Someday you will be able to do as you like."

"I do not want to have to wish him dead to be happy," Lucrezia had said sadly. "Why must he be so difficult?"

Alphonso had shrugged. "He is no different with Isabella. He simply does not like to part with money."

"But it is my money, not his."

Alphonso did not answer.

When Lucrezia began cultivating the company of Ercole Strozzi, a handsome man in his thirties, Alphonso protested.

"But he is a famous poet," Lucrezia said quickly. "At home I had Vincenzo Calmeta. Here I have no one."

"You have me," Alphonso reminded her.

"I am used to having a salon," Lucrezia said stubbornly. "Your sister has already had everyone's ear. No one is friendly."

"All right," Alphonso said finally. "But watch him. He has a way of twining himself around a woman. I don't like it."

Strozzi did indeed have a way of fastening himself to women, one woman at a time. He came from Florence, of a very good family. He had great style, elegant manners, and an eloquent way of speaking. He seemed to sense a woman's moods and adapted himself to fit them. Knowing how Lucrezia felt about her sister-in-law Isabella, he set out at once to criticize her. "She is dumpy and frumpy and confuses freakishness with flair," he said to Lucrezia. "She really prefers young boys to men and is not averse to women either. As for her personality, I don't know why anyone puts up with her." What he did not tell Lucrezia was that he and Isabella had had their differences and that this new friendship was a form of vengeance.

When Isabella, in Mantua, heard of their friendship she was furious. "What right has she, mindless idiot that she is, to cultivate a man of letters!"

For Lucrezia, Strozzi bridged the gap between Fer-

371

rara and Rome. He became her favorite, gaining access to her apartments whenever he liked. He had a slight limp, which endeared him to her even more. She felt that he was mysterious and that he had suffered. Men generally did not care for him, nor he for them. He much preferred the company of women.

Strozzi generally turned up around eleven in the morning. Then, while Lucrezia had her breakfast and decided what to wear, they made plans for the day.

Alphonso came back from the hunt one morning to find Strozzi stretched out on the foot of the bed while Lucrezia sat against the pillows, having her morning meal. Every so often she would toss him a dried fig or an almond, which he would smilingly catch and eat, looking at her intently all the while.

"Why can you not receive him in the salon?" Alphonso asked her later.

"Because," she replied, "it is not the fashion."

"He is a fop!" Alphonso burst out. "He collects women the way a squirrel collects nuts, using them as he needs them."

"What difference does it make? He is using me and I am using him. Isn't that as it should be?"

"Well, watch out," Alphonso said lamely. "You are just another nut in his cheek. Remember that."

"And you," Lucrezia said angrily, "are jealous!"

Although her allowance was not as large as she would have liked, Lucrezia was able to make Strozzi costly little gifts which she knew delighted him.

When Alphonso heard about the gifts, he bit his lip and said nothing. After all, it was her money. She should be able to spend it as she liked. He thought of speaking to his father about Strozzi, but then he remembered that the old Duke thought highly of him, highly enough to sponsor him. Ah well, he supposed that the poet was an intellectual ornament at that. He would have to try to be more tolerant of him. There was nohing else he could do.

Soon Strozzi was supervising Lucrezia's wardrobe. "Your sister-in-law gets herself up like a circus. She would eat fire or swallow swords to ensure an audience. You, milady, have no need of such tricks." He encouraged her to dress simply, wearing only one important piece of jewelry at a time.

A few weeks later Strozzi sat at the foot of her bed and told her that he was going to Venice.

She stopped peeling the orange she was holding. "Why? Are you not happy here?"

"Of course I am. It is just that I have friends there whom I have not seen for several years, and at the same time I thought I might do some buying for you. There are things in Venice that you simply cannot find anywhere else."

Her interest was immediately piqued. "What sort of things?"

"Oh, brocades, silk shawls, leather goods so fine that they fit like a second skin."

"When are you planning to leave?" she asked slowly, already feeling a sense of loss.

"At once. The sooner I leave, the sooner I will return."

"Yes," she said, wondering how she would spin out her days without him.

"Before I leave," he said, sensing her mood, "I will make a list of books for you. And you must promise to read them all while I am gone so that we can discuss them when I return."

"Yes," she said, "and you must buy me the loveliest and most extraordinary things you can find."

Once in Venice, Strozzi took his time, amusing himself as he saw fit. First he visited his friend Pietro

373

Bembo, the humanist. For one week they did nothing but drink together and discourse endlessly into the night.

The next thing on his list was a Venetian woman, a great beauty, with whom he'd been carrying on for some time. He wanted to break it off before Lucrezia heard about it; he did not want to lose her and the old Duke as patrons.

After a week of indolence he went back to Bembo's house, and in a grand manner granted audience to all the silk merchants in the city. He fingered and sniffed, laying the fabrics against his cheek to test their fineness. He ran one bolt of silk over the bridge of his nose, discarding it after a snag in the material chafed his skin. The merchants waited, rubbing their hands together anxiously. Finally one of them, in order to cinch things, threw in a bolt of fine brocade, remarking shrewdly that Strozzi could keep it for himself if he wished. He made his selections slowly, choosing with care the colors he thought would suit Lucrezia best. His purchases far outweighed the purse she had given him, but he waved his arms, declaring that the old Duke was good for it.

In the end he bought on credit, receiving from each merchant something for himself. If the old Duke did not pay, they reasoned wisely, Alexander would. His generosity to his children was well known. Strozzi's last purchase was a magnificent cradle for the child Lucrezia was expecting. All in all, it had been a good trip.

Lucrezia had just finished her bath when the courier arrived with a large bundle from Venice. She pried open the seals and out tumbled a jewel-like profusion of colors. She invited the ladies of the court to come in afterward and see them. They fingered the fine fabrics, their eyes bright with envy.

When Alphonso saw them, he was furious. "Do you

realize that you have spent nearly a year's allowance?"

"It's all right," Lucrezia soothed. "He has bought it all on credit. Isn't he clever to have thought of that?"

Alphonso's face turned dark. "Very clever," he said as evenly as he could. "Do you realize you have gone against my father's wishes in this?"

Lucrezia looked at him, her eyes clear of guile. "That is true, but then your father has gone against my father's wishes in not granting me the whole of the allowance provided for me in my dowry."

Alphonso looked for a moment as though he were about to say something. Instead, he turned on his heel and left.

Lucrezia, giddy with happiness, arranged to have dresses made on credit as well. After all, she reasoned, if she didn't use it, it would all go to waste. She had twenty dresses made, all richly embroidered, with little caps and shoes to match. When Strozzi returned from Venice, she thought, she would give a large dinner party in his honor. It would be fun to show off her new clothes and, she thought spitefully, it would be fun to flout the old Duke and Isabella, whom she would invite as well.

Strozzi arrived home with a gift for her. It was a miniature of himself painted by one of the foremost artists in Venice. She was so pleased with it that she completely forgot to ask him for an accounting of all the coin she had given him.

When the time for the dinner arrived, the old Duke, with a sour face at the whole proceedings, sat in the place of honor Lucrezia had accorded him. She and Alphonso sat on either side of him. Next to Alphonso she put Isabella and her husband Francesco. Next to herself she put Strozzi.

Lucrezia had used the gold and silver service from all three dowries, and the tables looked magnificent.

375

She watched with satisfaction as the Duke and his daughter examined everything and said nothing.

Lucrezia, aware of the effect this brilliant display created, lost no opportunity to speak of her father and his great generosity. Finally, looking straight at the Duke, she said loudly, "You need not trouble yourself about the cost of all this, for I have never lacked for resources."

Ercole smiled faintly. "No," he said courteously. "I never presumed that you did."

When they were alone later, Alphonso took her to task. "I don't know what you hope to gain by such behavior. You were unpardonably rude. And if I know my father, he will not forget it."

"Rude!" Lucrezia burst out. "I am simply repaying them in kind. Your sister has never given me one kind word, and your father delights in thwarting my every wish!"

Alphonso sighed. "No one is trying to thwart you. He is simply a thrifty man. He expects nothing of you that he does not expect of himself. Why can you not understand that?"

"He may live as he likes," Lucrezia shouted. "And I shall live as I like!"

The relationship between Lucrezia and her father-in-law grew more strained. Whatever she asked for now, he refused to grant. In June, feeling that the cooler air at the park in Belfiore would be better for her than the summer heat at Ferrara, she asked the Duke for permission to take her court there.

"I am sorry," he said coldly, "but I am having work done there and you would only be in the way of the workmen and painters."

"What about Belriguardo then?" she asked, testing him.

The Duke hesitated. He had just received word that

Cesare Borgia had taken Urbino, divesting the Monte-feltro family, who were avid art collectors, of all their belongings. This was a terrible blow. After all, the Montefeltros were related to Isabella by marriage, and Lucrezia had stopped there to visit on her way to Ferrara.

"My father would not want me to be uncomfortable in my present condition," Lucrezia said firmly, ignorant of what Cesare had done.

The Duke hesitated no longer. "All right, you may leave at once."

Lucrezia returned to her room to pack.

Alphonso was waiting for her with a gloomy face. "We have just received word that your brother Cesare has taken Urbino. Just how far does he intend to go?"

"He does not keep me informed," she said as evenly as she could. She was shaken by the news. The Montefeltros—especially Elizabetta—had been very kind to her. Suddenly she burst into tears. Cesare's long shadow followed her everywhere, even into her new life.

Alphonso took her into his arms and attempted to comfort her.

"What does he want?" she murmured brokenly.

"*Omnia, omnibus, ubique,*" Alphonso answered softly. "Everyone, everything, everywhere."

Isabella, who had returned to Mantua, was furious when she heard of this. Not only did she feel sorry for her sister-in-law and brother-in-law, who fled to her for protection, but she was furious at the thought that their valuable art collection would undoubtedly end up in Rome. She listened with tight lips as Elizabetta told her tearfully how Cesare had ordered his men to pull up the beautiful carpets, tear down the tapestries, and inventory the collection of silver and art. Her eyes hardened as she thought of the famous *Sleeping Cupid* by Michelangelo, which Cesare had probably sent to

Rome by now. Was there any way of obtaining it for herself, she wondered. She would write to Cesare and see, under the guise of wanting to return it to the Montefeltros. After all, the relationship between Cesare and herself had always been a cordial one ...

Cesare wrote back: "Unfortunately, I have sent the *Cupid* and the little *Venus* to Lucrezia. They seemed so right for her somehow. Had I but known of your interest in them," he added, seeing through her plan to obtain them for herself, "I would have been only too happy to have given them to you." He sent her, by way of compromise, a beautiful tapestry which she recognized as having hung in Elizabetta's private apartments. Saying nothing of this to Elizabetta, she rolled it up carefully and put it away. There would be plenty of time to enjoy it after her sister-in-law left.

When Lucrezia received the *Venus* and the *Sleeping Cupid*, her first instinct was to return them to the Montefeltro family.

It was Strozzi who dissuaded her. "Don't be a fool," he exclaimed. "They are priceless! Besides, they don't expect to get them back. It would only set a precedent. And if you return them to Cesare, he will only send them on to Isabella. Is that what you want?"

"But I am so ashamed," Lucrezia said.

"You are not responsible for your brother's behavior," Strozzi said firmly. "Everyone is aware of that."

Isabella, unable to contain her anger and jealousy, wrote to her father to try to intervene. For once the old Duke told her to mind her own business. After all, he reasoned, as Lucrezia was now a member of the Este family, the booty belonged to them as well as to her. Realizing that Cesare would not go against his own sister and attack Ferrara, he began to treat her better and advised Isabella to do the same. "She is a guarantee of immunity against attack," he wrote her. "Be careful how you treat her." He began to bestow little gifts upon her and to inquire solicitously after her health.

Lucrezia, who could melt at a kind look, was grateful. She wanted nothing more than to be accepted and loved.

Toward the middle of July there was an epidemic of fever. Lucrezia, more susceptible because of her condition, became ill immediately. The old Duke was terrified. If anything happened to her now, where would his protection lie? Sparing no expense for once, he sent to Florence and Venice for the best doctors available. Alexander had been informed immediately, and had responded by dispatching his own physicians, Gaspare de Torre and Bernardo Bongiovanni. Then he sent for Don Constabili, the Ferrarese ambassador to Rome. "If anything happens to my daughter," he told him, "I will not be responsible for what Cesare does in Ferrara."

Constabili sent out a courier to Ercole in Ferrara. "His Holiness is greatly concerned about his daughter's health," he wrote. "He blames undue melancholy for the illness, saying that it was brought on by your refusal to honor her dowry. I earnestly beseech and advise that you do everything in your power to hasten her recovery, since her father and brother Cesare would take her demise as an unforgivable affront."

Alexander, not content with this, also sent word of her illness to Cesare at the French court.

The old Duke was really frightened. "I did not realize that four thousand gold ducats a year meant so much to her," he said to Alphonso, who was worried to distraction about Lucrezia's health. "Tell her that it is hers to do with as she pleases, with two thousand more thrown in for good measure from me, as soon as she recovers." In the privacy of his study, the Duke fell on his prie-dieu, calling upon God to save her. "It will

379

not be suitable if she dies—for the time being," he added fervently.

Alphonso was sorry now that he had not taken Lucrezia's part more actively. He loved this wife who was so like a child. Now that he could not have her, he missed her bed, her silliness, her laughter. Let her just get well, he resolved, and everything will be different. He would try to be more understanding, more like Strozzi. The poet still set his teeth on edge. He lounged outside her door like a spaniel, his face pulled long by a grief that Alphonso was certain he did not feel.

A week after Constabili's message, two emissaries, Troche and Remolino, arrived from Rome. They put their noses everywhere, into the food, the drink, and the medicines, jotting everything down in a large notebook.

The old Duke eyed them stonily but said nothing, fearing that anything he said might be misconstrued. He could understand Alexander's concern for his daughter. Even though their relationship had been strained, he felt a certain fondness for her. She did, after all, impart a certain sunniness, a spirit of lightheartedness. Trying to make amends, he had fresh delicacies sent to her every day. Lucrezia looked at the large grapes and the choice peaches and smiled. She could not eat them, but she knew that they were a gift of love.

On the second week in August, Cesare made an unexpected appearance at Ferrara. The old Duke and Alphonso greeted him with every show of hospitality.

He looked at them haughtily. "I have come to see for myself how my sister is." When he saw her, pale and wasted against the pillows, he ran to her and took her into his arms. "My own sweet love," he cried hoarsely, not caring whether anyone heard or not.

Lucrezia opened her eyes and smiled weakly, the

tears sliding down her cheeks. If Cesare were here, it could mean only one thing . . . she was dying.

He sat by her bed the entire night, unwilling to leave her even to eat a meal. She seemed to take strength from his presence, and the two of them talked in their native Valencian dialect until dawn. Then Cesare took her into his arms once more and kissed her tenderly, saying loudly so that all might hear him, "Do not forget to send me the ring if you need me." Then he was gone.

Two weeks later she gave birth to a stillborn child. As if that were not enough, she developed puerperal fever. Maria stayed by her side, sponging her hot body with water while she laughed and cried alternately, prattling on and on about the cradle which Strozzi had ordered for her. "I will lie in it," she said with empty eyes. "I will lie in it myself."

Alphonso for once was completely distracted from his war games. His toy soldiers stood idle on the painted wooden battlefield. During the day he rarely left her side. At night he slept on a cot at the foot of her bed. "Only live," he whispered to her. "Live and everything else will be all right."

The old Duke did everything in his power. There were a dozen doctors in attendance. They applied poultices and bled her, then plied her with noxious purges to rid her of impurities. Then they stood aside and waited. "God has laid His hand on her," they said gravely.

Lucrezia's face already had the look of the other world. Her skin, waxy and transparent, was pulled tightly over the small bones of her face. Her eyes were sunken and staring. Her once beautiful shining hair was limp and lusterless.

Cesare returned late one night, just as they were bleeding her for the fourth time. He came straight from the court of the King of France, from where he'd been summoned, with his brother-in-law Cardinal d'Albret and a company of French nobles. He took one look at Alphonso's tragic face and ran to her room, taking the stairs two at a time.

Almost out of her head with fever, she nonetheless smiled when she saw him. Seeing the discomfort she was in, he held her in his arms, murmuring words of comfort and endearment. The members of the Ferrarese court, having heard what an unnatural monster he was, could not believe their eyes.

"So that is the Borgia fox," the old Duke muttered to himself. "Well, even a fox has a heart, it seems."

Toward evening she had difficulty breathing, and they gave her Communion, as Alphonso wept at the foot of her bed.

Cesare held her in his arms, rocking her gently, as though the movement would keep her alive. Sometime during the night the fever broke. Cesare felt the dampness saturate her body. "Sponge her," he whispered to Maria.

A few minutes later Lucrezia opened her eyes and looked about her calmly. "Have I died?" she asked.

By midday she was well enough so that Cesare could leave her. He took the small hand that lay on the coverlet and pressed it to his lips. Then he rose, looking at Alphonso and the Duke.

"I am going now because I must. I leave behind my most valued possession. Need I say more?"

Alphonso and the Duke watched him leave. Then Ercole turned to his son.

"Go to Lucrezia now and tell her that she may have the twelve thousand a year. And give her this," he added, handing him a leather pouch with two thousand gold ducats in it, "and tell her that it is a get-well gift from me."

CHAPTER 33

Alexander was entering a period of his life that was completely foreign to him. At seventy-two years of age, he was beginning to suspect that he might not live forever. The thought of death and dissolution had never entered his mind in the past. He had always lived vigorously, at full tilt. But only a few months ago he had been with a woman and nothing had happened. It was the first time for him, and although he was aware of the fact that it happened to other men, he could not take it lightly. At first he had laughed, pleading a full stomach and fatigue. But after the woman had done everything she could think of to stimulate him, without arousing the flaccid organ between his thighs, he had slapped her good-naturedly on the behind and told her to be off, adding that he was no longer in the mood. He had not tried it since then for fear of failure.

It was not that the sight of a pretty face or a full breast did not arouse him; they did, and because they did he grew increasingly irritable. Unlike his former genial self, he began to carp at small things, taking his servants to task over nothing. At night he lay awake listening to the beat of his heart. He would lie thus in a cold sweat for two or three hours, finally falling into a fitful sleep just before dawn.

"I think I will go to Ferrara this summer to visit Lucrezia," he announced suddenly as he and Cesare sat one day at the noonday meal.

Cesare looked at him shrewdly. "What is it, Father? What is troubling you?"

Alexander looked away from the sharp, probing eyes of his son. He even managed to laugh. "Nothing. But who knows? Next year at this time I may be dead."

Cesare put down the cheese he was holding and wiped his mouth with his napkin. "Not you. You've made a pact with the Devil. Everyone knows that."

Alexander laid a trembling hand on his arm. "Do not joke about a thing like that. I have had several dreams recently. That thing, for instance, about Cardinal Ferrari, that was a bad piece of business."

Cesare lifted his brows. "Since when have you become so finicky? The old man died and left you three hundred thousand gold ducats. You would have been a fool not to take it."

Alexander wet his lips nervously. "But people are beginning to talk. They say that his death was not a natural one."

Cesare smiled. "Nonsense, Father. He died as a natural result of having been poisoned, and so you have a perfectly natural death. What could be more simple?"

"I think I am getting old," Alexander said apologetically. "A year ago it wouldn't have bothered me."

"Tut," Cesare said. "Nor should it bother you now."

Alexander said nothing. He poured himself a little more wine. That would make him feel better.

Cesare sat watching him. "You showed no such

384

compunction about dispatching Cardinal Michiel, as I recall."

"I've already told you. I felt differently then."

"Ah yes, so you did. If I remember correctly, the wretched man died after forty-eight hours of the most excruciating cramps and vomiting. He was even happy to go. There was a rumor at the time that while he was in his death agony you had the entire place stripped of valuables."

Alexander drank his wine quickly. "I only did it for you."

Cesare inclined his head gratefully. "Thank you, Father. Your generosity is overwhelming. But there is nothing sadder somehow than an aging monster. I liked you better before."

Alexander looked enviously at this strong son of his who feared nothing. "You are right," he said. "I sound like an old woman. But perhaps an old man is not so different from an old woman after all."

Cesare flung his napkin on the table and rose from his chair. "I do not like to hear you speak like that!" he said severely. It was true, he did not. After all, he was concerned at this moment with carving out an empire for himself, and in order to do that he needed a strong Pope behind him.

"I do not trust Louis," Alexander said that evening at dinner.

Cesare paused, barely able to control his irritation. After all, the French king was a trusted ally and friend. "What is it now?" he asked.

"French influence is on the wane," Alexander said slowly. "Perhaps you ought to look to Spain for protection instead."

"Louis is all right," Cesare said calmly and continued eating.

After three and a half years of warfare with Louis as

an ally, he had accomplished a great deal. He had succeeded in crushing all rebellion in the Italian states and bringing them under Vatican rule. He ruled fairly as well, granting a form of justice that the peasants had never known under their former rulers.

For his part, Louis was aware that Cesare's fortunes were riding high. Cesare had friends in high places everywhere. Was he becoming too strong, Louis wondered. Later, he reasoned, when he no longer had need of him, he would cut Cesare down to size, but not until then.

The summer of the year 1503 was an unusually hot one. The sun blazed day after day with a pitiless heat, shriveling flowers and shrubs and burning the skin of the peasants in the fields. The people of Rome stayed indoors, waiting for the cool of evening before they went out into the streets. Even then, most of them held wet scented rags to their faces, for the city was suddenly full of fever. Men and women dropped in the streets and died without absolution. Children eating their morning meals of bread and cheese would be dead by evening. The air was heavy with the sound of tolling bells.

"It is the Pope's doing," the superstitious peasants told one another. "We are paying for his sins and the sins of his son Cesare."

Resentment burned in their hearts along with the fever. Every time there was a death, a fist was shaken in the direction of the Vatican. After a while common pits were dug and the unwashed bodies were thrown in and covered with lime, for the carpenters could not keep up with the demand for coffins.

At the Vatican palace many of the servants were stricken and died. Alexander, newly vulnerable to death, was glum. He had little appetite for food, but

386

proceeded to stuff himself anyway in order to reassure himself that he was in good health. "A corpse has no appetite," he proclaimed, belching.

To lighten his mood, he surrounded himself with jongleurs and dwarfs, preferring not to be alone. They slept on the floor of his bedchamber, rolling up their pallets as soon as he awakened and turning their handsprings and somersaults and looking foolish. He had guests to dinner each night, and plied them with sweetmeats and wine afterward so that they would remain late.

When he and Cesare received an invitation to dinner from Cardinal Adriano da Corneto at his vineyard estate on the slopes of Monte Mario, he immediately accepted for both of them. It was the first week in August, and the hottest month so far. Because of the heat, their host had had the tables set out-of-doors on the terrace. There was a profusion of ice-cooled drinks, which Alexander gulped endlessly.

An hour later, with dinner already under way, the sun, an angry red ball, sank beneath the hills. The air was aswarm with insects, and Alexander alternately slapped at his face and swallowed huge amounts of iced wine. After dinner the air cooled somewhat and the insects disappeared. The party sat in the starlit garden, looking down at the city below them, watching a torchlight procession of monks wend its way through the miasma that rose from the swamps.

Alexander rose suddenly. "I am tired," he said heavily to his host.

A week later, as he was celebrating Mass in the Sistine Chapel, he began to feel unwell. Within a few days both he and Cesare were ill with the fever. Doctors were immediately summoned to Alexander's bedside.

"He must be phlebotomized at once," Gaspare de

387

Torre advised, paying no attention to Cesare's illness, since he was younger and stronger.

Alexander was accordingly relieved of a pint of blood. This seemed to make him feel better, and so they immediately removed another pint. He was feeling so much better afterward that he was able to sit up in his bed and watch the cardinals in attendance playing at cards.

A few days later his condition worsened. This time de Torre not only bled him, but fed him a stew compounded of arsenic, antimony, and aconite, which Alexander immediately expelled.

Gaspare de Torre stood by his bed, a handkerchief at his nose. "There seems to be a morbid flux of viscous fluid. I do not think he will live."

Alexander was seized alternately with fever and chills. He was barely coherent. He was unaware that Cesare had not been to see him, or that Cesare was himself ill.

Toward evening he became lucid. "Life is fatal," he murmured. Then his eyes closed and he dozed off. When he awakened, he was hungry. "Bring me a roasted bird," he ordered.

When it was brought from the kitchen, a napkin was tied under his chin. He gobbled the bird greedily and called for some wine to wash it down. He had no sooner drunk it than he began to choke and vomit. When he was through, he fell back weakly against the pillows, breathing shallowly.

During the night he became delirious. He thought he saw a large baboon leaping about his bed. He began to shriek that it was the Devil come to fetch him away. "Only a little while longer," he beseeched, "and I will come."

Alexander continued to mutter the entire night, doz-

388

ing and waking. Burchard, who was standing in a corner, would not approach the bed.

On the morning of August 18, Alexander realized he was dying. The Bishop of Carinola came running to hear his confession. When it was over, Alexander lost consciousness. Toward afternoon he opened his eyes. "A peach," he said plaintively. "If I could just have a peach."

A peach was sent for and peeled. The Bishop pressed it to his lips. Alexander looked at it, a frothy sputum hanging in the corners of his mouth. Then his eyes rolled back in his head and his breath was expelled in a hoarse sigh. He had never once asked for Cesare.

Burchard went in toward midnight, as was his office, to oversee the preparation of Alexander's body for burial. The night was warm. The windows had been thrown open, but the heat had hastened decay so that the air of the room was fetid with the stench of death.

Burchard held a linen cloth to his nose and went over to the bed. In the uncertain flickering light the corpse looked monstrous, so swollen that the features were grossly misshapen. The eyes bulged from their sockets.

"They will not stay closed," one of the servants complained, crossing himself.

It is the pressure from inside, Burchard thought. "Do the best you can," he murmured, anxious to leave.

A dresser of the dead had been summoned from Strasbourg. He had been cooling his heels for a week now, waiting for Alexander to die.

"He is a veritable magician," the Bishop of Carinola said. "There is nothing that he cannot do with a corpse."

Burchard nodded on his way out. "It will take a magician to make this one presentable."

389

The body was washed and dressed. Then it was carried to St. Peter's, where it lay in state on a black velvet catafalque, the bare feet protruding through a sort of curtain so that those who wished to could kiss them in obeisance. No one stayed to keep vigil as was customary. Even Burchard, who went entirely by the book, refused to stay.

When he came in the morning to open the chapel to the public, he found that a horrible transformation had taken place during the night. The dresser's magic had vanished and in its place lay a swollen, blackened corpse. Burchard, retching, made his way out to the steps. A crowd of people waited to enter. One look at the awful thing before them was enough. Several women screamed and fainted.

"It is the Devil himself!" one shrieked. "Run for your life!"

They almost crushed one another in their haste to leave. After that no one was allowed in. Burchard summoned coffiners to box the corpse without delay.

The Bishop of Carinola remonstrated with him. "Cesare will want to see his father one last time."

"Cesare is out of his head with fever," Burchard said reasonably. "The body will not keep in this heat."

Cesare lay staring up at the ceiling, his mind detached and drifting. The fever had left him weak and disoriented. He raised his hand and looked at it curiously. It was thin and wasted and it shook. Is that my hand, he wondered, idly and uncaring. He could not remember days or nights or hours. He could remember de Torre saying "There is a superfluity of blood" before they bled him. He could remember being plunged into a vat of ice water up to his neck so that his teeth rattled in his head. Then as his fever cooled, he seemed

390

to hear Lucrezia's voice at his ear, calming him into sleep. When he awakened the fever had broken.

When Burchard entered his room and saw the hollow eyes set in the gaunt, bearded face, he crossed himself, for Cesare looked exactly like Jesus Christ lying against the pillows.

Cesare attempted to raise his head, but it was so heavy on his neck that he fell back weakly, gasping with the exertion. "How is my father?" he whispered finally.

"He is dead."

Cesare's eyes closed against the shooting pains in his head. "When?" he asked hoarsely.

"He was buried yesterday."

Cesare raised himself with difficulty. His head felt as though it would burst. "Summon Don Michelotto. There will be looting."

"There has already been looting," Burchard said softly.

"What was taken?"

"I have a list," Burchard said coldly. "The servants started to loot as soon as the body was cold."

Cesare's breath was coming in short spurts now. "Give me the list," he gasped. "I want the guilty ones punished!"

"I will let Don Michelotto attend to that," Burchard said distastefully.

Cesare peered at him sharply. "You smelly old fool. You're not sorry that my father is dead, are you?"

Burchard looked at him and said nothing. Then he walked from the room.

CHAPTER 34

In Ferrara, Lucrezia was steeped in sorrow. Her father's death had dealt her a serious blow. Although he was old, she had always thought of him as being somehow invincible. Now he was gone, and she could no longer turn to him for protection. What would happen, she wondered sadly, to little Rodrigo now that his grandfather was no longer there to watch over him? Cesare's position was even more precarious. He had been able to confiscate a hundred thousand or so gold ducats and some valuable gems and art objects from his father's apartments before the looters took everything. But his problem was with the people. All of Rome seemed to have turned against the dead Pope and his son, blaming them for the fever, seeing them as the Devil's own messengers on earth.

Cesare was distraught. "I had provided against everything that might occur in case of the Pope's death," he wrote to Lucrezia, "but I could not have foreseen that at such a time I myself would be almost dead."

Lucrezia tried to think. Without her father, and with

Cesare's influence at a low ebb, what would her position be now?

When Isabella heard of the sacking of the Pope's apartments, she was jubilant. It was, after all, nothing that he and Cesare had not done many times themselves. Now there would be much less for Lucrezia.

It was Alphonso who finally brought her out of her misery. "You are truly one of us now," he said tenderly. "You have been all along. Your father's death will do nothing to change that, I assure you."

She had received a letter from Cesare only a week before her father had been taken ill. In it he had written: "What after all is the fret, the hurry, the stir? It all ends in nothing."

Lucrezia showed Cesare's sad letter to Alphonso. "I think that I should go to him. There is no one else who cares."

"I think you had better wait and see what happens," Alphonso said wisely.

The events of the next week bore him out. The deposed lords came riding into Rome, demanding their properties back. Cesare, his teeth still rattling with fever, defied them. In retaliation they sacked and burned almost a hundred houses in the Spanish section of the city, a direct insult to Cesare and his Spanish blood.

The Sacred College, meeting to elect a new Pope, suggested to Cesare discreetly that he convalesce at the estate in Nepi while the conclave met. He saw the wisdom in what they said and left immediately. The good country air would restore his ravished body.

All of Europe watched and waited. When Francesco Piccolomini of Siena was elected Pope, Cesare breathed a sigh of relief. He had been afraid that Giuliano della Rovere might be elected. If that had happened, he thought, it would have spelled the end for him. As it was, Pius III, as the new Pope called himself, was eighty-four years of age and suffered from gout and ulcerations of the leg. It was only a transition vote, Cesare realized, for Pius would not be in office long, but at least it gave him the time he needed to reform his army and defend the territories he had taken from their rightful owners.

Four days after taking office, Pope Pius announced publicly that Cesare Borgia was to continue as Captain General of the Church. Shortly afterward he granted Cesare permission to return to Rome.

Cesare was at dinner when the news of Pius' death reached him. He dropped his napkin and turned ashen. The Pope had died too soon.

For two days he waited for news of what was happening. Then he was summoned to the Vatican to meet with della Rovere, Cardinal of Vincoli.

The Cardinal smiled. If Cesare could see his way to influencing the Spanish conclave in his favor, then Vincoli, if elected, would arrange it that Cesare continue in his role as Gonfalonier and that all his principalities would be returned to him. He did not tell Cesare that he had made a different deal with everyone concerned.

Cesare consented. He had no choice. Machiavelli, the Florentine statesman who had been sent to report on the proceedings, wrote to Florence: "The Cardinal of San Pietro in Vincoli has been proclaimed Pope. The reason for his unanimous election is said to be that he promised everyone whatever he asked. Now the difficulty will be to keep his word." The new Pople proclaimed himself Julius II.

For a time the new Pope was all smiles. He might not keep his promises, but no one would know it yet. He invited Cesare to occupy apartments in the Vatican once again. To allay his fears completely, Julius next informed the people of Fano and Faenza that they were to support Cesare as their overlord, referring to him as "my beloved son."

A week later Julius was speaking from the other side of his mouth. "Those states," he said, "which our predecessors have unlawfully alienated from the Church must be returned to it." Everyone breathed more easily now. He had merely been playing for time. Cesare had finally met his match.

Cesare became aware, little by little, that his prestige was slipping. No one deferred to him anymore. When the ambassadors and prelates passed him in the halls of the Vatican they merely nodded briefly or not at all. And although he lived luxuriously in the Vatican, he realized that he was in effect being held a prisoner.

Cesare's position worsened by the hour. He could not act, he could not issue orders of any kind. He became irritable and suspicious, looking over his shoulder and searching faces for motives. He flew into rages over nothing and was afterward ashamed. He made the fatal error of apologizing for something to one of his servants. The contempt in the man's eyes appalled him. He had never before apologized to anyone.

Machiavelli, noticing the change in him, wrote to Florence: "The blows of fortune which he is not accustomed to bear have stunned and bewildered him."

In Ferrara, Lucrezia was taking this news badly. Although the Borgias had suffered ill fate before, it had seemed unthinkable that Cesare could be defeated. Her family's turn of fortune filled her with sadness. Although she had had no sympathy in the past for Cesare's aggressions, her heart was sore for him. "He is like the beasts of the forest," she said to Strozzi. "He cannot help how he behaves any more than they can." She wrote to him to bolster his spirits, starting her letters with "My Dearest Cesare" and ending them with "Lucrezia who loves you unceasingly."

Turning one day to Alphonso, she asked him tearfully if Cesare might not be allowed to come to Ferrara to stay.

Alphonso considered. "You may ask him if you wish," he said finally. "But I do not think that he will want to come."

"I will come when I can," Cesare wrote back diffidently, "but I do not know when that will be. I have much to occupy me here, and Julius leans on me heavily for support. Please know that I carry you always within my heart."

In Rome, Cesare schemed how he could best recoup his losses and bring back his days of glory and triumph. He discarded one plan after another. He had been backed into a corner from which there was no escape. Losing all control, he even lashed out at Machiavelli, his only friend, whom he admired and respected.

The Florentine statesman, aware of how little company Cesare had nowadays, had come to pay him a visit. But he had been imprudent enough to suggest that Cesare give up all idea of conquest and retreat to the estate at Nepi, where he could live in peace and luxury for the rest of his life. "You would be safe there," Machiavelli continued wisely, "and in time they will forget all about you."

This idea so enraged Cesare that he burst out without allowing him to finish. "You have always been my enemy," he shouted illogically.

Machiavelli looked at him with pity. He left the room without saying anything more.

Cesare was shaking so hard that his whole body trembled. It was the fever, he thought hopelessly, that was making him lose control. He had always been so cool-headed in the past. He was horrified and depressed by what he had become.

Cesare poured some wine to steady his nerves. He

396

was sorry he had shouted at Machiavelli; he was one of the few people who wished him well. Had it not been for Niccolò's friendship through all of this, Cesare felt, he might have let go of his mind. He took a draft of wine to clear his head. There was only one route open to him now. He must leave Rome and take his men to the Romagna before everything slipped away from him. He had two hundred thousand gold ducats available to him in a Genoese bank. That would be enough to recruit more men. All he needed now was Julius' permission to leave.

To his amazement, Julius was more than willing. "We shall of course be sorry to see you go," the Pope said, turning his head so that Cesare could not see the relief in his eyes. To Burchard he confessed later, "I have never granted anything with more willingness. It is now out of my hands entirely."

Machiavelli attempted once more to change his mind. "It is not prudent," he insisted. "Nepi is the only answer."

Cesare smiled and embraced him. "You have been a good friend, Niccolò, but I must listen to my own dictates."

Machiavelli nodded. "Then it is good-bye, I suppose."

Cesare laughed with something of his old confidence. "No, my friend. It is merely *au revoir.*"

Cesare had no sooner left Rome than Julius was informed that Venetian troops had infiltrated the Romagna and that the people of the region, incited by the Venetians, were rising against the Church.

"I should never have let him go," Julius exclaimed. "For if he sides with Venice as he has threatened to do, then we are lost." He sent two cardinals to overtake Cesare and ask him to promise he would not bear arms against the Church.

Cesare was at Ostia, ready to set sail. When cardinals Remolino and Soderini approached him with Julius' message, he was astounded. "Are you all mad?" he shouted, sparing nobody's ears. "I would as soon forfeit my life as forfeit my interests!"

"So be it," Julius said grimly when Cesare's answer was reported to him. He sent word to the captain of the fleet that Cesare was to be returned to Rome under armed guard.

Lucrezia received the news of Cesare's incarceration with something close to hysteria. Not only had she been deprived of a loving and generous father, but now Cesare was in jeopardy.

"Use your influence," she implored Alphonso. "Surely there is something you can do to help him."

Alphonso looked away from the torment in her face. "What would you suggest I do?" he asked "Tell Julius that he need not fear him? You know that is not true."

Lucrezia clasped and unclasped her hands. "There must be something that we can do!"

"There is nothing we can do," Alphonso said firmly. "And he has only himself to blame."

To add to Cesare's misfortunes, Julius appointed Guidobaldo Montefeltro, Duke of Urbino, as the new Captain General. Cesare's past misdeeds were coming back to haunt him.

"Any person who wants to enter the good graces of His Holiness the Pope has to pay court to the Duke of Urbino," Burchard said to him with satisfaction. Burchard knew as well as anyone that Cesare, having once ousted the Duke from his castle and confiscated all his treasures and holdings, would receive no consideration from this man, reputed though he was to be fair. "I would advise you to banish all thoughts of an audience," Burchard warned him. "After all, the man is only a duke, not a saint."

Cesare brushed this aside. He would seek an audience with him and throw himself on his mercy. What did he have to lose?

When he disclosed his plan to Machiavelli, the Florentine was astounded. "Do you really expect him to give you an audience after what you have done to him and his family?"

"That was a long time ago," Cesare said impatiently. "He has probably forgotten all about it by now."

"Forgotten?" Machiavelli repeated in wonderment. "You throw a man out of his house, confiscate all his worldly goods, and expect him to forget such a thing? Cesare," Machiavelli said softly, "promise them that you will retire to Nepi and live in peace. Believe me, it is your only chance."

Cesare turned on him fiercely. "Would you ask a hawk not to fly? Would you suggest to it instead that it stay on the ground and scratch for its food like a chicken?"

Machiavelli dropped his eyes. "Do as you will, my friend. There is no one left who can help you now."

Cesare sent two requests for an audience with the Duke of Urbino, both of which were ignored. In desperation he entered his chamber unannounced and threw himself at his feet. The Duke was so taken aback by this that all he could do was stare. Finally he recovered himself and bade him arise, asking coldly what had brought him.

Cesare, with no thought now for his dignity, and ignoring the stares of the courtiers, burst out with an apology for his past behavior. "I attribute such lack of feeling to my youth and my inexperience," he said humbly, his head bowed. "But more than that, I attribute it to the undue influence of my father, whose greed and bestiality were well known."

399

At the mention of Alexander's name, the Duke's eyes widened.

Cesare, mistaking shock for approval, babbled on, not knowing or caring what he was saying at this point. "Alexander was a horrible man and it was he and he alone who ordered me to do that terrible thing in Urbino. But forgetting all that, look what I have done for the Church. I have vanquished its enemies and restored peace to the Romagna. And as for the things that I have taken from you under the express orders of my father . . ." He would have gone on interminably, except that the Duke, who was already visibly embarrassed at the reference to the dead Pope, now became annoyed. Cesare, seeing this, tried to finish quickly. "I have been waiting all this time for an opportunity to make amends. Believe me, nothing would make me happier."

The Duke coughed.

"I will make full restitution of everything that was taken," Cesare continued anxiously, "with the exception of course of a few little trinkets which I have already dispensed as gifts . . ."

The Duke stared at him and said nothing.

Cesare finally had no choice but to stop talking and bow his way out under the amused glances of his former compatriots, who, as soon as he had quitted the room, began to mimic him. *"The bestiality of Pope Alexander!"* they shrieked in falsetto, until brought to order by the Duke.

"There is nothing so sad," he admonished them, "as a fallen giant. There is a lesson here for all of us."

Cesare's new quarters in the Vatican were the rooms in which Alfonso of Bisceglie, Lucrezia's husband, had met his death. If such a thing bothered him, he gave no sign. He did not believe in ghosts, and furthermore, he had his own problems. He was now quite alone, for Julius had made it clear that he would look with extreme disfavor on anyone who attempted to befriend Cesare. With nothing to do and no one to talk to, he took to lying on his bed and gazing off into space. In despair he wrote a letter to Lucrezia, imploring her to use her influence in his behalf with Alphonso and Ercole.

Lucrezia was once more reduced to tears over her brother. Forgetting his hand in her dead husband's murder and his numerous aggressions, all of which had mortified her, all she could think of now was his misery and how she could help him.

"Perhaps they would release him to us," she suggested.

"Absolutely not," Alphonso was firm. "He would not be here five minutes before he started taking over the affairs of state and the entire household. Let him stay where he is."

Cesare wrote next to Francesco Gonzaga, Isabella's husband.

"Do nothing," Isabella advised him when he told her of it. "He is no longer worth the trouble."

Then something happened which no one expected. Louis's hopes of conquest in southern Italy were permanently squashed by Gonzalvo de Córdoba. The Spanish victory was a boon for Cesare. The Spanish ambassador, feeling this was a good time to intervene on behalf of a fellow Spaniard, pressed Julius for a decision regarding Cesare. Not wishing to antagonize the Spanish at this time, Julius made a concession. If Cesare would surrender all claims in the Romagna and promise never again to take up arms against the Church, he would be free to leave Rome and live in peace.

Cesare absolutely refused to surrender his claims. In

a pique Julius had him incarcerated in the heavy fortress at Ostia. There, in that lonely wasteland near the Tiber, he was left to reflect. He knew the thick stone walls of captivity would destroy him. After seven weeks he could bear it no longer. He sent word to Julius that he would surrender unequivocally, whereupon Julius made him sign a paper testifying to the fact that he would never again march against the Church. Then the gates were opened and he was free to leave. He embarked for Naples.

Once there, he forgot all about his imprisonment. His cousin Cardinal Juan Borgia welcomed him with open arms. He gave him magnificent quarters in his palace and assigned him servants proper to his rank. Cesare was instantly surrounded by a growing crowd of admirers; even Sancia came to pay him homage. It was very much like old times. He strutted and preened, conscious once more of cutting a fine figure before envious eyes. He needed this audience, needed to see himself mirrored larger than life in men's eyes. Nepi indeed, he thought. He would not play to an empty house. No actor worth his mettle would.

Two weeks of adulation were enough to restore his old confidence. He would show everyone that he was far from beaten. As for honoring the promise of non-aggression that he had made to Julius, he would simply close his eyes to it and do as he pleased. He had no trouble finding a few hundred men who would follow him. Encouraged by this, he bought some artillery and chartered several ships to take him and his men to Tuscany.

In Ferrara, Alphonso reacted to this piece of news with disdain. "That brother of yours never knows when he is well off," he told Lucrezia. "He is giving Julius the very excuse he needs to destroy him."

Lucrezia, who was doing a bit of needlework,

402

pricked her finger at this, then sucked away the blood. "It is not his fault that he cannot live any other way. What would you have him do?"

"I would have him live like a gentleman on the estates at Nepi. It is a good enough life for me. Why isn't it good enough for him?"

"Cesare is not a gentleman," Lucrezia said calmly, taking up the piece of work once again. "He is an adventurer. He must live by his wits or not at all."

"He is thirty-three," Alphonso said stubbornly. "He is no longer so young. He should try to make a life for himself with Charlotte and have some children."

Lucrezia looked at him then. The word "children" always made her think of Rodrigo in Rome. But each time she spoke of him, Alphonso looked away and busied himself with other things. The child would always be an ache in her heart. "Cesare would never be content to spend the rest of his life playing toy soldiers," she said, putting the thought of the child away from her.

Alphonso said nothing more.

In Rome, Julius acted immediately. He sent a letter to Isabella and Ferdinand of Spain complaining of Cesare's treachery. Those two, anxious for the new Pope's good will, directed the Grand Captain in Naples to stop Cesare.

A week later he was imprisoned again, this time in the underground dungeon of Castel Nuovo in Naples. He was permitted no visitors and no comforts of any kind.

"Let him rot!" Julius had ordained.

To a man like Cesare, this betrayal was the supreme indignity. After several weeks of captivity he was moved across the bay to the fortress on the isle of Ischia. There he shouted and beat his fists against the

403

stone walls. But there was no one to hear him or to care. Peculiarly enough, the only one of his enemies to pity him was Caterina of Forlì, the amazon whom he had humiliated publicly and treated so badly. Only a wild spirit like hers would appreciate his imprisonment. "I would rather die!" she said when she heard of it.

It was the end of a golden era, the end of the Borgia rule.

CHAPTER 35

Lucrezia mourned for her brother as though he were already dead. Alphonso, who had tired of all her pleas in Cesare's behalf, eagerly seized upon his father's suggestion that he settle a dispute which had arisen in one of their provinces. He told her that when he returned he hoped to find her in a more reasonable frame of mind.

Alphonso had been gone over a month now and Lucrezia was bored. After a while Cesare's imprisonment began to weigh less heavily on her, and she was starting to chafe.

"I was not made to do without a man for this length of time," she grumbled to Maria.

"Then take a lover," Maria said lightly.

Lucrezia pinched her mouth in thought. "There is no one around who interests me," she said seriously. "Some women can live without men, but not me. If only little Rodrigo were here to keep me company."

It was Strozzi who unwittingly provided the man and the moment. Since they spent a great deal of time together, it was not unusual for him to do his correspondence as she sat at her needlework.

"To whom are you writing?" Lucrezia asked, reaching for a sweetmeat without looking up from her work.

"To a friend," Strozzi replied evasively.

Lucrezia looked up immediately. "Ah, and who is that?"

"Pietro Bembo. You wouldn't like him," Strozzi added quickly.

She was suddenly all interest. "And why wouldn't I?"

Strozzi considered. "Well, for one thing, he is very selfish. He is only interested in matters that concern him. His poetry, for example."

"I see," she said, putting her frame to one side. "What else?"

"Well, for another thing, he is always posturing and preening."

"Tell me more," she said, intrigued.

"There is nothing to tell. He lives by himself. He is really quite a solitary fellow, not at all given to social affairs."

"Well," she said thoughtfully, "we must remedy that at once. Invite him to visit."

Strozzi was astounded. "But you don't even know him."

She smiled. "From what you've told me, I feel as though I know him already."

Strozzi tried to dissuade her. "I don't know why you should be so interested in someone you've never met," he said peevishly, feeling that his own position was being threatened.

Lucrezia, who had already read everything that Bembo had written, said, "He seems to know a great deal about women."

"He is a great womanizer," Strozzi agreed sourly.

"That business between him and the Venetian woman, Helena, when he wrote to her: 'Love me, love me, love me a thousand times over. Love me if you can. May it please you to love me a little more than you do.' I should love to be loved like that." She had memorized it from one of his books of poetry.

Strozzi made no answer other than to say that Bembo probably considered those lines to be a literary exercise of some sort.

Bembo's reply to her invitation came a week later. He regretted that he could not come. His health was delicate. Perhaps later in the year . . . ? In the meantime he thanked Her Highness for her good thoughts and her kind invitation.

Strozzi did not try to hide his satisfaction. "He is always indisposed. I told you so. He is probably busy with some woman or other and does not wish to be disturbed."

In the end it was Ercole who was responsible for Bembo's visit. The old Duke had not been feeling well for some time and needed cheering. Pietro Bembo was one of his favorites, and Ercole fed Lucrezia's curiosity about the Venetian poet, glad that she was finally coming to share some of his interests.

"Why don't you ask him to come and visit?" Lucrezia suggested innocently. "His presence would be a tonic for you."

"Would you really like me to do that?" the Duke asked, his eyes filling with pleasure.

Lucrezia replied that nothing would make her happier.

Ercole sent him a letter.

"He is coming," he told Lucrezia two weeks later.

"He said expressly that he is looking forward to meeting you."

Lucrezia readied herself by washing her hair once a day. She sponged her face with honey and cream and whitened her teeth with salt, rubbing her gums so hard that they bled. Then she looked critically at herself in the large glass. She had by now had two miscarriages, but her body was still attractive. In fact, her breasts had rounded and so had her hips. She looked seductive, she thought. "I wonder what sort of woman he likes best," she mused aloud to Maria.

Maria did not answer. She wanted no part of it. If Lucrezia had innocently fallen into an adventure, she would have shrugged her shoulders and understood. But this cold-blooded plan of seduction soured her blood. "You should find another outlet for your feelings," she said finally. "I will say one thing more to you, and then you will never hear another word from me. I know that you are still in mourning for your father, that Cesare's exile breaks your heart, that your husband's absence weighs heavily on you. But what you are about to do can only make matters worse."

"Never mind," Lucrezia said, looking quickly away. "This is what I need right now and I mean to have it. I am bored to death here."

Lucrezia was entirely unprepared for Pietro Bembo. She had never met anyone like him, she thought. When he took her hand and kissed it, she noticed that his eyes were deer-soft and brown. His lips smiled, but his face did not. His mouth was tender, but carved with a man's strength. All this she saw at once, and was both smitten and ashamed. She began to stammer. Then she blushed and said nothing.

Bembo, although he gave no sign of it, was similarly intrigued. He spoke to Ercole about his new projects. He was polite and charming to everyone at the court, but his eyes strayed toward Lucrezia, taking in the soft flower of her face, the gentle shifting of her golden hair.

"I have heard that you take a great interest in the arts," he said to her when they finally had some time together. He had directed this statement politely to the corner of her nose, but she continued to look at him until he was compelled to look back. Her eyes caught and held his. Are they more blue or more gray, he wondered. No matter, they were the eyes of a child set in a woman's face. How attractive, he thought. He took her hand and kissed it lightly to hide the tumult in his chest. "I will prepare a list of poems for you to read," he said casually. "Pieces that I think you will enjoy."

"Thank you," Lucrezia said evenly. Then, inexplicably, she left his side to speak to someone else.

Spring had come suddenly to Ferrara. One day it was warm and everything seemed to burst into bloom. Lucrezia had felt it the moment Bembo walked into the room. Everything in her seemed to flow and come alive. The flowers slowly budding into petals and filling the air with fragrance, the bright chirp of birds by her open window, only intensified the soft flow of feeling within her. So far Bembo had given her no indication that she had any effect on him whatsoever. And she had tried to keep her quickening feelings to herself. Where before his visit she felt like gambling on something new, now she felt frightened and solemn, aware of emotions over which she had no control. The poems he had given her to read were unashamedly romantic ones.

Strozzi, who had been out of sorts ever since Bembo's arrival, remarked that the poetry was intended to seduce her mind so that he could then go to work on her body.

Lucrezia colored. She was sitting by an open window, a volume of poems on her lap. "You shouldn't be so envious of Pietro. You both have different gifts to give."

"Yes," Strozzi agreed, "but my gifts do not sit between my legs."

"It is not like that," Lucrezia said thinly.

"Not yet, but soon."

Lucrezia had been in mourning ever since Alexander's death. "I will never again wear anything but black," she had told Maria in tears.

"You will change your mind," Maria had answered. "Nothing is for all time."

When Pietro Bembo first saw her, she was dressed in a thin black tissue taffeta that stood out stiffly from her small body and emphasized the translucent pallor of her skin. She looked altogether romantic and melancholy, her lovely blond hair caught up in a black velvet snood worked with tiny black rosebuds, her feet shod in black satin slippers, her only ornament the ruby and diamond brooch Cesare had given her.

Now, for the first time since Alexander's death, she felt as though she wanted to wear some color, but it was still too soon. But on second thought, black was better after all. It was more becoming and more romantic. What was it that Strozzi had said about Bembo trying to seduce her with his poetry? She laughed softly. Was it possible, she wondered, taking up a black organza and spreading it out on the bed for Maria to brush. And if he did try to seduce her, would she allow him to? Of course she would not. She was, after all, the Marchioness of Ferrara. And although Alphonso was away, he was still her husband.

She thought of Alphonso and a feeling of sadness settled over her. She loved him, but she resented his absence. Throwing on a light wrapper, she went onto the balcony with her brushes. She wished she were a child again. Then Papa would still be alive, she thought, and Cesare would run and tease her. The sun drenched her with its warmth. She sat and dozed, feeling small once again, and happy. Why had she not realized how wonderful everything had been then? Why had she let it all slip away like quicksilver, without trying to catch it in her fingers and keep it with her always? Why was she growing older so quickly?

That was it, she thought with a shudder. It was horrible to grow old. She would rather die first. She opened her wrapper to the sun and examined her body with satisfaction. Her breasts were still high and round. Her belly was flat and her waist was tiny. She was so engrossed in self-scrutiny that she did not notice the figure on the balcony next to hers. It was only when the flower fell at her feet that she looked up to see Pietro Bembo watching her with his soft brown eyes. He saluted her gravely, then he went inside.

Maria, noticing her high color later, said sharply, "What is wrong with you? Do you have a fever?"

"A fever," Lucrezia repeated dreamily. "Yes, I think I have a fever."

She dressed carefully, surveying herself anxiously in the glass. Maria had dressed her hair so that it hung simply about her shoulders, framing the narrow oval of her face. The head gardener had found some lovely roses. She selected two of the pale pink ones and pinned them carefully to her waist.

When Lucrezia entered the salon, she found everyone assembled and sipping wine. Pietro Bembo, who was discoursing with the Duke, his back to the door, turned around as though sensing her presence. His eyes held hers and she found herself moving toward him. She kissed her father-in-law, keeping her hand in his.

411

How fragile he has become in the last year, she thought.

Pietro bowed. "I was telling His Grace that I was inspired to write a poem this afternoon."

Lucrezia felt her face grow warm.

"It is about a sportive nymph," he continued, "who amuses herself by appearing as nature made her in front of a simple woodsman."

"It sounds a dreadful bore," she said quickly. "Do you not think so?" she asked, addressing herself to the Duke.

"At my age," he said, watching her closely, "I think it's delightful." He took her by the arm and invited Pietro to do the same, saying with a smile, "You are surrounded by youth and romance on the one side and by age and wisdom on the other. Truly no one could be better served."

At dinner she was seated next to Bembo and conscious of his eyes seeking hers. She was determined not to look at him. She would not give him the satisfaction. She ate little, tasting nothing, aware only of a rising feeling of ecstasy. All sensation seemed to be centered in her groin. When she bent to retrieve the napkin she had dropped, she felt warm fingers mingling with hers.

"You want me," he said, his mouth against her ear. "You want me as much as I want you."

She retrieved the napkin and placed it on her lap.

He turned away from her then and spoke to the Duke as though nothing at all had happened.

She moved slowly. The black organza lay on the chest, the roses wilted and crushed. She had not even bothered to remove them. When Maria tried to help her undress, she sent her away, her eyes strange and vacant. She loosened her hair and brushed it, sweetened her mouth with cloves, and sprinkled her pillow with

412

lavender. Then she lay in her bed waiting, her body burning with its own fever.

The door opened and shut so quietly that she was not certain she had heard it. Her heart beat high in her throat; she was almost choking. The bed sagged suddenly.

"Pietro?" she whispered. Her voice was hoarse. She did not even recognize it.

The hands that grasped her were rough and bruising. She would have cried out except for the fever of her body. The mouth that covered hers was sharp and tearing, leaving her with the salt taste of her own blood. When he entered her without foreplay, the pain was so intense that she beat at his chest with her fists. He slapped her breasts and pinned her arms to her sides, thrusting his outsized member so far within her that she nearly retched. He moved furiously, tearing and burning the raw dry flesh. She cried out for him to stop. He sent his fist crashing against the side of her face, and as blackness descended over her he ejaculated with a low animal groan.

When she came to, he was gone. She remembered then hearing him leave, laughing that he had had his first marchioness and that she was no different from a kitchenmaid. Her eyes filled with tears. She hurt; she hurt all over. Alexander's face swam before her. "Papa," she cried suddenly. "Papa, I need you!" Her body was wracked with sobs, tearing her chest, hurting her throat.

In the morning Maria's hands comforted her. She laid soft wet strips of linen against her forehead. "Up," she whispered frenziedly. "Can you get up? We must clean you."

Lucrezia tried to raise her head, but it ached from the blow. "I can't," she said weakly. "Let me rest."

Maria's voice was firm. "There is no time for that

413

now. Do you want your husband to smell another man on you?"

Lucrezia's breath caught in her throat.

"He arrived late last night. I told him that you were not feeling well and could not be disturbed. God only knows what he thought!"

"The sheets," Lucrezia whispered. "We must change the sheets!"

"That won't be necessary." Alphonso's voice stabbed at her like particles of ice. "I will not be sharing your bed tonight—or any other night."

CHAPTER 36

How Alphonso had found her out, she did not inquire, nor did she wish to know. The humiliation of his rejection was utter and complete.

Like a child who has fallen out of favor, she pondered how best to win him back. She was thus engrossed when Strozzi entered the room.

There was a smile on his lips. "Pietro has gone home," he said, rubbing his hands together. "He has more tail than teeth, it seems."

Lucrezia said nothing.

"It was really very foolish of you," he continued, enjoying himself. "The pedestals he erects for women have nothing whatsoever to do with his own erections."

"Do not preach," she said wearily. "What's done is done."

Strozzi appeared to pick a piece of lint from his sleeve. "He has left a final poem for you. I did not bother to open it. It is probably sealed with semen."

Lucrezia made no move to take it.

"Your husband is furious with you," he said cheerfully.

"How does he seem?" she asked anxiously.

"Thin," he avowed tonelessly. "Thin and pale. But that is probably from sorrow, since it seems that he left your side to meditate on how best to live happily with you."

"Happily?" she repeated, the tears starting from her eyes.

Alphonso stayed away from her bed. When he addressed her at all, it was formally and had to do with the business of the house. For Lucrezia this was an agony not be borne.

Strozzi watched her through narrowed eyes. "I think it's possible," he said, "that you are falling in love with your own husband."

It was true. Alphonso grew more desirable to her with each passing day. She was smitten by the sight of him as he passed her in the halls or in the Grand Salon. How had she never noticed, she thought, how proudly his head sat upon his shoulders, how neatly his jaw was formed, how well his eyes were set? He seemed to stand straighter than ever in his misery. Could anyone die of love, she wondered.

A month later she was certain she was pregnant.

"Don't worry," Maria soothed her. "We will find a way to get rid of it. A little mandrake root in a *tisane* and he will never know of it."

"I am going to tell him," Lucrezia decided.

"Fool," Maria hissed. "If you tell him, you'll never get him back!"

"I must tell him. I'll never deceive him again in anything."

It was a strange pregnancy. Her appetite decreased, and in place of a sense of well-being such as she had experienced with Rodrigo, she felt nauseous and ill.

She grew pale and thin. If Alphonso noticed any of this, he gave no sign.

It was at this time that the old duke Ercole fell ill.

Alphonso found Lucrezia sitting by a window, sewing. It was autumn now, and the late afternoon sun touched her hair with added gold. He stood watching her for a while before he spoke. "It seems that my father is very ill. He has asked if you would be good enough to attend to him."

Lucrezia, her heart jumping, put her sewing aside. Perhaps now he would relent and take her into his arms.

Alphonso's voice was toneless. His eyes were directed to the wall beyond her. For all he cared, she realized, she might be a picture on the wall. She folded her work neatly and put it into a basket. A small sigh escaped her.

She found the Duke lying propped against a profusion of pillows. He looked so weak and frail that she ran to his side and put her face against his. Tears seemed to come so easily to her now.

"There," the Duke said, patting her awkwardly. "I am not dying just yet. But sit in that chair and let me look at you. The sight of you sitting there and doing your work will make me feel better. She makes a pretty picture, does she not?" he asked Alphonso.

Alphonso said nothing.

"I cannot do anything about Alphonso right now," she said to Maria later. "My father-in-law needs me and that is more important."

The next time she and Alphonso were together in the Duke's room the old man looked at his son and said, "Please send in the musicians. They will ease my mind."

Alphonso went to fetch them.

The Duke waited until he had left the room. Then

he looked at her slyly. "Well, is he sharing your bed yet?"

Lucrezia shook her head.

"He is a stubborn boy; he always was. Perhaps my death will soften him."

"You are not going to die," Lucrezia said quickly.

"I am going to die, my dear. I feel it . . . a gradual slowing down and cessation of things. It is all happening very quietly within me, but I can feel it all the same."

Lucrezia's eyes filled with tears. Since the death of her father she had come to rely on the Duke and to feel a very real affection for him. "You cannot die," she said simply, her voice breaking. "There is no one who loves me now but you."

"Come here, my child." Ercole stroked the soft strands of her hair. "My son loves you. He may not wish to know it, but he does."

They were clasped so when Alphonso returned to the room. He affected not to notice. "The musicians are here, Father. I trust they'll cheer you somehow."

Lucrezia spent all of her time now with her father-in-law, having had a cot moved into his dressing room. She took all her meals with him, leaving him only to bathe and to change her clothing.

The autumn days had lengthened into winter and the old Duke grew no better.

"I think that Isabella should come to visit," Lucrezia said to Alphonso one gray afternoon when Ercole's breathing seemed especially labored.

"Isabella has already been sent for," Alphonso said shortly.

Lucrezia awakened one morning to find the Duke going over some notes he had made of the writings of Plutarch. "You should be resting," she said affectionately, straightening the coverlet and adjusting the pillows in back of his head.

"I will be resting soon enough," he said gently. Later in the afternoon he looked at her strangely. "I want you to summon the harpsichordist," he said. "There is a certain fourteenth-century melody . . . I want to hear it once more."

Lucrezia bent and kissed him, and sent for the musician. The sound filled the room with its beauty, and the Duke, his face transfixed, moved his hand feebly in rhythm with the music. When it was over, he lay still. He was dead.

Lucrezia was inconsolable. Another person who had cared for her was gone. If his father's death had softened him, as the old Duke had hoped, Alphonso gave no sign. Lucrezia's sobs fell on deaf ears. He stood straight and silent with never a word of comfort, his hands at his sides.

The bells of Ferrara tolled for two days. On the third day they rang to summon the Council of Savi to the election of the new Duke. Alphonso's father still lay in state, but Ferrarese law decreed that a new Duke be elected before the old one could be placed in the ground. There was much to do to ready the palace for the delegation. Lucrezia, setting aside her grief for the time being, and with Isabella to help, saw to everything with quiet dignity. She looked on with pride as Alphonso received the sword and the golden rod. She followed with the others as he rode out into the wintry day to be received by the people of Ferrara, who lined the streets. Although it was cold and the snow was deep, the streets had been cleared for Alphonso's passage and the entire town had turned out to celebrate.

Alphonso rode calmly through the streets, looking at his people and saluting them gravely, then on to the chapel for a High Mass.

419

Lucrezia watched, bundled in thick furs against the cold, from a balcony of the palace. She had spent the morning receiving visitors and well-wishers, some of them from the noblest families of Ferrara. When Alphonso emerged from the chapel, she hurried down to the doors of the palace to kiss his hand as was the custom. Face to face with him at last, she bent down in an attitude of total submission, her heart pounding.

Custom required that he raise her to her feet and kiss her brow, acknowledging her as his Duchess. Would he do that? An eternity passed and to her horror nothing happened. Then she felt herself being lifted by strong arms that held her fast. She raised her eyes to meet his. He bent his head to kiss her, not on the brow, but full on the mouth. Then he took her by the hand and led her into the Grand Salon, where the reception was being held.

Through it all, she could feel his eyes on her. Looking up from the conversation she was forced to make with the others, she met his gaze, fixed and steady. Her skin warmed, and she could feel the flush that rose to her cheeks. For the first time she dared to hope that she might win him back.

When it was time to go in to dinner, he offered her his arm. She took it, not daring to smile at him lest he think her giddy and foolish.

When he had seated her, he leaned over and breathed in her ear. "Eat well, my dear. You will need some strength for later."

Their lovemaking was savage. They came together like two wild things, tearing at each other's bodies.

Suddenly she pushed him away from her and looked full at him. "I must tell you. I am with child."

He looked at her with wounded eyes. "I know." His

420

mouth, which was hard and fierce, began to bite. Inflamed, she bit him back.

"I want to hurt you, to make you weep as you have made me weep," he muttered thickly.

She moaned with the pleasure of it.

"Bitch," he breathed against her hair. "I should put you in chains for what you have done!" Then, gently, "Come, my love, let us try for it together."

CHAPTER 37

Lucrezia awakened in the morning to find Alphonso raised on one arm, watching her. She smiled a bit self-consciously. "Was I sleeping with my mouth open?"

"A little," he said.

She reached over and took his hand in hers. Thank God, she thought, thank God it was over.

He took his hand away and turned on his back, staring up at the ceiling.

"What is it?" she asked anxiously. "What is wrong?"

"It cannot mend itself all at once," he said without looking at her. "We must give it time."

"Time?" she repeated. His words settled into her bones like lead. "But we've wasted so much time already ..."

"Nothing is wasted," he said tonelessly. "Time will take care of everything."

She sighed. "It will never be as it was," she said later as Maria was drawing her bath.

"Perhaps not. Nothing remains the same."

"And yet I am willing to do anything to make things right."

Maria looked at her. "You are still such a child. You think that just because you want something to happen, it must happen."

"But I am willing to do anything, anything at all."

"It is no longer up to you. He must go at his own pace. Then one day, if you are lucky . . ."

Lucrezia watched her as she squeezed the water from the sponge and put it on a tray. "If only Isabella would go home where she belongs and Alphonso and I were alone, then perhaps everything would be different."

She began taking special pains with her appearance. After all, Alphonso was a man, and susceptible to the temptations of the flesh. She looked critically at herself. "I am beginning to look like that cow Isabella," she grumbled.

"We can always bind you," Maria said soothingly.

"I will not be bound. I do not even want this child," she said brokenly. "It has come between us like a sword."

"It is too late to worry about that now."

"It is never too late," Lucrezia said, stamping her foot. "If necessary, I'll find someone to get rid of it for me!"

Maria's face darkened. "You will do nothing of the sort."

That evening Maria brought her a dose of ergot.

"What is it?" Lucrezia asked, eyeing the moldy mash with aversion.

"It is blighted rye, but at least it will not kill you."

Lucrezia swallowed it, retched, and brought it back up.

"Do you want it or not?" Maria asked sternly. "It is

423

still better than having someone remove the child a piece at a time."

In the morning Lucrezia felt a sense of heaviness within her. She looked down and saw a small trickle of blood. At last, she thought happily. "It has begun!" she called to Maria. For once she was grateful that Alphonso had left the bed before she awakened.

By the time Maria arrived, the bleeding had stopped. "Why has it stopped? Why am I not bleeding?" she asked anxiously.

"Because you are not. Now just lie there and wait."

At eleven o'clock Alphonso returned to the room. "Are you not feeling well?" he asked, seeing that she was still in bed.

"I am all right," she said, covering the sheet so that he would not see the blood. "I did not sleep very well last night."

He stood for a moment or so longer. "Very well then. I am going to ride out with Isabella. We will see you at the midday meal. By the way, she has consented to stay until you are delivered of the child."

As soon as he left, she threw back the covers and looked. Still no blood. She must do something, she thought, and quickly. She looked about the room. On the writing desk was a stiletto, the kind used to open seals. She looked at it and considered. It was really not long enough, but if she pushed it all the way up, perhaps . . . no, that would hurt. Once again she saw Alphonso's eyes looking at her coolly, impersonally. Oh God, she must change those eyes and make them warm. She grasped the stiletto . . .

"It was not the ergot," Maria explained afterward to a white-faced Alphonso. "It was that," she said, pointing to the sharp knife. "She did not want the child because it was not yours."

424

"Stupid woman!" Alphonso shouted, striking her with the flat of his hand. "Why did you not come and tell me!"

Lucrezia lay where they had moved her, her body jerking with shock.

"If she does not bleed to death, she may survive."

Alphonso turned to look at the small pimply-faced doctor who spoke. "If she does not survive, you will follow her to your death. Do I make myself clear?"

"Spirits," the poor man cried out. "Spirits and sheets! And where is that tub of boiling water?" As though on cue, six men stumbled into the room bearing a steaming caldron.

"The sheets," the doctor shrilled. "Immerse the sheets!"

It was at this point that Isabella swept into the room. "What is going on?" she demanded.

Alphonso seized her by the shoulders and propelled her firmly through the door. "You will be fully informed of what is going on at the proper time." The men dipped the sheets and wrung them out, their hands raw with heat.

"Wrap her," the doctor shouted. "Wrap her up!" Lucrezia did not even move as the steaming sheets touched her skin.

"More," he cried. "More!" As the tremors of her body began to lessen, he motioned for the spirits.

"It is the strongest we have," Alphonso said, handing him the French brandy which Louis had sent as a gift.

The doctor pried her jaws apart with his fingers and tipped the flask so that the fiery liquid slid down her throat.

"Take care that she does not drown," Alphonso warned as she began to choke.

The little man trembled. "You must either let me

425

treat her as best I can or else kill me now and be done with it. Verily, I can do no more!"

Alphonso's voice remained hard. "Do your best then," he said, turning his face aside so that the man could not see his tears.

Lucrezia's limbs finally ceased to tremble. She lay ashen and still.

"What is it?" Alphonso asked sharply. "What is happening?"

The doctor unwound the dripping sheets and uncovered her. "The bleeding seems to have stopped." He looked at Alphonso, his eyes filled with fear. "Either she is completely exsanguinated or it has just stopped of itself. I could cauterize the wound," he said, as though to himself, "or I could leave it alone. If I leave it alone, it could become infected . . ."

"Make a decision, my good man," Alphonso said coldly. "Only take care that it is the right one."

"Yes," the little doctor said. "Yes, I will cauterize. I will need a hot iron."

Alphonso, unable to bear watching what he guessed must happen, fled from the room, shouting, "Get on with it! Just get on with it!"

Standing outside the closed door, Alphonso heard a high, tearing scream. He braced as though he were receiving the thrust himself and fought to keep his stomach down.

After a few moments the doctor, looking himself as though he might faint, came through the door. "It is in God's hands now," he whispered.

Alphonso turned to him heavily. "So now you are leaving it with God. No, my good man. It is still in your hands." Together they went back into the room.

Lucrezia lay as though made of wax, a low moan her only indication of life. Throughout the day the doctor dozed in a chair by her side, coming awake every now and then to make certain she was still breathing. Alphonso sat at the foot of the bed, watching her closely. If she lives, he thought, if only she lives, I will make everything different.

At five o'clock that evening Isabella again pushed her way into the room. She looked stonily at the small figure that lay on the bed. "So this is where her passions have brought her. Why don't you go and rest," she said to Alphonso, laying a hand lightly on his arm. "The sooner she is belly-up for good, the better it will be for us all."

Alphonso turned and looked at her with eyes like ice. "Isabella," he said slowly, "nothing would give me greater pleasure at this moment than to run you through." He smiled at her quick intake of breath. "If you are not quitted of this place within an hour, I shall have you spitted like so much meat and thrown to the pigs."

Isabella's eyes widened in disbelief. "But she has brought this on herself. I don't see why . . ."

"Get out," he shouted. "Out!"

Toward midnight Lucrezia's fever began to rise.

"The afterbirth," Maria said fearfully. "I don't remember seeing it."

"There was so much blood," the doctor answered, "I simply assumed . . ."

"You assumed!" Alphonso shouted. "Why were you not certain?"

"I saw the fetus," the doctor recalled, "but I did not think of the afterbirth."

Alphonso grabbed the poor man and threw him to the floor. "On your knees and pray that she lives through your bungling. For if she doesn't, I shall take out your eyes with the same iron, then your tongue, which I'll pull out by the roots, and then your testicles, if you have any!"

"Give her some rue," the poor man shrieked. "If it is still in there, it will draw it out!"

Maria prepared a *tisane* of rue.

The doctor inserted a reed between Lucrezia's lips. He attempted to pour the rue into the reed, but his hands shook so much that very little of it found its mark. "I shall need a spout," he said finally.

"It is going all over the place!" Alphonso said impatiently. He pushed the doctor aside and with infinite care poured the liquid through the reed, wiping away the excess from the corners of her mouth.

Two hours later she began to babble, her eyes wide and staring.

Alphonso grabbed her arms and tried to bring her back to reality. "Little Rodrigo is coming—I've sent for him. You *must* get well!"

She gave no sign of hearing.

Alphonso seized the doctor by the shoulders and shook him until his teeth rattled in his head. "What have you given her? It is driving her mad!"

"No, it is only the fever."

Lucrezia had stepped back into the golden garden of her childhood. Cesare lay on the grass, waiting to tickle her with a long reed. He stuck it in her mouth. It tasted bitter. "*Paugh!* I shall tell Adriana, and she will have you punished."

He looked at her in that taunting way of his. "Adriana has gone mad, didn't you know?"

"Then I shall tell Carlos. He will know what to do."

"That poetaster. Don't make me laugh. Come," he said, pulling her to her feet. "I have a new game, I'll show you."

She looked at him, at his auburn curls, at the way his ears ran goatishly into his jaws. Then something inside her exploded in pain. "I can't run," she gasped,

428

holding herself with frenzied hands. "Something hurts so much!"

He was looking at her intently now, his face thrust close to hers. She could see the freckles standing out against his white skin. They seemed to be growing and growing. He thrust his hand under her skirt. She screamed. She was frightened. He always frightened her. Little tufts of hair grew from his ears. A pair of horns sprang stubbily from his forehead. She looked down at the grass and saw his hooves. "Cesare," she screamed. "Cesare!"

Someone held her close. It was Alexander. "Papa, I thought you were dead."

He looked at her and smiled. His skin was the color of tallow.

"Please help me, Papa. I hurt so much."

He gave her his Fisherman's ring to kiss.

She covered his hands with her tears. "Take me home, Papa. I promise to be good."

He was still smiling, but it was a smile she had never seen. His face swam from side to side. Then it cracked and fell apart.

"Papa!" she screamed. *"Papa!"*

Someone was still holding her, but now she was cold, so terribly cold, and she couldn't seem to get warm. And suddenly she knew why. She was lying on a catafalque in St. Peter's, and no one had thought to cover her. And Alfonso was lying beside her, her poor dead husband. She leaned over and traced his lips with her fingers. Alfonso, poor dear Alfonso. She kissed him softly, and he smiled without opening his eyes. She would tell Alexander what Cesare had done to him. She would see that her brother was properly punished. She looked at Alfonso once more, and then she saw the ragged hole in his tunic. It was crawling with worms.

"Papa!" she screamed. *"Papa!"* And his poor broken face swam before her. Cesare grinned at her. But he was dead, they were all dead!

Alphonso held her close to him, kissing away the tears that stained her face.

Lucrezia opened her eyes. "Why are you naked?" she asked him.

"So that the heat of my body could reach out to you and bring you back."

She lay against the pillows, her skin bleached and taut from the fever, her eyes two deep holes. "How long has it been?"

"A week," he said hoarsely, bringing her fingers to his lips.

"How long have you been holding me like this?"

"I don't know. An eternity perhaps."

She tried to smile, but her lips were cracked and they hurt. "I was with Papa and Cesare, but all the time I could feel there was someone holding me."

He smoothed her hair with tender hands and kissed her softly on the forehead.

She looked up at him, her eyes filling with tears. "I dreamt," she said weakly, "that Cesare was dead."

Two weeks later Cesare escaped from prison and fled to Navarre. He sought refuge with his brother-in-law, Jean d'Albret, who was King. To Charlotte's brother, Cesare's arrival seemed a stroke of good fortune. For the kingdom of Navarre was at this time being threatened by provincial insurgents led by one of the rebellious land barons, Louis de Beaumont, Count of Lerin. And Cesare, a seasoned general, had suddenly dropped into his lap.

D'Albret welcomed him with open arms. "God alone

430

has arranged this," he told him, "so that you can help me."

Cesare smiled. "God has come to help us both," he said simply.

A few weeks later he found himself at the head of ten thousand men, pushing on to Viana, the Count of Lerin's stronghold. He made his camp on the bank of a river, not far from the castle.

Early in the morning of March 12 a band of Lerin's horsemen, on their way back from Castile and bearing provisions, scuffled with some sentries, who sounded an alarm.

Cesare donned his armor and was on his horse in an instant. In no time he and his men had dispersed them. He sat tall and brooding on his horse, watching them flee, his polished armor catching the sun's rays. Then without any warning or reason, he set out after them, without waiting for his men to follow.

He pursued them furiously into a ravine, and was instantly surrounded. The melee that followed was bloody and swift. Cesare fought as though possessed, swiping left and right with his sword, his eyes filled with a strange and unholy light. When an enemy blade pierced his armor and unhorsed him, instead of begging for mercy he got to his feet and fought on, swinging unsteadily in all directions, his head pouring blood.

A hundred blades tore at him. He swayed on his feet, his clothing in shreds. In another moment it was over. The men on horseback stared for a while at the naked, battered body on the ground. Then they turned their horses and left him. His brother-in-law, King Jean, riding out an hour later, found him and covered him with his cloak.

Lucrezia was walking in the garden waiting for Alphonso. The illness of the past months had left her

431

weak and wan, but each day she awakened feeling a bit stronger. In a few weeks, she thought happily, little Rodrigo would be there. It was a warm day for April, and she moved about the garden in a light cloak, taking joy in the tender shoots pushing through the newly turned earth.

When she saw Alphonso walking toward her with a pale, dusty messenger in Spanish dress, she was struck with a feeling of dread.

"Tell her what you have told me," Alphonso said to him.

The poor man, who was plainly exhausted, sank to his knees. Lucrezia recognized him as one of Cesare's former pages.

"He is dead," she said simply. "Tell me how it happened."

When the messenger had told her everything, sparing her no detail, she lowered her head. Cesare's face came before her, mocking her. *And one day, when I am lying in a field, broken by the swords of my enemies, will you be there to comfort me?*

Alphonso, seeing her sway, reached out to steady her.

"It is all right," she said, raising her face to his. "It is what he wanted."

That night as she lay in his arms, she turned to face him. "Tell me," she said, stroking the line of his jaw lightly with her finger, "if I had died, would you have taken another wife?"

At first he made no answer. Then she felt his lips move against her ear. And the love words that he whispered were so tender and so fierce that she needed to hear nothing more, for she knew all at once that he was hers and that life for them was just beginning . . .

EPILOGUE

Lucrezia was happy with Alphonso. She genuinely loved him, for he provided the strength and stability and affection she so sorely needed. Aware of her childish ways, he kept her amused with gifts and trinkets, and busy bearing children.

In her thirty-ninth year, still beautiful and slender, she was delivered prematurely of a little girl. It was a difficult birth, and she developed childbed fever. She soon sank into delirium, confusing Alphonso with her father and brother, and complaining of the weight of her beautiful hair, of which she had always been so vain. Alphonso cut it off to ease her pain, for there was little else anyone could do to help her.

She died on June 24, 1519, in the first days of summer, her favorite time of the year.

Alphonso, who was by her side, was inconsolable. Taking her hand in his, he looked down at the small face which still bore its childish lineaments and murmured brokenly, "Life's fitful fever is over for her at last."

Less flattering was the epitaph attributed to the poet Pontanus: *In this tomb sleeps Lucrezia in name, but Thais in fact, Alexander's daughter, bride and daughter-in-law.*

Preview

SAMANTHA

Angelica Aimes

The following pages comprise the prologue of a new and exciting romantic novel set in the exotic orient, glamorous Paris and London, and the infant state of Massachusetts in the nineteenth century. *Samantha*, the story of a beautiful, determined girl, the men in her life and the one man she lives for, will be published in June, 1978.

Scorching fingers of flames like crimson spears leaped out in his path. Suffocating clouds of black smoke engulfed him. The shouts of men calling him back in many languages echoed like Babel in his ears. Still he fought his way through the rampaging inferno, battling the furious fire as if his only entry into paradise lay through the fatal blaze.

His tall, lean frame was bent almost double, his arms raised across his face in a futile effort to protect himself from the raging fire. Flames licked at his blond hair and singed his eyebrows and lashes. But he struggled on, hurling himself into the living hell that threatened to consume him, only to be driven back by a wall of intense heat as inpenetrable as a sheet of iron. Crying out in desperation and despair, he rushed into the fiery furnace again.

He woke up trembling, his body cold and clammy with sweat. He rubbed his eyes, trying to wipe away the memory of the terrible inferno that haunted his sleeping and waking hours, and instinctively touched the thin purple scar that ran from his left temple to his ear. Exhausted in body, tormented in soul, he stumbled into the night. Walking—walking the hills and winding roads of Macao—was the only release he had from the frightening nightmare which allowed him no rest, no peace of mind.

It was midnight. The streets and byways were deserted when the man began his desperate walk. He strode on for miles, unaware of his surroundings, of the steepness of the climb or the fragrance of the summer air—driven by demons he could not exorcise, by memories he could not escape, by passions he thought he would never know again. A faint ripple of far-off music added to the strangeness of the night and to his dangerous, feverish mood. He paused to catch the melody that seemed to waft in off the river. Lost in the eerie moment, he had not noticed the figure coming toward him until she was kneeling in his path, like a gift heaven-sent to deliver him from his torment.

He stared in amazement at the apparition on her knees in front of him, bathed in moonlight. She was dressed in an exquisite raspberry satin robe. Silver dragons danced in its graceful folds, and silver thread outlined its mandarin collar and long, full sleeves. Her jet black hair hung thick and straight to her shoulders. Her forehead was powdered a lily white, her mouth painted in a ruby bow. A satin mask, the same raspberry shade as her robe, hid the rest of her features. He held out his hand to help her up and the sweet scent of jasmine drifted over him. It was, he suddenly realized, the evening of Colonel Blackstone's masked ball, the highlight of the summer season in Macao, and the old soldier must have imported boatloads of the willing girls from the flower boats of Canton to pleasure his guests.

Released from his searing memories by this unexpected encounter, the man laughed aloud. *I don't have to suffer the boredom of the Colonel and his guests,* he thought, *to savor the delights he provides.* Pulling the girl to her feet, he pressed his mouth firmly against her crimson lips. She stood motionless, frozen in his arms. "I hope you're not on land because your rivers have run dry," he said in perfect Chinese as he kissed her again, lightly, curiously this time. Without further ceremony, he swooped her up into his arms, and then deposited her beneath the wide spread of a pomegranate tree.

The tree's heavy boughs blocked out the moonlight. Darkness closed in on them. He could no longer see the girl distinctly, could barely discern the outline of her figure. The suddenness, the mysteriousness of their meeting excited him and he fell on top of her, his eager hands searching her rigid body. Suddenly like a volcano long dormant, she erupted, tossing and rolling, biting and clawing like a tiger. The more she struggled, the more aroused he became. He had been on the flower boats many times and knew that a world of immeasurable pleasure floated on the Pearl River, exotic sex with beautiful women skilled in the fine art of arousal. Anything a man desired he could have from these girls, as well as some things he never dreamed of. "If you like to be hurt, I will hurt you. If you like to be forced, I will force you," he whispered savagely as she struggled with him on the shadowy hillside.

The passionate tussle with the silent, masked girl who had appeared from nowhere drove him wild with desire. He flung one strong arm across her heaving chest, pinning her beneath him. With the other, he lifted her dragon robe to her waist and ripped away her linen bloomers.

If there had been enough moonlight to see the girl clearly, he would have been shocked by what he had uncovered. For, instead of the wispy black hair of the Oriental flower girls, there was a luxurious crown of tawny-colored curls.

In the shadow of the tree, though, all he could see was the curve of her hip. His nostrils filled with the womanly aroma of her body. The sound of her gasping for breath beat in his ears, and he entered her roughly, his ardor driving him deeper and deeper.